A Song of Home

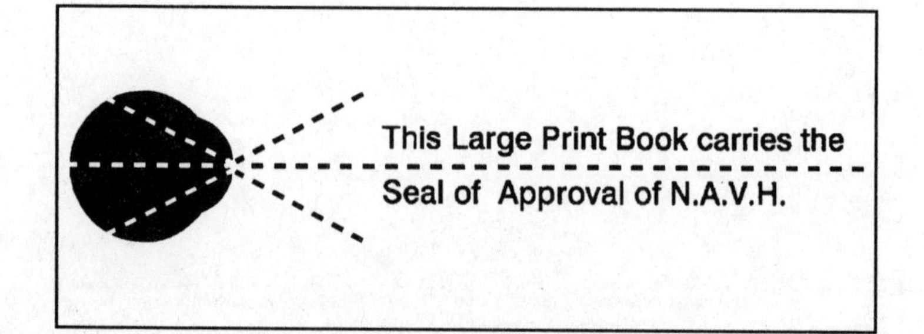
This Large Print Book carries the
Seal of Approval of N.A.V.H.

A Song of Home

A NOVEL OF THE SWING ERA

Susie Finkbeiner

THORNDIKE PRESS
A part of Gale, a Cengage Company

Farmington Hills, Mich • San Francisco • New York • Waterville, Maine
Meriden, Conn • Mason, Ohio • Chicago

Thorndike Press® Large Print Christian Historical Fiction.
The text of this Large Print edition is unabridged.
Other aspects of the book may vary from the original edition.
Set in 16 pt. Plantin.

LIBRARY OF CONGRESS CIP DATA ON FILE.
CATALOGUING IN PUBLICATION FOR THIS BOOK
IS AVAILABLE FROM THE LIBRARY OF CONGRESS

ISBN-13: 978-1-4328-4676-3 (hardcover)
ISBN-10: 1-4328-4676-0 (hardcover)

Published in 2018 by arrangement with Kregel Publications, a division of Kregel, Inc.

Printed in the United States of America
1 2 3 4 5 6 7 22 21 20 19 18

In memory of
Grandma Relf,
the original Pearlie Lou

ACKNOWLEDGMENTS

Writing Pearl's story has been one of the great joys of my life. There may have been sleepless nights and panicked moments of self-doubt. But through it all I've had a community of friends, family, and readers who have kept me writing. For each of them, I am grateful.

Sonny Huisman: The day you told me you were praying for this book was the turning point in my writing. If this novel points anyone to the mercy of Jesus, it's partly because of the time you invested in interceding. Thank you, my friend.

Ann Byle: From before I wrote the first word of this series to the moment I typed the last sentence, you believed in me. I cannot express how greatly I value your friendship. On days when I don't have the strength to keep writing, I remember your confidence in my abilities. Just that thought keeps me going.

Jocelyn Green: Whenever I doubt my worth as an author, I have only to scroll through the history of our Facebook messages. You refuse to let me believe I'm a fraud and you do so in the gentlest way. You are a gift from God.

The folks at Kregel Publications: You have given wings to Pearl's story. All the cookies in the world wouldn't be enough to show my appreciation.

Baker Book House: I do believe you have sold more copies of these books than anyone else. Your enthusiasm has kept me going on many a weary day. I know that I'm not the only author who has found a home in your store.

Elise, Austin, and Tim: You three have taught me more about love, mercy, and hope than I could have ever learned on my own. Being your mama is one of the best things in my life. I love you.

Jeff: I realize that you had no idea you were marrying an author fourteen years ago. Surprise! But you have taken to the role of writer's husband with grace, generosity, and energy. You make this possible with your support and love. I hope you know how much I treasure you.

My readers: I never could have imagined how sweet it is to have such wonderful people choose to read my humble offerings. You write reviews, send encouraging emails, and purchase stacks of books to share with your communities. You have become dear to me. I can't help but thank God for you whenever you come to mind, which is often.

Chapter One

Bliss, Michigan
December 31, 1935

It was no surprise to me that I'd lost track of time. The clock on the wall told me that soon I'd need to be heading on home for the evening. Seemed I'd only sat down in that velvety chair a couple minutes before. Instead it'd been a couple hours. A good story had that kind of power over me.

I turned the pages of my borrowed book to the very last story. There was a picture of a man, tall and lean, wearing yellow and red striped clothes and holding a flute to his lips. A river of rats followed along behind him. I knew without reading a single word that it was the story of the Pied Piper.

Leaning my head into the soft back of the chair, I closed my eyes. Much as I tried not to, I slipped just below the surface of asleep and awake. It was a shallow dream that floated along with me.

I didn't dream of rats and I was glad for that. But I did dream of the line of children, helplessly lining up behind the piper, lured by his song.

Then I pictured myself in that line of kids, following along unwillingly behind the piper. Away from home and away from what was safe and warm and good. I turned my head to see all the grown folks just watching us leave and not doing anything to stop us. Try as I might, I couldn't get my feet to step out of the line to go back home.

A woman came running out of one of the grimy old cottages, rushing toward all us kids, her mouth open and a melody lifting up and out of her. It was a song of home meant to call us all back to where we belonged.

Just as I was about to turn I felt two hands on my shoulders, jostling me, making me surface out of my dream with gasping breath and heart thudding so hard I was sure it was about to jump right out of my chest.

"Wake up, Pearl," Ray said. He stood over me with a big old grin across his face. "You was snorin' so loud I thought the librarian was fixin' to kick you out."

"Why'd you have to shake me like that?" I gave him my best scowl and shut my book hard so he'd know I wasn't all too happy with him just then.

"Don't you know you ain't supposed to sleep in the library?" He stood up straight and offered me his hand. "Come on. Your pa sent me to come get you."

"I can get up by myself," I said, slapping his hand away.

My aggravation wouldn't last too long. I never could stay mad at him no matter what he did.

Ray Jones was my best friend in all the world. Always had been since before I could remember. The way I figured, he always would be. Nobody understood me like Ray did. Seemed we shared an understanding that only came from losing so much.

If there was one good thing about moving away from Oklahoma it was that Ray got to come with us.

Ray and I made our way to the front of the library where Mrs. Trask sat at her desk, ready to help folks find just the right book. She smiled at the two of us and half stood. I wondered how it didn't hurt her to stand, the way her shoulders stooped and her back curved into a hump. But no matter how much it ached her, she always had a sweet smile to give.

"Oh, Miss Spence," she said, her voice

gentle and her thick-knuckled fingers resting on the top of her desk. "Would you like to check out that book?"

"No thank you, ma'am," I said.

"Then just put it here on my desk and I'll put it away in the morning."

"Thank you, ma'am," I said, putting the book within her reach.

"Happy New Year," she said, her eyes crinkling in the corners.

"You too, Mrs. Trask."

Ray waited for me to get bundled before we stepped out the library doors. He shoved his hands in the pockets of his coat and stopped once we got to the sidewalk.

"Hold on," he said. "I wanna show you somethin' before we go home."

"What?" I asked.

"You'll see." He winked at me. "Just come on."

He turned and I followed down an out of the way street. I wasn't worried about where he was taking me. If there was someone I could trust it was Ray Jones.

The American Legion was a big, square building that looked as old as most any other place in town. There wasn't a thing fancy about it other than the old cannon that sat at the ready by the front doors.

"You think that's a real cannon?" I asked.

"Don't know," Ray said. "Probably. That ain't what I wanna show you, though."

He nodded at the building. A group of young folks stood around the big double doors. Some of them smoked cigarettes and others talked real close to each other. Cars were parked along the sides of the road. As early in the evening as it was all the lights were on in the Legion and music boomed so loud I could hear it from on the walk.

"What's going on in there?" I squinted up at the old bricks as if I could see through the walls if only I looked hard enough.

"A dance I guess," Ray said. "Bet we could see in the window if we stood on top of that cannon."

I didn't give myself the chance to wonder if Ray'd had a good idea or not. I followed along behind him to the window. I even let him steady me while I climbed onto the cannon, but only because it was a little slick with ice. Holding onto the window sill, I leaned close to the glass.

The jolting and jumping music rattled the glass in its frame. I felt of it with my mittened hand. Ba-ba-booming drums set the beat, wa-wahing trumpets dragged out a note and then blasted another. The band was on the stage, clear on the far side of the room. From what I could see there were just a handful of instruments, but what they lacked in number they made up for in sound.

A line of people stood watching a man and woman dance like I'd never seen before. That pair pounded the floor with their feet like they were running in place, then they kicked to the sides and I wondered how they knew to do that at the same time. The lady's skirt flipped up, showing her thighs and the bottom hem of her underthings and I felt embarrassed for her. She didn't seem to mind, though. She just kept on kicking and moving her hips.

Using my mitten, I rubbed the steam from my breath away from the glass just in time to see the lady turn toward the man. He put his hands under her arms, lifting her so she could swing her legs from one side of him to the other. Then he dipped her down so she slid on her backside between his legs, her dress bunching up behind her, bloomers showing for everybody to see.

The man grabbed her hands, pulling her back up until she hopped to her feet. The folks in line cheered and clapped for them while they made way for another couple who waddled like a couple ducks to the center of the circle.

"Ray," I said, having to wipe the glass again. "It's Opal."

Opal Moon was the hired girl who'd taken care of us since Mama went away. She cooked and cleaned and watched after Ray and me so we didn't get into too much trouble. Seeing her there in the middle of the floor, dancing faster than I'd ever have thought possible, surprised me to no end.

And to see her with a boy who had white-blond hair and pale-as-paper skin only added to the shock. Even if Opal was only one-half Negro, it seemed against some kind of rule, her dancing with a white boy.

She spun, her skirts fanning up, and ducked under her partner's lifted leg. Shimmying and spinning and twirling, she danced like a wriggling worm. At the very end of their turn, the boy picked her up, throwing her over his shoulder like a sack of potatoes. She pretended to pound her fists on his back and she kicked her legs, but with a big smile on her face the whole time. Then her face turned toward the window.

Ray and I ducked just in time.

"Let's go," he whispered.

"You think she saw us?" I asked.

"Don't know." He grabbed my arm. "Ain't stickin' around to find out. We best get."

He was right. I knew Opal would be real

sore if she knew we'd been spying on her. We ran all the way home, even with the cold air burning in our lungs.

I didn't think I'd get the sound of the ba-ba-booming music out of my head all night.

Aunt Carrie had our dinner ready in the kitchen of the house on Magnolia Street. She'd made a pot of soup with big chunks of vegetables from her cellar and hunks of chicken from one of the birds on her farm. Uncle Gus sat across from Daddy, where Mama should have been.

If somebody'd looked at the Spence family tree they'd see that Gustav Seegert was Daddy's cousin. But to me he was Uncle Gus. And his wife was Aunt Carrie. It'd been so since the day we set foot in Bliss and I liked it that way plenty.

And I sure did like it when Aunt Carrie fed us supper. She never was one to scold us for slurping the broth or dribbling it down our chins. But when Uncle Gus would lift his bowl to his lips and tip it so he could swallow the last little bit, she'd shake her head and pretend to be upset.

The way her eyes sparkled at him, though, made me think she wasn't too sore, really.

After we finished eating, we cleared the dishes and Uncle Gus got a deck of cards out of his shirt pocket, shuffling them with his large hands. He didn't let even one of them fly out or tumble to the floor.

When he saw me watching, he moved his fingers to hide one of the cards, making it seem to have disappeared. When he flicked his wrist and the card reappeared, I clapped.

"You know any more?" Ray asked, eyes wide.

"Nope," answered Uncle Gus, smiling. "That's the only one I ever could get the hang of. My hands're too big for any of the others."

"Where'd you learn it?" I asked.

"When I was in the service." He started shuffling the cards again. "Had my ma known I was playin' cards in the Army she'd have come all the way to Europe and dragged me home to Oklahoma by the ear."

I didn't doubt that one little bit. Playing cards was just as bad as dancing, the way we'd learned from Pastor in Red River.

"Some days all we had to do was sit in the trenches and wait," Uncle Gus went on. "Playin' cards passed the time. French fella I met could do all kinds of tricks. He'd have somebody pick a card and it would end up in some other guy's helmet."

Uncle Gus dealt the cards and shook his

head. "Never did figure out how he done that."

"My pa taught me a trick or two," Ray said.

My eyes darted to Ray's face. He hadn't said so much as one word about his father since they'd found him hanging from the rafters of their dugout back in Oklahoma. He'd never been nice, Mr. Jones, at least not that I knew of. He'd been more the kind of man to smack Ray and Mrs. Jones around if he'd had too much to drink. How Ray ended up being such a good boy, I couldn't figure out. It sure wasn't any of his father's doing, that much I did know.

"Gus knew your pa," Daddy said, carrying a plate of cookies from the kitchen.

"Lord, yes," Uncle Gus said. "Good old Si Jones. I remember him bein' smitten with your ma. He couldn't hardly think straight when Luella was around."

"That true?" Ray asked.

"Yup." Uncle Gus put the remaining cards in the middle of the table. "Poor fella didn't eat for a week he had it so bad for her. His ma even sent him to see the doctor, she was so worried about him. Thought he had a worm."

Ray leaned forward so his chest pressed against the edge of the table.

"Weren't no worm, Doc said," Uncle Gus went on. "Just lovesickness. Him and your ma got married not two weeks later. Si and Lu. They run off and got married up to Boise City. Made their folks crazy."

Aunt Carrie came in with a couple bottles of Coke and a glass for each of us.

"I only known a handful of people so mad in love as your folks was," Uncle Gus said. "He sure was sweet on her."

Mean as Mr. Jones was when I knew him, I never could've imagined him doing much other than hurting Ray and his mother.

Hard times had the power to change people. I knew that. They could change them for good or bad. Thing was, nobody could tell somebody which way to go. Folks had to figure it out on their own.

Ray's mother and father, they'd gone the wrong way. Mama had, too. What I wanted to know was if somebody could come back after wandering off so far.

If there was a way, I sure did hope Mama would find it.

Aunt Carrie let Ray and me drink our Coca-Colas right out of the bottle and didn't say a word when we ate so many cookies our stomachs started to ache. We played cards well into the evening, the room full of our laughing.

Ray didn't even seem upset when he lost three hands in a row.

They didn't stay up all the way until midnight. Uncle Gus said he'd ring in nineteen-thirty-six with his eyes closed and in his bed. Aunt Carrie said the only noisemaker he needed was his snoring.

Daddy did let Ray and me stay up, listening to the radio as the seconds ticked away to the new year. Soon as twelve o'clock struck, Daddy told us it was time to go to sleep.

I kissed him on the cheek. "Goodnight, Daddy."

"Thanks for my new year's kiss," he whispered to me.

" 'Night, Mr. Spence," Ray said, going for the stairs.

"Happy New Year, Ray," Daddy said. "Go on, Pearlie. It's real late."

"Will you tuck me in?" I asked.

"Course I will." He smiled at me. "Get in your nightie. I'll be right up."

With my nightie on and the blanket pulled up to my chin, I made room so Daddy could sit on the edge of my bed.

"You wanna say your prayers?" he asked.

"I'll do them myself," I answered.

"That's fine."

"Daddy, are Negroes allowed to dance with white folk?"

"I suppose they can if they want to." He pushed his lips together. "There's no law against it in Michigan that I know of. Why do you ask?"

"There was a dance tonight."

"Down at the Legion?"

I nodded. "Ray and I peeked."

"Did you like how they danced?"

"Yes, sir." I smiled. "And I saw Opal."

"I bet you did." Daddy leaned over and kissed my cheek. "Now go to sleep, darlin'."

I shut my eyes. He stayed by my side a few minutes longer and I was glad. Having him near like that was safe. It didn't take long before I was deep asleep, dreaming of the new year.

Chapter Two

More than a few times a week I'd dream that Mama had never left. She'd be standing in the kitchen or the living room or looking into the mirror in her bedroom. Wherever I happened to find her in those dreams, she hummed a hymn and the light breeze from the open windows fluttered the fabric of her everyday dress.

That early morning dream found Mama setting the table. The dining room seemed to go on forever, a mile-long tunnel of a room. She moved along the table that was just as never-ending, placing plate after plate after plate. Somehow the stack of dishes in her arms never ran out.

"Mama," I said, my voice high and light.

She turned toward me, her face full of sunshine and smiles. But then her expression changed, her eyes lost their sparkle, opened wide, as if something had surprised and scared her. Without lifting her feet she made her way behind the pushed-in chairs, floating toward me. She opened her mouth to speak but I couldn't seem to hear her.

"What're you saying?" I asked. "Mama?"

Opening her arms she reached for me, the plates magically gone. A wail swelled up out of her, so loud it hurt my ears. She sucked in breath and shook her head over and over so her hair fell from its clips, curling up beside her face.

"Mama," I said again.

"I don't want you," she said. "All I've ever wanted was her."

She pushed past me, gliding her way to where Beanie's body was laid out. I called to her one last time but she didn't turn toward me. She was too busy moaning, sitting at the edge of her bed next to the motionless body of my sister.

Gasping, I woke up, curled in a tight ball on my bed. My heart thudded and didn't seem like to slow any time soon.

"It was just a dream," I whispered, blinking hard against the image of Mama that didn't want to fade from my mind. "It wasn't real."

Stretching out, I rolled onto my back and rested my hands on my stomach, feeling the way my breathing came in and out. In and out.

The morning was still too dark for me to get up but I knew I wouldn't fall back asleep even if I tried. That was the way of things whenever I dreamed of Mama. Some nights they were good, those dreams, other times they were awful. I didn't know which were worse, the bad ones or the good ones.

The dreams of Mama holding me or brushing my hair or smiling into my face made me fit to bust with happy feelings that steamed away just as soon as I opened my eyes.

At least the bad dreams never tricked me into having hope.

After a little bit, the darkness lightened and the sounds of the day beginning came from downstairs — the gurgling percolator and clomping of Daddy's boots on the wood floor. Turning my head, I glanced out the window for signs of sunrise. Just a tiny glow of orange that I hoped might soon burst into a sun-shine day.

I swung my feet off the bed and let them hang just over the floor. It would be cold on my bare soles, I knew it. Holding onto the edge of the bed, I tried to work up the nerve to shock myself with the icy cold. Even if I didn't have school for another week or so, I did have chores that needed getting done before I could go about my day.

Taking in a good breath I lowered my feet, then winced and cussed under my breath as a shiver traveled its way from my toes to the top of my head. I whispered a different curse word for every step I took to the closet.

Much as I tried, I couldn't seem to quit swearing even if I did know how it grieved the heart of God. I hadn't even managed to make it past the second full day of the new year with a clean mouth. At least I knew enough to do it in a quiet voice and never in front of any grown-up who might have a mind to make me taste a bar of soap for my language.

I got myself dressed as quick as I could, pulling on a wooly pair of socks before anything else. I buttoned up my everyday blouse and stepped into an old pair of overalls Ray'd grown out of. Last thing I wanted was to walk around in the snow wearing a dress and getting my legs frozen. Grabbing my warm and wooly sweater, I headed for my bedroom door.

I thought maybe if I helped Opal get breakfast together she might not make me do up the dishes afterward. It was worth a try, at least.

Mama had never been one for cooking big meals first thing in the day. She'd scramble a couple eggs if the hens gave or put out a plate of biscuits she'd baked the day before. Most of the time, though, she'd boil oatmeal to hold us over until noon. It never had bothered me, her simple breakfasts. She'd made do with what we had, just like all the other mamas in Red River.

Opal, though, was a believer in breakfasts of fried eggs and sausages, canned fruit and hash-browned potatoes. She'd fill the table with dishes of steaming food, all things we'd gotten from Uncle Gus and Aunt Carrie. Their farm meant we would never go hungry just so long as the hens kept faithful, the soil stayed good, and the seals on the canned things held tight.

I rushed down the steps and to the kitchen where I found Opal mixing up batter for pancakes, her griddle warming on top of the stove. Daddy'd given her New Year's Day off and I was eager to ask her the questions I'd been holding on to for a couple days.

"I'll set the table," I said, going to the cupboard for a stack of plates.

"Good morning to you, too," she said, looking at me over her shoulder. "Why are you up so early?"

I shrugged. "Couldn't sleep anymore."

"You'll be tired later," she said. "Didn't

you stay up until midnight on New Year's Eve?"

"That was two days ago." I rested the four plates on the counter. "I'll be all right. I never do sleep all that much."

"Maybe you should get a rest this afternoon." She turned back to her work. "The mayor's coming for supper tonight and I don't think your daddy would like you being grumpy when you have company over."

It was a good thing she had her back to me, otherwise she would've seen the stink face I made at the idea of taking a rest. I hoped she'd forget she even said it. There was nothing I hated more than Opal's rest times. She wouldn't allow me a book on account she said I needed my mind to be at ease. I'd end up staring at a wall, unable to sleep, and sore that I was wasting so much of my day.

"How was your New Year's Eve?" I asked, hoping maybe if I changed the subject she'd forget about me resting.

"Fine," she said.

"What did you do?"

"Don't forget the forks and knives," she said as if she hadn't heard me.

I pulled the drawer, counting out four forks and resting them on top of the plates.

"I saw you at the dance," I said, peeking

at her out of the corner of my eye.

"Did you?" She didn't so much as flinch. Instead she poured circles of pancake batter on the griddle. "What were you doing there?"

"Ray and I heard the music. We looked in a window." I stood with my hip resting against the drawer after pushing it closed. "You dance good."

"I dance well," she corrected me. "And thank you."

"Who was it you were dancing with?"

"You've got a lot of questions today, huh?" She shook her head. "If you've got to know, that was Lenny Miller. He goes to the high school."

"Is he your boyfriend?" I asked, raising my eyebrows.

"You'll need butter knives, too," she said. "And, no. I don't have a boyfriend. I don't have time with all my life spent making sure you get the table set like you promised."

"Yes, ma'am."

I counted out four knives, and spoons too for good measure. Then I rested my elbow on the counter, leaning my chin on my fist.

"Opal, how'd you learn to dance like that?" I asked.

She shrugged, taking the time to flip over a whole row of pancakes before answering me. "Just did."

"Will you teach me?"

She turned, spatula held up like she meant to swat at a fly. I half expected her to take a swing at me with it.

"I'm fixing roasted chicken for supper tonight. Got a fresh one from Mrs. Seegert," she said. "She said they got a little surprise when what they thought was a hen started crowing in the middle of the night and strutting around the yard."

"Is it plucked?"

Opal nodded. "But I gotta dress it and all." Then she nodded at the counter. "And I'll be peeling until kingdom come to make enough potatoes to fill up Mayor Winston."

"I'll peel them for you," I said. "And I'll even chop them."

"That would be nice," she said.

"If you want, I can do up the dishes after breakfast, too."

"Pearl Louise, I'm not teaching you to dance," she said.

"Please?" I said, trying to give her my most polite voice. "Pretty please?"

"You best get the table set." She nodded at me. "I'll have breakfast ready in a minute."

"I promise I wouldn't tell anybody if you taught me."

"It's not for kids." She turned back to the stove. "That kind of dancing is for grown-ups."

"You aren't that much older than me," I told her.

She turned her head and pursed her lips at me, raising both her eyebrows. "I am too, miss," she said. "A lot can happen in six years to make a girl grown."

I wanted to tell her all that'd happened to me in one year that made me feel grown, but I didn't because the last thing I wanted was her giving me a pity look just then. What I wanted was for her to give me a nod and tell me she'd start teaching me to dance that very afternoon.

"I'd help you with supper every night," I said. "I'd even scrub the pans."

"You don't give up easy, do you?" she asked.

"No, ma'am."

"I can see that." She lifted a stack of pancakes, piling them on a plate before turning off the burner. "But I'm just as stubborn as you, little lady."

There was a laugh riding along on her voice and I imagined she was smiling.

That was when I knew she'd teach me. Maybe not that day, but she would.

■ ■ ■ ■

Bert Barnett lived in the house across the street. He sat on his front porch most mornings, waiting for Ray and me to come out. Really it was Ray he wanted to see. As far as he was concerned, Ray had hung the moon and stars.

Me, he could've done with or without, at least that was what I thought.

"Hey ya, Ray," Bert called out from his front yard when we stepped out after breakfast. He crossed the street without even looking out for any cars driving through.

"Mornin', Bert," Ray said back, shoving his hands into his coat pockets. "Cold, huh?"

Bert scrunched up his face like he hadn't noticed before. Then he put his hands in his pockets, slumping his shoulders the way Ray did. Ray was two years older than Bert, but he was nice to him anyhow.

"I'm gettin' a dog," Bert said.

"That so?" Ray said, kicking at a mound of snow.

"Well, I think so at least." Bert toed a chunk of ice. "Dad said he was gettin' some kind of surprise for me from a trade."

Bert's father was the only doctor in town.

If anybody got sick or hurt, they'd call for him and he'd come, day or night, to help out. Problem was, most folks in Bliss didn't have money enough to pay to get a tooth pulled or a couple stitches put in. Instead of paying cash, they'd trade something they thought was equal to how Doctor Barnett had helped them. There always seemed to be somebody over shoveling their walk or fixing a shingle on their roof. And they always had plenty of meat and vegetables off one of the farms on the outskirts of town.

"One of the Litchfield boys stuck a pea up his nose," Bert said. "Dad had to help him get it out."

"Why'd he stick a pea up his nose?" I asked.

"Beats me," Bert said. "Their hound just had a litter of pups. I'll bet my toe that's what Dad's gettin' for me."

"What if it's not a dog?" I asked.

"What's it matter to you?" Bert asked, pulling a face at me.

I raised one of my eyebrows at him and tried looking the way Opal did when I talked back at her. He didn't seem to care.

"I'm gonna teach it tricks," Bert said to Ray. He pointed at his mittened hand as if he was counting off a list. "Sit down, roll over, speak, and play dead. Might even teach it to climb a ladder."

"Dogs can't climb ladders," I told him.

"I seen it in a newsreel once," Ray said. "They can learn about anything if you teach 'em right."

"I'm gonna," Bert said. "My mother said I'm real good with animals."

When Bert said that, I had to fake a coughing fit so he wouldn't know I was laughing at him. He was the kind of kid to bring home some kind of critter he'd found while tromping through the woods or fishing in the river. Problem was, for as much as he loved all the creatures God had placed upon the earth, Bert couldn't seem to keep one of them alive longer than a week.

I sure worried about that dog.

There was a back way to the library, one that followed a turning and curving road past a handful of houses and a wide-open field that in the winter was full of nothing but snow. That was where the boys sometimes played baseball or football when the weather was nice enough for it. It took longer, going the back way, but I didn't mind so much, especially when I wasn't in any hurry.

Aster Street was the name of it. Aunt Carrie'd told me an aster was the pretty purple flower that grew tall and wild along the roadsides all over Bliss. On that freezing, snow-covered day I had a hard time picturing what those flowers looked like. It would have been nice to see a little something colorful amidst the piles of snow.

Walking along, I stuffed my hands in the pockets of my coat and tipped my head down so the scarf around my neck covered my mouth and nose. It turned out the blue-sky, bright-sun morning had tricked me and the day was far colder than I'd expected. Every step seemed to pull me forward into chillier air.

We'd made the move away from Oklahoma so I wouldn't choke to death on the dust. But the way the frozen air burned in my lungs I didn't know that it was much better here in Michigan.

Good thing I was less than a block away from the library doors or else I didn't know if I'd make it. I started counting my steps. One, two, three.

Squinting my eyes against the cold, I thought how before, when I was smaller, I might've pretended to be an eskimo in the frozen wilderness of Canada. I'd have pretended I wore a coat of seal skin with the fur of a grizzly bear sewed inside to keep me warm enough. If I was playing eskimo,

I'd have imagined snowshoes strapped to my feet and a harpoon slung across my back just in case any wild animals had a mind to take a good bite out of me. Maybe I'd even have a wolf as a pet to keep me company. But I'd grown too old for such make-believe.

A powerful gust of wind blasted past, pushing the snow across the walk in front of me. So much like the dust back home in Red River. But the snow would melt come spring, unlike the dirt that wasn't like to leave Oklahoma anytime soon.

I shook my head against the picture of Beanie standing between me and the duster, her arms spread over her head like she meant to hold it back.

If I could've wished for one thing, I'd wish to be able to go back in time. I'd go all the way back to Palm Sunday, to the hour right before the big duster rolled over us, crushing everything and everybody. I'd have stayed home that day, I wouldn't have wandered off with Ray no matter how he begged. Me staying home would've meant Beanie did, too. She never would have gotten herself lost in the dust coming to find me. We'd still be in Oklahoma. Mama and Daddy would be together and happy because Beanie would be alive.

Maybe, if none of the bad had ever happened, I'd still be up for pretending. Instead of playing an eskimo, I'd imagine myself an Indian and instead of frozen wind whipping me in the face it'd be sharp dots of Oklahoma grit. Life never was perfect back home in Red River, but at least we'd stayed in one piece, dust and all.

Standing on the edge of the street with my eyes shut, I realized I'd stopped moving. The cold air scrubbed against the part of my face not covered by the scarf and I opened my eyes.

Turning, I looked at where I'd stopped. The only problem with me taking Aster Street was that I had to walk past that house, the one with white paint peeling and sad, off-kilter black window shutters. From what I could tell, nobody'd lived in that house for nearly a hundred years. All the kids in town said it was cursed, that house. They'd hold their breath when they had to walk past it, fingers crossed. They'd said if somebody did look, they'd be dead in a week.

I didn't believe that for one minute. Even so, something about that place gave me the heebie-jeebies and I crossed my fingers. I figured it didn't hurt to be careful.

Holding what little breath I could take, I

walked away from it, fast as my body allowed me. I looked back at it over my shoulder and a shiver tingled up my backbone.

I walked faster still, trying to talk myself out of being afraid.

My favorite seat by the fire was taken by the time I stepped foot in the library and I only had myself to blame for it. If I hadn't spent so much time missing Red River and getting spooked by that old house, I would've been in the cozy chair already, a book open on my lap and the warm flames flushing my cheeks. Just as well, I decided. It was as good an excuse as any to wander about the library to see if there were any corners I'd left undiscovered.

Holding my finger out to my side, I felt of the shelves as I passed them. There wasn't so much as a speck of dust. My fingers came up clean at the end of the row. As long as I had lived in Michigan, I still wasn't used to how clean things stayed with no fine dust seeping through the cracks all day long.

I wouldn't let myself think of how Mama spent the better part of her days trying to get rid of the dust in Red River. I just wouldn't allow it.

Around the corner I saw Mrs. Trask leading a young boy to the back of the library where I knew she kept the books for little kids.

"I believe I have just the book for you," she said, holding the shelves for support as she walked.

If there was one place in that building I knew I hadn't seen yet it was the upstairs. Whenever I asked Mrs. Trask if I could go up there, she'd just say it was full of old furniture and books that needed to be repaired. Then she'd say she didn't think I better go up there.

I told myself I wouldn't open a single door, but if there was one with the door pulled to, it wouldn't do any harm to peek in.

"We could maybe read a story or two together," Mrs. Trask said, her voice quieter as she took step after step away from where I stood. "I'd like that if you would."

I had plenty of time.

I made my way to the front of the library, through the lobby, then toward the stairs. They were the kind that led up to a landing before breaking in two for a second set. Holding onto the railing to be sure I didn't stumble, I rushed up that first set fast as my legs would go without my feet stomping on the steps.

Turning, I made to take the set of steps to the right, surprised by how out of breath I was. Doctor Barnett had called it asthma. Said it was just something that happens to some folks after they have pneumonia.

"When you get short of breath," he'd told me, "I need you to slow down. All right? Just slow down and try to breathe in as deeply as you can."

I didn't trust myself to slow down when I was still on my feet, so I sat on the second step, breathing down as deep into my lungs as I could.

"Go slowly," he'd told me. "You might feel like you'll suffocate if you don't breathe in fast, but it isn't so. You'll get better air if you take it slow."

I tried remembering that. But still I was struck with the temptation to huff in and puff out short air that only reached the top of my chest.

"Pretend that you're trying to fill up all the way into your stomach," Doctor Barnett had told me. "You'll be all right."

And then he'd given me a breathing treatment with medicine that'd made me jumpy and twitchy all the rest of the day.

It took me more than a handful of minutes sitting on that step to start breathing regular. Even then it felt as if somebody'd filled my lungs with wool, scrubbing it around to rub my chest raw inside.

I heard Mrs. Trask's voice at her desk, helping somebody check out a book most likely. Must've been a real short book she'd shared with that little boy.

She might've been an old woman with a breaking-down body and a thin memory, but she heard as well as an elephant. If I took one step up she'd know it. And if I tried going downstairs she might get sore at me for sneaking around. Last thing I needed was to have the librarian mad at me. I decided to stay put until she was off to help another kid find a book.

Turning, I rested my back against the banister and shut my eyes. I sure had a way of getting myself in a pickle. Darn curiosity of mine.

Opening my eyes I looked at a framed picture that hung on the wall. It wasn't a large painting and the frame was nothing but a regular old wood one. The colors of it were those of just-after-sunset, blues and oranges and blacks. It looked like a town or city, with tall buildings sprouting up on either side of a river.

It was wide, that river, and made me think of the day we'd crossed over the Mississippi on our way to Michigan. Over the painted river were dots of stars. I wished we could have been at the Mississippi at night. How nice it would've been to sit there beside the river looking up at the nighttime sky.

We'd been happy that day along the Mississippi, Mama, Daddy, Ray, and me. I tried believing that at least.

Forgetting about Mrs. Trask's sharp ears and the fact that I was someplace I wasn't meant to me, I stood and stepped close to the painting. I let my eyes take in every inch of it. The sky and the spires of what I imagined to be fine places, the bridge that spanned over the water, and the tallest of the buildings with a round clock face painted in yellow.

So small I almost didn't see them were four people. Their arms were spread wide like wings that helped them glide in the air over the river. A tiny glow of white dotted next to the boy in front.

Where were they going, I wondered. How was it they could fly without wings?

I imagined myself rising up from the ground, feet wiggling as I dangled in the air. I'd be sure to wear slacks that day so nobody below could see my underthings. Up, up, up nearly touching the clouds, reaching for them and barely grazing them with my fingertips. Then I'd take off flying to all corners of the earth, seeing the things I'd only ever dared dream of. The ocean where whales would spurt water out the tops of their heads. The mountains where I'd lower down to touch the tippy-top peak with my toes before zooming off to soar over valleys of green.

It seemed the very best kind of magic, flying wherever it was I wanted to go.

My daydream faded when I heard steps creaking from below me. I turned to see Mrs. Trask coming up slowly, holding tight to the railing.

"Hello, dear," she said. "I thought I heard someone up here."

"I'm sorry, ma'am," I said.

"No." She smiled. "No need."

When she got to the landing she kept her hand on the railing to keep from toppling backward. My heart flipped a little when I saw how close she was to the edge of that top step.

"Oh yes," she said, taking a step forward. "You've met Peter Pan."

"Who, ma'am?" I asked.

"What do they teach children these days?" she said under her breath.

Letting go of the railing, she pointed at the picture and stepped closer to it.

"This is Peter Pan." She pointed, holding

her finger over one of the flying children, showing me the boy at the front of the pack. "He's taking them to Neverland."

"Where's that?" I asked.

"Oh, I could tell you, dear," she said. "But I won't."

I turned to see her wink at me.

"What would be the fun in that?" she asked. "Follow me. We'll find the book together."

She took my hand and I walked as slow as she did down the steps, taking one last look at the picture.

I thought I'd like nothing better than to be friends with that Peter Pan.

Chapter Three

The minute I got home from the library Opal sent me up to bed for a rest. I snuck the book in the front of my overalls and climbed under the covers, hoping she wouldn't catch me reading when I should have been sleeping.

It didn't take me long to figure out that I liked Wendy Darling. She seemed a girl I might like to make friends with. She might have been the kind to like dressing up more than I did or one to want to play house, but that was all right.

Just so long as she was nice, I would've been able to overlook something like that.

Who I didn't like in that book was Peter Pan. I thought if he'd come in through my bedroom window right in the middle of the night trying to get me to give him a kiss, I'd have slapped him right in the mouth and told him to go back to where he'd come from.

I read all the way to where they flew out of London to Neverland where Wendy would play mama to all the boys who'd found their way there. On that page was a hand-drawn picture of them flying over that big river, like the one in the library painting, just without the color. Wendy's face held an open-mouthed smile like she was whooping as she flew. Her eyes were wide with wonder.

"Go back home," I whispered, tapping the page with my fingertip. "Wendy Darling, you go back home."

I stayed in bed reading that story until Opal came up to tell me it was time to peel potatoes. She saw the book even though I tried stuffing it under my pillow. She didn't say a word about it, so I knew she wasn't too sore.

Opal didn't stay to eat with us like she sometimes did. The way she hurried off, promising to get the supper dishes done up the next morning, I wondered if she was going to see that Lenny Miller boy again. I would have asked but I didn't want her thinking I was being nosy, even if I was.

She'd gotten everything on the table before she went, though, and just about bumped into Mayor Winston on the front porch.

"Guess I got good timing," he said, nodding at her and letting her know she didn't need to apologize. "Whatever you fixed sure smells good. Far as my nose is concerned you have nothing to be sorry about."

"Yes, sir," she said, smiling at him before tapping down the steps and into the dark evening.

"Come on in, Jake," Daddy said. "Pearl, you wanna get his coat?"

"Yes, sir," I answered, stepping forward.

"Thank you," Winston said after taking off his coat and laying it across my arms. It was wooly and tickled at the tender part of my wrist. He took off his hat and handed it to Ray. "Son, you'll take care of that for me?"

Ray told him he would.

"Y'all can put those in on my bed," Daddy said.

Ray and I stepped into the room that hadn't been slept in for all the months since Mama'd been gone. It was colder in there than the rest of the house on account Daddy kept the door closed most of the time. In the darkness of the room I could almost imagine she'd never left. I could pretend that behind the door of the closet were her dresses, hanging side by side. That her powders were still lined up on her vanity and her few pair of shoes stood against the wall.

I could have made myself believe she was still there. But I didn't.

I lowered Winston's wooly coat to the foot of the bed. Ray put the hat right on top of it. And the two of us walked back out into the brightly lit living room and the kind smile of Mayor Winston.

"I hear you're thinking of calling on Mrs. Wheeler," Winston said, dumping a heap of mashed potatoes on his plate. "That true, Tom?"

"Yes, sir," Daddy said. "Guess she's been wanting to have a talk with me."

"What's she want?" I asked.

"Now, I'm not sure. Might not be anything I could tell you anyway, darlin'. Some things folks would rather keep to themselves," Daddy said. "I'm thinking of going over tomorrow morning if you wanna join me, Winston."

"I might just do that," the mayor said.

"Pearl, you could come and have a visit with Hazel if you'd like," Daddy said, smiling. "I'm sure she wouldn't mind."

"That's all right," I said.

"Maybe next time then, darlin'." Daddy leaned back in his chair, crossing his arms over his chest. "She's not near as bad as you think."

What I wanted to tell Daddy was that he hadn't spent enough time around Hazel Wheeler to know a thing like that. But I thought better of it and kept my mouth shut so nobody could accuse me of being a gossip.

"She can be a real sourpuss," Winston said. "Isn't that right?"

"Yes, sir," I answered. "Aunt Carrie said everybody's got their troubles. Even Hazel Wheeler."

"That's so," Winston said. "That is so."

We finished our supper and nobody said another word about Mrs. Wheeler or Hazel or paying anybody else in town any kind of a visit. Daddy warmed up some leftover coffee for him and Winston to have in the kitchen and told Ray and me we could listen to a radio show if we wanted.

"I don't want you listening in to our conversation, hear?" Daddy'd said.

There wasn't one thing in the world that teased my curiosity more than being told I wasn't supposed to hear something.

I did fight the temptation to put my ear to the door as long as I could. I sat beside Ray on the floor, eyes on the radio as if there were pictures moving across it along with the words and music pouring from it. Every inch of me fidgeted, thumbs twirling and toes tapping and teeth biting at lips. I sat there long as I could, until I felt fit to burst from the curiosity.

"I need a glass of water," I told Ray, getting to my feet.

"No you don't either," he said, shaking his head. "You're just gonna eavesdrop."

"Am not," I said, putting on a voice like I was surprised at him. "I'm parched."

"You'll get yourself into trouble."

"For getting a drink of water?"

"You go on and pretend all you like," he said. "I know you better than you know yourself, Pearl Spence."

I stuck my tongue out at him and that only served to make him laugh at me. I hated that he could see through me so clear.

By the time I got close enough to the kitchen to hear the men talking, I could have sworn that Ray'd turned up the radio.

"Happy days are here again . . ." a crooning voice sang over top of a full band of blasting instruments.

I could've stomped right back to the living room and given Ray an even worse face than I already had, but I knew he'd just roll on the floor crying his laughter tears if I did.

"Lucky Strike features *Your Hit Parade . . .*" a man announced, just as I got my ear to the door enough to hear Daddy's voice.

I plugged the other ear to muffle the radio.

"You sure we have to have a meeting?" Daddy asked. "There's that many upset?"

"Tom, I've told you. This town's got a history," the mayor said, no smile in his voice. "And that history goes all the way back to when the first runaway slave crossed into Lenawee County. There are some who just can't see to treating a colored person right. You ask Mrs. Wheeler what happened to her sister and brother-in-law. I bet that'll convince you."

"You told me about that before, Jake," Daddy said. "But this is just a couple of dances."

"And that's just what I'll tell them at the meeting." He stopped talking and I heard a slurping sound I thought must've been him drinking from his coffee. "We're due one anyway. I don't think I've called one for at least a year."

"You won't want me to talk, will you?" Daddy asked.

"Nope, you don't have to get up," Winston said. "Just be there so the people see you're with me."

"I will," Daddy said.

"I'll let people speak their mind," Winston said. "Then we'll let them know how it's going to be. That's all there'll be to it."

"You don't think there's gonna be any trouble, do you?" Daddy said.

Winston sighed. "I hope not, Tom. There're some holdouts from the Klan. Not many, but a few."

"Who's that?"

I held my breath. I'd heard Daddy talk about the Klan before. They were white men that put on long robes and pointed hats and rode around on horses pretending to be the ghosts of the Confederates that'd gotten themselves killed in the War Between the States. I'd thought they were silly until Daddy told me there wasn't a thing silly about such dangerous men.

"Probably half of them moved away after what they did that night. That wasn't ten years ago, I guess." Winton hesitated. "I've got a list back at the office. I could give it to you tomorrow."

"They aren't still active, are they?" Daddy asked.

"Not too much," he answered. "Guess the last time they stirred up any kind of trouble was when Gus hired Noah."

"I imagine they thought he should've hired a white man instead."

"Yep," Winston said. "It's hard times. Men do desperate things when they're out of money."

"What did they do?" Daddy asked.

"Well, Gus got a letter that said they'd burn down his house if he didn't get rid of Noah."

"Must not have meant it," Daddy said.

"Nope."

"Any idea who wrote it?"

"Some thought it was Stan," Winston answered. "But he can't hardly write his name. It wasn't him."

"Stan?" Daddy asked.

"Fitzpatrick," Winston said. "Lives out in the chicken coop on the west end of town. You know the one?"

My eyes grew wide. I knew Delores Fitzpatrick. Sat beside her in school. And I'd seen the chicken coop-turned-house they lived in. They were the very poorest of anybody in Bliss.

"Yeah. I know that place," Daddy said. "Wish we could get them into something better."

"Well, Stan wouldn't let you if you could."

"I understand."

I heard the creak of a chair and the slurping of somebody taking in a good drink of coffee. Daddy offered another cup and Winston accepted. Other than that, the two men were quiet for at least a full minute.

"Tom, we've got some good people here in Bliss. They'd do anything for anybody. But as good as most of the people here are, there are some —" Winston stopped and I imagined he was taking a drink of coffee. "There are some who'd think splitting the dances was just the start. I know of at least two families who'd like nothing more than to have Jim Crow up here."

"Well, I do have faith you'll be able to settle them in that meeting."

"I hope you're right, Tom."

The sound of chairs scuffing against the floor got my heart to racing. They were about to come out of the kitchen.

Quiet as I could, I rushed back to the living room and my spot right in front of the radio.

"That was one long drink of water," Ray said, not looking at me.

"Yeah, yeah," I said, pretending to listen to the radio show.

After Mayor Winston left, Daddy sat in his chair and smoked a couple cigarettes. Ray'd since turned over to a comedy show that had the two of us laughing and wishing the program could go on all night.

Daddy sent us up to bed, telling me I could stay up to read a bit if I wanted. Just as I got settled under my covers with the Peter Pan book open on my lap, Ray came in. Without me even saying anything, he sat on the edge of my bed.

"Aren't you tired?" I asked.

"What's Mrs. Wheeler got to say to your pa?" he asked. "You know?"

I shrugged. "How would I know?"

"Didn't you hear nothin' through the kitchen door?"

"Probably just got some kind of ax to grind," I said. "She's got Hazel for a daughter. Isn't that enough to make a woman complain?"

"That ain't nice."

"Hazel's not nice," I told him.

"You think she's scared of somethin'?" he asked.

I wanted to tell him about what Winston'd said about the Klan doing something to Mrs. Wheeler's sister. But I thought better of it. I wasn't the kind to go around spreading stories I only knew half of.

Instead, I asked if Ray wanted me to read to him. He said he'd like that and leaned back so his shoulders were against the wall beside my window. His hair had grown shaggy around his ears and when he clenched his jaw I saw a shadow of his father in him. Seemed strange I'd never thought of how he'd end up looking like his father someday.

"What?" he asked, lowering his eyebrows at me.

"Nothing."

"Why're you staring at me like that?" He got a little smirk on his face the way he did when he was fixing to tease me. "You think I'm pretty special, don't ya?"

I rolled my eyes and shook my head, flipping through the pages to the beginning of the book. I didn't figure he'd want me to read out of the middle of the book where I'd gotten to.

"You ever get scared still?" Ray asked.

"Scared of what?" I looked up from the first page.

"Don't know." He turned his head toward me. "Maybe what happened before?"

I knew he meant what Eddie'd done to me, so I nodded my head. "I get bad dreams sometimes."

"Yeah?"

"Don't you ever get scared?" I asked.

"Sure I do." He bit at his bottom lip

before going on. "Some days, though, I feel more mad than scared."

"You mean about your pa?"

He nodded and I didn't make him go on. I knew very well how his father'd treated him. And I didn't figure a boy could get by seeing his own pa dead the way he had without feeling something or another about it.

"Does it ever make you feel mean?" I asked.

Again, he nodded.

"But you're never mean to anybody."

"Don't wanna be."

He turned his eyes down to the page of the book and I knew that meant he was done talking. So I went ahead and read that story to him, all the while thinking on how Ray could've been the meanest boy in the world if he'd wanted to. He was strong and stubborn and smart enough to think up ways to bully any kid between Red River and Bliss. But he didn't.

I thought Ray Jones knew more about being a good person than most anybody else I'd ever known.

Chapter Four

All morning I was in a sour mood. Seemed just about every little thing that could go wrong did. First I'd tried making fried eggs by myself before Opal got to our house. All I'd managed to do was to get three eggs stuck to the bottom of one of Mama's best pans and fill the house with a nasty burnt smell that I was just sure would take the better part of the year to clear out.

It all seemed to roll on downhill from there. My warmest stockings had a hole in the toe and I couldn't manage to get my bedsheets tucked in the way Mama'd taught me. My hair was full of snarls and Opal'd threatened to wash my mouth out for the cuss I said as she pulled a brush through them.

To top all that off, Bert'd asked Ray to go along with him to get whatever it was his dad had traded the Litchfields for when he got the pea out of their kid's nose. I knew very well there was plenty of room in Doctor Barnett's car for me. But I also knew that there were some things boys wanted to do without girls around to pester them.

"You just need to make a few friends of your own," Opal told me. "There has to be somebody."

I shook my head and told her I'd rather drink castor oil than be friends with any of the girls in Bliss. She just told me I was being difficult and went back to scraping egg off her pan.

It seemed the only reasonable thing to do was stomp up the stairs and pout in my room for the rest of the morning.

Ray knocked on my door not an hour later, calling for me to come on out and see what Bert got. I tried ignoring him, but my darn curiosity got the better of me and I bolted out the room and down the steps. Opal had my coat laid out on the couch for me with my scarf in hand to wrap around my face. Out to the porch and down the steps, Ray and I went.

"Button up all the way," Opal called.

I hollered back that I would, then we crossed the street to Bert's house.

Bert was out back, standing in the doorway of a little shed where his father kept his tools. Big as Bert's smile was, I could tell he was happy.

"Hey there, Pearl," he said, hardly able to stand still for all his excitement.

"How do, Bert?" I said back. "What you got in there?"

"You got a guess?" Ray asked.

"It's a pigeon," Bert blurted out before I had the chance to even think on it. "It's a girl pigeon."

"How do you know?" I asked.

"Mr. Litchfield told me." His eyes were round as dinner plates and near as wide. "Wanna see her?"

I shrugged, hoping not to seem too eager even though I was.

"All right. You just can't let her outta her cage," he said.

"I won't."

"Promise?"

"Course I do." I put out my hand and shook on the promise so he'd know I meant to keep my word.

A brass birdcage sat on the workbench along the back wall of the shed. The bird made a warbling coo, her throat puffing out. The way her feathers caught what little light came in through the door made them look green and purple and blue. I never would have thought a pigeon was so pretty.

Right away I regretted promising not to

open the cage. I'd have liked to hold her in my hand and feel of her feathers.

"What would happen if she got out?" I asked, taking a step toward her.

"She'd fly off," Bert said, standing between me and the cage as if he worried I'd lift the latch and set her loose. "Dad said she'd fly all the way back to the Litchfield farm."

"Nah, she wouldn't," I said. "How would she know the way?"

Bert shrugged. "Guess she just does."

I looked at him sideways, figuring he was pulling my leg. But Bert never was one for kidding. I didn't know that he was clever enough for something like that.

"Mr. Litchfield said that's her way," Ray said. "Said if you took her five hundred miles away she'd end up right back at their place."

"You aren't teasing?" I asked.

"I ain't." Ray leaned a hip into the workbench beside me and stuck a finger in through the cage to feel the bird's feathers. "You can go on and ask Mr. Litchfield hisself."

"How does she know the way, though?" I asked.

"Beats me," he said.

"What's her name?"

"Sassy," Bert said. "You like it?"

"Sure I do," I said, wishing I had the courage to touch her the way Ray had.

We stood there just a couple minutes more. I wondered if that bird was upset about being taken away from where she'd lived all her life. I wondered if she even knew enough to miss her home.

Since Ray and I were already bundled up, we decided we might as well go on to the farm to visit Uncle Gus and Aunt Carrie. Mama would've worried that we were imposing on them, going over without an invitation. She'd have told us we were fixing to wear out our welcome.

But Aunt Carrie'd told us more than once that we were welcome whenever we wanted to come. I knew she meant it by how she'd smile when she first saw us. If there was one place in all of Bliss where I felt at home it was on the farm with Uncle Gus and Aunt Carrie.

We found Uncle Gus and Noah Jackson out by the chicken coop mending a bit of fence. Uncle Gus held the chicken wire to the post while Noah drove the nails in. They stood up straight as Ray and I got closer, Uncle Gus waving us over and hollering out a howdy.

"Bet I can guess what's new," Uncle Gus said. "Bert got himself a bird, didn't he?"

"How'd you know?" I asked.

"It's a small town." Uncle Gus rubbed his nose with the back of his gloved hand. "Word gets round fast."

"What do you think of that pigeon?" Noah asked, pulling a couple nails from between his front teeth. "It's something, ain't it?"

"Would it really go back home?" I asked. "If it got out?"

"Yes, miss," Uncle Gus answered. "It sure would."

"Didn't they use them birds in the war?" Noah asked.

"Sure did," Uncle Gus said. "I seen them when I was over in France. English fella had a couple in the trenches with him. He'd put a little message into a capsule and tie it to one of the pigeon's legs. Then he'd let the bird go and it'd fly right back to where the generals were. Always found its way, I hear. Every single time. Even with the Germans shootin' at them. See? Smart birds."

"Can they find anyplace they want to go?" I asked.

Noah shook his head. "Nope. They can only find home, right Gus?"

"That's right," Uncle Gus answered. "Only place they go is back home."

■ ■ ■ ■

Aunt Carrie had a hot cup of milk in the kitchen for me once I went inside. I was sure grateful for the warm drink and that she let me take it in what she sometimes called the parlor. She told me to curl up on the davenport and then tucked a soft afghan around my legs. I hadn't realized how sleepy I was until I'd gotten comfortable.

"Could you please tell me a story?" I asked before sipping at my milk.

"I'd be happy to." She took a seat at the other end of the davenport, turned so she was facing me. "What kind of story?"

"A fairy tale," I said. "Maybe one with birds?"

"Hmm. I think I know one like that." She smiled before she began. "Once upon a time there was a young man named Wilhelm and a young woman named Marta. They were deeply in love and planning to get married, but don't worry, this isn't a story with too much kissing in it."

Aunt Carrie gave me a wink before going on.

"One day, in their joy at being young and in love, they went for a long walk in the woods," she said. "You know nothing good can come from fairy-tale characters wandering in the woods, don't you?"

I nodded.

"Suddenly, Marta felt a sinking feeling, like her heart was breaking," Aunt Carrie went on. "She cried, but didn't know why or what could make her so sad. Wilhelm tried to comfort her, but it was no good. Marta's heart had broken, shattered like glass inside her chest."

"Did she die?" I asked.

"No. But something else happened." Aunt Carrie took another sip of coffee. "As soon as her heart was in too many pieces to ever have a hope of being mended, she turned into a bird."

I put a hand over my mouth so I wouldn't be tempted to talk and interrupt the story.

"Just a tiny sparrow of a bird, she sat in Wilhelm's hand, singing the saddest song ever sung in all the history of the world." Aunt Carrie let the room grow quiet and I thought she was every bit as good at telling stories as Daddy and Uncle Gus. "But then, from deep in the woods came another voice, one not so beautiful as that of the sparrow Marta. The voice was shrill and horrible, calling for Marta to follow it away from Wilhelm. He tried to wrap his fingers around the small bird, but it was hopeless. The voice from the woods was more powerful, too strong. Marta had to fly away."

Aunt Carrie told of how Wilhelm tried to follow her, but the woods were too thick and the night growing too dark. He'd trudged through the woods, never resting and never stopping to eat even, searching for his beloved Marta.

"Was she lost to him?" I asked.

"Ah, but one can never be too lost to be found by true love."

Wilhelm climbed mountains and crossed streams, calling for his Marta by day and by night until he found a cabin, deeper in the woods than he'd ever been.

"An old hag hobbled out of the cabin. Wilhelm asked if she had his Marta and the witch nodded her crone's head and told him the only way to get her back was to mend her broken heart."

"How could he?"

"The witch told him it would take something precious made of sand." She smiled at me. "Would you like to guess what that is?"

"A pearl?" I whispered.

"Of course. A pearl," she answered. "Wilhelm was wise enough to know that, too."

He traveled all the way to the edge of the land where it touched the sea, and there he found a pearl to give to the witch to heal

Marta's heart. It took him so long, though, he feared his love was lost. Still, he went on.

"His love was stronger than fear," Aunt Carrie said. "He showed the pearl to the witch, begging her to release his Marta and restore her to the young lady she'd been. The witch tried to take the pearl in her gnarled and veiny hand and cackled at him when he closed his fingers over it. He demanded to see Marta before letting go of the pearl. The hag snarled at him, but then invited him into the cabin."

Once inside Wilhelm saw cages hung from every inch of the rafters and resting on shelves along all of the walls. Cages sat on every inch of the floor and bench and table in the cabin. Each of them with a different bird. Just by looking, he couldn't tell one from another.

The witch laughed with her ugly voice and I imagined it sounded more like a battle cry than anything.

"She told him he'd never find the right bird," Aunt Carrie said. "She said he could only have one guess which one was Marta. If he was wrong, he'd be sent into the sea where he'd found the pearl, never to return."

"What would happen if he didn't try?" I asked.

"He could go back to his life," she said. "He wouldn't have Marta, but he would live."

"What did he do?"

"He stepped closer to the cages and shut his eyes." Aunt Carrie squeezed her own eyes closed and put a hand to her chest. "He began to sing. It was a song he had sung to her by the river when they'd sat watching the rolling current or when they'd sat together in the sunshine, feeling its warmth on their faces. It was a song only the two of them knew."

I imagined him singing a line then waiting. One little bird trilled out the tune in echo. He sang a second and a third, a fourth and a fifth. The little bird repeated every note back at him. He kept on singing and listening for her calling back to him until he found her in a cage all the way to the back of the cabin.

"He reached her cage, knowing it was her by their shared song," Aunt Carrie said. "The witch screamed in fury, but she was powerless to stop him from freeing Marta. He held the pearl out in the palm of his hand and the bird picked it up with her beak, hopping out to the dirt floor of the cabin. As soon as she was free of the cage and her heart mended, she turned back into her human form."

"What about the other birds?" I asked.

"The witch warned them, saying they ought not release any more." Aunt Carrie smiled. "But it little mattered what she threatened or how she warned. One by one, Wilhelm and Marta released those birds. With each one the witch grew weaker and weaker until she herself was nothing more than a chirping bird in a cage all her own."

"Did they live happily ever after?" I asked.

"Yes, dear," she said. "They most certainly did."

That night I dreamed of Mama. She'd gotten herself five hundred miles away from us in a place I'd never seen before. I dreamed that tall buildings grew out of the ground all around her and that cars zoomed from here to there past her, making her skirts rustle around her legs.

She didn't notice all the hustle and bustle. Didn't hear a bit of it. She kept her eyes closed and lifted both hands over her head. Slow and gentle and graceful in the middle of the wild city, Mama rose up off the ground, her toes pointed until her whole body stretched out, like she was lying on the air.

She opened her eyes, but not because she needed to see. Every bit of her knew the way.

She knew the way home.

Chapter Five

I didn't make Opal ask me to help her get supper together. Matter of fact, I'd been following her around that whole day, hoping she'd find work for me to do. She'd found plenty, but kept looking at me like I'd sprouted a toe out the top of my head. I'd been doing odd jobs all day long hoping she'd see how big a help I could be to her. Maybe then she'd be obliged and offer to teach me to dance out of the goodness of her own heart. But when time came to cook supper I'd plumb run out of patience.

"Opal?" I said, watching her set a pan on the stovetop.

"Hmm?"

"Aren't you ever going to teach me how to dance?"

"Well, I thought you'd forgotten about that," she said. "You haven't asked for days."

"Will you?"

"Get the cutting board out."

"You're the best dancer I've ever seen," I said. "I'll bet you'd be a real good teacher, too."

"Don't be so sure," she told me, shaking her head. "Besides after the meeting tonight, I'll probably be forbidden to dance in this town again."

"Nah, they wouldn't do that," I said.

"You don't think so? You know they're meeting because of the dances," she said. "Hand me that washrag, would you?"

I did as she asked.

"I was the only Negro at that dance." She took care to fold the damp rag into a square. "I know they don't want me dancing with their white kids."

"But you're not all the way Negro," I said. "Just half."

"That's more than enough for most people." She shook her head and rubbed at a spot on the kitchen counter. "If I'd known it was going to cause such a stir I would've just stayed home that night."

She handed me a couple carrots and the chopping knife. "Make them thin," she said. "They're for soup."

I couldn't cut up anything near as fast as she could without fear I'd take off the end of my finger. Still, she didn't sigh at me for being slow the way Mama would have. Opal just went back to mixing up the cornbread she'd started.

"Opal?" I said, stopping my knife before setting to work on my second carrot. "You think they'll split up the dances?"

"Who's *they*?"

"I don't know," I said. "Some folks and Jim Crow."

"Well, first off, Jim Crow isn't a person. They're laws about what colored folks can and cannot do in the south," she said. "Keep your eyes on your knife. You'll slice your thumb off."

I looked back at my carrot.

"We don't have Jim Crow laws here, thank goodness." She cleared her throat and poured the cornbread batter into a pan. "And some folks are just busybodies. That's all."

She looked at me over her shoulder.

"You don't have to tell anybody I said that," she said.

"I won't."

"People who hate Negroes so much should move to Mississippi, if you ask me."

I didn't know what she meant by that, but didn't ask. She'd started humming and I kept right on working until all the carrots were chopped. She told me to go ahead and put them in her stew pot. I did, liking the way they clunked on the bottom.

The cornbread in the oven and the soup on to simmer, Opal did up what few things were dirty in the sink and I dried them. She thanked me for helping her.

"Opal, can I ask you something?" I asked.

"I guess so."

"If they do split up the dances, which would you choose?"

"I don't know." She pushed a curl back into her loose bun. "Maybe I'd just have to start my own."

"I'd come," I said.

"That would be nice."

Daddy told Ray and me we'd best stay home from the town meeting. He'd said it would just be a bunch of grown folks bellyaching about not getting their own way and it would only serve to bore us right out of our minds.

"Opal's gonna stay with you until I get home," he said. "You'll mind her, won't you?"

We said we would.

"Now, I won't be too late," he said, putting on his coat. "Y'all can stay up until I get back and I promise I'll tell you about some of the meeting."

After Daddy left, Opal turned on the

radio, finding something nice and calm and slow. She said it was so Ray could concentrate on the letter he was writing to his mother and so I could read my book. Really, I thought it was so I wouldn't bother her to teach me how to dance.

Even if she'd offered to give me a dance lesson that night, I would have told her no thanks. At least that was what I told myself.

I peeked at her every now and again out of the corner of my eye to see if she was giving any sign of wanting to dance. A toe tapping or a head bobbing. The way I figured, if she got into a dancing mood, she might just teach me a step or two after all.

But nothing. I knew it was a lost cause when she took up Mama's mending basket and got to work on one of Ray's socks. Somehow that boy could find a way to work a hole in his socks with every single one of his toes.

I just turned my eyes back to my book.

Ray beat me at four out of five games of checkers. And I was pretty sure he'd set me up to jump his last few pieces in the fifth game.

"You let me win," I said, shaking my head.

"I never did," he answered back. "I was just listenin' to the radio."

"You don't have to let me win," I said.

"I didn't."

"Don't bicker," Opal said, putting the mending down beside her chair and getting up. She checked the clock on the wall. "It's getting late."

"Can't we stay up until Daddy gets home?" I asked. "Please?"

"He said you could." She shook her head and went to the kitchen, letting the door swing closed behind her.

Ray went to the radio and bent at the waist, eyes level with the dial as he turned it up and down, trying to find something worth listening to. As fast as he moved it, I didn't know how he could figure out what was playing. I didn't care, though. I wouldn't have admitted it to Opal, but I was tired.

Dropping onto the davenport, I leaned my head on the back and stared at the ceiling. There was a crack that went all the way from one wall to where a light hung right in the middle of the room.

"Ray, if you could pick anywhere in the whole world, where would you live?" I asked.

"I don't know, Pearl," he said, still monkeying with the radio.

"I'd live in the library," I told him.

"Seems as good a place as any."

"You'd go out to California, wouldn't you?" I asked. "Or Florida?"

He shook his head then settled on a radio program. He plunked down cross-legged, facing me.

"Would you go back to Red River?" I asked.

"Would you?"

I nodded.

"Then I'd go with you." He bit at his bottom lip and shrugged. "Guess I'd just go wherever you went."

We were all he had, Daddy and me. And, when I thought about it, he was all we had, too.

I slid off the couch and took the half step toward him. I settled into the spot on the floor right next to him.

We sat there, the two of us, listening to some program that I knew I'd never remember. What I would remember the rest of my days was how important Ray Jones was, and how having him around made me feel brave enough to face anything.

I could make it through just about anything so long as Ray was there with me.

Back in Red River the telephone had never rung. At least not that I remembered. The dusters had knocked over all the poles that held the lines. The wires had snapped at one point or another. Besides, most folks in town couldn't have afforded to keep a telephone in their home even if the lines had been up.

So, there in the house on Magnolia Street, I still jumped whenever the telephone rang. My heart would beat fast and I'd feel like the very best thing to do was run and hide under the bed.

That night, the ringing surprised me even more because Daddy wasn't home to let me know it was all right.

"Who's calling?" I asked Ray.

He shrugged. "You gonna answer it?"

"Should I?"

"Might be your dad," he said.

"What if it isn't?" I turned toward the telephone where it sat on a table against the wall. "You answer it."

"No thanks."

"Well, if you're scared . . ." I started, thinking he might take my bluff and pick up the receiver.

He didn't. He just reached out and turned down the radio. "There, now you'll hear the ringing better."

I rolled my eyes and pushed myself up off the floor.

I picked up the receiver and held it to my ear, feeling the weight of it in my hand.

"Hello? Spence residence," I said, just the way Opal always did.

"Pearl?"

"Yes, ma'am," I answered, trying not to drop the receiver for how my hand had started shaking.

It was Mama.

Chapter Six

Mama had played the piano for the church services in Red River as long as I could remember. She'd pound out the hymns while Pastor stomped across the stage, his arms waving to and fro, singing the words at the top of his lungs.

Every week she'd practice and once in a while I'd sneak over and sit on the church steps listening to her play. I'd close my eyes and imagine those fingers of hers were dancers, leaping from one piano key to the other.

I always wished she'd teach me to play. I never asked her to, hoping she'd offer. She never did. I wondered if it was something she'd wanted to keep just to herself, playing songs the way she did.

In my Peter Pan book it said that Wendy's mother had a kiss in the corner of her lips that she didn't give to anybody. Not to her children or her husband even. I'd tried picturing what that might look like. Seemed to me Mama not offering to teach me piano was something akin to that held-back kiss of Mrs. Darling's.

One day while Mama practiced at the church, I'd sat on the steps as usual expecting to hear her playing loud and fast the way Pastor liked all the hymns to be. But instead, she played light and slow, like she felt the sounding of each note all the way down to her toes. I'd imagined the music fell from high up in the sky like stars, twinkling and sparkling as they came.

Then Mama's voice had filled the sanctuary, rich and smooth, singing of stardust and love and lonely nights. She didn't belt it out, that wasn't Mama's way. And she didn't hold out the notes like some folks did when they wanted to show off. She just opened her mouth and the sound sailed out, drifting along on the air all the way to where I sat.

I couldn't help myself from stepping inside so I could watch her. Her eyes were closed as she played, her fingers not straying to a sour chord, not hitting a wrong note. Every once in awhile she'd move her head from one side to the other or rock forward as she moved her hands along, tapping her foot on the pedal to make the piano sound hold out as long as she could.

She finished, not taking her hands off the keys but letting them rest there until the piano fell silent. I'd thought how pretty she was. The prettiest mama in all the world, as far as I knew. Turning her head, she noticed me.

"Hi there, Pearl," she'd said, her voice gentle and her face full of sunshine.

I remembered that while I stood in the living room in the house on Magnolia Street, holding the telephone receiver to my ear. I wished Mama'd had a little sunshine to her voice that night, too. But she didn't.

"Hi, Mama," I said.

"Is your daddy home?" she asked, her voice cool and short.

I swallowed, trying not to be too disappointed that she hadn't asked how I was or said how she missed me. Even if it wasn't true, her missing me, she still could've said it. I'd have made myself believe it.

"No," I answered. "He's at a town meeting."

"Are you home alone? At this hour?"

"Ray's here," I said. "And Opal, too."

"All right." She made a sound like she was sniffling and I wondered if she was crying.

"Are you okay, Mama?" I asked.

"Fine," she said. "I'm fine. How about you?"

"Yes, ma'am." I tried thinking of something to say to her that might make her want to come home. Something exciting or new. Nothing came to mind, though.

"You know when you're expecting your daddy home?"

"I don't, ma'am."

"Well, you have him call me when he does," she said. "You'll remember?"

"Yes, ma'am."

"He has the number."

"All right." I held the cord of the telephone with my free hand, feeling how smooth the wire was. "Mama?"

"Yes?"

"Are you coming home?" I asked.

"Pearl . . ."

"Are you?"

She sighed and I imagined she had closed her eyes. "It's not that easy."

What I wanted to ask was if it was easy for her to leave us. But when I thought about it, I didn't think I needed to know the answer to that. It would've hurt too much.

"I'll tell him you called," I said.

"Thank you, Pearl," she said.

"I love you."

But I'd told her too late. She'd already hung up.

Daddy waited until Ray and I had gone up to bed before he called Mama back. I didn't try to listen in and I didn't let myself imagine what it was they had to talk about. What I did was work at convincing myself that I just did not care.

But when I heard Daddy walk up the steps and come in to check on me, it took all my self-control to pretend to be asleep and not ask him what Mama had wanted.

From the way he didn't stay at my bedside longer than it took to pull the covers up over my shoulders, I thought he wouldn't have wanted to talk about it anyway.

Chapter Seven

Daddy told Ray and me that he was going over to Adrian to pay a visit to Mama. That she'd asked him to come when they'd talked the night before.

His eyes were bright like he'd gotten a good night's sleep for once, and he sat up straighter in his chair at the table. Seeing Daddy almost back to himself was good for my heart. I tried holding out hope that we might just be okay after all, but it wasn't too easy after how Mama talked to me on the telephone the night before.

His smile was quicker to pull up the corners of his mouth. I wondered if that was the way Wilhelm from Aunt Carrie's story had looked after finding the pearl that would heal up Marta's heart.

"Opal's going to stay the night with you," Daddy said to Ray and me over his morning cup of coffee. "I expect you both to help her out, hear?"

"Won't you come home?" I asked.

"Well, of course I will." He took a gulp of coffee. "But in case it's real late by the time I get back, I'll just have Opal here."

"Can we go?" I asked. "Ray and me? We'd be good, wouldn't we, Ray?"

Ray looked from me to Daddy and nodded his head.

"We don't got school tomorrow," Ray said.

"I promise, we'd stay out of the way," I added. "Please, Daddy."

Daddy had a way of sighing when he was thinking of how to say no in a gentle or kind way. He would push the breath out of his nose and make a deep humming sound and sometimes rub at his chin, making a scratching noise of calloused hand against stubble. When he did that, I knew I wasn't about to get my way.

Still, I had to give it a try.

"I want to see Mama too," I said.

"Not this time, darlin'," Daddy said.

"May I be excused?" Ray asked.

"Sure," Daddy said.

After Ray took off, Daddy finished his coffee and looked at me from across the table.

"What's on your mind, Pearlie?" he asked.

"Mama said she wasn't coming back," I told him. "When I talked to her last night. She said it wasn't that easy."

He breathed in deep through his nose and blew it out his mouth. He rolled his head from one side to the other like his neck was stiff.

The hope had faded right off his face and all because of me.

"Well, that may be," he said. "It's not what I'd like, but she might just stay away, I guess."

"Is she going to ask you for a divorce?"

I'd never said that word before, and it sounded like a curse coming out from between my lips. I'd heard it plenty of times from Pastor down in Red River, saying that God hated divorce. The Lord Himself had said as much to Moses when they were carving the Commandments into those two tablets of stone.

God hated divorce, that was Bible truth and I knew it. I wondered if He hated the folks that got them, too. If God ever decided He didn't love my daddy anymore, it would've broken my heart.

"Pearlie, I don't want you worrying about that," Daddy said. "We can't be worrying about something that might not even happen."

"What if she wants to?" I asked. "Do you have to do it?"

He ran both hands through his hair, pushing all of it back off his forehead.

"How about we don't borrow worry?" he said, his voice smooth. "We don't have to even think on that just yet. All right, darlin'?"

I nodded.

"When're you going?" I asked.

"Just as soon as I can."

"Promise you'll come back?"

"Course I will, darlin'. Wouldn't stay away for all the world."

Bert had asked Ray to stay the night at his house. I knew it never would've been right, me sleeping over at the Barnetts' with the two of them on account I was a girl. Still, it stung, not getting invited even to come visit with the pigeon or tell scary stories like I knew they'd do.

Opal had promised she'd play cards with me. I'd never seen her play so much as a hand of poker before and I thought it was because she wasn't much for games. Seemed to me she'd agreed to play with me out of pity. That was all right by me, though. I didn't mind pity just so long as she didn't beat me too many times.

We'd had our supper in the kitchen because it was just the two of us. All she fixed was fried eggs and a couple slices of bread.

It was the kind of supper Mama would've snubbed her nose at. She'd have said breakfast was only to be had in the morning. But Opal said she'd not wanted to fuss.

I didn't mind. Besides, she'd left my yolks runny so I could swab it up with my bread.

"I'll do the dishes," Opal said. "You go on in and find something good on the radio. I'll be right in."

I did as she said, turning the dial slower than Ray would ever have patience for until I found a song I knew right away. I pulled my hand back so I wouldn't turn it by accident and lose the song. Sitting flat on my behind, I even tried breathing without making a sound. I wanted to hear every word and every note.

Back when I was real young, Mama'd sing that song to Beanie and me sometimes before bed. She'd tuck us in and kiss us on our foreheads before starting in on the melody.

"Stars twinkling up above you," she'd sing. Then she'd whisper, "Make a wish."

I'd close my eyes, thinking of what I wished for more than anything in the world.

"They flicker and I whisper —" She'd stop, waiting for me to finish the line.

"I love you," I'd say in a whisper.

"I love you, too," she would answer,

touching Beanie and me both on the tips of our noses with her fingers. "Bird sing a song so pretty and new."

She'd raise her eyebrows and wait for me to make a chirping sound.

"All I ever dream of is you," she'd sing. "I get a thrill when you kiss me."

Lowering her face, she would wait for Beanie and me to kiss her on either check.

"Say once again how if I left you'd miss me," she'd sing. "I'll never go as I love you so, all I ever dream of is you."

I didn't realize I'd started crying, sitting there in front of the radio, until I felt the warm drops streaking down my cheeks.

For as much as I only let myself remember the bad times with Mama, there were plenty of memories that reminded me of who she'd really been. She'd been a good mother. She had loved me.

"Oh, what's wrong, baby? Why are you crying?" Opal asked, coming in the room.

I felt her hands, dried but still warm from the dishwater, wrapping around my arms. Opening my eyes I saw she was stooped down beside me. She pulled me to her and held me close.

"What happened?" she asked. "Did you hurt yourself?"

I lifted my hands to cover over my face,

feeling the wet tears and my hot breath on my palms. "Nothing," I managed to say. "Nothing happened."

"Then why are you crying?" she asked, pulling back from me and pushing my hair away from my face.

"I miss her."

She didn't say anything and I thought that was because she understood.

Holding my wrists, she moved my hands away from my face and I felt the worn-soft cotton of her apron dabbing under my eyes and wiping at my cheeks. She was so gentle with me and that helped me to get a good breath in and stop my hiccup-coughing.

"You miss your mama?" she asked.

I opened my eyes and nodded.

"I know how that feels," she told me. "Sometimes I miss my mother, too. And my dad. It's hard, isn't it?"

"Yes," I answered. "Where's your mama?"

"Up in Detroit."

It never had occurred to me that Opal had a family somewhere and that she might miss them. All I thought of about Opal was how she took good care of us and knew how to make me smile most days.

"Your daddy, too?" I asked.

"Uh-huh," she answered. "And my brothers and sister. Three brothers and a sister."

"They're younger than you?"

She nodded. "Yup. I'm the oldest."

"Why don't you live with them anymore?" I asked.

"Come on and get up off that cold floor, huh?" She took my hand and led me to the davenport.

The song ended and another started, one with a singer of warbled voice so I couldn't have understood the words even if I was paying close attention.

"I left home when I was fifteen," Opal said. "My parents, they couldn't feed all of us and I was the only one old enough to find work. So I packed my bags and left."

She told me how she had hitched rides, hoping to get all the way to Toledo. But after a while she couldn't find anybody else to pick her up. That landed her in Bliss.

"I didn't realize until later on that I was close enough to walk to Toledo if I'd wanted to," she said. "But by then I had this job."

"I'm glad you stayed," I said.

"Oh, and before you get an idea in your head, don't you ever let me hear about you hitchhiking, do you understand me?" she said, giving me her dead-serious face.

"Yes, ma'am," I answered.

"It's dangerous." She shook her head. "I

never should have taken the risk. But I had to go."

"Why?" I asked. "Why did you leave if your family was nice to you?"

"My mother was already giving up her portion of meals for us," she said. "That wouldn't have changed if I'd stayed. And I knew they'd never take money from me if they could help it. It's easier for them, with me gone. It's hard enough for them as it is."

"Why?"

"Because my mother's colored and my dad's white," she said. "Not everybody likes that."

I understood what she meant. Mama would've said we should stick to our own, that God had meant for it to be that way. Otherwise He would have said in the Bible that the races should mix. I didn't know if she was right about that or not. But then again, I wasn't sure Mama was the best to speak on matters of who should marry who.

"Anyway, it's easier with one less person to care for," Opal said.

"Do you ever write them letters?" I asked.

She shook her head. "I never have."

"Why not?"

"If they knew where I was, they'd come for me." She leaned against the back of the davenport and crossed her arms. "They'd make me come home, and I know that I'd just be a burden."

"I don't believe you would," I said. "I bet they'd be glad to have you back."

"That's nice of you to say." She reached up and wiped under her eyes.

"Do you think that's why my mama left?" I asked. "Because she thought she was a burden?"

"I don't know," she said. "I don't know why she'd ever leave somebody like you. Leaving your parents is one thing. That's the way it goes. But it's another thing to leave your kids."

I thought Opal would make a good mama someday. She'd never be mean to her children and she wouldn't leave them.

She used her warm hands to smooth my hair and looked me right in the eyes and smiled at me. She asked if I was all right and I nodded.

"Opal?" I asked. "Do you ever wish your problems would go away?"

"Sure I do," she said. "I think most people do. Wouldn't it be something to be able to forget about everything awful?"

"I wish I knew how to forget." I shrugged. "No matter how I try, I just keep remembering the bad."

"When I dance, I don't think of anything but the music," she said. "I don't even think of what my feet are doing. Not really. All I do is keep my mind on the beat and my body goes along. For just a few minutes, I put everything else out of my mind."

"That sounds nice," I told her.

"You still want to learn how to dance?" she asked.

I nodded, hoping she might see the eagerness on my face.

"All right," she said, smiling. "We can start Monday after school. But you've gotta promise to help me get supper on."

I promised and we shook on it, sealing the deal tight as could be.

We spent the rest of the evening before bedtime listening to the radio and playing hands of poker for matchsticks. Opal popped some corn and even drizzled a little melted butter on top. It was a treat Aunt Carrie'd sent over and I knew Ray wouldn't get something like that over at the Barnett house.

I'd stayed up later than Daddy might've let me. Opal had said it was all right with her just so long as I wasn't sour to everybody the next day. I promised I wouldn't be.

When I did get to bed, I could hardly keep

my eyes open long enough to change into my nightie.

I slept fast and without dreaming at all.

Chapter Eight

What woke me in the middle of the night was the sound of Daddy's truck, the low rumbling of its engine, pulling up to the house. As much as I wanted to hear how Mama was, it was still dark out and I was tired enough to shut my eyes and doze off again.

Next thing I knew, I woke in the morning. When I opened my eyes I looked right out the window. The sun rose on the other side of the house, but I could see the pink and orange glow on the bare naked trees and the otherwise stark white snow in the back of our yard. It must've been a real pretty sunrise. I had half a mind to run over to Ray's room and watch it out his window.

But when I rolled to my other side and saw Daddy sitting on my bedroom floor, his back against my bed, I forgot all about the sun and Ray's window.

Daddy was breathing in and out through

his mouth like he couldn't get enough air or push it out fast enough. He had his knees bent up and an elbow rested on one of them, his hand holding up his head. If I hadn't known any better, I might have thought he was crying.

Daddy'd told me more than once that if he could, he'd have taken all the hurt in the world so I wouldn't ever have to feel it. I did believe he spoke true. It hadn't been a year before that he'd given himself over, almost getting killed so I could live.

There in my bed, I blinked away the picture of Eddie DuPre, his gun pointed right at Daddy. And I wished I could plug my ears so I wouldn't hear Daddy telling Eddie, "I don't want her to see this."

My daddy would've done anything for me, I knew that was true.

Just then, though, I wished I could take whatever sadness he held and push it right into my own heart.

I put my hand on his back. "Daddy?"

He breathed in through his nose and wiped at his eyes with the heel of his hand before turning toward me.

"Hey there, Pearlie," he said, his voice sounding pinched like he wanted to steady it. "You can go back to sleep. I just didn't think I should be downstairs. Opal's sleeping on the davenport."

"You can stay in Ray's bed," I told him. "He's at Bert's house."

"Might just do that, darlin'." He tried at a smile, but it didn't stay on his face but a second.

"Did you see Mama?" I asked.

He nodded and bit at his lower lip. "I did."

"She doing all right?"

He nodded again. Then his face scrunched like he was about to break into a crying fit. But he didn't. He held strong.

What I wanted to tell him right then was that it would've been okay with me if he'd wanted to cry, that it wouldn't bother me one bit. And I wanted him to know that I'd never tell a living soul if he did.

But men didn't like crying, especially in front of their little girls. I knew it might've ruined his pride for me to say such a thing.

"I tried getting her to come home," he said. "Thought she was going to. But she just couldn't."

"Why not?" I asked.

"I'm sorry, darlin'."

"Why wouldn't she come back?"

"You've just lost so much. I never wanted that for you."

"Is she mad at me? Is that why she won't come home?"

"No, darlin'," he said. "It's me she's mad at."

He turned toward me and used one of his trembling hands to move a wisp of hair off my forehead. Even in the low light of the room I could see his knuckles were swollen and an angry shade of purple.

Then I moved so I could see his face closer. His lip was fat and his eye was blackened.

"Daddy?" I said, my voice a whimper.

"I'm all right, darlin'."

"Did you get in a fight?" I pushed myself up so I was sitting, looking down at him. "Who'd you fight?"

"It wasn't right," he said. "I shouldn't have."

"Did you fight Abe Campbell?"

I knew I was right on account he didn't answer me, but instead looked away.

"I hope you whupped him, Daddy," I said, my voice hard and icy. "I hope you clobbered him something awful."

"Pearlie . . ."

"He stole Mama."

"Nobody stole her, darlin'." He licked at his sore lip and winced. "She went on her own."

Still, I hoped he'd broke Abe Campbell's nose. It would've served him right.

■ ■ ■ ■

The next day I tried no less than a half dozen times to write a letter to Mama. In them I either asked her to come home or told her I never wanted to see her again. I begged her to call or used every cuss word I knew how to spell to let her know I no longer cared what she did.

I tore every single one of them into shreds and tossed them into a fire Ray kept going in the living room. The paper curled before turning to flame to ash to dust. Mama would've said it was a waste of perfectly good paper, burning it like that.

She'd have been right. It was a waste.

There was no making somebody come home when they'd just rather stay gone.

Chapter Nine

Daddy didn't make us go to church that Sunday. He said it was because I'd been sniffling all weekend. I wondered, though, if it was because he wasn't up to seeing folks and shaking hands. As it was, the few people who'd seen him with his shiner and busted lip had got to talking already. I was sure he didn't want to invite more gape-mouthed stares than he had to.

"Besides," he'd said, "all anybody wants to do is bend my ear one way or the other about the meeting the other day. It's hard for a man to sit and listen to a sermon when he's got half the town staring at the back of his head."

It didn't bother me one bit, not going to church that morning. Daddy'd let us stay in our pajamas and I didn't even bother putting a comb through my snarled-up hair. How we moved around that morning was lazy and slow and it felt awful good to me.

Daddy put together a hot breakfast of chunked potatoes, bits of sausage, onion, and scrambled-up eggs. He made sure we said a prayer together before we ate.

I couldn't take more than a couple bites before my stomach felt full to busting. Ray didn't seem to mind. He ate the last of my breakfast like he'd never seen such good food before in his life.

"Daddy," I said. "Can you please tell us a story?"

Daddy nodded and took a sip of coffee. "Yup," he said. "I reckon I can."

He leaned back in his chair and crossed his arms, pushing his lips upward so they almost disappeared under his mustache.

"Now, a man named Isaac married a woman named Rebekah. After a while they found out they were going to have a baby," Daddy started. "But instead of just one, they had themselves two."

"This is from the Bible," I said.

"Yes, ma'am. Telling stories is the only kind of preaching I know how to do and it's Sunday. So this is our sermon," Daddy said. "Now, those twin babies wrestled around inside the womb, fighting over who was going to be born first."

Ray put an elbow on the table, resting his head against his fist, still shoveling food into his mouth but not taking his eyes off Daddy. His folks never had been ones to drag him to church or to read out of the Bible after supper. Lots of the stories that were old to me were brand-new to him.

"When it came time for those babies to be born, it was Esau that won the race." Daddy lowered his arms, resting his hands on his lap. "But Jacob, he had a hold of Esau's ankle, like he meant to pull him right back inside so they could keep on fighting."

"Babies can do that?" I asked.

"Course they can," he said. "I mean I guess I wouldn't know from experience exactly."

I tried picturing it, but wasn't all the way sure how any of it worked, birthing babies, that is. As curious as I was, there was no way in heaven or on earth I was about to ask Daddy. Especially not with Ray sitting right there. Just the thought of it made my cheeks burn.

"Now, Esau was hairy as a bear even then on his first day," Daddy went on. "But Jacob was bald as a badger. Esau ended up being a hunter and Jacob stayed at home with his mother most days."

"Jacob was her favorite," I said.

"That's right."

"Mothers shouldn't have favorites."

"No, darlin', they shouldn't," Daddy said. "One day, when the boys were grown, Esau went off hunting like he always did. Jacob, of course, stayed home making soup."

I imagined Jacob standing at the cookstove, bone broth bubbling in a big old pot over the fire. He stirred it every now and again, adding a pinch of salt or a shake of black pepper. Maybe he chopped onion and carrot to add in the mix, letting them get soft in the simmering liquid. I decided he hadn't bothered putting on an apron. Daddy never wore one when he was cooking.

"Esau came home, starving near to death," Daddy said.

Esau would've come staggering into the kitchen, not from being drunk but from being fall-down tired. His shirt sleeves were rolled up above his hairy arms and his beard was grown out down to the middle of his chest.

Loud as Esau was, panting and heaving and with his stomach growling like a mad dog, Jacob wouldn't turn to him. He just pretended not to know his brother had entered the room.

"Esau begged Jacob for a bowl of that soup," Daddy said. "Jacob, though, he didn't believe anything was free. Not even a sip of broth for a starving man."

I pictured Jacob to have a nasty curl of the lip and a wicked narrowing of the eyes.

" 'I'll trade ya,' Jacob told his brother." Daddy leaned forward. "Esau, he was so desperate he would've agreed to anything."

That sneak Jacob ladled up some soup, letting the steam carry the smell of it to his twin. He'd give him that bowl, and maybe even another, for the promise of Esau's birthright.

"What's a birthright?" Ray asked.

"Esau was oldest," Daddy explained. "That meant he'd get everything — all the land and sheep and such — after their father died."

"Did they have a lot?"

"Yup, son, they sure did." Daddy nodded. "Now, Esau was sure he was just about to die of hunger anyhow, so he didn't care about giving up his birthright. He agreed right away. Nobody in the history of the world ate soup so fast as Esau did that day."

I thought Esau'd forgotten about his sold birthright as soon as he had a full tummy and went off to rest. Jacob, though, he wasn't like to forget. Not that ankle-grabbing cheat.

Daddy went on to say that it was getting close to the time when their father would pass on. He lay on his deathbed, calling for his son Esau to come on and get the blessing due him.

"But first, he sent Esau out hunting," Daddy said.

"What was he huntin'?" Ray asked.

"Don't know," Daddy answered. "Maybe some deer or something. Whatever it was, Esau was supposed to make it into a stew for his father."

"They eat a lot of soup in this story," Ray said.

"You're right about that. You are." Daddy nodded and smiled. "Well, soon as Esau left, the mother got to scheming. Jacob and Esau's father was just about blind. She thought they could use that to their advantage."

She'd told Jacob to get dressed in animal skins that would make him pass as his brother. I wondered if he stood in his room, the fur strapped to his arms stinking to high heaven of outside and sweat and musk, and if he had even a flicker of a thought that he ought not trick his father.

If he'd had such an idea he sure hadn't given it a second thought.

"So Jacob, wearing his Esau costume, took some stew his mother'd made and spoon-fed it to his father," Daddy said. "And Isaac, convinced it was his firstborn son, went on and gave him the blessing."

Jacob's hand under his father's thigh, his mother looking on. The blessing only given once, placed on the head of the wrong son. They were just words out of a dying man's mouth, but once they'd been said, there was no taking them back.

"Esau came back and brought his own stew to his father," Daddy said. "By then it was too late. Jacob was so scared, he went running, swearing he'd never come back just so long as his brother was there."

I wondered if Jacob had even bothered to take the fur off his arms before he went.

Daddy left off there, saying something about us cleaning up the breakfast things. I knew Opal would've said we should leave them to soak until the next morning when she could do them up. Daddy didn't like doing such a thing though.

He washed, Ray dried, and I put away the dishes. All the while I thought about the day when Jacob finally went on home. Only reason he'd returned was because God told him he'd better. He shook in his boots all the way there, sending his wives and children and servants out ahead of him like a coward.

I'd never felt sorry for that lying weasel Jacob.

But then Esau'd come rushing through

the crowd, making a beeline to his brother. Instead of socking him a good one in the nose or shoving him to the ground, he threw his arms around him and welcomed him home.

The prodigal brother had made his way back.

Chapter Ten

We sat in our rows at school, all of us wishing the teacher would tell us to pull our chairs closer to the radiator so we wouldn't freeze to death in the too-cold room. It wouldn't have made much difference, anyway, I didn't think. Only time that radiator ever did warm anybody was when they bumped their arm into it and got a burn branded into their skin.

Miss De Weese sat at her desk, a little girl in the chair next to her. That little girl stumbled all over the words in the book the teacher had asked her to read. She didn't seem to mind too much, Miss De Weese didn't. She was real patient, which was good. And she never got mad, either. Miss De Weese wasn't one for hollering or smacking hands with the broad side of a ruler. The only kid she'd put in the corner yet was Bob, and that was for tripping Delores Fitzpatrick while she walked past him to get to her desk.

I would've fattened his lip myself for doing a thing like that except he was the biggest kid in the school — at least twice my size — and I wasn't so sure I could've reached his face with my fist if I'd wanted to anyhow.

Delores Fitzpatrick was the mousiest, dirtiest, poorest kid in all of Bliss. Everybody knew it. And because she and her family were so poor the other kids teased her something awful. She'd have fit right in if she'd been born in Red River. Down there, everybody was poor as dirt and knew it. But there in Bliss, it seemed folks didn't want anybody else knowing they were out of money. And they had more than enough to say about folks like the Fitzpatrick family, that was sure.

Meemaw'd always told me folks make fun of what they don't understand. I sometimes thought they even make fun of what they're scared of. And I thought those kids, and some of the grown folks in Bliss too, were scared of living in an old chicken coop and having hardly anything to scrape by on.

Delores hadn't come to school that day, and I didn't blame her one bit. It was the coldest kind of weather and her coat wasn't warm enough to keep her from freezing to death on the walk from way out on the edge of town where she lived. I just hoped they had some kind of wood stove or something, to keep them warm in that coop-house of theirs.

Miss De Weese had asked us to write letters to somebody and all our pencils scratched across the paper. I'd picked Millard Young back home in Red River. I had written about Bert's pigeon and the town hall meeting and about Opal agreeing to teach me how to dance. Much as I'd wanted to, I didn't ask him to leave Oklahoma to come live with us. Partly because I didn't want to put upon him and partly because I knew it wouldn't do any good. Red River was as much a part of Millard as his hands or feet or his brain even.

Of all the things I missed about Red River, I missed him the very most.

I finished my letter, looking it over to be sure I spelled everything the best I could. Done, I put my pencil in the groove at the top of the desk. All there was to do then was look around the room, trying to occupy my mind until everybody else was done.

Ray sat in the desk to the right of me. I watched him work at forming the letters on his page, his fingers holding the pencil just so and the tongue sticking out the side of his mouth the way it did when he was concentrating real hard. When he caught me staring at him he pulled his tongue back into his mouth and lowered his brows at me like he wanted me to leave him be.

"Cut it out," he whispered. "You're makin' me nervous."

"I'm done," I said, my voice quiet, too.

"So what?"

"I'm bored."

Ray rolled his eyes before going back to his work.

"Miss Spence?" Miss De Weese called to me from the front of the class. "Come here, please."

Quiet as I could, I got out of my desk, hoping nobody else had heard me get called to the teacher's side. I especially didn't want Hazel Wheeler to know about it. She'd never have let me live that down.

Hazel's father owned the general store in Bliss and they lived in the biggest, fanciest, most beautiful home in town. She hardly let a day pass without reminding somebody that her however-many-greats grandfather had founded Bliss years ago.

Hers was an important family. I knew because she'd made a point of telling me so no less than a dozen times.

I made my way to Miss De Weese's desk,

putting my hands behind my back so as not to let her see how they shook. I was just sure I'd be in trouble for whispering to Ray.

The little girl she'd been helping stood, her book hugged close to her chest. And she smiled at me.

"Pearl, if you're done with your letter, would you mind listening to Gwendolyn read a story?" Miss De Weese asked. "You can sit over beside the window."

"Yes, ma'am," I said.

The girl named Gwendolyn made her eyes big as saucers and she made a tiny clap with her hands, dropping the book in the process.

As Gwendolyn read aloud, I glanced out the window. All of the outside world looked to me like the picture shows, gray and black and too-white. I wondered if the whole winter would be so gloomy, so colorless. What I wouldn't have done to see even a hint of blue trying to break a crack in the clouds or a shoot of green forcing a hole in the snow.

"Let us be friends," Gwendolyn read, slow and clear. "What's this word?"

I looked at the page.

"Because," I told her.

"Because I am like you," she went on.

She kept reading and I turned my attention back out the window, not that there was anything to see. Not really.

Gwendolyn finished and I told her she'd done a fine job.

"You want to hear it again?" she asked.

Before I could answer, she opened the book to the first page and started over at the once-upon-a-time. It was fine by me. I was happy to stay there staring out the window.

From where I sat I could see the houses that ran up and down the streets nearby. That was where most of the kids in school lived. Daddy'd told me the men in town worked in a factory up in Adrian when there was a job for them to do or as field hands around harvest time. Nobody in Bliss was rich, expect maybe the Wheelers, who Hazel said had old money.

I didn't know how old money could help anybody or where they'd keep such a thing. But by the store-bought dresses Hazel wore and the parties they put on every once in a while, I thought maybe they were better off than most. At least they showed off like they were.

I watched out the window and saw somebody coming on the road toward the school. It was a small somebody wearing a gray coat and some kind of stocking cap. The closer she got, the more I could see the patches on that coat and how ill fitting it was.

Delores Fitzpatrick had made her way to school after all.

"All right, children," Miss De Weese said. "You're dismissed for lunch. I'll see you this afternoon."

It'd taken Delores all morning to get to school. It seemed a real waste that she'd just have to turn around and walk back home in a couple hours.

All the kids rushed to get their coats on. Most of us went home for the noon meal on account we lived so close. I knew Delores would sit in the classroom with the teacher and eat her folded piece of bread with butter spread thin as paper on it.

As for me, I didn't hurry. I knew Ray'd wait for me. Bert might, too. As much as I could, I put off being out in that cold-snap air. I took my time getting to my coat and putting it on. Once I got out to the schoolyard I saw most of the kids standing in a circle.

Through a gap in the circle I saw Delores with her eyes to the ground, holding her lunch pail to her chest, and the boy named Bob standing in front of her with a nasty smirk on his face.

"Leave her be," Ray said, stepping into the circle with them.

"I'm not hurting her," Bob said. "I'm not, am I, Delores?"

She didn't answer.

Ray stepped to Delores's side. "Come on," he said to her. "I'll walk you in if you want."

She turned from him like she wasn't sure if he was teasing her too.

"What's in your lunch?" Bob asked, putting out a hand to grab at her pail. "Let's see what your ma packed you."

"Cut it out," Ray said, slapping Bob's hand away.

"I seen your name on the list for taking handouts," Bob said.

"Most people're on that list." Ray stepped right between Bob and Delores. "Ain't nothin' wrong with it."

Bob moved forward, putting both hands on Ray's shoulders, shoving him back and back and back.

"Nobody asked you to get in the way," Bob said. "She's nothin' but white trash."

"No she's not," Ray hollered.

"You don't know," Bob said, getting real close to Ray's face. "Her dad's a bad man. The worst."

"That don't make her bad," Ray said, his voice as full of gravel as I'd ever heard it.

"Yeah? What do you know?"

Bob turned, reached for Delores's pail and

tipped it, making her pitiful lunch fall into the snow. Delores dropped to her knees, digging in the snow, trying to find her food. Ray gave Bob one last sharp look before lowering to a squat beside Delores.

"Don't worry," he said to her. "Leave it. You'll come eat with us today. All right? Mr. Spence won't mind. I promise."

Ray picked up her pail, empty except for the snow that'd fallen in. He helped her to her feet. She walked beside him to leave the schoolyard, Bert following behind with wide eyes.

I thought about stomping on Bob's foot as I walked by, but didn't know that I had the strength to run away from him if he came after me. Instead I gave him my strongest sneer. All he did was roll his eyes and shake his head.

"Pearl," Ray called to me over his shoulder. "Come on."

Delores slumped her shoulders like she was trying to make herself so small nobody'd be able to see her. I thought she'd have been content to disappear. I couldn't have blamed her.

"Coming," I said back.

"He's right," Bert said, grabbing me by the arm as I caught up. "Bob's right. Mr. Fitzpatrick's bad."

I jerked my arm away from him and followed after Ray and Delores, leaving Bert behind me.

There was a handful of things I knew to be true. One was that Jesus lived in my heart and another was that Daddy loved me deeper than an ocean. I knew the sun would come up every morning, even if I couldn't see it for the thick Michigan clouds.

And I knew without a shadow of turning that just because a man was bad didn't mean his kids would be too.

The man whose blood ran through my veins was wicked as the devil himself.

I refused to believe I could be even a little like him.

Bert called after me but I just kept on walking.

Chapter Eleven

Uncle Gus often said that it took a fool to find a way to starve in a place such as Bliss. The soil was good, the woods were full of game, and the stream busy with wiggling fish, when it wasn't frozen over, at least.

"All's a body needs to make it here is a handful of seeds, a good rifle, and a warm coat," he'd say. "And maybe a good woman who don't mind puttin' stuff up for winter."

Seemed, though, if there was a way to starve, the Fitzpatrick family had found it.

I expected Delores to gorge herself on what Opal served up on her plate. Thought she might not know what to do with her napkin or how to hold a fork the right way. Boy, was I ever wrong.

Turned out Delores had the kind of table manners Mama'd always wished for me to have. She kept her napkin spread on her lap and never dribbled her gravy on it. She didn't even slurp when she drank her milk.

Her mouth stayed shut as she chewed and every bite she took was just the right size so she didn't have to open up too wide.

I never would have guessed that a girl who'd grown up in a chicken coop could be such a lady.

We had chipped beef in gravy poured over the top of bread that was probably on the stale side. If I had to guess, we'd have milk toast for breakfast the next morning to use up the last of it. Opal never did waste a single thing. Everything had a use, even if it was a couple days past fresh.

Ray made sure Delores had everything she might need, offering her the salt and pepper shakers and asking if she would like more to drink.

"We always got plenty of milk," he told her. "Mr. and Mrs. Seegert make sure of it."

Delores took whatever it was he offered and whispered her thanks to him, her voice so quiet it was almost covered over by the clinking of forks on plates.

Opal came and ate with us after a minute or two. Delores snuck looks at her out of the corner of her eye like she wasn't sure what to make of her. If Opal noticed, she didn't act like it. She just got to eating her meal and drinking her glass of milk.

"Delores, you've got a brother and a couple of sisters, don't you?" Daddy asked, pushing a blob of white gravy over a bare edge of bread.

Delores nodded in answer, putting her fork down between bites. She glanced up at his face and I thought she wondered about his bruised eye. Either she had too good of manners or she was just shy. Either way, she didn't ask about it.

"They're younger than you, aren't they?" he asked.

Again she nodded.

"What're their names?" Ray asked, smiling at her.

Delores waited until she'd finished chewing and she dabbed at the corners of her mouth before talking.

"Nathanial, Helen, and Lizzy," she answered. "Lizzy just started walkin'."

"Is she a baby?" I asked.

Delores smiled and nodded. "She felled down a lot at first. Mother said she'd get it like all the rest of us done. She was right."

"There's nothing like seeing a baby walking for the first time," Daddy said. "I remember both times when my girls started wobbling about. Always made me smile."

We finished our food and Opal told us to leave the dishes. I knew that was on account we had a guest. Any other day and she'd have asked us to stack our plates in the sink. We bundled up and Daddy said he'd give us a ride back to the school.

"I'll walk with Bert," Ray said.

"You sure?" Daddy asked.

Ray nodded and turned toward Delores. "Hope you'll come round again sometime."

She lowered her eyes so fast, like she was afraid to look him in the face. "Thank you," she said.

I thought I saw a little blush rise in her cheeks.

Delores didn't come to school the next day and I imagined her sitting at home, watching little Lizzy walking around the chicken-coop-house. The way I pictured it, the whole family sat on straight-backed chairs or on the edge of a bed, all of them watching that baby tottering with her arms out for balance. The tiny girl would have little brown colored wisps pulled into rag ribbons and her cheeks full and round with just the right amount of pink in them. With every step the family would clap their hands.

I thought of how nice it might be if Delores invited me over some time. Not for lunch or supper or any kind of food. I knew enough to know that they wouldn't have enough to feed an extra mouth. They'd have been embarrassed by what little they had, though, and they'd apologize for their lack. I'd tell them it was no bother, that I'd had a big lunch at home before I'd come.

Delores would show me around. In the front room there would be a couple chairs and the one bed that they pushed to the side during the day like a lot of the sharecroppers had done back in Red River. I thought maybe there'd be a picture or two hanging on the walls. Old folks looked out from inside the tarnished frames, not a one of them smiling and all of them with their eyes looking black in the shadows of their deep brows.

Mrs. Fitzpatrick would come into the room with an apron tied around her tiny waist. It would be dirty, that apron. Her dress would be, too. Scrubbing laundry inside wouldn't have been so easy, especially since she didn't have any room to set up her wash basin.

I'd tell her it was all right, that it didn't bother me to see her grimy clothes. And I'd offer for her to bring her dirty things on by the house whenever they needed being done. I'd tell her that Opal wouldn't care about scrubbing a handful of extras.

But even in my daydream I knew Mrs.

Fitzpatrick would have just looked at me and shook her head. She never would've wanted so much help, especially not from a girl like me. A girl with a clean and starched dress that fit me right, if not a little too big. She'd not want pity from somebody who got fed more than she could eat or who could take a hot bath whenever the fancy struck her. There was no way that a mother like Mrs. Fitzpatrick wanted somebody like me feeling sorry for her.

Even if she was married to a bad man.

Chapter Twelve

I'd rushed home from school fast as I could. So fast, I was plumb out of breath by the time I got to the front door and Opal made me sit and rest awhile before she'd even think of starting the dancing lesson.

"You're going to need all the breath you've got," she said. "The lindy-hop goes fast."

"The who?" I asked.

"This dance is called the lindy-hop." She raised one of her eyebrows. "You're sure you want to learn?"

I let my eyes grow wide and I nodded my head.

"You ready?"

"I think so," I answered.

"All right." She reached over the davenport to pull the curtains closed over the window.

"Why're you doing that?"

"I have caused enough stir already, don't you think?" She looked at me over her shoulder. "I don't need to lose my job over this."

"Daddy wouldn't fire you for teaching me to dance," I said.

"If it makes too much trouble for him, he just might." She got to the middle of the living room and put out her hands. "Come on over here."

"Should we turn on the radio?" I asked, getting up and going to stand in front of her.

"Not yet." She took my hands and pulled me closer to her. She put her right hand on the middle of my back and held my hand in her left the way I'd seen dancers do in the movies. "Not too tight. Stay loose."

"Like this?" I asked, wrapping my fingers around her hand.

"Looser. That's it," she said. "Now, follow my lead, okay? And don't tense up."

I nodded and tried to relax even thought my heart pounded hard.

"This first move is called the groove."

"The groove," I repeated.

"All you have to do is put your right foot out. Yup, like that." She smiled. "Keep both feet planted, all right? Don't pick them up just yet. Now, rock back and forth. Like this. Bend at the waist and bend that right knee."

She guided me, the two of us leaning

forward and back, forward and back.

"Like this?" I asked.

"You're getting it," she answered.

We did that at least ten times before she told me to bounce at the knees whenever I rocked one way or the other. She counted to eight more than a couple times as we moved.

"You like it?" she asked, still guiding me in the groove.

I sure did.

"Try tapping your toes as you go."

I was a little off the beat she counted. She didn't stop, though. Didn't get frustrated or give up on me. Opal just kept on going until I started feeling it, the one-two-three-four, until I moved in time to the five-six-seven-eight.

"That's it," she said. "Ready for the next part?"

"Yes," I answered, not sure if I was or not.

"Now, watch me. Keep your left foot where it was, all right? Then step back with your right. Like this."

Counting to eight, she slid her right foot so it was even with her left, twisting her body and guiding me so we were standing side by side. Then she stepped forward, pulling me so I faced her again.

"Got it?" she asked.

"I think so," I answered.

I tried moving my body like she'd shown me, her holding my hand and gently pushing on my back. The first couple times I about got my legs tangled up and I couldn't seem to remember which foot was supposed to go where.

"It's all right," Opal said. "We've got plenty of time. Once you get this, you'll be able to do anything."

I didn't know about that, but I still gave it a few more tries, almost catching up to Opal's counting.

"There you go," she nodded, leading me through the move a couple more times. "Miss Pearl, princess of the double-back."

She was just being nice and I knew it, but I didn't care. I hadn't felt so good in a long time.

"Want to put that all together?" she asked. "We'll do two counts of eight for the groove then one count of eight for the double-back. Then we'll stomp our foot and peck three times."

"Peck?" I asked.

She smiled wide and jutted her head out back and forth like one hen going after another. I couldn't help but laugh before trying it for myself.

"That's the way," she said. "Ready for the

whole shebang?"

We moved through those three steps half a dozen times, her calling them out as we went. Each time they felt more and more natural. After a while I realized Opal wasn't counting anymore. Instead she was singing — not words, but she made noises like "dah-dah" and "bum-bum-bum" and "wah-waaaaaah." She sounded like an instrument and I felt like we could have gone on like that forever.

"You did good," she said, letting go of my hand and stepping back. "Best partner I've had in a long time."

"Better than Lenny Miller?" I asked.

She chuckled and nodded. "He's too full of himself to be a great dance partner."

"Can you teach me more?" I asked, trying not to let her see how hard I was breathing and hoping she couldn't hear the light wheezing from my lungs.

"Tomorrow," she said, looking up at the clock on the wall. "Now we need to see to supper."

I didn't say a word of complaint when she had me peel the potatoes and chunk them. In my head I kept hearing Opal's voice, counting out from one to eight, and let my toes tap to the beat.

I thought I'd be happy if I could go on dancing all the days of my life.

Chapter Thirteen

Delores didn't come back to school until that Friday. She wasn't as late as usual and her hair looked fresh cleaned. I smiled at her as she walked past my desk. She must not have seen me, though, because she didn't smile back.

We finished up our arithmetic lesson and Miss De Weese dismissed us for lunch. I waited in my seat until all the other kids had filed out and the room held just the teacher, Delores, and me.

"You wanna come to my house for lunch?" I asked, turning in my seat to look at her.

Delores shook her head but didn't look at me.

"You sure? Opal's making chicken and dumplings," I told her. "It'll be real good."

Delores didn't move, not to shake her head or shrug or anything. Not even to breathe, it seemed. It made me think of how a deer could sit still for hours so nobody'd be able to see them. I wondered if she was hoping I'd just stop talking to her and leave her be if she didn't bat an eyelid.

"Come on, Delores," I said. "Daddy said you could come for lunch any time you want. It's no bother."

She pulled her lips in between her teeth and bit down on them. Then she peeked at me real quick.

"Does she always eat with you?" she asked.

"Who?"

"Your girl," she whispered.

"You mean Opal?" I asked. "Course she does. We don't make her eat in the kitchen."

"My mother said I can't go to your house no more," she whispered, turning her eyes down to her hands folded in her lap.

I leaned closer to her. "Why not?"

"She said I ain't suppose to eat with them."

"With who?" I asked, knowing who she meant but wanting her to have to say it.

"With people like her. She tries passin' as white, my mother said, but really she's a . . ." She paused and took in a breath. Then she looked to be sure Miss De Weese wasn't listening before opening her mouth again.

Of all the cuss words I knew to use there was only one I'd never dared say. It was one

Daddy'd warned me not to let slip out of my mouth, threatening a lick of a switch to my behind if I did. Some folks'd used it back in Red River, but never Daddy. Not once.

When Delores opened her mouth, she used that word for Opal. Even in her small, whispered voice it sounded like a growl.

"Don't call her that," I whispered, trying to keep my voice calm even though it wanted to break into a holler. "Don't you ever call Opal that."

It was a good thing I felt sorry for Delores. Had anybody else called Opal that word I would've given them a bloody nose.

Instead I left her to eat her sad little lunch all by herself.

Still, I didn't feel good about it.

No matter how much I tossed or how many times I turned, there was no falling asleep for me that night. All I could see was the way Delores's lips had moved around the bad word she'd called Opal and all I could hear was the "grrr" of the word grinding out of her mouth.

When Daddy came to check on me like he did most nights, I didn't pretend to be asleep. I just kept my eyes open and said hi.

"I thought you'd be sleeping," he said,

stepping into the room.

I shook my head and propped myself up on my elbow.

"What's bothering you?" he asked, sitting on the edge of my bed. "You feeling all right?"

I nodded.

"You'd tell me if something was wrong, wouldn't you?"

"Yes, sir," I answered.

He gave me a grin and told me he hoped I would.

"I don't want to go back to school," I said. "Can I stay home? I can learn everything from here. There's plenty of books I can get at the library."

"Darlin', you gotta go to school," he said. "I'm fixing to see you graduate from high school. You know, you could even go on to college if you wanted."

I sighed and made sure he heard it. "I don't want to be in school all my life."

"I thought you liked school."

"I guess," I said. "It's all right."

"Somebody giving you trouble?"

I shrugged.

"Something happened today?"

"I guess so." I turned my face up so I was looking at him. "Why's *that* word so bad?"

He wrinkled up his brow like he was

thinking hard. "Which word?" he asked.

"The bad one."

"Can you spell it for me?" he asked.

I shook my head. "You'd whup me."

"That bad, huh?" He nodded. "I think I know the one you mean. It starts with an 'N'?"

I nodded. "It's a real bad one, isn't it?"

"Sure is," he said. "And you wanna know why it's so bad, right?"

"Yes."

"Well, darlin', far as I know it's another word for Negro."

"That's not so bad."

"But it's more than just the definition. It's what's behind the word," he said. "When somebody calls another man that word, he's saying that man is worth hardly anything at all. It takes away a man's humanity to call him that. Do you understand?"

I nodded.

"Calling a man that is saying that he has no soul, that he wasn't made to be like God," he said. "It's saying he's no better than an animal."

"Why would anybody say something like that?"

"I guess maybe they don't have any love for the person they'd say that about." Daddy let out air from his mouth and shook his head. "Did you hear somebody say that word?"

I nodded. "Delores said it."

"Hmm. Well, I imagine she doesn't know better."

"She said Opal was one."

"And we know that's not true," Daddy said. "We know Opal's a good person, don't we?"

"Yes, sir," I said. "Delores told me she can't come eat with us anymore because we let Opal sit at the table."

Daddy nodded. "Well, we aren't going to change what we do, are we?"

"Mama wouldn't let her eat with us," I said. "Remember?"

"I do." Daddy stood before bending over to kiss my forehead. "I want you being as kind as you can be to Delores, hear?"

I nodded. "I'll try."

Chapter Fourteen

January ended even colder than it started. It didn't seem to matter how many pairs of socks I slipped over my feet or how hot I let the water get for my baths, I couldn't manage to thaw out.

February didn't start off any different, either. In fact, I heard folks grumble that it just kept getting colder and colder by the day. I started doubting whether or not spring would ever come.

Millard had written at the beginning of the month to say that Pastor and Mad Mable had packed up and left.

"I don't know where they took off to," he wrote. "There's just a few of us left sticking it out here. Sure is lonely and I miss y'all something awful."

"I do wish he'd come live with us," Daddy'd said, folding up the letter. "Wouldn't it be nice?"

Ray and I both agreed. But if there was

one thing we knew wouldn't happen in a hundred years it was Millard Young moving away from his Oklahoma home.

After church most Sundays we'd have dinner at Uncle Gus and Aunt Carrie's table. We'd spend the better part of the day there, the men listening to the radio and snoozing in their chairs or poking around at this or that in the barn. Once we got the dishes done up and put away, Aunt Carrie and I would visit the hens until we couldn't stand the cold anymore. Then we'd sit in her room reading, she in her bed and I in a chair pulled into a corner, both of us bundled in blankets and quilts.

That day she had her favorite book of poetry and I had the last couple pages of Peter Pan to finish up.

Peter and the mean old fairy Tink sat inside the nursery of the house where Wendy and her brothers had lived before Neverland. They were hoping to keep Wendy and the boys from coming back to their family. If anybody'd asked me, I would have told them that Peter Pan was the most selfish boy I'd ever heard of. It wouldn't have bothered me one bit if he'd gotten himself swallowed by that gator, the way he treated the lost boys and Wendy. He was the kind

Mama would've had no trouble whupping on a regular basis.

He'd never had a mother to care enough to give him what for, though. Just the thought of that made me sad for him.

Still, he wasn't as nice as he could have been.

He and Tinkerbell listened while Mrs. Darling played on her piano. She played, not knowing anybody was listening. Even though the song didn't have any words, Peter knew Mrs. Darling was using it to call out for Wendy to come on home.

"You will never see Wendy again!" Peter had hollered.

I shut the book right then. If I could have, I'd have taken that book right back to the library, marching myself up to Mrs. Trask's desk and letting her know that the book was foul. That I didn't want to read anymore of it.

I'd gladly read a book of her choosing rather than spend one more minute with a story about Peter Pan. Even if her book had swishy skirts and women swooning on their couches over men that said just the right words at just the right time.

It was the third time I'd read the Peter Pan book to that very point and stopped short of finishing. Something had kept me from going on every time.

All I could think of was how I wished Mrs. Darling would get up from her piano to check the window. She'd stand there with her hands on the sill, looking out into the night for her children to come rushing back in. But then she'd hear something in the room. A little tinkling bell from the tiny fairy and the breath of a little boy.

Turning, she'd see Peter there.

She'd ask him how he got into the nursery and he'd tell her he'd flown through the window. Mrs. Darling wouldn't scold him for being rude or for not calling her ma'am. She'd know just by looking at him that the boy didn't have anybody looking after him.

Nobody had ever cared for Peter Pan. Not really.

Taking a step toward him, she'd ask where his mother was and he'd clam up. Peter'd look at Mrs. Darling — her soft smile and pinned-up hair, clean clothes and fresh scent — and he'd realize that he wanted her to be his mother. Not Wendy or any other little girl. He wanted that grown woman as his mama.

I only hoped Mrs. Darling would have taken him by the hand and told him he was welcome to be her child. He'd follow behind her, learning how it felt for somebody to care for him. He'd be her son and she'd be his mama. And she wouldn't ever walk away from him. She'd be a true and good mother.

She'd never leave him.

Aunt Carrie held the book of poems to her chest before placing it on the stand right beside her bed. Then she swung her legs off the side and let them dangle there.

"How was your book?" she asked.

I told her it was all right.

She nodded.

"What happened to his parents?" I asked.

"Oh, that's an interesting question," Aunt Carrie said. "One of the other Pan books, *Peter and Wendy,* if I'm correct, tells of how he flew away when he was a baby. When he was older, he tried to come home but found the window locked. When he looked in through the glass he saw a new baby in his place. He left again, believing they'd replaced him, that they no longer wanted him."

"But did they?" I asked. "Did they want him?"

"What do you think?" She licked her lips.

"I think they wanted him back."

"I do too," she said.

"Then why did they let him fly away?"

"I don't know that they could have

stopped him if they'd tried," she answered. "He wanted to go."

"That must've been real sad for them," I said.

Aunt Carrie nodded. "I believe it was."

I decided right then and in that chair that if ever I had a baby, I'd watch him close and love him deep so he'd never even have a thought of leaving.

Aunt Carrie insisted we stay for a light supper before going home for the night. I helped her put out sliced bread and leftover ham for sandwiches. She'd even let me put out a jar of her spicy pickles that she'd put up last fall. She said we should eat in the kitchen and she pulled out the table and lifted the drop leaves so there'd be room for all of us to sit.

"You fellows bring in a chair each, please," she called to Uncle Gus, Daddy, and Ray. "I hope you don't mind eating in the kitchen."

I didn't mind at all. There was just something about Aunt Carrie's kitchen that made me sit more comfortably and laugh a little easier. Besides, Uncle Gus and Daddy were more inclined to tell stories while sitting in the warm kitchen, their bellies full of food.

They didn't disappoint me that day, either.

"Y'all goin' to that Valentine's Day dance?" Uncle Gus asked, slathering mustard on his bread.

"There's a dance?" I asked, leaning forward so my chest rested against the edge of the table.

"Sure is," Uncle Gus answered. "Legion's gettin' everythin' ready for it. Don't got a band yet, but we'll make do anyhow."

"Who's invited to the dance?" I asked, trying not to sound too eager, but feeling like my heart was about to thump all the way out of my chest.

"Everyone," Aunt Carrie answered.

"Even Opal?"

She nodded. "Especially Opal."

"So, Tom, what d'ya think?" Uncle Gus asked, giving me a wink. "Y'all gonna come?"

I looked to Daddy, hoping he'd say that we were. He nodded and gave me his crooked smile.

"I suppose we can," Daddy answered, piling a couple slices of meat on his bread.

"Tom, you remember that dance we had back in Red River?" Uncle Gus asked. "Lord, you and me must've been fifteen or so."

"You might've been fifteen," Daddy said. "I'd have been thirteen."

"Always gotta remind me I'm older, huh?" Uncle Gus grinned. "You remember?"

"Sure I do."

"There was a dance in Red River?" I asked, knowing full well how my mouth hung open. All my life I'd been taught that dancing was as much a sin as drinking liquor, fornicating, and spitting on the sidewalk. Those were things faithful Baptists didn't do if they wanted to stay in God's good graces. Sometimes I wondered about the spitting part. Seemed to me that might've been something Mama'd made up to keep me from embarrassing her when we walked out in public.

"We didn't have more than the one," Uncle Gus said. "Only reason our mamas allowed it was Jed Bozell was the one running it."

If ever I could listen to stories about one man for the rest of my life, I'd have picked the ones about Jed Bozell. Daddy'd told me stories about old Jed and his traveling sideshow all my life. I never did find out if any of those stories were true. Didn't matter to me much if they weren't. Stories about Jed Bozell just plain old made me smile.

"Had to call that dance a square step, though," Daddy said. "If any of us called it a dance our mothers'd come after us with their wooden spoons."

"Everybody got gussied up," Uncle Gus said. "Don't recall what I wore but I do know I took a bath that day."

"I remember." Daddy crossed his arms. "You had on a shirt all buttoned up wrong and pants that were a good inch too short for your legs."

"Well, I was tryin' to start a new way of dressin'." Uncle Gus nodded. "Besides, who wants to trip up on your pant legs when you're tryin' to square step?"

"You got a point," Daddy said. "As for me, it was lucky I got out of the house at all for how Meemaw'd made me scrub behind my ears and scour under my nails. That was one thing she'd never abide, a dirty child."

"I do recall you being so scrubbed you'd shine on a bright day," Uncle Gus said.

"That I did." Daddy nodded and took a sip of his milk. "Wonder if that was how old Jed saw me through the crowd that day to call me up on stage."

"What'd he want you to do?" I asked.

"I'm getting to that. Hold your horses." He leaned back in his chair, tipping it up on two legs. "Old Jed was calling out the usual steps, hollering along with the music for the folks to swing-their-partner and circle left. He kept time with the fiddle."

"Who played the fiddle?" Ray asked.

"I do believe it was Millard's wife," Daddy said.

"That's right." Uncle Gus smiled. "She sure was somethin' else. First woman I ever loved."

Aunt Carrie cleared her throat and gave him a look like she was about to smack him. But I knew she was teasing him by the way her face broke into a smile like she just couldn't help it.

"Didn't matter none anyhow," Uncle Gus said. "Her heart was for Millard. Besides, she was old enough to be my mother."

"Anyhow," Daddy said, going on with the story. "I was a little bit shy about girls. There wasn't a way in the world I was about to go up to one and ask her to dance. I stayed clear to the side of the room."

"Why would you ever be scared of girls?" I asked. "Ray's not scared of girls."

"I was scared one of them was gonna bite me."

"Son," Uncle Gus said to Ray, "there's a bit o' wisdom to that. Be careful of some ladies. They'd be more like to bite you than say howdy."

Ray blushed and smiled.

"Jed, he looked out over the crowd and

saw me, back against the wall and skin glowing fit to light up the whole night." Daddy shook his head. "He waved me over to him and whispered in my ear between calls."

"What'd he say?" I asked.

"Well, I don't know that it's nice to say in front of mixed company," Daddy said, nodding his head at Aunt Carrie.

"Tom, I'm married to Gus Seegert," she said. "Anything you have to say, I promise I've heard it before."

"All right then," Daddy said. "Poor Jed had to use the outhouse. Said he'd eaten too many of Meemaw's apple dumplings and had himself the skitters."

I wrinkled up my nose and tried not to laugh too loud. I didn't want to miss out on one word of Daddy's story.

"He told me to just have the folks do-si-do round and round until he got back. Said he wouldn't be a minute."

Uncle Gus had a wide smile on his face and he rubbed at his chin, watching Daddy as he went on.

"So I did as he said and hollered out for everybody to keep do-si-doing. Over and over I called it." He shook his head. "They couldn't help but obey me. That's the first rule of square stepping — you gotta obey the man calling the steps."

"I was partnered up with some girl," Uncle Gus said. "Can't remember her name off the top of my head."

"It was Mable," Daddy said. "Remember? That was before she'd married Ezra."

"That's right." He put his hands up like he was dancing. "We went round and round, Mable and me gettin' dizzier by the minute."

"Jed didn't come back," Daddy said. "I didn't know any of the other calls and I didn't know what to do. So I kept telling them to go on with their do-si-do. Seemed like a whole hour'd passed and Jed was still gone."

"One hour?" Uncle Gus said. "More like three. I started worrying that I wouldn't get home to milk the cow."

"Why didn't y'all just stop?" Ray asked, his eyebrows pushed down low.

"Son, you can't just stop a square dance like that," Uncle Gus said, his voice serious. "You gotta wait until the ending's called. Then you gotta bow. Them's the rules."

Ray snickered and Uncle Gus winked at him.

"All the skipping round and round each other caused a powerful wind on account the women's skirts were working like wings, stirring up the dirt in Red River. It lifted up all the topsoil in town, swirling into one big roller that twisted and spun its way across the plain," Daddy nodded. "You ever wonder why the dust got started?"

"That ain't why," Ray said. "Is it?"

"Might be," Uncle Gus said. "Just might be. And we all got Tom to thank for it."

"Finally, after five hours of folks circling their partners, Jed came back. He got big in the eyes and hollered out for the folks to allemande, promenade, and bow to their partners so they could stop." Daddy shook his head.

"Millard made them swing their partners the other way for a couple hours, just to get them unwound," Uncle Gus said.

"Still, for a couple *years* after, nobody walked in a straight line."

I imagined the upright citizens of Red River weaving down Main Street like they were all tipsy from moonshine and it made me giggle.

"You know, Meemaw always warned of the dangers of dancing, but I never believed her," Daddy said. "Not until that night."

"You dance," I said. "I've seen you."

I thought of the times when he stood close to Mama, her humming a tune, and the two of them swaying together like they were one person. Any smile I'd had on my face fell just then.

"Guess I didn't learn my lesson," Daddy said. He looked me in the eye and gave me a smile like he knew what I was thinking.

I didn't doubt he did.

Chapter Fifteen

All that week and into the next, the only thing anybody in town could talk about was the Valentine's Day dance. At school, the girls went round and round about what they were going to wear and the boys went on and on about how their mothers were making them go.

I'd sit to the side of them, listening to their chirping and chattering, thinking how their jaws would drop when they saw me lindy-hopping across the dance floor. I didn't think it would matter if I had on a nice dress or if Opal let me brush a little color on my cheeks. The only thing they'd remember from that dance was how jealous they were of my swinging and swaying. I wasn't one for bragging or thinking more of myself than I ought, but I was getting pretty good at dancing.

I didn't say one word to them about it, either. I wanted them to be surprised.

Opal had helped me pick out a dress for the occasion. It was one that'd gotten just a little too small on her. Eating at our table once or twice a day had done her some good. All she had to do to that dress was hem it up an inch or two. I only had to twirl to make it swoop up away from my knees. It was pink with white polka dots and a pretty white collar she'd bleached fresh just for me.

"I'll do your hair if you want," she'd said. "I could put it in curlers."

"Yes, please," I'd said, hoping I'd end up looking just like Shirley Temple.

As for Ray, the only reason he was coming was because he'd heard there was going to be a cakewalk. For a nickel he'd get to walk around until the music stopped. Depending on where he ended up, he could win a cake. I knew for a fact that most the ladies in town had gone without sugar in their coffee to be able to make those cakes.

When I'd asked Aunt Carrie why they'd do something like that, she'd said sometimes all it took was baking a pretty cake to make a woman feel like times were normal again.

"It reminds us of how things were," she'd said. "Back when times weren't so hard and baking a cake was the most normal thing in the world to do. I think it helps us have hope

— even a little bit — that times can be like that again."

"Do you think they ever will?" I asked.

"No. Not completely." She'd smiled at me. "But they might just be better. We'll have to wait and see."

I thought I understood because whenever I imagined what it might be like to dance in the American Legion, I felt that maybe things weren't so bad as I sometimes thought they were. When I visited those daydreams I forgot about Mama being gone and about the way Hazel sneered at me from across the classroom or even how Delores stared like a scared little deer whenever I said a word to her. The only thing I thought of was how good it felt to dance. Every bad feeling shuffled back into a dark corner of my mind.

If only I could've swept them all the way out I'd have been a whole lot better off.

Every once in a while Daddy'd drive me home from school. On the coldest days it didn't matter how many layers of scarf I held over my nose and mouth or how I worked at breathing nice and easy like Doctor Barnett had told me to, the freezing air still got to me, making my lungs tighten up and causing me to struggle for breath.

It was a Tuesday and Daddy'd not only dropped me off at school, but he'd told me to wait inside for him to get me that afternoon. He didn't want me sitting out in the schoolyard for fear I'd catch my death from how the wind whipped. Those days were hardest for breathing, like the rushing wind would've liked nothing more than to steal the air right out of me.

"And I'll see you after I get done at work, okay?" he said after driving me all the way up in front of the house on Magnolia Street. "Go right inside, hear?"

I nodded, putting my hand on the latch to open my side of the truck.

"Pearlie?" he said, reaching over and squeezing my hand that was closest to him. "I love you, darlin'."

"Love you, too, Daddy," I said, smiling at him over my shoulder before pushing open the door and stepping out.

The wind smacked me right in the face and I tried not to gasp at how freezing cold the air was. Rushing toward the porch, I tried my very best not to slip and fall on any hidden patch of ice. Turning, I waved at Daddy just before opening the front door and stepping inside.

On the other side of the door, I untied my boots so they wouldn't get snow on the living room floor. In my stocking feet, I padded my way to the closet to hang up my coat.

Opal came from the kitchen, wiping her hands dry on a towel.

"Have a good day?" she asked.

"Sure I did," I answered. "How about you?"

"Just the normal." She smiled. "Just a couple more days until the dance."

"I know."

"You think you're ready?"

"Might be."

"How about we work on those triple steps today?" she asked. "Maybe try doing a few underarm spins?"

She didn't have to ask me twice.

That night I dreamed of dancing. Trumpets blasted and drums boomed. My shoes tapped on the dance floor as I made my way to the center. I swung my arms at my sides, making circles with my hands in the air and shimmying for all I was worth. Kicking my feet, I caused my skirt to swish from one side to the other.

And that skirt was of the deepest purple, so deep it almost looked black.

I stomped and spun and hopped. All the folks standing around me in a circle cheered out, hollering my name, whistling and clapping and moving their shoulders to the beat.

But then the music changed. The clarinets held out one long sour note. The trombones groaned and the trumpets sighed. All the dancers in the circle went on with their clapping like nothing had changed.

Then the floor dropped out from under me and I fell, the skirt of deepest purple flew up so it covered over all of me except my legs and underthings. I tried pushing it down, tried getting free from it, but the fabric tangled me as I fell, fell, fell.

Down, down, down.

All of the sudden I was on the floor of the living room. Mama stood in front of the davenport, carpetbag in hand. Without looking at me she walked to the door and opened it, then stepped out to the porch.

Then she was back, standing in front of the davenport again, same carpetbag hanging from her fist. She walked to the door, opened it, stepped out.

Back to the davenport. Leaving. Back. Leaving. Over and again and over and again. It must've been a hundred times I watched her walk away from me just to come right back to that same spot, her feet firm on the living room floor.

And from somewhere above me the music went on and on.

Chapter Sixteen

The last couple days leading up to Valentine's Day were full of whispers about who'd get a heart-shaped card from one of the boys. Hazel was sure she'd get at least three of them and the other girls looked like they'd about melt into a puddle if she did.

When I'd asked Ray if he'd thought of making a card for a girl, he'd looked at me like I'd lost my ever-loving mind.

"Why would I do a thing like that?" he'd asked.

I was half glad he'd not thought to get a Valentine for any of the other girls, and half sore he hadn't thought to get one for me. But I wasn't about to tell him so.

Opal taught me more steps to the dance, teaching me to shuffle and spin on the toes of my shoes. She showed me how to move my arms when I wasn't holding hands with my partner and what to do if I missed a step. She'd even turned on the radio so we could put the steps with music.

When she told me I was getting it, I'd smile. When she said I was a good dancer, I'd believe her.

All that week the ladies in town went to see if Mr. Wheeler had sugar and flour for them to buy and they took home just enough to bake for the cakewalk. They went without other things on their lists so they could spend five cents for a little sugar and another five cents for flour.

Ray's mouth watered every time he thought about the chance of winning one of those cakes. He'd decided he wanted one with chocolate frosting and he did not care what kind of cake it was.

As for Opal, she shook her head when she heard they were putting on a cakewalk.

"Can we bake a cake for it?" I asked, helping Opal stretch the fresh-washed fitted sheet over my mattress. "I'll help. I know how to sift flour and crack eggs."

"I don't want any part of it," she told me. She stood straight and let me finish the work myself.

"Why not?" I tilted my head like I did not understand a word coming out of her mouth.

"Because I know what they mean." She crossed her arms and pushed her lips together tight, the way she did when she wasn't happy about something at all. "Back a hundred years ago they were a way for white people to laugh at their slaves."

She wasn't mad at me and I knew it. Still, I didn't say a word for fear the wrong thing would come out of my mouth. Instead I tucked the top sheet in at the foot of the bed the way Mama'd shown me when I was smaller. It never would be smooth as Mama would've liked, but Opal never said a cross word to me about it.

"My mother told me back in the days when people held slaves, they'd get their colored folks dressed up nice and tell them to act civilized for once," she told me. "And then they'd judge who did the act the best and give them a cake."

"Wasn't that good?"

"No, baby," Opal said, her voice soft. "It's never good to make fun of somebody for being some way they can't change. Not even if you do give one of them a piece of cake for their troubles."

The night before the dance Opal put my wet hair up in rollers. I'd been happy to let her do so until she started tugging at my hair, wrapping it round and round so I worried I might not have any left on my head by the time she was done. I didn't dare complain, though, not if I might have movie star curls after all that suffering.

I couldn't hardly sleep that night. Partly because I was so excited for the next day. Mostly, though, it was because of those rollers poking at my scalp.

The morning of Valentine's day I ended up being glad for how curly my hair was. Little ringlets bobbed around my face and I thought I did look like Shirley Temple after all. Opal had even bleached my warmest stockings so they'd be nice and bright to go along with my dress.

When I came down for breakfast, Daddy stood up from his seat and put both hands over his heart, tilting his head and looking at me.

"Oh, Pearlie Lou," he whispered.

I couldn't understand how seeing me dressed up like that could get his eyes watery. But the way he smiled warmed me all the way to my toes.

"You look nice," Ray said.

"Thanks," I said back.

Opal followed behind me, fussing with a curl on the back of my head. "Don't spill anything on yourself," she said. "There's toast you can have. No jam."

All through breakfast I caught Ray sneaking peeks at me. I pretended not to see.

Daddy'd offered to drive me to school so my dress would stay nice and my curls wouldn't get ruined by the wind. Ray'd wanted to walk to school like usual, Bert hopping along by his side. Besides, he'd taken it on himself to be sure that pigeon of Bert's didn't perish from the earth due to his owner's smothering love.

Only reason I could figure the pigeon'd made it so long was on account of Ray. Even then, the bird had flown back to the Litchfield's place three times. It hurt Bert's feelings on each occasion.

Daddy turned the truck onto the main street and tipped his head to somebody standing on the corner.

"Might need you to walk home after school," Daddy said. "I'll have plenty to do for the dance tonight. You think you'll be all right?"

"Yes, sir," I said.

"By the way, I did what you asked me to," he said. "Took your package out to the Fitzpatrick place just yesterday."

Looking at him out of the corner of my eye, I nodded and told him my thank you.

"It was good of you, darlin'. Real good."

Having Daddy take one of my good

dresses over to Delores's house was my way of turning a cheek for her saying that nasty word about Opal. Meemaw had always said it pleased the heart of God when one of His children got insulted or hurt and didn't fight back, but gave them another chance.

If there was something Delores Fitzpatrick needed, it was a chance.

I did hope Delores would wear the dress to school, maybe to the dance even. I thought it would be sad if she didn't come because she didn't have something nice to wear. I was glad she'd have at least one.

Hazel stood against the outside of the school, puckering her lips and rubbing them together so the dark red would get everybody's attention. Her eyes looked me over from curly head to polished shoes, then turned back to the girls around her, all of them fawning over how lucky she was to wear lipstick to school.

Not a one of them dared tell her she had a smudge of red on a front tooth.

When Miss De Weese rang the bell, we lined up and walked into the school. The girls took notice of each other's dresses once we got our coats off and I tried not to be sad that nobody said anything about mine. I hung up my coat and felt of my curls, glad that they hadn't drooped since I left home.

Just as we were all going to our seats, Delores walked in. Her hair was clean and pulled back into a tight braid, a scrap of cloth tied into a ribbon at the bottom. When she took off her too-thin coat, I saw she was wearing the dress I'd had Daddy take over. The green and yellow flowers looked prettier on her than I'd imagined. It hung looser on her than it ever had on me, but it still looked real nice.

More than a few eyes were on her, and Delores seemed to fold up on herself, not liking the attention just then. I tried making my way over to her, but the other kids walking to their desks blocked me. She saw me coming, but looked away before I could smile at her.

That was when I saw Hazel walk past her.

"Nice dress," Hazel said, her voice hissing. "Who'd you steal if from?"

I opened my mouth to let loose a string of bad words I knew weren't fit for the classroom, but never got the chance to say a single one of them. Miss De Weese called us to our seats.

Slipping into my desk, I tried thinking of something to say to Delores, but my whole body was shaking from being angry and nothing right came into my mind.

Ray, though, he leaned across me and caught Delores's eye.

"You look pretty," he whispered to her.

I'd never seen anybody blush so deep a red.

The way I imagined it, I'd rush out after Hazel just as soon as Miss De Weese dismissed us for lunch. I'd grab her shoulder and swing her around to face me. Without even giving her a chance to say a word, I'd tell her to leave Delores alone or else.

I wouldn't hit her, much as I'd like to. And I wouldn't call her a nasty name even if a whole list of them was right on the tip of my tongue. Still, she'd nod and agree, promising not to say another mean word to Delores as long as she lived.

But I didn't get to give Hazel so much as a dirty look. As soon as I stepped out of the schoolhouse and into the yard I heard Bert calling after me.

"Pearl," he said. "Wait up."

I turned and watched him half trip down the steps toward me, and I wished I could die right then. In his hand was a big old piece of paper cut into a heart shape. He'd taken the time to color red all along the edge of the heart.

Once he got close enough he held out the

card for me to take. Then he ran past me before I could even tell him thank you. I watched him go, fast as if the devil himself was after him.

Ray walked up to me and looked over my shoulder at the card. "He's been workin' on that all week," he said.

In the middle of the heart Bert had drawn what I guessed was a cat but looked more like a possum. Whichever it was had a heart in its mouth between jagged teeth. Above the critter were letters written in the best hand I thought Bert could manage.

I read it out loud. "I sent along this little kitty to let you know I think you're pretty."

"Well, that's nice, ain't it?" Ray said. I could tell he was working real hard at not laughing.

I shrugged.

I didn't want Ray to see how embarrassed I was.

I got back to school a good half hour early. Opal'd packed a couple things for me to take to Delores. Nothing special. Just a biscuit with a dab of jam on it and a hunk of good cheese. I hoped she was still hungry enough to eat it and walked right to the classroom.

Before I stepped in, I spied her and Miss

De Weese sitting on either side of a table near the front of the room. Delores had a nice, round, shiny apple she was taking dainty bites off of and a big sandwich on a napkin right in front of her. Gifts from the teacher, I knew it.

She put the apple down and stood, holding out the skirt of her new dress and turning so Miss De Weese could see it. The teacher put her fingers to her lips and declared it the prettiest dress she'd ever seen.

I stepped away from the door. They didn't need me snooping on them and I didn't want Delores to be embarrassed that I'd seen how much she liked that dress or to feel like she had to thank me for giving it to her.

It was enough to know that turning the other cheek did feel good after all.

Seemed every time I looked at the clock for the rest of the afternoon only a minute or two had ticked away. Eternity's passing was how it felt.

When it was finally time to go, Miss De Weese gave each of us a tiny candy heart as we walked out the door.

"Pearl," Miss De Weese said, putting the pink candy in the palm of my hand. She leaned close and whispered in my ear, "You're a good friend."

"Thank you, ma'am," I said.

"Delores told me about the dress."

I nodded, feeling the wilting curls brush against my face.

"That was kind," Miss De Weese said.

I dropped the candy into my coat pocket, saving it for a time when my stomach wasn't so troubled, when I might be able to enjoy it, and I walked out of the classroom door, Ray right behind me. I could tell he was already sucking the sweetness out of his candy heart. I wondered if he'd even bothered to read what it said first.

Delores was last to leave and I heard Miss De Weese ask if she'd be going to the dance that night. We walked out of the schoolhouse before I heard Delores's answer.

If I could've changed the way of things, Delores would have gone back home with Miss De Weese where she stayed with the preacher and his wife. They wouldn't mind having Delores there. All their kids were grown and moved away to start their own families.

They'd give Delores a whole closet of dresses their daughters had outgrown ages ago but were still real nice and clean. Miss De Weese would let Delores use a brand-new cake of soap, scented with rose, to take a bath with. Then she'd brush out Delores's hair — one hundred strokes — before giving her a nice supper that had steam rising up off it.

Delores would smile and her eyes would stay bright. She'd have somebody looking after her. Somebody to take care of her.

And Miss De Weese would tell Delores stories of pirates or wizards or fairies until bedtime, when she'd show her a clean bed to sleep in. She'd have a room to herself with soft pillows and maybe even a rag doll to hold through the night.

She'd sleep well there, no ghosts of chickens to haunt her and no hungry stomach to keep her up.

Delores would shut her eyes and have nothing but the sweetest of dreams.

"Bert and me's gonna go over to the farm," Ray said.

"Huh?" I asked, just then realizing we were standing right in front of the house on Magnolia Street. "Oh. Yeah."

"You all right?" he asked.

I nodded.

"You wanna go with us?" he asked. "Mr. Seegert said he's got a way to make the pigeon stay to home."

"Nah," I answered. "Think I might go in

and rest a spell."

Ray shrugged and turned to cross the street to collect Bert.

"Ray?" I said.

"Yeah?"

"Why do you think everybody hates Delores so much?" I asked.

"Don't know," he said. "Why does anybody do anything?"

I didn't have an answer to that question.

"Hey, tell Bert I say thanks for the card," I said. "Would you?"

"Sure I will."

He gave me one last look before going across the street.

Chapter Seventeen

Somehow I'd managed to keep my pink polka dotted dress clean all day. As for my Shirley Temple curls, those had loosened only an hour or two after Opal had pulled the rollers out. It was all right, though. Aunt Carrie'd said she'd come over before the dance to help me get ready.

"That way Opal can have time for her hair, too," she'd said.

Aunt Carrie sat on the davenport and had me settle in on the floor, my shoulders against her knees. She was gentle when she brushed my hair and didn't pull too hard where there was a snarl. I told her it didn't hurt me, working tangles out of my hair, but she apologized for tugging anyway.

"I'm afraid I haven't had much practice at this lately," she said. "I always liked playing with other people's hair."

"Whose hair did you play with?" I asked.

"Oh, years ago I had a friend named

Ruthie." She worked her fingers through my hair, parting it down the middle with a fine-toothed comb. "Ruthie had long, thick hair. It was red and she never let anyone say a cross word about it. Have you ever heard that redheads have hot tempers?"

I nodded, thinking of Hazel and her ginger-colored hair.

"Well, it's true," she said. "I think it has less to do with the hair and more because they get teased about it. Anyway, Ruthie was a spitfire."

"Did she climb trees with you?" I asked.

"Of course she did. We had such fun," Aunt Carrie said. "Ruthie would let me brush her hair and put it in all kinds of braids while she told me all her secrets. I told her a few of mine, too."

"I've never had a friend like that," I whispered.

"Oh?"

"Except Ray," I said. "But he doesn't play with my hair."

"I wouldn't think so," she said with a laugh. "But he is a very special kind of friend, isn't he?"

"He's the best kind," I said. "What ever happened to Ruthie?"

"She moved away," Aunt Carrie said. "Long ago. At least it feels that way."

"Do you ever see her?"

"No, dear," she said. "I'm afraid she'll never come back to Bliss."

"What happened?" I asked, turning. My hair slipped out of Aunt Carrie's hands and swept over my shoulders.

She sighed and folded her hands in her lap. "Some things are just too difficult to talk about."

I turned back around and let Aunt Carrie finish up with my hair. She braided it and pinned it across the top of my head the way I liked.

We didn't talk about Ruthie anymore. Still, I understood.

I knew what it was to hold onto a bad memory.

CHAPTER EIGHTEEN

Daddy said we could stay at the dance until eight o'clock. I hoped he'd have such a good time, though, that he'd forget about the time. If I'd had my way, we would be the first ones there and the very last to leave. I did intend on dancing all night long even if it was the same dozen steps over and over.

It seemed like forever before Daddy put on his coat and let us know it was time we headed out for the Legion. Ray ran out ahead of us and opened the door of the truck for me, waiting until I slid to the center of the seat before climbing in and pulling the door shut.

The whole ride over I shivered, half from the cold and the other half because I was just so excited.

There weren't all that many cars parked around the American Legion building when we got there. Not near as many as there'd been on New Year's Eve and I wondered if most people had decided just to stay at home where it was warm and quiet.

"It's early yet," Daddy said. "Folks'll come."

We followed up the walk behind a lady carrying a wide cake on a long platter. Ray rubbernecked to get a look at that cake as he passed her to get the door.

"Thank you, young man," the lady said, nodding at him as she walked through the door.

"Let me get that for you," Daddy said, bending to slide his hands under the plate.

"Don't tip it, now," the lady said.

"I won't." He smiled at her. "I'll be real careful."

The woman caught me looking at her and gave me a thin-lipped smile. I gave her one back even though I didn't want to. She seemed the kind to say nice things to a person's face just to turn around and say nasty things behind that same person's back.

"Be sure it gets a good place on the cake table," she told Daddy, turning her face from me. "Everyone in town says I make the best cakes."

"I'll bet this is the finest in town, Mrs. Ritzema," Daddy said, using the sticky sweet voice he usually saved for folks he just could not stand.

Never in my whole life had I heard Daddy call another grown person Missus or Mister. Back in Red River he'd talked to everybody using their first name the way friends did. But one look at Mrs. Ritzema's pinched face told me she was a woman who'd have none of that kind of familiar nonsense.

Under the lights in that hallway I got a good look at the cake she'd made. The lumpy top sunk here and there under the spread-too-thin frosting and one corner of it was singed and crusty looking. If I'd wanted to place a wager, I'd have bet that Mrs. Ritzema's cake would be the very last picked at the end of the cakewalk.

Ray and I walked behind Daddy and Mrs. Ritzema and I couldn't help watching the way her round behind hitched up with every step, her dress stretched over it so tight I worried it might split the seam.

"I hope they don't plan on playing any of that jungle music tonight," Mrs. Ritzema said to Daddy, louder than she needed to, her voice bouncing against the hard walls. "I read that kind of music stirs up all sorts of bad instincts in young people. We don't need to have our children stirred, wouldn't you agree, Officer Spence?"

"Well, I guess I'd have to read on it," Daddy answered. "Doesn't seem to do much harm when I let my children listen to it."

"What's she mean by 'jungle music'?" I whispered to Ray.

He shrugged.

"If you ask me, these kinds of dances cause all kinds of trouble. Don't you think so, officer?" Mrs. Ritzema turned toward Daddy so I could see her profile, her sharp nose tipped up and her thin lips pushed into a tight line.

"Nah," Daddy said, his voice as nice as could be. "Gives the kids something to do. They aren't hurting anybody."

"Not yet." She turned her face back the direction she was walking. "You'll see."

"Yes, ma'am," Daddy said. "Suppose I will."

"Make sure that cake is in a good spot. I don't want it getting hidden behind anybody else's."

"Yes, ma'am."

The work it must've taken for Daddy to be kind to her was more than I had patience for. But he was a kind man, Daddy was. If there was anything I'd learned from him it was that gentleness wasn't a show of weakness. Sometimes it took more strength to be gentle than Samson possessed even on his very best day.

▪ ▪ ▪ ▪

Most of the kids from school had come a couple minutes after we did, their mothers arriving with cakes of all different kinds. Hazel had put on a fresh face and her troop of girls stood around cooing about her hair that did hold a curl, unlike mine. The boys lined up by the wall, like Ray, shoulders slouching and looking like they'd about die of boredom.

I sat in a chair, watching the three brave couples that moved about the floor to the slow and easy music. Crossing my legs at the ankles, I swung them back and forth, hoping maybe I'd get the nerve up to dance.

I sure was glad when Aunt Carrie came to me with a cup of punch. She pulled up a chair beside me, saving me from being all by my lonesome.

"Are you enjoying yourself?" she asked.

I shrugged, taking a sip of the punch. It wasn't as sweet as I expected.

"Do you think more people might come?" I asked.

"Yes, I'm sure of it." She smiled. "Do you think you might dance later?"

I nodded, hoping it was the truth.

"Opal taught me how to lindy-hop," I said.

"Did she?" Aunt Carrie's eyes widened. "How nice of her."

"Aunt Carrie," I said. "What's jungle music?"

"Where ever did you hear that?"

I told her about how Mrs. Ritzema had said it as we were walking in. Aunt Carrie breathed in deep through her nose and closed her eyes for just a moment. Then she opened them and shook her head.

"Well, it doesn't surprise me that she'd say something like that," she said, leaning in closer to me. "She means jazz."

"Oh," I said.

"It isn't a very nice thing to say, you know."

"I won't say it, then."

"That's good."

We sat and listened to the boring old ordinary music and watched the few dancers sway on the floor so slow that I wondered if they were asleep on their feet.

I tried so hard not to feel disappointed.

By the time just half an hour had passed, the dance hall was full of people. Some of them even took up space on the dance floor, moving together along with the music. There wasn't a band on the stage. All they had was a phonograph with a microphone positioned right by the horn to catch the sound. A couple older kids took turns changing the records between songs.

With all the punch I'd had, I needed to visit the lady's room. Girls bigger than me traveled in and out the door two by two. I couldn't hardly help but think of the critters making their way to Noah's ark in pairs. Something told me, though, that those animals wouldn't have stared into a mirror primping and preening quite so much as those girls did.

They touched up their lipstick or fixed their finger-waved hair. They chirped like birds the whole time, talking all at once. I didn't even try to follow along.

I finished up as fast as I could and hoped none of those girls noticed that I didn't wash my hands. There wasn't a single open sink and I sure didn't want to ask any of them to shimmy over for little old me.

Seemed funny to me, they'd gotten themselves dolled up at home just to come and fuss with their hair and faces all over again in the ladies' room. Far as I could tell, being ladylike was just one hassle after another.

Still, I smoothed my skirt and stood up tall before walking back into the dance hall. I sure hoped my hair was holding in the braid Aunt Carrie'd folded into it. And when I sat in one of the chairs at the edge of the room I made sure to keep my knees together.

From the chair I'd picked I could see Opal dancing with Lenny Miller. It was a slow dance, one without much tapping or swinging. They were real close, the two of them, in a way that made me wonder if they knew folks watched them. She'd insisted over and over that she didn't feel all that much for him, but the way she smiled when he whispered in her ear made me think otherwise.

I remembered Mama and Daddy dancing just like that in our living room back in Red River. Her pale-skinned hand in his rough one. Sometimes she'd even rest her head on his chest and I imagined she was listening to his heart beating.

I wondered if she ever danced with Abe Campbell that way. Just the thought of it turned my stomach sour. Shutting my eyes, I tried clearing that idea from my mind.

The slow song ended and I opened my eyes. A couple pairs left the dance floor, holding hands, and the next song started, one with a man and woman singing together.

"What are they doing here?" a girl sitting near me asked her friend, looking toward the door.

I turned to see who it was she was making a stink face at. There, standing right inside the dance hall, was Noah Jackson followed by a couple other men and three ladies.

If some of the people in Bliss had raised a stink about Opal joining in the dances, I knew they wouldn't like Noah and his friends being there on account they were all full Negro.

Uncle Gus walked right up to Noah and it seemed the whole room caught its breath, holding it and waiting for what might happen next.

The two men shook hands and Uncle Gus reached around and patted Noah on the back.

The steady, tame song from the record player ended and everybody clapped even as they whispered about the new arrivals to the dance hall.

"How's about something with a little swing to it?" Lenny hollered up at the boy standing at the phonograph, pulling a little attention from Noah and his friends.

Lenny ran over and jumped up on stage and rummaged through the stack of records, finding one that he handed to the boy running the phonograph.

"Play this one the rest of the night, dig?"

Lenny asked.

The boy looked at him like he'd just said something in Italian.

"Just put this on and don't stop it, all right?" Lenny said before sitting on the edge of the stage, looking over the room. "How about a little Benny Goodman, folks?"

More than a couple people called out their approval and Lenny grinned.

The music started up hard and fast, the kind that got my heartbeat thumping. Pairs formed and made their way to the edges. A couple that'd come in with Noah half ran to the center of the dance floor. Noah took Opal's hands and she nodded like she was willing to dance with him.

Lenny stayed on his perch, watching Opal and Noah. From the way his grin turned to a smirk, I didn't think he was too happy about her dancing with somebody else. The way Opal smiled up into Noah's face and how he smiled back, I wouldn't have been surprised to find out that Lenny was more than a little bit jealous.

Of all the couples dancing, Opal and Noah were the fastest, the best. They moved smoother, worked in more twists and hops. They didn't stumble and they didn't slow. They moved like their lives depended on it. I didn't think I'd ever be able to dance so quick without fainting from breathlessness. And I wasn't so sure of being tossed around like Noah was doing to Opal.

Still, I wished I'd had the nerve to go do what few steps I knew. I just stayed put in my chair, not moving so much as a toe even with how the music tempted me.

They danced the whole song that way. Some of the pairs around them started dancing furiously too. The ones who didn't moved to one side or the other to make sure they didn't get kicked. When that song ended, the kid on the stage didn't change the record, he just let it keep on going like Lenny'd told him to.

More people rushed out to the floor, even Aunt Carrie and Uncle Gus. They didn't go near as quick as some of the others, but they kept time with the music well enough.

"Pearl," Opal called, waving me over to her.

I shook my head.

"Come on," she said, nodding.

She shuffled over and grabbed both of my hands.

"What'd we spend all month practicing for if you're not going to dance to even one song?" she asked, pulling me to my feet. "Just remember to feel the beat all the way from your head to your toes. You'll do fine.

All right?"

I nodded, letting her lead me to the floor.

She put her hand on my back.

"Ready?" she asked.

I knew she meant to twirl me and I told her I was. The room swirled past me in a blur of colors and lights and the sound of the music. Faster and faster I went, Opal directing me like she was stirring a pot of soup. Cool air rushed up my skirt and I knew it was fanning up in pink and white around my legs and I didn't care one bit if the whole world saw clear up to the bottom of my underthings.

If ever in my life I'd felt like I was flying, it was right then.

We made our way through all the steps more than a couple times. We grooved and doubled back. We shook our hips and waved our hands in the air. By the end of the song we were side by side, our feet kicking, moving faster than I ever did at home.

Before the last note of the song I was out of breath already and wheezing, but I didn't want to stop dancing.

Song after song, I danced. With Lenny Miller, who seemed to have gotten over his sore feelings at Opal and Noah and hollered out cheers all during the song, and with Uncle Gus who made me laugh with all the faces he pulled. Daddy'd even taken my hand, leading me in a smooth dance when the song turned slow.

"How about a little punch?" Daddy asked after that song ended. "You're looking a little flushed."

I told him that would be nice and he showed me a chair where I should sit and rest a minute. As much as I'd loved dancing, I was glad to have a break. Besides, a cool glass of punch sounded awful good right about then.

It wasn't until I was in my seat that I saw Hazel and her group of girls walking right in my direction. Hazel stood in front of me and made a face as if I was a three-legged elephant in a jelly jar. I'd have said something smart to her about how she was staring at me, but I didn't have the wind to.

So I just looked her square in the eyes and raised my brows.

Hazel opened her mouth, but there wasn't the sneer that was usually on her upper lip. And her eyes grew round.

"How did you learn that?" she asked. "To dance like that?"

All the girls around her leaned in close to hear what I said.

I shrugged. "Oh, just here and there," I said.

"Will you teach us?" one of the girls asked.

"Ethel," Hazel scolded her, giving her a stink-eye. Then she turned back to me. "So, will you?"

"Maybe," I answered. "I'll have to think about it."

Hazel looked me up and down one more time before turning to go. But then she looked over her shoulder. "Your dress is pretty."

"I like your hair," I said back.

I thought maybe we didn't have to be enemies after all.

Our time at the dance was done and I knew begging Daddy to let me stay longer wouldn't do any good. He'd said eight o'clock and I knew he'd hold firm to that. Besides, he'd already gone out into the cold night, saying he was getting my chariot to take me on home.

Before, when I'd been younger, I might have pretended I was Cinderella, rushing away from the dance before the clock could strike midnight and my carriage turned back into a pumpkin, my pink and white polka-dotted gown back into rags. But I didn't play at such things anymore.

Aunt Carrie helped me with my coat and kissed my cheek. "You dance beautifully," she told me.

"Thank you," I said.

"Did you have a good time?"

"Yes, ma'am." I nodded. "When's the next one?"

She gave me a twinkle-eyed smile.

"I don't know, dear," she said. "But you are always welcome to dance in my kitchen."

Aunt Carrie wished me a good evening and said that she wouldn't mind if I came for a visit the next day. Seemed she missed me, at least that was what she said. I told her I'd come and turned toward the hallway.

Ray stood there, the cake he'd won balancing across his arms. He was like to drool all over it.

"Come on, Ray," I said.

"I'm fixin' to eat this whole thing tomorrow," he said, walking alongside me to the door.

"You'll get sick."

"Won't either," he said. "Even if I do I'll be happier than a magpie in the silverware drawer."

"That doesn't make any sense," I told him.

"Doesn't have to." He turned and bumped the door open with his backside, holding it so I could go out. "Watch for ice."

Daddy had the truck running right at the end of the walk. He held the cake while Ray and I climbed in. Daddy asked if we were ready before driving us away.

Leaning my head on Daddy's shoulder I could still hear the music playing in my ears.

Chapter Nineteen

For a full week after Valentine's Day I had daydreams of dancing. Every day. Try as I might, I couldn't hardly keep from slipping into them even in the middle of class. They were the kind a girl didn't like being pulled from.

In my imagination I saw a mighty big band had formed on the stage of the American Legion dance hall, one with every kind of instrument ever made. They'd be the kind to play fast and loud, never slowing it down for a cheek-to-cheek song. The song leader would dance in front of the band, wild and without a shred of embarrassment.

I'd walk into that room, my hair long again and full of curls like I saw on the women in Aunt Carrie's magazines. My dress would be short and full of swishing, so when I moved it couldn't help but dance along.

One of the grown boys would come and

take my hand, leading me out to the floor. Not Lenny Miller, though. He wasn't allowed in my daydreams on account he was just too cocky and I didn't like the way he looked at Opal. Whoever it was I'd paired up with, he'd spin me and lift me and smile all the while. The other pairs would stop, forming a circle around us. They'd clap and cheer until the song ended.

Somebody from Hollywood, California'd come all the way across the country to find himself a new star to dance and sing and bat eyelashes into the movie camera. He'd come to me while I sipped at my punch, telling me how much money I could make. Telling me I'd be famous.

I'd let him know I couldn't sing worth snot. He wouldn't care. I'd tell him I wouldn't leave without Daddy and Ray, and that we'd best pick up Millard along the way. That movie man would say he knew a deal when he heard one. He'd put out his hand and shake on it.

In my dream Mama would find herself a nickel for a movie. She'd find her way to a theater, holding that five-cent piece tight in her hand so she wouldn't lose it. She'd sit down, her legs crossed, the mended stockings on her legs showing their wear. Her eyes'd grow wide and her mouth fall open when she saw me on that screen in black and white and gray. Pressing her hands to her chest, she'd get teary for missing me.

Not giving it one thought more, she'd catch a train, traveling all day and all night for as long as it took to get to California from Michigan. It wouldn't matter if it took a month or a year even, not the way she wanted me. Wanted to be my mama again.

She'd come walking, head hanging, to the front door of the big house I'd bought from my movie money. Standing there on the porch she would look up at all the windows, wondering which one I was behind. And in her heart of hearts she'd know that she'd done wrong by me. She would know that she needed to look me in the face and try just a little to show me she was sorry.

She would knock on the door and that was where my daydream ended every time.

For the life of me I couldn't figure out what I would do if Mama came home.

Chapter Twenty

February melted away and March came in with a little more sunshine and a little less chill to the air. What Uncle Gus had called a cold snap seemed to have broken right in half and let the warmer days through. I was glad for that. Seemed all of creation agreed with me the way the birds swooped through the sky and the squirrels chitter-chattered in the tree branches. Most folks even smiled easier.

Most days before class I'd meet up with Hazel and a couple of her friends to dance in the schoolyard. We'd pair up and take turns being the lead and the follow. I never would've thought Hazel could giggle, but she did. When she did, the sharp, pinched up look on her face dropped away and I saw how pretty she really was.

Sometimes I imagined we'd become friends, Hazel and me. The kind of friends that shared secrets and played with each other's hair, like Aunt Carrie's friend she'd told me about.

But then she'd snap at her partner for stepping on her toes or glare at Delores when she made her way to her desk, and I'd remember how nasty she was.

"Folks is as they is," Meemaw might've said. "Ain't like to change this side of heaven."

After all my eleven years of living, I had to think she'd have been right about that.

Every once in a while Bert would come over and watch us dance, hoping we were unevenly paired. When we were, I'd have him dance with the younger girl named Gwendolyn. She seemed just pleased as punch to be dancing with him even if he did stomp on her feet more often than not.

When I wasn't at school or home helping Opal with chores, I was out in the woods that stood between the house on Magnolia Street and the apple orchard behind Uncle Gus's barn. I'd climb over snow-buried stumps or clumps of leaves. I'd try to climb into the branches of trees I thought had been there since God spoke Michigan into being. There, not too high above the earth, I'd read out of a book I'd stowed away in the wide pockets of my coat. It wasn't near warm enough to be sitting out in the air like that and Mama'd have pitched a fit seeing me there with my skirts all bunched up on my legs.

But Mama wasn't there to see me. She was off who-knew-where doing who-knew-what with Abe Campbell. She'd not called or so much as written a note since the time Daddy'd gone off to see her.

It was just as well. We didn't need her. We were doing just fine living the way we were.

At least I talked myself into believing that just about every other day when my heart tried to trick me into missing her.

A couple days a week Opal still gave me a dance lesson. She'd keep the radio off, the only music was her counting off the rhythm. Then we'd go to the kitchen to get supper around, Opal putting the radio on in the background. Every once in a while a good song would come on and we'd both put down whatever it was we were chopping or stirring and we'd dance with small swings of arms and kicks of feet so as not to knock over anything from the stove or the counter.

It was a Thursday and Opal had put the casserole in the oven. Her other chores for the day were done, so we went out to the living room and danced for a couple songs before one of them made Opal stop right in the middle of a step. She went over to the radio and put her ear up to it, shutting her eyes with a smile tipping up the corners of her lips.

"What's wrong?" I asked.

"Hush," she answered. "It's Cab Calloway."

Even though my heart was pumping loud and my body still wanted to move, I settled in next to her, our ears close to the radio to listen to that man as he half sang, half hollered out a whole bunch of nonsense words.

The way Opal knit her brow and sighed while listening to that song, I would've thought that Cab Calloway had set the earth to spinning. She put her hands to her chest and slumped back against the radio stand as if the very thought of him made her weak and unable to put together any words, just sighs and swooning.

"If I ever make it to New York, I'll find him," she said after the song ended. "I promise you I will."

"You'd go to New York?" I asked. "Why would you do that?"

"Oh, I don't know how to explain it," she answered. "I guess it's easier for somebody like me in a big city, Pearl. There are more who look like me and think the way I do."

I did not understand what she was talking

about, but I didn't say a word to her about it.

"There's a club on every block in the city. At least that's what I've heard." She smiled, closing her eyes like she was dreaming. "I bet I could go to a different place every night of the week and never get tired of it. Can you imagine?"

"Do you think you'd get famous if you went there?" I asked.

"Maybe." She opened her eyes and raised one brow. "They're always looking for dancers out there for the shows. I could make a little money to send home."

She stopped and bit on her bottom lip.

"Do you think you'll ever go?" I asked.

"Probably not." She reached up and fussed with the back of her hair. "I'd never have enough money to make it there."

I thought if I could scrounge up all my nickels and dimes, I could save until I had enough to buy her a train ticket or a seat on a bus. Maybe I'd even hold back a little so I could get her a store-bought dress so she wouldn't have to wear one of her flour-sack ones in the city. While I was at it, I didn't think it would take too much more to get her a brand-new pair of shoes — the kind she could dance in.

I imagined her getting off the train or the

bus, looking at all the buildings that reached up to touch the clouds, her neck craning to see the top of them. It would be loud, New York would be, with lots of people bustling down the road. But Opal wouldn't be scared about it. And she wouldn't be nervous. Not one little bit.

She'd feel right at home there. Nobody'd look at her funny, trying to figure out if she was white or colored. They wouldn't look at her tight curls and her full lips or her bright eyes and her fair skin and think of how she didn't belong. They'd just see her, how her eyes lit up when she smiled and walked and how her hair bounced. What the folks in New York would see was Opal.

And that was good enough.

She'd be walking down the street, paying too much attention to all that was around her to see what was right in front of her. With a thump and a bump, she'd run right into a man wearing the most beautiful suit she'd ever seen.

He'd put his hands on her shoulders and ask if she was all right. She was and would tell him so. But then she'd move her eyes up to his face.

"Cab?" she'd ask, feeling weak in the knees the way women in the movies sometimes did.

He'd nod. "That's right."

He would ask her name and say it was just right, the kind of name that should be on a marquee somewhere. Opal Moon. A name meant for flashing lights. That would make her blush and smile her prettiest of smiles.

"Say, you wouldn't happen to dance, would you?" he'd ask. "One of my girls is out sick with the flu. I could use a gal like you in my show tonight."

Opal would tell him she did dance and he'd believe her. Taking the suitcase out of her hand, he'd give her his arm and they'd walk down the road together, not even noticing the cars speeding by or the people rushing past them on either side.

She got up, Opal did, from in front of the radio, saying she needed to check on the casserole, and left me sitting there on the living room floor, the radio playing a song that made me feel sad for some reason I couldn't put my finger on.

As much as I would have liked to keep Opal with me, I knew she couldn't stay forever. She'd have to go back to her family or strike out for a new town, maybe even a big city like New York.

There had to be someplace that would be more home to her than Bliss ever could be. I just had to believe there was.

Chapter Twenty-One

It'd been the kind of March day that could make a person forget how bitter cold winter had been. The sun had been kind and Ray and I'd stayed out all day in it at the farm.

I'd always been taught that Sundays were for Sabbath rest. Running around with Uncle Gus's tan dog and exploring in the barn, climbing trees and feeding the hens out of the palm of my hand seemed about as holy as a day got.

When I'd told Aunt Carrie that, she'd smiled.

"You think that's all right?" I'd asked.

"God sees even the smallest of sparrows," she'd said. "Chickens too, I imagine. And if He takes notice and delights in them, then isn't it sacred for us to do the same?"

I told her that sounded real nice.

As was usual on the farm, time got away from us. Daddy called for Ray and me to get in the truck so we could head to the house on Magnolia Street. I dragged my feet, wishing we didn't have school the next day. One thing about warm weather, it sure made me long for summer.

We rode home in quiet, the three of us just letting the goodness of the day rest on us. Daddy had the windows rolled down just enough that the sweet smell of almost-spring air danced around us, mussing up our hair.

Once we pulled onto our street we saw Bert and his dad out in their side yard. The pigeon was in its cage, placed under the tree.

"Now what do you think they're doing?" Daddy asked, cutting the engine of the truck.

"Looks like he's puttin' together a coop for that bird," Ray said. "Bert's been talkin' about it for a month."

"Huh. How about that." Daddy nodded. "Think I'll go over and see how it's going."

"Yeah," Ray said.

They both got out of the truck, before I budged an inch. Ray dashed ahead of Daddy and crossed the street. They said their howdies to the doctor and Bert who was holding a hammer in a way that made me mighty nervous.

"Hi ya, Pearl," Bert called over to me as soon as I slid off the truck seat.

I put my hand up in a wave and turned to go to the house. Ever since he'd given me that heart-shaped card, I'd done my best not to pay him too much attention. I didn't want him thinking I was in love with him the way I imagined he was with me.

And I especially didn't want him or anybody else to know that I'd hidden that card away in my dresser under an old blouse that didn't fit so well anymore. Or that I took it out every couple days to look at that cat he'd drawn and the words, "you're pretty." I'd never gotten a Valentine before.

Holding the porch railing, I made my way up the steps, breathing in the last little bit of that spring day. As far as I'd been concerned it could not have been a more perfect Sunday.

I'd forgotten how often the best of days were followed up by awful ones. I'd let myself think how good it was and always would be, not paying any mind to my gut that told me it couldn't last.

I opened the door and stepped inside, feeling the comfort of being back home. The sinking sun let a beam of light break through the window in the living room that made it look even warmer than it already was. I pushed my hand into the stream of sunshine, trying to catch the dots of dust on the air but only managing to stir them up.

I thought of how Beanie would sit and stare at the dust as it danced in the beams of light. She'd sit on the floor of our bedroom, her legs stretched out in front of her, just staring straight in front of her for what might have been hours.

When I'd ask her what she was doing, she wouldn't answer me. She would just make her grunting sounds like she did when something had her attention.

I wondered if she was doing that very thing in heaven just then, looking at the dust in the tubes of sun that streamed into whatever kind of mansion Jesus had built just for her. But that dust wouldn't be made of earth. Heaven dust was made of gold and silver.

Beanie would like that very much, I was sure of it.

Closing my eyes, I hummed the tune of a song we'd sometimes sing back in Red River. I couldn't remember the exact words. But I did remember something about Jesus holding us in His strong and righteous hand. Not a sparrow fell but He knew about it. And I did believe that He'd seen Beanie and held her right in the palm of His hand.

I hummed that song until I heard a sound from the direction of the kitchen. Like a drawer being pushed shut. There shouldn't have been anyone in the house. Daddy and Ray were across the street and Opal had that day off.

Another sound. Like a cup set on the counter. Then the faucet, rushing water. A footstep.

Flashes of fear zipped through my body and my heart pounded. A sickening ache clenched my stomach and my breathing shallowed.

Another footstep. It was from a hard-soled shoe. Not Opal's, I knew. Her shoes didn't make near so much noise.

Holding my breath, I waited, listened. Heard no other sounds.

"It's nothing but your imagination," I whispered to myself. "There's nobody here."

Then the kitchen door swung open and one footstep clomped and another. The steps drew nearer and I opened my eyes, ready to fight for my life if I had to. Ready to scream bloody murder if I had to. It wouldn't take half a minute before Daddy'd be there to save me.

Turning, I saw who it was.

Mama.

Chapter Twenty-Two

Meemaw liked to tell the story of the woman caught in sin and dragged out into the streets of old Jerusalem by the Pharisees. As to what her sin was, I'd never asked Meemaw, but I was sure it had to do with fornicating by the way Meemaw's voice lowered to a whisper when she mentioned the word sin.

"Them men pulled her out and threw her right in the dust," Meemaw'd say, shaking her head.

I imagined that woman's clothes were torn from them dragging her and her hair a mess, too. She'd have been crying, streaks of tears cutting through her dirty face. Scared, she'd fold up into herself, maybe even cower, ducking her head just in case a rock came through the air at her.

"Now, it was at Jesus's feet them men threw her," Meemaw'd go on.

Jesus would have known what she'd done.

Far as I'd been told, He knew everything in all the world that'd ever happened and everything that was to come. He'd look at the woman, I was sure of it, feeling pity in His heart for her.

"Them men wanted Jesus to condemn that woman," Meemaw would say. "They wanted Jesus to say it was all right for them to stone her."

I'd heard enough Bible stories in my days to know that throwing rocks was how they punished somebody in old Israel. I never did think it was a nice thing to do. Couldn't hardly understand how it came to be that God put it down in the law of the land. When I'd asked Meemaw to explain she'd just told me that God was God and He got to make up whatever rules He saw fit.

Meemaw'd told me that Jesus bent Himself down and wrote a little something into the sand. When I'd asked her what it was He'd written, she shook her head and told me that nobody knew.

"That'll be a question for you to ask once you reach heaven, darlin'," she'd say. "It don't matter so much what He wrote as what He said."

Jesus, the tip of His finger dusty from His writing, stood upright and looked at the men. I always wondered if His face held anger or sadness or maybe a little bit of both.

"Then, the Lord said, 'Whoever is without sin may throw the first stone.' " Meemaw'd close her eyes like she wanted to think on those words for a minute or two. She'd put a hand to her chest and she'd shake her head back and forth, her lips trembling. "And not one of them fellas so much as picked up a pebble, let alone a stone. They all turned tail."

Jesus hadn't watched them go, but in His never-ending wisdom, He knew they'd left. He looked at the woman. She'd have stopped crying, not sure what to make of what had just happened.

He asked her where the men had gone, if none of them had stayed.

She'd shake her head. I imagined she'd have had a hard time finding her voice just then.

"I don't condemn you," He'd say to her. "Go. Don't sin anymore."

I wondered how clean that woman lived after that.

We stood facing each other in the living room, Mama and me. Neither of us had bothered to take our jackets off. I still had the sunshine of the day warming my skin and she held her old carpetbag in front of her, letting it bob against her knees.

Not for a second did I take my eyes off her face. And not even once did she look at mine.

I didn't want to throw stones at her, but I sure didn't feel like forgiving her.

"Hi, Mama," I whispered.

I let myself take a good look at her. She seemed different to me. Not messy, but shabby, like she hadn't been taking care of herself as much as usual. Her pale face, sunk-in cheeks, and the purple under her eyes were all new. A flutter in my heart made me worry that maybe she was sick. At the very least she looked like she hadn't slept in all the time she'd been gone.

She took another step closer to me and put down her bag. She rested her hands on her chest like she wasn't sure what else to do with them. I looked from her face to her hands.

As hard as Mama had always worked at scrubbing and folding and picking and dusting, her hands had always been beautiful. She'd kept her nails trimmed and filed into perfect arches and she'd put salve on her knuckles to keep them from getting cracked in the dry weather.

But that day, her hands were red and cracked and her fingernails were short like they'd all broken off. An ache spread from my chest to my stomach, making me feel like I might just get sick for the deep sadness that set in all the sudden.

For all the times I'd imagined her coming home, I'd never thought it would make me so sad.

"I need a glass of water," I told her, stepping around her toward the kitchen.

Turning, I watched over my shoulder to see if she'd follow. She did, looking around the dim living room as she walked. She even ran two fingers across the table in the corner by Daddy's chair.

"Opal keeps the house real clean," I said, turning from her. "You won't find any dust."

"I'm glad," Mama said, but her voice sounded flat and empty like she wasn't glad at all.

In the kitchen I took a glass from the cupboard and drew cool water from the tap. I sipped at it so Mama wouldn't get after me for gulping or slurping. But she didn't even look at me. She stood with her fingertips on the countertop, feeling of it like she couldn't believe it was real.

"Did you have supper?" she asked. "I can cook up something for you."

"Yes, ma'am," I told her. "We ate at Aunt Carrie's house."

"That's fine."

"Are you hungry?" I asked, pushing my hip against the counter.

She shrugged. Mama had never been one to shrug. She'd always said it was too common a thing to do and made her think whoever it was doing the shrugging didn't give proper thought to whatever it was they were asked.

But she'd shrugged and didn't look me in the eye.

"You want me to hang up your jacket?" I asked.

"That's all right." She moved her hand up to clutch at the collar.

"Are you staying?" I asked.

"Pearl . . ."

"If you aren't going to stay you should just leave now," I said. "Before Daddy sees you. I wouldn't even tell him you were here."

"Pearl Louise." It wasn't a scolding like I would have expected. Instead, my name came out of her like a sigh she'd been holding a good long while. Then she looked up at me, meeting my eyes. When she said my name again it was with more edge to it.

"I won't have you hurting Daddy again," I told her. "Not anymore, Mama."

"Listen here —"

I didn't stay there to hear what she might have to say to me and I didn't stay put to have her give me a bar of soap to bite for being a sassy-mouth little girl. It felt like power, walking away from her like that. I knew it wasn't right, but I hoped it hurt her even a tiny bit as much as her leaving us had broken me.

I didn't want to throw stones at her, that was true. But I didn't mind if she hurt, even just a little. It was what she deserved.

I waited until I was up in my room with the door closed before I let myself cry.

Ray and Daddy came inside not half an hour later. By then my eyes were dry and I was nursing a powerful headache. I heard Daddy tell Ray to go on upstairs and before I knew it, my door opened.

"You all right?" Ray asked, his voice a whisper.

I told him I didn't know and he nodded like he understood. If ever there was a gift that Ray Jones gave me, it was that he knew me through and through.

Without having to say a word the two of us went to the register in the floor, lowering down to put our ears to it. If Mama and Daddy talked clearly enough, we'd be able to hear most every word.

We laid on our sides, Ray and I, facing each other.

"Why didn't you let me know you were coming?" Daddy asked. "You could've called."

"I was afraid," Mama answered. "I wasn't sure I'd end up here. I was just afraid."

"Of what?" Daddy's voice sounded strained. "Of me? When have I ever given you cause to fear me?"

There was a pause and Ray blinked a bunch of times fast like he did when something made him nervous.

"I was scared you'd tell me not to come," Mama said. "That you'd say you didn't want me anymore."

"Mary," Daddy said. "You can always come back home to me."

"I don't know that I can," she said.

"What do you mean?"

"I think this was a mistake," she said. "I can't stay. I shouldn't have come in the first place."

"Why did you then?"

"I didn't know where else to go," she answered. "Pearl doesn't want me here. She told me as much. I should just go."

Hearing her say my name made me get up off the floor. Before I knew it I was at the bottom of the steps. Then I was moving toward the kitchen. I could see the light that glowed around the closed door. I leaned against the wall beside it, letting my head rest back.

"She's hurt, Mary," Daddy said. "Did you think she'd run to you?"

"I don't know." She sighed. "I guess not. I just hoped."

For a moment all I heard was the ticking clock from the living room and a couple sniffles I supposed had come from Mama.

"I won't have you come and go," Daddy said. "If you're staying, that's fine. We'll make do. But if you're fixing to go again, you might as well just go now."

They went quiet again and I held my breath, waiting for what one of them might say next.

"Abe left me," Mama said, her voice small and hardly breaking the silence. "A few weeks ago."

"Where'd he go to?" Daddy asked.

"I don't know."

"How have you been making it?"

"I've done some work," she said. "There's a hotel up in Adrian I've been cleaning."

"I never would've left you like that, Mary," Daddy said. "I never would've had you working like that."

"I didn't have much choice, did I?"

Daddy sighed and I heard his heavy boots on the floor when he took a couple steps.

"He left me a note." Mama's voice shook. "Like I left you."

I imagined Mama walking into the apartment or house or lean-to or wherever it was she'd been staying. There on the dresser or desk or table was a note, folded in two and sitting up like a tent or in an envelope under a paperweight. Her name was spelled out across it in black ink.

"I just couldn't believe it," she said.

I pictured her reading that letter and having to sit down to deal with the bad news. What I felt thinking on that wasn't pity for her. If somebody'd asked me, I wouldn't have been able to tell them what it was, that tightening of my stomach and throb in my head. All I knew was that I didn't feel sorry for Mama. Not even a little.

"He never cared about you, Mary," Daddy said, his voice flat. "Not like I always did. Like I always have."

"Tom, don't."

"I was nothing but good to you."

"Until Beanie . . ." Mama started. "You never held me after. You never comforted me. You blamed me."

I knew that wasn't true. It couldn't have been. But Daddy didn't talk back to her or stick up for himself. He'd never been one for that sort of thing. If I'd had any spine at all, I'd have pushed through that kitchen door and given Mama a piece of my mind.

She wasn't the only one who'd lost Beanie. It was well past time she heard that.

But I didn't move from my spot. I didn't have the courage.

Neither Mama nor Daddy made even the slightest sound for more than a minute and I thought they were both frozen, turned to stone so they wouldn't break into a hundred pieces from grief and heartbreak.

"Stay here, Mary, with us," Daddy said. "This is your home as much as it is mine."

"I don't expect you to put me up," she said.

"You're my wife," Daddy said. "I've gotta keep my promise I made to you on our wedding day. I won't have you staying out on the streets."

"I can find a place," she said. "I could take in laundry or something."

"You're still my wife, Mary."

"I'll manage."

"You'll stay here," Daddy said.

"Tom," she said. "I'm expecting."

It seemed all the air'd gotten sucked right out of my chest and I worked at pulling some in. The sick feeling in my stomach got stronger and the room started to spinning.

I knew what it meant that a woman was expecting. All the grown folks used that word when they were talking about a woman who was going to have a baby.

Mama was expecting a baby.

As many times as I'd asked God ever so politely to give me the gift of a little brother or sister, I hadn't thought I'd be so broke up upon finding out He'd answered my prayers.

"What?" Daddy asked, his voice sounding every bit as baffled as I felt.

"I hid it as long as I could," Mama told him. "Abe told me over and over he never wanted to be a father."

"Is it mine?" Daddy asked. "I've got to know. Is it mine?"

"How could it be?"

"That night," he said. "When I came to see you."

She didn't answer him.

"It could be," he said. "Couldn't it?"

"Tom."

"Just tell me, Mary." His voice was thin, sounding like it could break at any moment. "Is it mine?"

"No."

"How can you be sure?"

"Because I already knew about the baby,"

she said. "I'd known for a week or two."

"And you still let me be with you?" he asked. "Lord, Mary. Why'd you let me if you knew that?"

"I missed you."

"Then why didn't you come home with me?" he asked. "That night, you could've come home."

"Because being with you made me remember all the hurt." Her voice seemed far away, wispy, like a breath of wind. "I shouldn't have come back here. I should have known better."

"You'll stay, Mary," he said.

"Everyone will know," she said. "They'll all stare at me."

"Don't know what I can do about that. Stay anyway."

"I don't deserve it," she said. "Being here. With you."

"It won't be like before." His voice sounded firm.

"I know."

"I'm not ready to forgive you."

"I don't expect you will."

"Yup."

The kitchen door swung open and Daddy stepped out. He stopped when he saw me there. Running his hands over his face, he let out a deep sigh.

"You can talk to her if you want," he said.

I looked in at her. She'd taken her coat off since I'd gone upstairs and I could see she had on one of her dresses that I'd always liked best. It wasn't anything fancy, just a cotton dress with little green flowers all over it. She'd even made one like it for me out of that same fabric. I'd long since grown out of it, but I still remembered how proud I'd been to walk down the street in Red River, matching my mama like that.

She'd gotten so thin around the shoulders and arms, though, that the dress hung. Her eyes fell to mine and she put her hand on the slight roundness of her stomach.

She didn't smile and she didn't frown. She just held her face blank.

I set my face away from her and toward Daddy.

He walked with me up to my bedroom.

CHAPTER TWENTY-THREE

There'd been no fat calf slaughtered to cook after Mama came home, and no ring put back on her finger. Daddy hadn't draped a new robe over her shoulders. We hadn't gathered all the town to come and celebrate the return of Mama.

We just turned out the lights and went to bed.

The next morning, before I'd come down for breakfast, I heard Daddy make Mama promise not to try and find Abe Campbell. She wasn't to write a letter or make a telephone call. He didn't want her going looking for him or inviting him to come find her.

"He's gone, Tom," she said. "I wouldn't even know where to look if I wanted to. Which I don't."

"Still," Daddy said. "I don't want you even trying."

"If it'll make you happy I won't even think

of him," Mama said.

"I wish I could make you promise a thing like that."

Once Ray and I came down they stopped talking. They didn't even look at each other. I thought I'd choke on how thick the air in that room felt.

Opal stayed in the kitchen while we sat at the dining room table. She'd hardly looked at me when she brought out the pot of oatmeal Mama had asked her to fix.

"Do you want to eat with us?" I asked her.

She lifted her eyes to mine and shook her head. The way she didn't smile at me made me think she was upset with me. I couldn't think of what I might've done that would get her mad at me.

Not even Ray ate much of his breakfast that morning.

It wasn't until Ray and I had stepped out on the porch to go to school that I said another word.

"Why do you think Opal was upset?" I asked. "Did I do something wrong?"

"Nah, you didn't do nothin'," he answered.

"Then why was she so quiet?"

He shrugged. "Probably 'cause your ma came back." He inhaled deep and looked across the street. "What's Bert doin'?"

Bert was standing in that new-built pigeon coop, the door of it wide open behind him. Even from where I stood I could hearing him talking to that bird like it was a baby.

"He don't have that bird outta its cage, does he?" Ray asked.

"Why's he got to keep her in the cage?" I crossed my arms.

"So it gets used to the coop." Ray jumped off the porch, landing flat on his feet like he always did, and rushed over to Bert. "Put it back in the cage."

Bert turned soon as he heard Ray and held up his cupped hands with a big old smile spread across his face.

"She likes it in here," he said, loud enough for me to hear him even.

Just then, as if she'd been planning it, that pigeon lifted herself up out of his hands and through the wide-open door.

"Sassy," Bert hollered after her, making his way out of the coop. "Come back here."

I stepped down off the porch, watching that bird light on the top of the coop and listening to her trilling away as if she meant to scold Bert for yelling at her. She bobbed her head, the morning sunlight catching the purple of her neck feathers.

I watched the boys for a minute or two, my arms crossed and shaking my head at their foolishness. Bert was trying his darnedest to get up to the roof of that coop and Ray was trying to give him a boost. All the while, the both of them hollered out for her to come back. With how red their faces were, I thought they were both plenty sore with that bird.

After a minute I made my way across the road. Looking back at the house to be sure Mama wasn't spying out the window at me, I tucked my skirt up the way Aunt Carrie'd taught me so I could climb without the whole world seeing my underthings. All it took was pulling myself up on one branch and reaching over for another before I was within reach of the bird. She only pecked me once or twice, smacking my hand with one of her wings a little, and then I had her, the feathers of her wings and underbelly soft against my palm.

"Why are you flying away from those silly boys, huh?" I asked, keeping my voice smooth as I could to soothe her. She pecked at my thumb, but it didn't hurt so much that I was going to let her go. "You cut that out, all right? Now simmer down, would ya? That's a girl. Good. Calm. Good."

Ray and Bert stood at the base of the tree looking up at me. I shook my head when

Bert put out a hand for me to give him Sassy.

"Y'all need to learn a thing or two about how to talk to ladies," I said. "They don't take so kind to being hollered at, you know."

"We'd've caught her," Bert said, trying his hardest to sound like Ray. I thought he was hoping to impress me. "She was just playing with me."

"Yeah, I'm sure," I said, my fingers curled around Sassy's body. "You better be careful. This girl's liable to fly on back to the Litchfields again if you don't treat her nice."

"I'm nice to her," Bert said.

"You shoulda kept her in the cage like you were told," Ray said. "She ain't used to the coop yet."

Bert looked up at Ray with a hurt look like he was fixing to boo-hoo. "Why doesn't she like me?"

"She's just gotta get used to you is all." Ray put out his hands for the bird. She didn't fight him one bit when he took her from me. "You just gotta be gentle with her."

Bert's forehead wrinkled and his fists clenched as he watched Ray take the pigeon into the coop and put her back inside the cage.

"She likes you better'n she likes me," Bert said, a whine to his voice so heavy it almost made me laugh.

"Nah," Ray said, shaking his head and closing the coop door. "She don't neither."

"Does too." Bert turned and stomped away from us, up the porch steps, and into his house. He didn't slam the door, and I thought that was on account his mother would've let him have it for such a thing.

Ray and I just watched him go.

"You think he'll be sore at us for long?" I asked, climbing back down from the tree.

"Maybe half an hour or so," Ray told me. "Maybe a couple minutes more."

"He's a funny kid." I untucked my skirt and smoothed what wrinkles I could out of the fabric.

"Yeah. He sure is." Ray wiped his nose on his sleeve. "We best get goin'."

"We gonna wait for Bert?"

"Nah," Ray answered. "He'll find his way all right."

Before we left the Barnetts' yard to take Magnolia Street to the main road, I turned and looked back at our house. Mama stood in the big front window, her arms crossed and eyes on me.

My chest tightened and I had to force myself to take a good breath. She'd seen me up in that tree with my skirts all bunched up. As much as I wished I didn't care what she thought of me, my thud-thud-thudding heart told me different.

Miss De Weese had got it in her mind to teach us a song in the French language. Back in Red River we'd never sung anything at school, let alone something in a different tongue. She'd told us it was about plucking a bird and she'd drawn a hen on the board. All the body parts were labeled and didn't sound anything like I would've guessed.

We sang about plucking feathers off the head, neck, and back and I tried not to think of Bert's pigeon all the while. The part of the song I didn't understand was how a person was going to pluck feathers off a bird's beak or eyes. That didn't make any sense to me, and I wondered if French birds just grew their feathers different than American birds.

After we finished the song, I about put my hand up to ask but thought better of it. It didn't matter, not really. What did matter was how that song had served to take my mind off Mama, if only for a little bit.

Besides, Miss De Weese said it was about time for us to get going for lunch. I had to look at the clock twice to be sure she was right. All that singing in French had made the last bit of the morning speed away from me.

Bert seemed to have forgotten about Sassy getting loose that morning and her liking Ray and me more than she liked him. Either that or he was mighty quick to forgive. Either way, he just about hopped all the way back to our neighborhood alongside Ray, telling him this or that about something or another.

Whatever it was, it seemed Bert could think of nothing on earth quite so important right that moment. When I turned and looked at Ray's face, it was all smiles and I thought he was near to laughing at Bert. Not out of meanness, but because of how Bert's voice grew louder and louder the more he went on.

Even after we got to our street, Bert kept going. And he didn't stop talking just because Ray'd turned toward our house and he'd gone toward his own.

"You think he knows you're not there anymore?" I asked Ray.

"Don't think it matters to him much," Ray answered, shaking his head. "Let's go in. I'm half starved to death."

Ray let me go inside first. Soon as I opened the door I saw Mama and Daddy standing in the living room facing each other, both red in the cheeks and tense in the shoulders. They quit talking soon as we walked in. Mama turned and rushed out of the room, the kitchen door swinging open and closed behind her.

Daddy crossed his arms and bit at his lower lip before looking at Ray and me.

"Go on and get washed up," he said.

Ray did as he was told right away. As for me, I stayed where I was, watching Daddy put his coat on and take his hat from the rack on the wall.

"You aren't staying?" I asked.

His hand on the doorknob, he looked at me over his shoulder and shook his head.

"I need to get back to work," he answered.

"You'll be hungry," I said. "Won't you?"

"I'll manage fine."

He pulled the front door open and put his hat on before stepping out. I followed him to the porch.

"Daddy," I said. "You can't leave us with her."

Stopping, he shut his eyes for a tick of the clock before turning his head toward me.

"Darlin', you're going to be all right," he said. "I'll be back for supper."

"Do you promise?"

"Of course I do."

What I wanted to say was how scared I

was right then in that very moment that he was fixing to climb into his truck and drive away. That he wouldn't stop or even think of turning back until he got all the way to Oklahoma. By then it would be too late for him to change his mind. The fear of him leaving us made it so hard to breathe that I wouldn't have been able to say anything if I'd tried.

"I'm just going to the station," he said like he'd read my mind. "If you need me, that's where I'll be. Hear?"

"Yes, sir," I whispered.

He gave me a wink before going down the porch steps and on his way to the station. I stood on the porch, arms wrapped around myself, and watched Daddy until he turned a corner and I couldn't see him anymore.

The table was already set and the food dished out on the plates by the time my hands were scrubbed clean and I stepped into the dining room. I didn't tell Mama that we usually took our noon meal at the table in the kitchen unless we thought we might have company. I didn't think she'd want me giving her suggestions like that by the way her lips were puckered like she was fixing to work up a good spit.

But ladies didn't spit and they didn't bother their mothers with silly ideas. At least that was what I imagined Mama would have said if I'd dared tell her that.

"Is Opal gonna eat with us?" I asked, holding my skirt tight against my backside and pushing it under me as I took my seat at the table.

"Does she usually?" Mama asked.

Ray lifted his eyes to mine from across the table. I knew what his look meant, the way he made his eyes just the tiniest bit wider and the slight back and forth movement of his head.

"No, ma'am," I answered, hoping God wouldn't hold that lie against me on the day of judgment.

Mama took her seat and spread her napkin across her lap. She didn't even say a blessing before eating.

After a silent meal, Mama asked me to help clear the dishes from the table. I did as she said and stacked our three plates, laying the silverware across the top.

"I can help," Ray said, picking up his glass and mine.

"No," Mama said. "Leave those. Pearl and I can do this. You go on outside until it's time to go back to school."

Ray met my eyes like he wanted to see if I'd be all right with him going. Just as soon as I nodded he moved toward the front door and his hung-up coat.

I backed my way into the kitchen, pushing open the door with my behind. When I turned toward the counter I expected to see Opal there, elbow deep in sudsy water or sitting at the kitchen table, eating her lunch.

"Hi, Opal," I said.

But nobody was there to say hi back to me. The only trace of Opal was the apron she'd always worn hanging on the hook by the icebox. Not paying attention to the dishes I was carrying, I laid them on the countertop and reached for that apron. It caught a bit of the sunshine coming in through the window and the light showed how faded it had gotten after all the times it'd been scrubbed and hung to dry in the sun.

We'd brought it from Oklahoma. I remembered Mama folding it and laying it gently in one of the boxes Daddy'd packed in the back of the truck. Our old life moved to where our new life would get started.

Mama'd let Opal wear that apron when she'd started working for us not long after we'd gotten to Bliss. There it hung on the hook, not around Opal's waist like it should've been.

"Where's Opal?" I asked when Mama came into the kitchen with the cloth napkins bunched in her hands.

Mama went right to the table, lowering the napkins and wiping her hands on the apron she wore tied up so it was above her round belly.

"I sent her home," she said. "We don't need her help anymore."

"Why'd you do that?" I didn't care if I sounded disrespectful or if questioning Mama would earn me a smack in the mouth. "She helps us."

"I'm here now."

Mama moved across the room to the sink and let the water run until it was hot. She plugged the drain and put a dot of soap in the stream to make suds.

"We need her," I said.

If I'd been brave I would've told Mama that she had no business doing such a thing as sending Opal away. If I'd had even half an ounce of courage, I'd have said that it was Opal who had taken care of us when Mama'd run off. And I'd have let her know that I'd rather have Opal than her.

But I was nothing but a coward so I just stood there, holding the soft cotton fabric of the apron hanging on the wall in the beam of sunshine.

"She came in the front door," Mama said. "Like she lived here."

"Daddy told her she should," I answered.

"She should have come in the back, Pearl. That's just how it works."

"Opal belongs here." I crossed my arms. "She's been good to us."

"You should go back to school," Mama said, then tensed her jaw like she was fixing to lose her temper. "Go on now."

I did obey. Not because I knew it was right, doing what I was told, but because if I stayed in that room any longer I knew I'd say something nasty to Mama.

I walked away from her, fast as I could.

It wasn't until I was halfway to school that I realized I'd forgotten my jacket.

Chapter Twenty-Four

The minute school was over I stomped my way down the street and stormed into the police station and right up to Daddy's desk. When he saw me, he folded up his paper and smiled.

"How was school?" he asked.

"All right, I guess," I answered.

"Learn anything?"

"A couple things."

"That's fine." He tipped back in his chair and crossed his arms. "You doing okay?"

"Mama sent Opal home," I told him.

He nodded and looked down at the paper on his desk. "I know she did."

"What'd she wanna do that for?" I tried keeping my voice steady.

"She says she can do for us now she's home." Daddy closed his eyes. "I'm sure there're other folks Opal can work for."

"She isn't going to come by anymore?"

Daddy shook his head. "Your mama didn't

think we needed the help."

"But we do."

He leaned forward, his chair creaking from the move. Elbows on the desk, he rubbed at his eyes with the meaty part of his hands.

"Your mama said she'll make do," he said. "She told Opal as much after breakfast."

"Is that why y'all were fighting?" I asked. "When we came for lunch?"

He turned his eyes up to me. "You don't need to worry about that, Pearlie. That's between your mama and me."

"Did you tell her no?" I asked, afraid of how bold I was just then, but unable to keep from asking. "You should've told Mama no."

"Pearl Louise," Daddy said with warning in his voice. "I don't like it either. But I'm trying my hardest to keep the peace."

"I want Mama to go away." I felt how my lips shook and the way the anger throbbed in my temples. "I don't want her coming back again."

Daddy put his hands together right in front of his mouth like he was about to start praying. He let out a long stream of air from his nose and then looked me straight in the eye.

"Pearl, your mama is my wife," he said, his words quiet and even. "And I'll have you remember that, darlin'."

If I could've melted right there into the floorboards, never to be seen again, I would've. Nothingness seemed a better end than being put in my place by Daddy.

I tried thinking of something to say, but there wasn't a single word that came to mind.

"And she's your mother," he went on. "You will respect her, hear?"

"Yes, Daddy," I whispered.

"Like I said, I don't like it any more than you do," he said. "It's hard on me, too."

"Then why are you letting her stay?"

"Because it's right."

I thought of Daddy finding me, a little hours-old baby on the steps of the church in Red River. How he had loved me just as soon as he'd picked me up. How, even then, he'd known I'd be his, blood or no blood. He and Mama, they'd given me a home and a family and a name because it was the right thing to do.

I just wished in that one case, where it concerned Mama, Daddy wouldn't be so sure to do what was right.

"What if Mama leaves again?" I asked.

"We'll have to make do." His eyes softened. "It's scary, isn't it? Not knowing what's going to happen."

I nodded and felt how my face pulled down into a cry. Daddy came around the desk and put his arms around me. He'd taken lunch at Shirley's, I could tell by how he smelled of too-strong coffee and greasy food. It seemed a strange thing, smelling that on him when I was in the middle of boo-hooing.

"I don't love her anymore," I sobbed. "I don't."

Daddy shushed me and reached his hand up to cradle the back of my head.

"Do you still love her?" I asked, between stabs of crying.

"Yes, darlin'," he said. "Couldn't stop even if I tried."

For some reason I didn't know, hearing him say something like that made my heart break even more.

Opal Moon lived in an apartment above what had been the Bliss newspaper. Nobody used those offices anymore, not since Abe Campbell had closed up the press and run off with Mama. It was just as well, that paper going unprinted all that time. He'd been the kind to put out a list of all the folks taking assistance from the government and shame anybody who'd lost their home to the bank just because he could.

If I lived to be a hundred years old I'd never understand what Mama ever wanted to do with that nasty man, even if he did look at her like she was a movie star and said things that made her laugh.

In my mind he was every bit as much a monster and villain as Captain Hook or the Pied Piper.

I made no bones about kicking at the locked door of that old newspaper office. It felt good to me even if nobody else saw me do it and I ended up with a sore toe for my efforts.

I knocked at Opal's door and waited for her to ask who it was.

"It's Pearl," I said.

Opal answered the door and I saw that her eyes were red and the skin below them seemed swollen. I wondered if she'd spent the whole day crying.

Still, she did her best to let her face raise up into a smile. "You came," she said as if she was surprised.

"Course I did." I stepped in when she moved to the side. "You all right?"

"I will be."

By the way she stood with her shoulders held back and her chin up, I had no doubt she'd be better than okay in time.

"Mama had no right —"

"She did," Opal interrupted. "She had every right, Pearl. It's her house."

"But she left."

"And came back."

On the table Opal had a burner coil that plugged into the wall. A pot of water sat on it and she switched it on.

"I don't have any cocoa or coffee," she said. "Don't even think I have tea. But I can give you a cup of hot water, if you'd like."

"Yes, please," I said.

"I'm sorry I don't have more."

"Don't be sorry."

"You can go ahead and sit on the bed." She nodded toward the corner where there was a mattress right on the floor. "I don't have any chairs."

It was a small room. Aunt Carrie might have said it was quaint or dainty. Really, it was just one square room where Opal had done her best to make a home for herself.

She handed me a chipped cup with steam ribboning up off the surface of the water. I wrapped my fingers around it. I could have sworn her apartment was colder than it was outside.

"Thank you," I said.

"You're welcome."

"What're you going to do?" I asked. "Are

you going to get a job somewhere?"

"I'm trying to figure that out." She sat beside me on the bed.

She didn't pour a cup of hot water for herself and I wondered if it was because she only had just the one cup. I made sure to drink the water while it was still hot so she'd know how kind it was of her to give it to me.

"Who's that?" I asked, pointing to a gold-colored picture frame hanging on the wall.

Opal smiled and looked up at the photograph.

"Those are my parents," she said.

Reaching for the frame, she took it from the nail on the wall and held it on her lap. A Negro woman in a white dress and white shoes stood beside a white man wearing a black suit and tie. He had his hand on her back and her hand was on his chest right over where his heart would be. They both looked off at something, their mouths held open like they were laughing.

"This was on their wedding day," Opal told me. "They couldn't have a church wedding, of course."

"Why not?" I asked.

"Neither of their pastors approved." She shrugged. "His pastor said it was outside of God's will to marry someone from a different race. Her pastor said it would cause trouble, the two of them bringing mulatto children into the world."

She felt of the glass over the photo, tracing the lines of her mother's hair. It was full of tight curls, like Opal's. In fact, Opal looked so like her mother, if I hadn't known any better, I'd have thought it was her in the picture, just with darker skin.

"It's been hard for them," Opal said. "When the market crashed, the factory fired the colored workers first. They said my father was just as good as a Negro because of his wife and children. They told him to leave."

"That's not right," I whispered. "He isn't a Negro."

"No, he isn't. But wasn't it wrong of them to fire the colored men first? Even if they worked harder than the white workers?" Opal licked her lips. "A good worker's a good worker no matter what color his skin is."

I nodded, not knowing what to say.

"There wasn't anyone who would be willing to take their part. Nobody wanted to stand up for a bunch of Negroes. They were all too scared of losing their jobs, too." She shook her head. "Dad hated having to move us out of our house. It was a beautiful place."

"Did you have a yard?" I asked.

"We did. A big one. And we didn't want for anything then, not until he lost his job." She took in a long breath. "Then we had to move into an apartment. The good thing about it was that across the street was a jazz club. Never had to pay a penny to sit and listen to them play. We'd just open the window if it was warm enough outside. Sometimes, if we were lucky, some of the dancers would come outside where it wasn't so stuffy. We could watch them dancing right there on the sidewalk."

"Was that how you learned to dance?"

"I suppose it is."

She leaned forward, resting her elbow on her lap and holding her head in her hands. "My dad used to take my mother to listen to the music sometimes," she said. "Just the two of them, when he could scrape together a few dimes. They wouldn't get anything to drink, that would have been more than he could afford. But they'd dance."

"Are they good dancers?"

"Yes. Beautiful." Opal sighed. "I miss watching them."

I nodded but didn't say a word about how I'd always loved to see Mama and Daddy dance. I tried not to even think about it.

"My father said once it was the only place they could be, aside from home, where nobody said a thing to them about their different skin. They can't even step in church together and feel so at home."

I stayed at Opal's apartment just a minute or two more. Just long enough to be sure she wasn't fixing to pack her things and leave. She said she didn't have anywhere else to go and no money to get there if she did. Not just then, at least.

I didn't even mention that she could've gone home to her mother and dad. That Daddy would have been more than happy to drive her so she wouldn't have to pay for a bus ticket or hitchhike. She could have been back with her folks before the sun set on the day if she'd wanted.

Something in me knew she would just say it wasn't possible.

One thing I'd learned was that sometimes home was the hardest place to go back to.

Chapter Twenty-Five

Opal had told me I should get going, that Mama would be worried about me. I tried telling her I didn't think Mama cared much where I was just so long as I was home for supper. But Opal had just given me a look that said I needed to believe her.

I took my time getting home, though. If I'd gone the straight way it wouldn't have taken me five minutes from Opal's door to the front porch of the house on Magnolia Street. But I'd gone any way but straight that day, circling around the block and looking in the windows of the shops I passed more than once.

I'd even walked past the abandoned house some of the kids believed to be haunted. I didn't hold my breath and I didn't go by fast as I could. In fact, I thought of marching right up to the window and taking a good look inside to see if it was as spooky as everybody said it was. But I wasn't near as brave as I could've been and I just kept on walking, trying not to give it a second thought.

When I finally did make it home, I turned the handle on the front door as slow and quiet as I could, hoping to sneak in and get to my room before Mama could stop me.

I didn't know how to talk to her. I didn't have anything to say. It was like a stranger had come into our house, making herself at home in our kitchen or living room. If I could have my way, I'd only see her at meal times when Daddy and Ray were around, too. Maybe not even then.

I wondered if I could keep that up for the years I had left until I moved away. It seemed an awful way to live.

Soon as I opened the front door, though, I saw there was no use sneaking.

Aunt Carrie sat on the davenport, a cup of coffee on her knees, and Mama in the rocking chair looking paler than I thought I'd ever seen her.

"Hello, dear," Aunt Carrie said, her voice as regular and kind as if nothing was even a little bit out of the ordinary.

"Hi, ma'am," I said. "Mama."

Mama's eyes flicked up to my face like she'd just realized I'd walked into the room.

"Where have you been?" Mama asked,

sounding sore as all get out.

"I was just talking with a friend," I answered.

I wasn't sure if it was a lie or not, saying that. Opal was my friend. But I knew Mama'd have pitched a snit fit if she'd known I was in Opal's apartment without asking her first.

"That's fine. I'm glad you've made a friend," Mama said. "Go on up to your room while I visit with Mrs. Seegert."

"Can't I sit and visit?" I asked. "You wouldn't mind, would you, Aunt Carrie?"

"I said go on up," Mama said before Aunt Carrie could answer.

I looked at Aunt Carrie who nodded and gave me a smile that made me think she wasn't happy about it either.

"I'll call you down for supper later on," Mama said.

I knew better than to put her to the test again. I went up to my room, but I didn't shut my door. I hoped there would be at least a few things I might overhear of what she and Aunt Carrie talked about.

All I could hear for more than a couple minutes was the clinking of Aunt Carrie's coffee cup on its saucer and the creaking of the chair as Mama rocked it.

I stood in the doorway of my bedroom,

working the buttons of my coat through their holes, wishing I'd thought to take a roll or a slice of bread on my way up the stairs. Supper wouldn't be for hours and there was no convincing my stomach to wait that long.

"She's grown," Mama said after a while. "Pearl has."

Aunt Carrie mm-hmmed at her. "She's becoming quite the lady."

All Mama had ever wanted was for me to be a lady. Not to spit, to keep my knees together, to never cuss or lie or scream, to walk slowly in the house, and say all my best-manners words whenever I was speaking with a grown-up.

She'd railed at me more than a dozen times over how I'd never make a nice young lady. But Aunt Carrie believed I was already, and she'd been the one to teach me how to tuck my skirt up so nobody'd see up my dress when I climbed a tree. And in our bare feet, even.

Aunt Carrie saw what was best in me. I knew it was wrong, maybe even a sin, but I wished Mama'd just go away and let Aunt Carrie be the one to raise me until I was grown.

"She missed you," Aunt Carrie said.

"Can I get you a little more coffee before

you go?" Mama asked.

"No, thank you," Aunt Carrie answered. "I wouldn't sleep a wink if I had a sip more."

"Let me get your coat for you," Mama said.

"No need. I can find it myself, thank you." Aunt Carrie's voice was clipped and cool in a way I wasn't used to hearing it. "I appreciate the coffee, thank you."

With the creaking of the rocking chair followed by the clonking of shoes on the hard floor, I imagined Mama taking Aunt Carrie's cup. Aunt Carrie would slide her arms into her coat and button it up before reaching in the pockets for her dress gloves.

Mama'd just stand there watching, waiting, hoping she'd be gone soon. That was the way I pictured it, at least.

"You're invited for dinner after church on Sunday," Aunt Carrie said. "Tom and the kids usually come. I would like it if you'd join us too."

"Thank you."

"Well, thank you for the visit."

The front door rubbed against the frame, letting me know it'd been opened. I wanted to run down the stairs and beg Aunt Carrie to stay just a little longer. Or I'd ask if I could go home with her to the farm where it seemed nothing bad ever happened.

But I stayed right there in my bedroom for fear that Aunt Carrie would tell me no. And worried that Mama would be angry as a bee if I did something like that.

"This isn't easy for me, you know," Mama said. "Being here is harder than I'd expected it to be."

"I know, Mary," Aunt Carrie said. "Give it a little more time. It's hardly been a full day."

"How am I supposed to fix it?"

"I don't know that you can."

"Then what do I do?" Mama asked.

"Love them," Aunt Carrie answered. "It can't make it back to the way it was, but I know it can't hurt, either. Just love them."

The door stuck in the frame when Mama shut it.

Chapter Twenty-Six

Mama knocked on my bedroom door not long after Aunt Carrie left. She asked if she could come in and I got up off my bed to open the door for her.

She had one hand resting on the slight slope of her stomach, fingers rubbing at one certain spot.

I remembered how jealous I'd been of Ray after his mother'd had Baby Rosie. Seemed all the other mothers were having babies. All the other mothers but mine. I'd begged Mama to have another, promised to be a good big sister. I'd even said I'd scrub out the diapers for her.

It had to have been a hundred times I'd asked. But every time she'd said the same thing.

"I'm happy with you and Beanie," she'd say.

I would pretend to see shooting stars in the sky so I could make a wish for a little sister. I'd even have settled for a brother if I'd had to.

But that day, Mama standing in the doorway of my bedroom, hand on her stomach, I regretted all the times I'd begged, all the wishes I'd cast. I didn't want any baby that had no part of Daddy.

"Pearl," Mama started and then worked up a swallow. "Would you like to go to the store with me?"

"Yes, ma'am," I said, not thinking I had the choice to say no.

"I only need a few things."

"I can go for you."

"The fresh air might do me some good," she said. "I don't mind going. Just don't want to go alone."

"Are you scared to go by yourself?" I asked.

She licked her lips and nodded. "Yes. But I can't stay cooped up in here until summer."

"Is that when it's coming?" I asked, looking down at her stomach.

"I think so."

"Will you wear your coat?" I asked. "To the store?"

She nodded. "I'm not sure I'm ready for everybody to know yet."

Wrapping both arms around her middle it

looked like she was trying to protect the baby from anything in the world that might want to harm it.

It was wrong and I knew it, but I felt more than a little jealous of that baby just then.

Mama had picked quite a time to walk down the main street of Bliss for the first time since she'd been back.

The way gossip sparked and spread through that town, I was sure most folks knew she'd returned already. But hearing a thing was nothing compared to seeing it for yourself, and boy did the people on the street that day get themselves an eyeful.

Nobody stopped to tip a hat or give her a smile. Not one person told her "how do." They all just glared out of the corner of their eyes and whispered behind their hands to whoever might be standing close enough.

But Mama didn't turn back to the house and she didn't cry. She just kept on walking toward Wheeler's general store, her hand on my shoulder like she meant to guide me in the way I should go.

There was no line at the store, no other customers waiting to get their bag of flour or can of beans. Meemaw had often told me that most days were so full of God's mercies we passed them by without knowing. That empty store, though, I saw as God being kind to us and I made sure to tell Him thanks for it. And to ask that nobody else would come in just so long as we were there that day.

Mr. Wheeler turned toward us when the bell over the door tinkled its announcement that we'd come. His arms were full of tins of baking soda and he finished stacking them on a shelf before coming to the counter to attend to us.

His sharp eyebrow jerked upward, forming wrinkles in his skin that ran all the way up his forehead.

"May I help you?" he asked, his voice dry and flat.

"Yes, please," Mama started.

She spoke her list to him — salt and dry beans and some noodles. Before he turned to collect the items, he reached below the counter for his ledger.

"I assume you want this on credit," he said.

"Yes, sir," she answered. "If that's no trouble."

"Oh, no trouble at all. I'll just need to know, is this under Tom Spence's account or Abe Campbell's?" He touched the end of his pencil to his tongue and I caught a glimpse of the meanest smirk tugging up at his lip. "Because Abe Campbell's account is past due. Any idea of where I could find him?"

I thought of every dirty word I knew that I could've said to Mr. Wheeler. But I held those ugly words in my throat. Mama'd done at least one thing right and that was to teach me to hold my tongue when it came to grown folks. I would have gotten myself in a world of trouble if I'd let loose on that man the way I'd wanted to just then. Instead, I held my teeth together so tight I thought I was like to crack a molar.

"This is, of course, under Tom Spence's name," she said, holding her own voice tight so she'd at least sound calm. "And as for Mr. Campbell, I have no idea where he might be, so if you'd kindly collect my groceries I would be ever so grateful."

At her side, her hand trembled.

I took hold of it. She squeezed my hand.

Mama didn't say a word about what had happened at the store. She didn't cry and didn't slam the cupboards the way I might have. When Daddy'd asked how her day had been she'd said it was fine.

I imagined she was embarrassed about it and wished she could just forget that it had ever happened. I didn't blame her for that one bit.

She served up supper and washed the dishes and sat to listen to the radio with the mending basket in her lap.

If I hadn't known better, I might have thought life was back to normal. That she'd never gone in the first place. Except that when she went to bed she didn't ask Daddy to come with her, and he didn't give her a second look when she left the room.

I laid in my bed later that night, the house so quiet I couldn't sleep.

CHAPTER TWENTY-SEVEN

I stopped just at the edge of the woods before stepping in. It seemed that beyond those two pines where the trail began was a world far away from Bliss and Mama and the sharp eyebrows and nasty smirk of Mr. Wheeler.

If ever I was tempted to play make-believe still, it was when I was there under the cover of the trees' branches where only God had His eyes on me.

"Not a sparrow falls without God seeing it," I whispered when I took a first step into the woods.

I didn't know if that was Scripture, but I remembered the way the hymn always made me smile when we sang it in church. Just then, with the quiet of the woods around me, it seemed a comfort, God watching me, knowing every time I'd ever stubbed my toes and skinned my knees. What I wondered was why He didn't stop me from getting hurt in the first place.

Meemaw might have said that was something I wouldn't know until I got to meet Jesus face-to-face.

Along the path through the forest were muddy spots where the snow had melted and the earth was still working on drinking up all the water. I jumped over the puddles that were small enough and stepped around the ones that were too wide for me.

I reached the twisted tree that stood tall right in the middle of the woods and felt of its bark that wound up to the tip-top branch. If I'd been a bird I'd have lit way up high at the top of that tree. I'd look out over all of Bliss and beyond. The folks below would look so small, like ants, and I'd watch as they went about their day.

I wondered if that was the way God saw us, like so many critters scampering around. Seemed to me He looked down from His heaven into every moment of our struggling and striving and just shook His head at the many ways we were getting it wrong.

I shut my eyes, my fingers still feeling of that winding bark, and thought of what Meemaw might've said to that. I pictured her face in my mind — the way her eyes were a faded color of blue and how every inch of her skin was full up of wrinkles. I imagined her smile and the spots in her mouth where her teeth were missing. And I saw the way she'd always worn her long hair in a braid or a tight knot at the back of her head.

"Darlin'," she would say to me. "God ain't far off. Don't matter how you feel 'bout it. He ain't far at all."

She'd put her crooked-fingered, blue-veined hand over mine.

"He don't watch us from heaven. No, miss." She'd smile and maybe rock back and forth on her heels the way she'd always done when she was in the Spirit. "He's here. Right here."

She would touch my chest with her fingertips, just over where my heart beat, and tap it three times.

"Always there with you, darlin'," she'd say. "It's where He sets up home. No matter where you're at, you got home with God right there."

I opened my eyes, missing Meemaw so hard I could've cried.

Uncle Gus was out among the apple trees with his shirt sleeves rolled up to his elbows. He stood under the branches of one of the trees, looking close at it and feeling of it with his fingers. In his other hand he had a big pair of clippers.

When he saw me coming he stepped away from the tree and tipped his hat back on his head.

"Now, I was hopin' you'd come by today," he said. "How're ya doin', Pearlie Lou?"

"I'm all right," I told him. "Whatcha doing?"

"Prunin' the apple trees." He lifted his hand and grabbed hold of the branch above him. "I put it off longer than I ought've. Should be okay, though."

He squinted as he looked up into the tree.

"Soon enough they'll start flowerin'," he said. "Smells so good when they do. Some days I just like sittin' here, breathin' in how fresh spring can smell."

"I can't wait to eat an apple," I said.

"Not till fall, sweet girl," he said. "But that'll be here quick too. Might not seem so to you, bein' young as you are, but time goes by faster than I can keep track of."

I thought of how before I knew it we'd have a brand-new baby in our house, one Mama could truly call her own. If I could have made a wish, it would be that time slow down a little bit.

"How's that pigeon doin'?" he asked. "Still flyin' back home?"

"Only when Bert leaves the door open," I

told him.

Uncle Gus smiled and laughed out his nose. "Tell you what. Have Ray carve a couple eggs" — he used his fingers to show the size — "yea big by yea big. Then have Bert put them in the girl's nest. That'll keep her to home."

I tilted my head so he'd understand I didn't know what in the world he was talking about. "Won't she know they aren't real?"

He reached into the pocket of his work pants, pulled out a hanky, and wiped at his nose with it.

"Well, seems I heard once if a homing pigeon like her got sent out thinkin' she's got an egg to sit on, she'd make it double-time back to her coop." He nodded. "Bet if Bert's girl had an egg or two, she'd think twice about goin' off."

"Why?" I asked.

"It's part of a mother's nature. She'll hurry on home as long as she knows she's got a young one to tend to."

I walked away from Uncle Gus, leaving him to his trees. And I thought of Sassy and how she'd come back, even if that egg wasn't really hers. She'd come on back.

Somehow, she'd remember the way home.

Chapter Twenty-Eight

Aunt Carrie was in the kitchen where I'd hoped to find her. Standing at the counter, she rolled out dough for a crust. She didn't mind me standing close at her elbow to see the way she wrapped it up on the rolling pin and put it real gentle-like into the tin.

"It took me years to learn how to do that," she told me. "My poor mother would get so frustrated with me. I tore so many crusts."

She smiled at the memory.

"Good thing mother was long-suffering and crusts can be fixed easily," she said. "Hand me that jar if you would, please."

I did, the apple slices in cinnamon syrup looking so good they about made my mouth water.

"This will be for tomorrow," Aunt Carrie said. "Do you think your mama will come for dinner after church?"

"She might." I watched her pour the fruit into the crust and breathed in the sweet and spicy smell of them. "We went to the store yesterday."

"Did you?" she asked, using a spoon to push the apples around so they'd be evenly spread in the pie.

"Yes, ma'am."

I told her about all the folks looking at us and what Mr. Wheeler had said about Abe Campbell. About how Mama had acted like nothing'd happened at all.

"She didn't even tell Daddy," I said.

"She must have been mortified," Aunt Carrie said.

"She had on her coat the whole time," I told her. "So nobody'd see."

I touched my own stomach, not knowing the right way of saying the state Mama found herself in.

Aunt Carrie nodded. "I think I understand."

She was quiet as she put the top crust on. She pinched all along the edge so it looked like one long, round wave. Then she took a sharp knife and cut slits in the middle of it before putting it into the oven to bake.

"I think your mama is very brave," Aunt Carrie said, collecting the crust scraps from the counter and rolling them into a ball. "And I think Mr. Wheeler behaved like a churl. He had no right to say such a thing to her. Especially not in front of you."

"What's a churl?" I asked.

"A poorly mannered person in possession of a mean spirit," she answered. "In short, a bully."

I thought of Hazel and wondered if she'd gotten her mean spirit from him. It would not have surprised me in the least.

"Why're they all so mean?" I asked.

"Who's that?" Aunt Carrie asked, turning toward me.

"The Wheelers."

"Well," she started. "I don't know that they're exactly mean, dear. They do mean things, yes. They behave badly, indeed. But there's always a reason for people to do the things they do."

"They don't have to be mean," I said.

"You're right. How we choose to treat people says much about us, don't you think?" Aunt Carrie asked, patting a fine dusting of flour onto the small lump of leftover dough. "Especially when it comes to people who have hurt us."

"Like Mama?" The words were out of my mouth before I could catch them. I hoped so hard that Aunt Carrie wouldn't think me a dishonoring daughter for saying a thing like that.

But she didn't so much as flinch. Instead,

she used her apron to wipe the loose flour from her hands. Then she put them on my cheeks, her palms warm and smelling of dough.

"My Pearl," she said.

I was surprised by the way her eyes got watery and her voice trembled ever so slightly.

"Forgiveness is the hardest gift to give," she said, reaching up to push away a tear from her own cheek with her knuckle. "It can cost us so much. But I've always believed that it's worth the struggle."

"Why are you crying?" I asked.

"Because it's difficult to see you hurting." She gave me half a smile. "But it will get better, dear. I believe this family will make it. I have faith that your heart will heal."

I nodded, knowing that God'd heard Aunt Carrie's words. Not from far away somewhere in the sky. But that He'd been a witness to Aunt Carrie's gentle hands and soft words. I did believe if I could've seen God just then I'd have watched Him nodding His head at what she'd told me.

"Now, how about I teach you how to make cinnamon snails?"

I told her I'd like that.

She let me roll out the leftover dough and sprinkle cinnamon and a little sugar all over it. Then we folded it into a log, cut off inches of it, and put them on a cookie sheet to bake.

They sat in the oven along with the pie, the whole house filling with the smells of butter and cinnamon and the sweetness of apple. When they came out, that scrap dough looked like perfectly coiled snails, a shade of golden Aunt Carrie declared to be just right. I hoped she might let me taste one of them. Maybe two even.

She did. And with a big glass of milk.

Aunt Carrie wasn't one to let somebody down.

Chapter Twenty-Nine

The stained-glass windows were dull on account the sun was hiding behind thick, gray clouds. A gloomy day like that one didn't bother me just so long as it brought showers with it. There was something about the sound of rain on the roof and windows that brought comfort.

But the rain had yet to come, so the day just made me feel slow and tired.

Mama had come to church that morning. She'd even taken her coat off, which surprised me. Her stomach didn't show so much, not under the dress she'd picked to wear. Still, if anybody'd taken the time to look real close, they'd have been able to figure it out.

I was between Mama and Aunt Carrie in the pew feeling for all the world that it was the very last place I wanted to be. If staring eyes had a weight to them, we'd have been pinned to the sanctuary floor for how nearly every pair in that church was looking over at our pew. Peeking up at Mama I saw that her eyes were closed and I thought that was awful smart of her.

Much as I wanted her to feel bad about what she had done, I didn't want the whole town of Bliss holding judgment over her head.

"Go ahead and throw one stone. Any of y'all without sin, go on ahead," I dared them. But only in my head, of course.

In my mind I was far braver than I ever could have been in real life.

I worked at listening to the voices around me singing about the soft and tender calling of Jesus.

The preacher stood behind the pulpit all during the hymn-singing time. He sang as he opened his Bible and arranged his pieces of paper that he'd written his sermon on.

Back home in Red River, Pastor never put his Bible down for anything while he hollered at us. And his sermons had never seen a sheet of paper. They just came streaming out of his own mind and mouth. Whatever he thought to say, he did. Meemaw'd say he'd got the Spirit and would go on until the Lord told him it was time to stop.

More than once I'd prayed for God's great mercy to make Pastor hush up, especially on hot days when even a paper fan didn't stir up cool air.

I liked that Bliss preacher's ways, even if he did wear robes and even if he did preach with a soft voice. He smiled out at us and told us that God wanted us for His very own.

After the hymn ended and we sang the long, dragged out a-a-men, the preacher put his hands up, palms facing us, and lowered them so we'd know we could sit down. The wood pews crackled as every backside settled in.

Aunt Carrie put her arm around me, pulling me to her side like she did most Sundays just as the sermon began. I didn't mind being held that way at all. But the way Mama cleared her throat made me think she wasn't all too pleased by it.

I couldn't seem to figure out a way of making both her and Aunt Carrie happy though, so I just didn't move. Not an inch.

If anybody'd asked me the truth, I would've said how it would've been nice for Mama to reach out for me, too.

It wasn't unusual for all the folks to stand about after church and catch up before heading home to their suppers. Back in Red River, Mama'd enjoyed that time. She'd go from one circle to another, listening in on the gossip or adding a juicy tidbit of her own. If one of the women at the church was having a particular struggle, she knew to go to Mama. Mama was the one to help make things all right just with her listening ears and sympathetic nodding.

That day, though, I could tell she'd have rather jumped off the tip-top of the tallest building in Bliss than face the ladies waiting at the back of the sanctuary, eyes on her and hands shielding whispering lips.

"Feels like I got a red letter A on my chest," she murmured in a way that I thought was just to herself.

"Don't you let them bother you, Mary," Aunt Carrie told her. "Keep your head up."

"They all know, don't they?" Mama's eyes were wide and her chin trembling. "They know what I've done."

"Never you mind what they do or do not know." Aunt Carrie slipped her hand through the crook of Mama's elbow. "It is none of their business."

"But —"

"But nothing," Aunt Carrie said. "I've known most of these women all my life. Believe me, we all need the same measure of grace, Mary. We all do. Now, would you please be willing to come to my house and help me get dinner on the table?"

Mama nodded as Aunt Carrie pulled her past the gawking ladies to where our coats were hung up.

Before any of us knew it, we were all packed up between Uncle Gus's car and Daddy's truck on our way to the farm.

Uncle Gus prayed the blessing over the roast and Aunt Carrie made sure we all filled our plates with potatoes and carrots and rolls. Mama took so little, I wanted to let her know we had plenty. She didn't have to take less than anybody else like she'd done sometimes in Red River. In Bliss we had more food than we could ever eat.

But the way she pushed the cooked carrots around the plate made me think maybe that wasn't why she took so little. Sadness sometimes had that way with folks. She kept her eyes down even through all the talking around her. I wondered if she heard a word of any of it.

"Gus says there's to be another dance this weekend," Aunt Carrie said. "Seems like they're becoming a regular occurrence."

"Don't I know it." Daddy shook his head and put his fork down on the edge of his plate. "All I ever hear about these days is those dances."

"And all on account of the good ole boys at the Legion," Uncle Gus said, raising his glass of milk like he was making a toast.

"Can we go?" I asked, knowing full well that I was speaking without being spoken to. But Mama didn't even flinch.

"I think so, darlin'," Daddy answered, putting a potato chunk into his mouth.

"It's gonna be a spring dance," Uncle Gus said. "Even found a band that'll come play it. Ain't chargin' us as much as they might, either. Real good fellas out of Adrian."

"Do they play jazz?" I asked.

"Might just," he answered.

I hoped they did.

"Got stopped by Gladys Ritzema in town the other day," Daddy said between bites. "She just about jumped out in front of my truck when I was making my rounds."

"You hit her?" Uncle Gus asked, perking up. "Sure would be a shame for this town to lose such a fine and sweet woman."

"Gustav," Aunt Carrie said, shaking her head.

"Nah, I didn't hit her," Daddy said. "Sure am glad my brakes aren't bad, though. She took me by surprise."

"What'd she want?" Uncle Gus asked. "She got somebody for you to arrest for spittin' on the sidewalk?"

"Gus, be mindful," Aunt Carrie said, raising an eyebrow at him. "Little pitchers have big ears."

"We won't tell nobody," Ray said, stabbing a carrot slice with his fork. "Will we, Pearl?"

I shook my head on account my mouth was full of food and I didn't want Mama getting after me for neglecting my manners.

"She wanted to talk my ear off about the dance this weekend," Daddy said. "Says it's bound to attract the wrong kind."

"She's still hung up on that, huh?" Uncle Gus pulled his head back and narrowed his eyes. "Guess she ain't fixin' to let it go, is she?"

"I can't imagine she is." Daddy glanced at me.

"Don't know why she's gettin' a bee in her bonnet about it," Uncle Gus said. "Ain't been no trouble, has there?"

"Nope. Not one fight, not one kid getting drunk. Nothing like that," Daddy said. "It's that they're mixing she's still up in arms about. She said now that there's more Negroes coming to the dances she wants separate dances for white and colored."

At that Mama turned her head to look at Daddy for just a moment before looking back down again.

"Now, that's just bologna," Uncle Gus said. "If she don't like them so much, why's she always gotta come?"

"Well, Gus, I don't know the answer to that." Daddy shook his head. "Tell you what, next time she comes to me in a snit, I'll send her your way so you can ask her yourself."

"Go on and do that, Tom." Uncle Gus sawed at his roast beef with his knife. "You just have her come out here. I'll give her a piece of my mind."

"You'll do no such thing," Aunt Carrie said. "You're too kind."

"Well, I know it," Uncle Gus said. "Lord, but does that woman make me riled. It's nineteen thirty-five —"

"Nineteen thirty-six, dear," Aunt Carrie corrected him.

"Even so," Uncle Gus went on, "all's they're doin' is dancin'. They ain't doin' nothin' wrong."

"What does she expect you to do about it, Tom?" Aunt Carrie asked, putting another slice of bread on Ray's plate.

"I suppose she wants me to talk to Jake Winston," Daddy said. "Guess he told her he won't have her in his office anymore."

"That's why I vote for him every election," Uncle Gus said.

"No one ever runs against him," Aunt Carrie told him.

"Don't matter. I'd still vote for him."

"Winston told me he isn't inclined to do anything about it just so long as the Legion keeps holding them and there's no fighting or such," Daddy said.

"Good for him. Let them kids have a little fun, that's what I say." Uncle Gus said. "Pearlie, could you pass the butter, please?"

"Maybe I'll try talking to her," Aunt Carrie said. "I might be able to talk some reason into her."

"Better you than me," Daddy said.

"Wouldn't it just save them trouble?" Mama asked. "Having separate dances?"

"Well . . ." Daddy started, but didn't finish his thought.

Mama put her hands in her lap. "Just seems if most folks don't like the mixing, maybe they shouldn't do it."

Ray went on eating but nobody else moved an inch. I could've sworn I heard the crackling of the roof settling for how quiet it was the rest of dinner.

After helping Aunt Carrie and Mama with the dishes, I put on my sweater and went out to visit the hens. I had a bucket of scratch for them, and once I stepped into the coop they came to me, a'clucking and a'pecking at the pail.

It'd started raining but that didn't seem to bother the hens all that much. As for me, I knew Mama'd only abide me being out in the weather for a minute or two before she'd come out, fretting over how I'd catch my death from being soaked like I was.

I ducked into the coop and scattered the leftover bits of food for the girls on the floor, leaning down to pat one or two on the back and talking softly to them the way they liked.

Something peaceful there was about being squatted down with those hens pecking at the floor for a scrap of crust or a tossed-aside bean. Maybe it was just knowing they didn't think anything of me except that I had food and that made me their friend.

"I best get," I said singsong to the chickens. "I'll come and see you later in the week. Promise."

They didn't seem to care about me stepping out, which was fine by me. I took my empty bucket and headed back to the house.

Across the yard I saw Daddy, Uncle Gus, and Ray bothering an old tractor just inside the wide-open door of the barn. Ray bent at the waist and reached up under the machine, fiddling with something or another. He shook his head and said something to

Uncle Gus. They both stood tall, hands on hips, and stared at that tractor like that might jog their brains as to what was wrong with it.

Ray turned and saw me watching them. He gave me a big old goofy grin, one that spread all the way across his face. I tried thinking back to a time when he'd been that kind of happy back in Red River. Sure, he'd smiled then, but never so big it made his whole face scrunch up.

It did my heart good, seeing a thing like that. It was all the sunshine I needed on the gray and rainy day.

I stepped in through the kitchen door, slipped out of my shoes, and shivered. Then I walked, drip-dropping along over the linoleum toward the door that led to the living room. Behind it, I heard Mama and Aunt Carrie talking.

"It will take time," Aunt Carrie said. "And patience. For all of you, Mary."

"They don't need me," Mama told her. "They've been fine without me. I know it. Don't tell me they weren't."

"Opal did a fine job keeping the house and watching after the kids. I'll give you that." Aunt Carrie used her warm and gentle voice. "But that's not all there is to a family."

"I can't do much else for them. All I can do is cook and clean. That's it," Mama said. "As far as I can tell they were better off without me getting in the way."

"That isn't true."

I tried seeing them through the tiny gap between the kitchen door and the frame, but all I saw was the arm of a chair and a corner of a table.

"I don't know that they'd notice if I went away again," Mama said.

"You know they would," Aunt Carrie told her.

"Half the time I can't figure out what to say to them. It's like we're all strangers living under the same roof. No . . ." she paused. "I'm the stranger. They all know and like each other and I'm the odd one out that nobody cares for."

"Give it time."

"I'm just a burden."

"That's not so, Mary."

"But Tom —"

"How about Pearl? And Ray?" Aunt Carrie's voice was sharper. "You'd break their hearts all over again."

"But —"

"No, Mary. Stop," Aunt Carrie interrupted her. "She's been through enough. Can't you see that?"

"Of course I know," Mama said, her voice weak and shaking. "But I'm not the only one that hurt her."

"She needs you."

"I wish I could believe that."

I stepped back from the door and made my way to the table. The chair Aunt Carrie always had for me to sit in was still in the dining room from the after-church meal, I guessed. There was just a space where it should have been. I stood there, my hands on the table.

A calendar was tacked to the wall. Every night before bed Aunt Carrie would mark an X through the day that'd passed. She'd told me it was how she kept track of the date.

That day was the fifteenth day of March and I wondered just how many days would be slashed through before Mama left us again.

I wished she'd just save us all the bother and be gone before we woke up the next morning.

It was an ugly thing to hope for and I knew it.

But the sooner she went away, the sooner I'd stop missing her.

CHAPTER THIRTY

If ever I'd believed God might go back on his promise to never destroy the earth with flood waters again, it was that week. The rain came down all day and all night for more days in a row than I could remember.

Mama didn't want me to so much as step out into all the rain for fear it might get me sick. When I'd pointed out Bert was splashing in the puddles even though his father was the doctor, Mama'd told me not to talk back.

But there was no anger in her voice, no sharpness to her face. She almost looked like she'd plain given up.

We heard on the radio about a flood in Pennsylvania. There'd been more than one hundred people who'd died in it. I tried not to allow my imagination to take hold of that and picture the ways there were to die in a flood. My heart just could not take something so sad as that.

When I'd asked Daddy if he thought the flood might spread all the way to Michigan he'd shook his head and said he hoped not.

"What would we do if it did?" I asked after supper one night.

"Well, darlin', I guess we'd figure it out then," he answered. "I don't want you worrying about it."

"Bert said it don't flood much here," Ray said.

"Doesn't flood much," Mama corrected him.

"Yes, ma'am," Ray answered back. "He said the river might get high, but that's about it."

"I'll tell you what, the farmers aren't upset about this rain," Daddy said. "Not for now, at least. Gus said Pennsylvania's getting a hundred-year flood, is all. It's not normal."

Still, every time I looked out the window I checked to be sure we still had a yard and a porch and that the street hadn't turned into a river.

Seemed about time for something to go wrong.

That night I dreamed of water. It rushed and roared, splashed and rippled along the street right in front of our house. It rose all the way to the window in my bedroom, surrounding the whole house.

I tried calling out to Mama and Daddy, wanting to scream for them. Hoping they still had their heads up above the rushing water. But the only sound that came was choking and gagging, as if something was stuck in my throat.

Pulling and tugging, I tried to open the window, thinking if I could just get to the roof I'd be safe. I could holler out for help. But the window wouldn't budge and even my fists couldn't smash through the glass.

Out that window I saw Mama being dragged away by the rush of the water. She flailed her arms and her head bobbed up and down, under the water and then back up into the air. Going, going, going, she wouldn't have been able to get back home even if she'd tried.

Daddy went after her, beating at the water with his hands and kicking his feet up and down, up and down. He went faster than any man had ever swum before. Putting my hands on the glass I watched, not blinking, hoping he'd get to her in time.

One more swing of his arms, one more flipper-flap of his feet and he'd have gotten her. But just before he could grab hold, she jumped at him, using her hands and pushing him under the water.

I screamed and screamed, calling out for her to let him up. To let him go. Slapping at the glass I thought sure I'd break through. But even if I did I never could have helped him. Not in time.

Daddy didn't fight her. Didn't try to come back up. He just let her push him under where she held him until there wasn't anymore life in him.

The whole time she kept her eyes on me.

I woke, gasping and fighting the blanket off me. My throat stung like I'd screamed myself raw. Sitting up straight, I had to blink hard and whisper to myself, "It was just a dream. Only a dream. It's all over now."

But I knew it would be the kind of dream to stay with me all day long. Like a canker sore in my cheek that my tongue kept poking at, that dream would stay in my mind and I wouldn't be able to stop thinking on it.

It was still dark but I couldn't fall back to sleep.

I didn't know that I'd have wanted to anyhow.

Chapter Thirty-One

The rain hadn't let up, and come Monday the ground in the schoolyard was nothing but mud puddles and slick grass. So we got permission to practice our dance steps in one of the unused classrooms. Miss De Weese'd said it was fine just so long as we paid extra attention during our lessons.

The days leading up to the spring dance were visited by the best-behaved kids any teacher in Bliss had seen since the founding of the town. At least that was how I imagined it.

We'd pushed the dusty desks and chairs to the edges of the room and swept the floor. Somebody'd even wiped down the windows with an old piece of newsprint so the light would shine through and we could see what we were doing.

It wasn't so big as the schoolyard, our makeshift dance hall wasn't, but it was good enough just so long as everybody kept an eye out for their neighbor's swinging arms and kicking feet.

Bert came too most days that week, even though some of the other boys had made fun of him. He'd pretend not to hear them calling him a sissy or hollering something or another about him tripping on the hem of his dress.

I'd have smacked those boys in the mouth for saying such nasty things, but Ray said it wouldn't have helped Bert one bit.

"They'd just make fun of him harder," he told me.

I knew he was right.

The rest of that week, Ray came along with us in the mornings, saying Bert was the smartest boy in town, spending his time where all the girls were. He didn't dance, he just sat on top of the pushed aside desks with a discarded reader he found in the classroom.

By Thursday he was counting to eight to keep us in rhythm, waving his finger in the air all the while, like a conductor.

We danced right up until Miss De Weese rang the bell, calling for the beginning of the school day.

"Hey, Pearl," Bert said to me, tapping me on the shoulder before I stepped out of the room.

"Yeah?" When I turned to him I could about see him shaking from head to toe and his eyes were wider than I'd ever seen them before.

"Pearl," he said, his voice cracking a little. "You promise to save a dance for me tomorrow?"

If he'd asked me something like that just two years before I might've pushed him down and told him I'd rather suck an egg. A year before and I probably would have walked away from him without saying so much as a word.

But I'd learned a little something about being a friend. I'd learned that being kind didn't cost me a single cent. And I'd come to know that it took more strength to be gentle than it did to be hard.

"Sure," I said, giving him a closed lip smile.

As red as his face turned, I worried he might boil his brains.

"I promise I won't step on your toes," he said.

"That's fine."

He flashed me a silly smile before taking off to get to his desk.

I wouldn't have admitted it to anybody, but I felt a blush in my cheeks, too.

■ ■ ■ ■

Mama hadn't wanted me to go to the dance. All that week she'd come up with one argument after another, trying to convince Daddy I should stay home. And he had an answer for every single one.

"She's too young," she'd said.

"Whole town's invited," he'd said back to her. "I hear they're even letting babies in if they want to come."

"She'll wear herself out from all the excitement," she'd said.

"Nah," he answered back. "Doc Barnett thinks she's doing just fine. A little exercise never hurt anybody."

"I don't want her getting hurt."

"Nobody's gotten hurt at any of the dances," he said.

"Not yet, anyway."

"I'll keep my eye on her the whole time."

"It's not a crowd for a young girl to be around."

"There's not been one problem since we started those dances."

By Thursday afternoon she'd given up and resigned herself to the fact that I was going whether she liked it or not. But she sighed whenever we said one word about it, and I knew she hoped I'd give in to her and stay home that Friday night.

But no amount of sighing or slumping of shoulders would make me miss out.

Mama'd had errands to run after I got back from school. She hadn't told me what kind or how long she'd be gone, but it little mattered. For the first time since she'd come home, I had the house to myself. Daddy was working and Ray was off wandering around with Bert.

It was just me in that big house and I knew just what I wanted to do.

Turning the dial on the radio, I moved it up and down until I found a good song, one with a good deal of what Opal would've called swing. I got myself to the middle of the living room and tapped my right toe, counting up to eight over and over until the rhythm set itself in the beating of my heart.

Opal had showed me how to do the Charleston not two weeks before, with all its forward-and-tap-and-back-and-tap mixed with step-and-tap-and-step-and-tap and arms going side-to-side-and-side-to-side.

"Now just add a spin here and there and a stomped foot and you'll have a whole new set of moves," she'd told me. "And you don't even need a partner holding you back. This one you can do all on your own."

I sure had liked the idea of that.

I imagined the music coming out of the radio to be made by a band that'd set up in the corner of the living room which had turned into a dance hall by some great act of magic. In my daydream I did not care one bit if I was all alone. There was just something about dancing that made me feel free. The trumpets and drums and my moving feet were all there was in the whole wide world.

The sides of my hair fell loose of the braids Mama'd crisscrossed on each side of my head earlier in the morning and my dress kicked up. But it just did not matter. Besides, there wasn't a soul in the house to see me dancing.

I didn't hear the door open even though it probably made its clunking and rubbing noise against the frame. And I didn't notice the bags she'd put on the floor by the closet door. It wasn't until I felt her take my hands in hers and smelled the rose of her powder that I realized Mama'd come home.

I stopped right then, breathing shallow and scared she'd get after me for dancing.

"Don't stop," Mama said. "I haven't done the Charleston in a coon's age."

"You know how?" I asked.

"Course I do." She nodded at me.

"You sure you should?" I looked down at her belly.

"It won't hurt a thing." She smiled. "Ready?"

We danced to the end of that song and into another, our swiveling feet moving us all the way up to our hips and our kicking almost knocking us both off balance but for each of us holding on for dear life to each other's hands.

"Oh," she said. "I'm feeling a little dizzy."

Mama stopped, still holding my hands, and smiled right into my face.

"You all right, Mama?" I asked.

"Yes. I'm good, Pearl." She looked down into my eyes. "Just need to catch my breath."

"You dance nice."

"I had a good partner," she said, winking at me. Then she touched her stomach. "Oh, he must've liked that. He's dancing around in there."

"It's a boy?" I asked.

"Well, I'm not sure. I'm just guessing." She put out her hand to take mine. "You want to feel it?"

"I'll be able to?"

"Yes." Her eyes lit up as she put the palm

of my hand, spread open, onto her stomach. "Now wait just a half minute."

I shut my eyes so I could put all my mind toward feeling whatever it was Mama wanted me to. Against my hand was the soft cotton of her dress and the warmth of her body under it. Her breath cooled the back of my knuckles and then I felt her hand moving mine to another spot.

Then a bump, so light I might have missed it. And another. And another. It was nothing more than a moment, nothing more than a gentle touch. But I'd felt it.

I couldn't remember the last time I'd been so happy.

Opening my eyes, I looked right into Mama's. Hers were watery and her mouth was spread in a wide smile. The best one I'd seen on her in far too long.

"Did you feel it?" she asked.

I nodded. "Was that the baby?"

"It was, darlin'."

"Do you think it knows I'm here?" I asked.

"I don't know," she answered. "But wouldn't that be something?"

She moved my hand again so I could feel more and more. I would have stood there with that baby bumping up against my hand all day if I could have.

And I let my imagination open up. I

pictured myself sitting on the davenport, holding the baby wrapped in a yellow and green plaid blanket, singing softly to him until he fell asleep, his tiny fingers wrapped around one of mine. Then holding him once he was stronger, face-to-face with me so I could make him laugh. I imagined his dark eyes squinting up and his gummy smile wide and full of gasping baby laughs.

I'd be the one to get up with him in the night, sometimes at least. I'd soothe him with stories and soft words and gentle kisses.

When he was big enough, I'd kneel on the other side of the living room, hands out and ready to grab him after he tottered across the room. I'd show him how to use a spoon and drink out of a cup and how to say "Pearlie."

My heart felt fit to bust for how much I loved that baby that I'd not even seen yet, no matter if it was a boy or a girl with dark eyes or light. And I would always love it no matter if it was Abe's by blood.

I would love that baby all the days of my life.

"Isn't it wonderful?" Mama asked, her voice just a whisper.

I nodded, afraid that if I opened my mouth I'd start crying and never stop. Instead, I smiled up at her and she grinned back at me.

It was her. It truly was. She stood there, the Mama I'd known before. I kept my hand on her stomach even though I couldn't feel anything anymore. It didn't matter. I had her and I wasn't like to let her go.

I was sure she was back to stay.

CHAPTER THIRTY-TWO

I gave the first dance of the night to Bert, to make good on my promise. We took it slow so he could get all his footwork in without tangling up and tripping on his legs. He didn't look at my face the whole time but kept his eyes on my shoulder. That was fine by me. I thought if he'd let his eyes meet mine he might've realized what he was doing and lost the rhythm.

As it was he counted to eight over and over under his breath. I didn't mind one bit. I did like Bert Barnett. Maybe not in the Valentine card and nervous dancing sort of way. But he was an all right kind of boy and the type of friend I was glad to have.

The band that'd come to play was set up on a stage to the far end of the dance hall. They were good enough to keep a pounding beat and steady tune and that was all we needed. I wished they'd had a singer, somebody to croon out the slower songs or holler out the faster ones. But it was all right.

The girls from school had gathered in a corner of the floor, following the steps I'd taught them, pairing up among themselves. I felt the kind of pride I guessed Miss De Weese might've felt when we learned how to work out an arithmetic problem or used our best penmanship.

And when Hazel caught me watching her dancing with Ethel, she didn't give me a stink face or roll her eyes. Instead, she gave me a smile. The kind friends might share with each other. I gave her one back.

It didn't cost me anything at all.

Opal had danced with Lenny all night long, and the way they looked at each other I'd have thought they believed there was nobody else in all the world. Their feet moved quick and their arms flew all over the place, but their eyes never broke from each other.

I decided the next time she told me he wasn't her boyfriend I'd let her know I thought that was a pile of bologna.

I found Daddy sitting all by himself off to one side of the dance floor. He had a cigarette between his fingers and a glass of punch resting on his knee. He smiled when I walked over to him and took the empty seat to his left.

"You having fun, darlin'?" he asked.

I told him I was.

"That's fine."

"How about you, Daddy?" I asked.

He shrugged and took a long pull on his cigarette, letting the smoke settle into the deepest part of his lungs before blowing it back out.

"I used to dance with your mama all the time," he said. Then he nodded at Opal and Lenny. "Not like that. I never was that good."

"You're a good dancer, Daddy," I told him.

"Thanks kindly, Pearlie." He winked at me. "We never danced like that when I was younger, though. All you kids take off faster'n a shot. In my time we were slower. Smoother."

"You think you'll dance with Mama tonight?" I asked.

He looked over to the other side of the room where Mama stood talking to Mrs. Barnett, her hand resting on the curve of her stomach. I wondered if the baby was moving around and I hoped he could hear the music.

"Nah," Daddy said. "It wouldn't be good for the baby, I guess."

"She danced with me yesterday," I told him.

"That so?"

"We did the Charleston in the living room."

"How about that?" He looked over toward Mama again, his eyebrows pushed low the way they did when something worried him.

"You think it hurt the baby?" I asked. "Us dancing?"

"Don't you worry about that, darlin'. I'm sure it's just fine."

The band started up another song, the last one before they took a break. It was a slow one and Lenny folded Opal into his arms, holding her almost too close. She rested her head on his chest and they swayed back and forth, round and round.

"Can I have this dance?" Daddy asked, standing and offering his hand to me.

I knew that giggling was for little girls, but I just couldn't help it.

As Daddy led our smooth kind of dancing I remembered when he'd have me step up on the toes of his boots. We'd shuffle around the floor of the living room in the house in Red River, the grit of the last duster grinding under the soles of his boots.

But I was too big for that anymore and I wondered if that made Daddy sad in a way.

If it did, he didn't let me know.

He pulled up my hand over my head and I knew he wanted me to twirl. I did, and when I stopped I saw Lenny and Opal dancing behind Daddy. They were giving each other a kiss and I knew it wasn't meant for me to see. So I let Daddy twirl me one more time. That time I kept my eyes closed.

I knew that song had to end but I wished so hard it would just keep on going. I'd have danced with Daddy for the rest of that evening. Being so near him felt like being home.

CHAPTER THIRTY-THREE

Nothing all that exciting happened after the Spring dance. There were no troubles in town and the ladies found little to gossip about after church come Sunday mornings. Most of all, folks talked about the coming planting season or the way March was going out like a lamb, even if it was a bit chilly still.

When I wrote my letter to Millard, I didn't have anything out of the ordinary to tell him. So I put down what happened most every day in our one-day-to-the-next life. I figured he'd just be glad to hear from us, boring letter and all.

I wrote how Mama got us up in the mornings for breakfast before sending Daddy off to work and Ray and me off to school and how Bert met us along the way to tell us the incredible things his pigeon had done since the afternoon before.

"Mostly it's just that Sassy started sitting

on her wood eggs or that she let him hold her without pecking him too much," I wrote. "Bert's proud of that bird even if he still can't let her out."

What I didn't write was how every once in a while Bert had a hard candy to give me or a stick of gum. It would've embarrassed me no end for Millard to know a boy'd taken a liking to me the way Bert had. It was bad enough, Ray knowing. He didn't tease me too hard about it, and for that I was grateful.

The rest of our days didn't hardly seem worth writing about. At school we sat in our seats doing our work until lunch when we'd go back home to eat. Then back to school, let out a couple hours later, and walk back home.

Library or Opal's apartment or wandering round the woods. Supper. Baths. Reading or listening to a radio show. Bed.

Sleep and dreams and quiet.

The next morning Mama was there still. Always there. Not leaving.

I'd gotten to like my normal, ordinary, boring life quite well, thank you very much.

Mama'd let me go with her to Wheeler's store to pick out which flour sack I wanted my Easter dress made out of. He'd put a whole stack of those bags in the window, Mr. Wheeler had, a handful of different patterns printed on them. I stood on the outside of that glass, trying to figure out which one I liked most.

"Go on in," Mama said. "Find the one you like. I need to stop by the post office. I'll be right back."

"Can I go with you?" I asked, hoping maybe there'd be a letter from Millard waiting there for me.

"Not today, Pearl," she answered. "Now, do as I say."

"Yes, ma'am," I said.

"And don't go anywhere until I get back, hear?"

I told her I'd stay put and watched her walk away from the store. I walked into Wheeler's, holding my hands behind my back so I wouldn't be tempted to touch anything.

"Can I help you?" Mr. Wheeler asked from behind his counter where he held a pencil over his ledger.

"Just come to look at the sacks, sir," I answered.

"Go ahead." He scribble-scratched his pencil across the page.

They sure were pretty, those flour sacks. Whoever made them never did have to print flowers in all different colors on them or patterns for a little doll to be cut out and stuffed with cotton. They did it to be kind. It sure seemed God would have a special blessing for whoever it was that had the idea to do such a thing for folks.

It didn't take me long to figure out the one I liked best. It was the color of the lavender flowers that grew by Aunt Carrie's back door in the summer. Dotted all over it were tiny white daisies. I put my finger on it so anybody coming in before Mama got back would know that was the one I'd be taking home.

I looked up when the bell over the door jingled just in time to see Delores walk in. Behind her was Mr. Fitzpatrick. He was a tall man. So tall he had to stoop to keep from knocking his head on the door when he came in. It was a wonder he could stand up straight at all for the way he must have had to walk, back bent, through that chicken coop of a house they lived in.

Delores looked at me out of the corner of her eye and gave me a smile.

"Hi," she whispered, so quiet I almost didn't hear her.

"Hey," I answered back. "You come to get a new flour sack?"

Soon as I said it I wished I hadn't. Delores

wasn't the kind of girl to get a new dress for Easter and I knew it. She slouched soon as I'd asked and shook her head.

"That's all right," I said. "It isn't something to feel bad about."

She eyed all the bright-colored flour sacks and I wondered which one she liked the most. If I could figure it out I thought maybe I could ask Mama if she'd make a dress for Delores, too. Mama before, back in Red River, wouldn't have had to think twice about such a thing as sewing together a dress for a little girl who didn't have one. Seemed to me that kindness wasn't all the way gone from her heart.

Just as I was about to ask Delores which color was her favorite, she turned at the sound of her father's voice.

"I ain't come for charity," Mr. Fitzpatrick said, his voice softer and quieter than I would've imagined it. He reached into his back pants pocket and pulled out his billfold. "I got cash money. I worked a job down in Toledo."

Mr. Wheeler made no small effort at holding his finger in the page he'd been writing on and putting down his pencil. He looked right at Mr. Fitzpatrick's face and pushed his lips together so hard I was sure they'd get stuck like that for all of eternity.

"You've got some nerve," Mr. Wheeler said, his one eyebrow pointier than I'd ever seen it.

"We just gotta have a few things to get us by." Mr. Fitzpatrick turned his head, looking at me and then lowering his voice. "I got money to pay."

Mr. Wheeler turned his back on Mr. Fitzpatrick and straightened a line of canned goods on the shelf behind him. "Nothing has changed. You are not welcome here."

Delores turned her eyes to the floor in a way that told me how embarrassed she was.

"Then I'll pay up. How much do I owe?" Mr. Fitzpatrick asked. "I know my wife's got credit here."

Mr. Wheeler looked at the man from across the counter with more bitterness than I'd ever seen him look at anybody. And he had plenty of nasty looks to give folks. The way he looked at Mr. Fitzpatrick made me think he'd like to reach over the counter and squeeze the life right out of him.

But instead of strangling him, Mr. Wheeler snapped the pages of the ledger and pointed his finger at a line.

"You're paid in full," he said. "Someone took pity on you."

"Was it the preacher?" Mr. Fitzpatrick asked. "I told him to stop taking up a collection —"

"No," Mr. Wheeler interrupted him.

"Who was it, then?"

"I was asked not to tell you that," Mr. Wheeler said.

"Well, you can just give the money back." Mr. Fitzpatrick pointed at the ledger. "I won't take it."

"I'm afraid I can't do that."

"I don't take charity."

I knew that wasn't true. The Fitzpatrick family was on the list of folks that took relief from the government. They'd accepted plenty of food from Aunt Carrie, and Uncle Gus always made sure to take milk to them every now and again.

But I didn't pipe up and say so on account I didn't want to embarrass Delores like that. I just stood there with my hand on the lavender colored flour sack I'd picked to be my Easter dress, waiting for Mama to come back and hoping with all I was worth that she'd hurry it up.

Mr. Wheeler rested his fists on the counter and leaned forward. He lowered his voice, but I could still hear him just fine.

"I tried telling her it was a bad idea, paying it off," he said. "I told her that it would only serve to allow you to stay in your lazy ways. But she insisted. My wife is a stubborn woman."

Mr. Fitzpatrick stood there, hands on his hips and the muscles in his jaw tensing. His large Adam's apple bobbed up and down.

"I don't know why she paid it up for you." Mr. Wheeler's words were sharp-edged and pulled tight. "You don't deserve it. I suppose it's because of your children. But you, you don't deserve to walk the same earth as her after what you did."

The two men didn't look away from each other, they hardly moved even for a good half a minute. Mr. Wheeler with his sharp edges and Mr. Fitzpatrick with his tensed jaw.

"It was a long time ago," Mr. Fitzpatrick whispered. "A real long time ago."

Delores took his hand like she wanted to run out of the store with him. I couldn't have said I blamed her.

"You're the same man," Mr. Wheeler said. "People don't change. Not after doing a thing like that."

"I didn't do anything."

"So you say." Mr. Wheeler turned his back and crossed his arms.

"Papa," Delores said, pulling on her father's hand. "Let's go home."

He looked down at her, his jaw clenched. I saw there was a wide scar that went all the way down his face and I wondered how it'd happened. Whatever had caused it, I would've bet it hurt like the dickens for a real long time.

When he turned to walk out of the store, I noticed he had a bit of a limp. Not so much that he had to jerk his whole body along like some folks I'd seen. It was just a small one, like his knee got caught and didn't bend just right.

Delores gave me one last look before they stepped out the door. If I could have found my voice, I'd have told her I'd keep all I'd seen a secret. That I wouldn't gossip about it at school or in the church after services. But I couldn't seem to say a thing.

The two of them left, leaving me standing there with my pointer finger on the lavender colored sack with tiny white daisy flowers all over it, feeling like the most helpless person in all the world.

Mama came in just a minute or two after Delores and her father had left. She'd been caught up chatting with somebody on the street and couldn't get away, that was what she said. But the way her cheeks were flushed, I wondered if she hadn't rushed from further down the road than just the post office.

"You all right?" I asked her.

"Just feeling a little sick," she told me, touching her stomach. "It'll pass. Now, which one did you like most?"

I showed her the sack and she said it would be just fine. I carried it, my arms wrapped all the way around it, when we left for home. Mama had her arms full of everything else we'd gotten.

Mama said she had dainty buttons in her coffee can that looked just like little posies that might be perfect with that fabric.

But even with the promise of a pretty new dress and Easter coming along with warmer days, I couldn't hardly help thinking of Delores and her father. I kept seeing them in my mind, the two of them holding hands and walking away from the store. Seemed to me their hearts were heavy for the things Mr. Wheeler had said.

I thought of the time the oldest Smalley boy back in Red River had told everybody at school that Beanie was stupid as a box of rocks. I'd punched him in the gut so hard he'd doubled over and sucked for air like a fish out of water for a full five minutes. I had remained of the opinion that he was bad through and through for what he'd said. As far as I'd been concerned, he'd never amount to anything on account of his saying a bad thing about my sister.

"Don't forget the apostle Paul," Meemaw'd said when I'd told her what I thought of that boy. "Ain't nobody outside God's reach. Ain't nobody."

I'd not understood what she meant.

"Come on, Pearl," Mama said, her coffee can of spare buttons in her hands. "Let's look through these on the table."

"Yes, ma'am."

We dumped the buttons on the table, sorting through them. Mama told me where she got a few of them. This one or that one had come off a dress she'd had as a little girl. A couple big brown ones were from a coat her mother'd worn while she was still alive. A few had even been strung together so they could be matched more easily.

All the while I sat with Mama, marveling at how she could take an old bag and turn it into a pretty dress for me to wear come Sunday.

If that wasn't magic, I didn't know what was.

It wasn't until after we'd put the buttons back into their coffee can that I noticed an envelope peeking out the top of Mama's sweater pocket. It hadn't been opened, and my curiosity got the wheels in my head turning. When she noticed I'd seen it she pushed it deeper into her pocket.

"Who's that from, Mama?" I asked.

"Nobody," she answered and got up from the table. "Would you like a drink of water?"

"No thank you," I answered, following her into the kitchen.

She ran the faucet, filling her glass. She sipped it slowly. I tried getting another look at the envelope in her pocket.

"It's not for you," she said.

It was the voice I'd remembered from Mama's worst days, the days not all that long after we'd moved to Bliss. The days when it was best for me to tip-toe around her and not do a thing out of order.

She'd not meant anything by it, I convinced myself. She was fixing to sew a pretty dress just for me with the best buttons out of her old coffee can. Mama was sweet, Mama was kind. Mama would never leave me behind.

I left her to sip her water in peace.

Chapter Thirty-Four

I had never been one to brag. But had I been, I'd have made it known that of all the dresses the girls wore to church that Easter morning, mine was the finest. Sure, Ethel from school had the same lavender with tiny white flower print on her dress as mine did. And maybe Hazel's had been store-bought from someplace in Toledo.

But mine had the pretty posy buttons and a ribbon of white that Mama had taken off one of her old dresses to sew all the way around the waist.

I looked all about the church that morning before the first hymn got started. There were more folks in the pews than usual. Aunt Carrie'd told me that would be the case. People always made sure to be in church on Easter Sunday. They might not come any other week of the year, but they'd hold down a pew to celebrate the resurrection of Jesus.

It was better than nothing, at least that was what I thought.

We sang more hymns that morning than usual, which was fine by me. The organ player had done something to make his music louder and I kept checking the ceiling to see if the roof was like to blow away for how loud he boomed on those keys.

The way all the folks standing in that congregation sang, it felt as if all the bad in the world had gotten itself made right and all the hurt healed up. Uncle Gus stood on the other side of Aunt Carrie from me but I could still see how he rocked on the balls of his feet when he sang "Up from the grave He arose," and Mama's voice to the right of me rang out so clear and loud I'd have believed nothing awful could ever happen again.

The preacher stepped out from behind the pulpit after the song ended and put his hands up, palms out. I waited for him to lower them so we'd all know to sit down, but he kept them up, a big old grin on his face and a warm sparkle in his eyes.

For being one of calm and soft voice, that day he didn't hold back. He spoke louder than I'd have thought possible for him.

"Christ is risen," he hollered.

"He is risen, indeed," the rest of the folks

around me called, almost making me jump in surprise.

"Christ is risen," the preacher called out again.

"He is risen, indeed!"

"Christ is risen!"

"He is risen, indeed!"

For some reason I couldn't have explained just then if I'd tried, my heart felt full and I worried that I was about to cry for how happy I was. I'd never felt love for anything or anybody like I felt it for Jesus just then. I swallowed, trying to hold the crying in the middle of my throat.

He was risen. He truly was.

The very best ending to any story ever committed to paper.

But, lowering down to the pew, smoothing my skirt under me so it wouldn't bunch up and wrinkle, I knew Easter wasn't the end of the story.

It was just the middle. And I'd read enough stories in my day to learn that the middle can trick the person reading it into thinking everything's going to be a-okay. That nothing bad is lurking around the corner just waiting to attack.

Jesus was risen. He was risen, indeed. And He'd spend time with His disciples and teach them a couple last things before getting Himself pulled up to heaven to get a place prepared for all His friends just beyond the pearly gates and a piece down the street of gold.

But for his disciples there were beatings to come and shipwrecks. His friends would get whupped and stoned and kicked out of town. They had more than their share of heartaches coming and they just did not know it. Because they were Easter-Sunday-happy they couldn't think anything would go wrong ever again.

I sat there in the pew between Mama and Aunt Carrie on that sunshine morning, fit to bust for how happy I was. And scared half to death of what bad thing might be waiting just around the corner.

I had no doubt, the bad would come.

Chapter Thirty-Five

Over breakfast the day after Easter, Mama said something or another about how she'd like nothing better than some fried chicken. So when Daddy'd brought home a whole bird from the butcher's she wasted no time in cutting it up to fry for supper. Hard as I tried, I couldn't seem to remember the last time I'd had Mama's fried chicken. What I did remember was how crisp the outside got and how juicy the meat stayed.

I thought when I grew up and had a family of my own I'd need to know how to make chicken just like Mama's. My husband, whoever he ended up being, would love me even more for the way I cooked it and my kids wouldn't leave so much as a scrap of it on their plates.

But first I'd need to learn how. I came to the kitchen and asked Mama if she needed any help.

"I'd like that," she said.

She let me help her sift the flour and dip the legs and wings and breasts in the buttermilk and then press it in the flour, then back to the milk, back to the flour.

"Why twice?" I asked, my fingers coated in a layer of the breading, making more of a mess than helping, I was sure.

"My mother always did it that way," Mama said. "I never could make it just the way she did. I think she added something she never told me about. Some kind of a spice or something."

"Why wouldn't she have told you?"

"I don't know," she said. "Maybe so my chicken wouldn't be as good as hers. She was funny about some things."

"What was she like?" I asked.

"My mother? Oh, I guess you wouldn't remember her. She wasn't around us much once you were with us." Mama pushed a piece of chicken into the flour. "She passed on when you were little."

"I wish I could remember her."

"She was a fine woman, I guess. Tough as could be. Course, she had to be, I suppose." Mama lowered the chicken into the bubbling oil with as much care as she could so it wouldn't splash. "She always said she was part Cherokee but I don't know about that."

I looked up at Mama's dark hair and eyes

and wondered if it was true, that she was part Indian. I wished there was a way to be sure. Next day at the library, I'd get myself a book about the Cherokee and see if they had any pictures on the pages. It would've been a great discovery if one of the squaws in the book looked just like Mama.

"Beanie was always scared of her. She'd cry whenever my mother got close. Didn't ever know why." Mama shook her head. "My mother never understood why we kept Beanie."

"What else would you have done with her?" I asked.

"My mother said we should've put her in some institution up in Boise City," Mama said. "One for mongoloids."

"What's that mean?"

"It was just another way of saying Beanie wasn't right."

"Beanie was just fine."

"She was. Yes, she was."

Mama fished the pieces of chicken out of the grease that were cooked through and put them in her covered dish to stay warm.

"I'm glad you didn't send Beanie away," I said, dunking a chicken piece into the milk.

"It wouldn't have been right." Mama blinked a tear loose. "She belonged with us at home."

I hoped Mama hadn't seen me peek at the calendar hanging on the wall. She'd circled one day out of all of the dates in April. It was a tiny circle, made with a pencil, around the number fourteen. I didn't remember the dates of everything that happened through the year. But that one I knew. That was the date of big, black dusters and lost sisters.

It would be a full year the very next day. It didn't hardly seem possible.

The stab of missing Beanie had changed over the months to an ache right in the middle of my chest whenever I thought of her. Aunt Carrie had told me once that having that kind of pain came because we still loved the person that was gone and that it never all the way left us. She'd said it was good to feel it and it was all right to still love Beanie so deep.

Mama felt it too. I could tell by the way she made her lips into a tight O and pushed out a thin ribbon of air.

We kept on making the chicken, Mama and me. Then we went on to setting the table, Mama telling me to put out an extra plate for Winston. I was glad he was coming. I hoped he'd tell us a story or two, maybe even a joke. And I hoped maybe he'd help us forget the sadness the next day would bring us.

We got changed into fresh clothes and Mama had me sit on her bed as she pulled a brush through my hair.

"It's growing out," she said. "It's pretty, darlin'."

She was more gentle with me than she usually was, careful not to tug too hard at a snarl or to push the bristles into my scalp. Soft and low, she hummed one of the songs she'd sing when I was smaller, one to keep me from being sad or scared. It was one I thought sure she'd made up herself on account I never heard it anywhere else.

"I'm glad you came home, Mama," I said, worried she wouldn't hear it because it'd only come as a whisper.

But she'd heard it. I knew she had by the way she paused in her brushing, just for a second, before going on. I looked at her reflection in the mirror on the other side of the room. She hadn't smiled and hadn't nodded. She'd closed her eyes and breathed in through her nose, pulling her lips in between her teeth.

She had to pull a hanky from her pocket to dab under her eyes.

CHAPTER THIRTY-SIX

Having Winston sitting at our table and filling our house with his big old voice and booming laugh made my heart feel fit to bust from happiness. He'd had only kind words for Mama's chicken and ate so much of it I thought we probably should have fried up two whole birds. He licked his fingers and wiped the grease off his chin with the palm of his hand, saying he'd never tasted anything so fine in all his life.

"I'm glad you liked it." Mama leaned back in her chair, her fingers laced together on the top of her stomach. "Pearl helped out, didn't you, honey?"

I nodded, feeling swelled up with pride.

"Some man's going to be lucky to marry you one of these days," Winston said, winking at me.

"Hold there." Daddy put his hands up like he was surrendering. "Let's not rush the girl, all right?"

The three grown-ups laughed and for some reason it made me feel embarrassed, like I should crawl under the table so they wouldn't look at me anymore.

"I read something the other day," Winston said, grabbing another drumstick for his plate. "There's girls waiting to get married until they're well into their twenty-second year. Can you believe that?"

"Why do you think that is?" Daddy asked.

"Don't have any idea." The mayor tore off a chunk of chicken with his teeth and held the drumstick up, using it to point as he talked, looking for all the world like a picture of King Henry the Eighth I'd seen in one of my library books. "But it don't seem natural, waiting so long to get married."

"I was seventeen when Tom and I got married," Mama said.

"Seems so young now we've got an eleven-year-old, huh?" Daddy asked, winking at me.

"I guess so," Mama said. Then she cleared her throat. "Maybe they can't afford the marriage license."

"Could be," Winston said. "Or they've just come to realize what I've been saying for twenty-some years. If the bachelor life was good enough for Saint Paul, it's good enough for me."

"Well, the bachelor life isn't for everybody. Myself included," Daddy said, raising his glass of water like I'd seen folks in the movies do with wine. "I'd toast you with champagne, but the town only gives me a tap water paycheck."

"You and me both, Tom," Winston said, raising his own glass. "You and me both."

Mama sat up straight as a stick and breathed fast, a little gasp. She half turned her head and looked down at the table.

"You all right, Mary?" Daddy asked.

"Yeah. Yes," she answered, hardly moving an inch. "Just a little twinge."

Daddy got up and poured some fresh water from the pitcher into Mama's glass.

"It's normal," Mama said, nodding. Then relaxing, she put on a smile and leaned back into her chair. "I'm fine."

"You sure?" Daddy asked.

She didn't answer him. What she did was look at everybody's plates and ask if anybody wanted more of something.

"I made plenty of potatoes," she said.

Nobody ate a bite more. Not even Mayor Winston.

Winston only stayed long enough for us each to have a good slice of the cherry pie that he had brought over from Shirley's diner and for the grown-ups to have cups of coffee. It was all right by me, though. Mama had said Ray and I couldn't stay up too late on account we had school the next day.

"Pearl, I'll have you help me clear the table," she said.

I did as she asked, scraping the plates and stacking them in the sink, shaking crumbs from the cotton napkins and putting them aside to be washed the next day. I lined the glasses along the counter, ready for Mama to swish them in her soapy water and rinse them clean. But Mama hadn't drawn the dishwater yet like she usually would. Turning to see what was keeping her, I saw she was leaning against the counter, her eyes closed.

"I can wash these," I told her. "You don't have to."

"You sure?" she asked, her eyes still closed. "I'm just so tired."

"It won't take me long." I turned on the tap, letting the water get steaming hot before plugging the sink up and putting a dot of soap in.

She was still standing there, hardly moving but to breathe deep.

"Why don't you go on to bed?" I said. "If you're so tired."

"Maybe I will."

Turning, I got started on the dishes, plunging my hands in the water and yelping for how it burned all the way to my bones. Mama didn't ask if I was all right, and when I looked over my shoulder I saw she'd already gone.

We sat in the living room, Daddy, Ray, and me, waiting for the news to finish so we could hear a radio play or comedy act. Mama'd already gone to bed, so there wasn't anyone fretting over us staying up so late on a school night.

The man spitting out the news talked fast and with a higher voice than any man I'd ever known. He spoke of tensions in Europe and a man taking hold of Germany and all manner of things I just did not understand.

But the way Daddy held his ear close to the radio and his eyebrows pushed down I thought it was no good, whatever was going on.

"You think there'll be a war?" Ray asked.

"Don't know, son," Daddy answered. "I sure hope not."

As soon as the radio show started, Daddy lit a cigarette and leaned back in his chair. He didn't laugh at the jokes or shake his head at the pickles the character in the show got himself into. His eyes seemed to be looking off at something far away.

His cigarette burned down and I worried he'd get his finger with it. He must have felt the heat of it. He reached over and dropped it in the ashtray.

"Daddy?" I asked. "What's wrong?"

"Nothing, darlin'." He looked down at me and smiled. "Just thinking."

I didn't have to ask what it was he was thinking about. Seemed plain to me.

Jesus had called all the weary and heavy-burdened folks to come to him, I knew that was so. And He promised that His way of living was easy and light. I sure did think Daddy could use a lighter load.

I'd made my best try at falling asleep. Seemed like I'd spent hours rolling to one side or the other to get more comfortable or clamping my eyes shut as I counted sheep. No matter what I did I couldn't manage to get my brain to slow down.

Back in Red River I could always blame Beanie for keeping me up with her tossing and turning, her kicking and stealing the covers. More than a couple times a week I wished I could have a bed all my own.

That night I would've given anything in all the world to have my sister back.

I scooted over to the edge of the bed, the side I would have occupied had Beanie been there. On my side with arms crisscrossed over my chest, I pretended she was there. I imagined like neither of us was sleeping the way Mama would have wanted us to. Instead, we shared quiet giggles, trying so hard not to get caught.

It wouldn't matter what was causing us to laugh. All that was important was being with my sister.

A smile on my face, I shut my eyes and held onto hope that she was all right. That she had a place in heaven where the pillows would be fluffed just right and nobody'd get too sore with her for making little noises in her sleep.

I didn't cry for Beanie just then, even though I could have. But I did hold a loneliness for her in my chest that seemed deep as a well.

I got myself up to see if Daddy was still awake.

There were no lights on in the living room and nobody making so much as a peep in all the house. Daddy wasn't in his chair or in the kitchen. I saw that the door to Mama's room wasn't closed all the way so I pushed it open, wondering if maybe she was awake. If she saw me, I hoped she'd invite me to come and sit with her a spell.

I didn't step in the room, though. Daddy sat on the end of the bed, elbows resting on his lap and his face covered by one of his hands. Mama was curled up tight on the far side of the bed like she was trying to take up as little room as she could.

In Daddy's free hand he held a photograph. The way he held it in a stream of moonlight made it so I could see that it was a man and woman in the picture, standing close together.

Daddy and Mama.

I knew the one even without getting a real close look at it.

It was taken out in front of our house in Red River. Before the dust had gotten real bad. Daddy had his arm around Mama, pulling her close into him. With his other hand, he'd tipped up her chin so they were looking right into each other's faces. She had that smile of hers, the one I could have sworn would stop the sun from setting. And he looked about as happy as could be, just having her close like that.

They had loved each other.

If I could've had a wish just then, it would have been that Daddy would put that picture down and that he'd climb in under the covers right beside Mama. That he'd have an arm draped over where her waist dipped down. Maybe he'd even feel the bumping of the baby like I had. Maybe then he'd decide to love it, too.

But even wishing on all the twinkle-twinkle stars in the sky couldn't undo much of anything.

"Pearlie?" Daddy whispered.

He stood and came toward me, putting a finger to his lips to let me know I should be quiet and dropping the picture on top of Mama's dresser. Pulling the door closed behind him, he steered me back toward the davenport.

"You all right?" he asked.

I nodded.

"That's fine, darlin'." He looked back at the bedroom door and crossed his arms. "Your mama wasn't feeling so good. I was just checking on her."

"I know," I said. "What's wrong with her, Daddy? Is it the baby?"

He turned back to me and wrinkled his nose and shook his head. "She's fine. Just not feeling good. It's normal."

"Should we get the doctor?"

"Nah." He shook his head. "She'll be right as rain tomorrow. You'll see."

"All right," I said, not sure if I believed him.

"Now, why'd you get up?" he asked. "Have a bad dream?"

"No, sir. Just couldn't sleep."

"I'm sorry to hear that," he said. "Tell you what. I'll tuck you back into bed. I can even tell you a story. That sound good?"

It did and I let him know by following him up the stairs and climbing right back into my bed. He pulled the covers up until just my face peeked out at the top.

"Can you tell me a story about Jed Bozell?" I asked.

Daddy knelt down on the floor right beside my bed. "Jed Bozell? You sure you wanna hear about that old cuss again?"

I nodded.

"I ever tell you about the lady old Jed liked to bring along with him?" Daddy asked.

"He always had ladies with him," I said. "Didn't he?"

"Well, you're right about that, I guess. But this lady, she was special. Not cause she was prettier than any other woman in the world. She never wore anything all that fancy like the others in the show. She was content to wear her gray dress and shoes. Most folks thought she was just a cook or maid Jed brought along to take care of the folks in the show." Daddy scrunched up his face. "Most just didn't pay her any mind at all."

"What was her name?" I asked.

"Smokey," he said. "Her name was Smokey."

"Because her dress was gray like smoke?"

"That and cause she'd be there one second and gone the next." Daddy grinned. "Smokey the Disappearing Woman."

"Did she really disappear?" I asked.

"Sure she did. At least I saw it a couple times. Guess you could ask Gus. I bet he'd tell you the same thing."

Daddy leaned in closer to me to go on with the story.

"Now, some folks said it was just a trick with mirrors and trap doors." He shook his head. "No, ma'am. They were wrong."

"They were?"

"Sure. They all were accustomed to magic shows. The kind where the magician would tell them to look one way so he could stuff a dove into his sleeve or something like that," Daddy said. "But that's not the kind of disappearing Miss Smokey could do. Her disappearing was real."

Daddy got up off his knees and used his hand to let me know I should scoot a little for him. He sat on the edge of my bed.

"I'm getting too old to be on the floor like that," he said. "Anyway. Jed told me once that he hated when folks asked to see

Smokey disappear. Said it always made him sick to his stomach with worry about her. But she never did seem to mind. Whenever the crowd would holler out to see her disappear, she'd walk right out on stage in that gray dress of hers and give them the show they wanted."

"How would she do it?" I asked.

"Well, she'd come on out with her arms held down at her sides. Smokey'd stand still as a statue, her eyes shut and her mouth moving."

"What was she saying?"

"Nobody knew," he answered. "Not even Jed Bozell ever knew that. It was some kind of ancient spell only she could recite. Everybody'd get real quiet, hoping to hear what it was she said, but they never did. She never made a sound, fast as her lips were moving. Never even made a whisper. Then, after she'd recited her silent spell, she'd look up, gray eyes wide as could be. That was when it happened."

"What?"

"Why, that was when she'd start disappearing," he said. "First, the smoke coming off her was gray. It'd curl up and get carried off by the breeze."

"Did it smell like a fire?"

"Nah." Daddy looked into my eyes.

"Smelled just like roses, if I remember right. The gray smoke turned to white. By the time all the white burned off there was nothing left of her but those gray shoes she'd had on her feet. For some reason or another, she never could seem to keep them on when she disappeared."

"Why not?"

"No idea," he said. "Maybe they were just too heavy."

"When she reappeared did she fall right back into them?" I asked.

"Nope."

I watched Daddy's face. There was sadness in his eyes, but a tiny spark was there too.

"Daddy," I said. "She did reappear, didn't she?"

"Now, I know that all the good magicians can make a rabbit disappear in a box and then reappear in his top hat. Thing was, Jed was no magician. And Smokey was no reappearing lady." Daddy licked his lips. "Only thing Smokey could do was disappear. That and put up a sideshow tent faster than you could say Timbuktu. Not that she'd lacked trying. She'd worked at it for years, trying to learn how to reappear. It was just part of the spell she'd never figured out."

"How would Jed Bozell get her back?" I bit at my lip, hoping that story wouldn't end up making me cry. "He got her back, didn't he?"

"Always did, darlin'. Always did."

"How?"

"I'll tell ya," Daddy said. "See, every time Smokey disappeared she'd wind up coming to somewhere else a day or two later. Not even she knew where she'd find herself. Sometimes she'd disappear in Chicago and wake up in Texarkana. Other times she'd disappear in Delaware and roll over on a bed in London, England. Jed never did know where that lady'd end up. But he always — every single time — went after her. He always brought her home."

"What if she wound up somewhere he couldn't get to?"

"He always found a way, darlin'," Daddy said. "Didn't matter if she was one hour away or all the way in the middle of Siberia, Jed would find a way to get to her. He'd climb mountains and swim across oceans if he had to. He'd make a way to get Smokey."

"Why?" I asked.

"Because he loved her." Daddy's eyes were soft around the edges when he said it and I was scared he might start crying. "After a while, she stopped doing the disappearing trick. She quit it. No matter how hard and loud the crowds hollered for it, she'd refuse. She'd just stay in the tent where her things were kept. And she was happy to stay."

"She was?"

"Course she was. She'd learned that when you got somebody that loves you, staying is better than leaving."

I waited, not saying anything just in case there was more to the story. But Daddy didn't say anything else. Just used a rough, calloused finger to push a strand or two of hair off my forehead.

"Daddy," I said.

"Yeah?"

"Mama got a letter. Before Easter." I swallowed before going on. "She wouldn't let me see it. Wouldn't tell me who it was from."

"That so?"

I nodded. "I'm not trying to tattle."

"I know it."

"Do you think it was from him?" I hoped he would know I meant Abe Campbell.

"I don't know, darlin'."

"She had it in her sweater," I said. "The gray one."

"You best get back to sleep, darlin'. Leave this to me, all right?"

"Are you mad at me?" I asked. "For telling?"

"No, darlin'. Not even a little."

I closed my eyes but didn't fall asleep for a long time. Daddy stayed right there beside me, sitting on the edge of my bed. I didn't move for fear he was watching me and would catch me faking that I was sleeping.

I imagined Jed Bozell crossing deserts and rivers and snow-covered fields to get Smokey. When I pictured his face he looked an awful lot like Daddy.

Chapter Thirty-Seven

I found Mama still in her bed. As far as I could tell she hadn't moved even an inch since lunchtime when I'd last checked on her. She was on her side and I could see in the mirror that she felt of her belly like she was hoping to find something there.

She didn't turn toward me when I said her name.

"You can come sit with me a minute," she said, her voice more a whisper than anything.

I sat at the end of the bed. Neither of us said anything, but that seemed all right just then.

Mama had a quilt covering her up to her waist. I recognized it as one we'd brought with us from Red River. Patchwork of every color. It was what I'd always imagined Joseph of the Old Testament's coat to look like.

Meemaw'd made it of scraps from this

and that. I thought all the stitching must've made her crooked fingers sore. But a little pain had never stopped Meemaw from doing what she wanted to. Daddy'd said more than a couple times that Meemaw was the most stubborn soul he'd ever encountered. I'd never doubted that for a minute.

It'd always been my favorite quilt. All those different colors and patterns gave me plenty to look at when Mama wrapped me up in it or when she asked me to fold it and put it away. More than a few of the patches had faded from washings and hours hanging to dry in the sun.

Beanie never had liked it, I remembered that. She'd said it was too itchy on her skin and I wondered if it was on account of all the stitches Meemaw'd had to make to piece together the various patches and squares.

Sitting on that quilt, Mama's toes wiggling right next to my leg, I couldn't help but smile, thinking of my sister.

Beanie Jean sure had been a stinker. And I missed her like the dickens.

It didn't seem possible that a year and a day could have rushed by so fast since I'd last seen her, standing between me and the duster like she could save me from it.

I blinked. Let myself think back to sitting beside her on the porch back in Red River, telling her the story of Hansel and Gretel for the hundredth time. She'd been pretending to sleep so I'd leave her alone for a little bit. I'd covered her hand with my own for less than a minute. And I'd told her I loved her.

She'd known. I was sure of it.

Even with all the things Beanie hadn't understood, she had known what love was.

Aunt Carrie took over Mama's kitchen. She cleaned up the dishes from breakfast and the noon meal before she got a good stew heating up on the stovetop. Soon the whole house smelled of salty beef and starchy potatoes. The way Ray's mouth watered, I would've thought he'd been starving to death for the last year or so. She put me to work cutting circles into the biscuit dough she'd rolled out onto the countertop.

"You didn't have to do that," Mama said, out of bed for the first time that day. She leaned one hip into the counter and kept her hands wrapped around her tummy. "We could have managed."

"Oh, it's no trouble," Aunt Carrie said. "I made the stew earlier today. All I have to do is get it nice and hot. It seems I'm always making far too much of it for Gus and me to eat by ourselves."

"Thank you," Mama said. "Will you stay and eat with us?"

"Would you like me to?"

Mama nodded and I was glad. There didn't seem to be anybody that could help us through the day so well as Aunt Carrie.

"I'll get Mr. Seegert," Ray said, peeking his head into the kitchen. "If you want me to."

"Yes, please," Aunt Carrie said. "Be sure to have him change into clean clothes, too, if you would."

Ray nodded before turning and running out the back door, jumping off the porch, and making his way across the yard to the woods.

"We could have called him," Mama said, turning to watch Ray out the kitchen window.

"I don't think Ray minds getting him." Aunt Carrie smiled. "It will do him some good, anyway. Boys are always moving, aren't they?"

"I guess so," Mama said. "I haven't been around many boys."

"The way you're carrying," Aunt Carrie said, nodding at Mama's belly. "I'd guess you'll have another running around this house soon enough."

Mama looked down at her stomach. "I

carried low with Violet, too," she said.

I turned, knowing the scowl that'd set on my face.

"She never liked that name," I said. "Beanie hated it when you called her that."

Mama gave me a look so cold I got the chills.

Good thing for me Aunt Carrie was there in the kitchen with us. Otherwise, Mama might have knocked me off my feet for sassing her the way I'd done.

Instead, Mama just told me I'd better mind my manners around my betters and told me to set the table. I knew I'd best not say a word back to her even if I wasn't done with the biscuits. Besides, I was right embarrassed to have her talk to me so harsh with Aunt Carrie standing right there.

I just did as she said, not because I was obedient, but because I was afraid.

Chapter Thirty-Eight

The next morning we went about getting our own breakfast, seeing as Mama was staying put in bed. I got the oatmeal cooking and Ray set the table. Daddy started brewing up his coffee before going in to check on Mama. When he opened the bedroom door, though, she just hollered for him to get out.

She didn't have to tell him twice. He shut the door, shaking his head. But he didn't walk away, not at first. He just stood, his hand on the doorknob like he was fixing to go back in. What he would've done, I didn't know.

"Do unto others as you'd like them to do unto you," Meemaw would've said. "That's in the Good Book, you know. How you wanna be treated is how you best do to everybody else. Even if they gone and hurt you. You still gotta do it. Praise Jesus."

Had I been upset, I'd have wanted somebody to use a soft hanky to wipe the tears out from under my eyes. I'd have hoped that somebody would sit on the edge of my bed saying soft words to me, soothing me. Maybe that somebody would read a poem to me or sing a song. She'd bring me a cup of warm milk with a little chocolate stirred in if she had any.

Something told me, though, that Mama would've just told me to leave her be if I tried even one of those things.

I spooned out a couple bowls of oats for Ray and me to eat real quick before we left for school.

I wasn't inclined to go home right after school, so I climbed up the old stairs to Opal's apartment and knocked on the door. She'd never once turned me away and I didn't imagine she was like to that day either.

But she didn't come to the door. She didn't even call out "Just a minute" or ask who was there. Figuring maybe she hadn't heard me, I knocked harder so it stung my knuckles more. Still she didn't answer.

"Opal?" I called out, feeling the doorknob to see if it was unlocked. "It's me, Pearl."

The knob didn't budge. That was when I knew for sure she wasn't home. Most folks in Bliss left their doors unlocked on account everybody knew everybody and had no reason to mistrust them. Opal'd told me she'd never get used to that.

Seemed living in a big city like Detroit made it so folks didn't trust each other so easy.

I took my sweet time going back down the steps and hopped off the last one to the pavement. For a good minute or two I stood and watched the people walking up and down the street, going in and out of the stores or stopping to chat it up a minute or two with somebody they met along the way.

Two ladies stood right outside Wheeler's store, just a package or two under their arms that I imagined to be fixings for supper. One of them had sad-looking eyes, the kind that told more than her mouth ever could. The other put a hand on the sad lady's shoulder. She made her face soft and moved her mouth around words I imagined to be full of pity and comfort.

I had to turn away from them and walk the other way down the street. Seeing the kindness made me sad on Mama's behalf. Back in Red River, she'd been the one with soft eyes and comforting words.

It sure didn't seem all that long ago.

■ ■ ■ ■

I ended up walking down the winding road toward the library. Even for as nice a day as it was, there wasn't anybody out and about down that street working on their yards or sipping an iced tea on their porch. That was fine by me.

It seemed all the sudden my eyes had gotten watery, and no matter how hard I clamped on the knot in my throat I couldn't keep the sadness pushed down anymore. It wasn't a noisy cry and it wasn't too messy, either. Still, it lasted longer than I wanted it to. I stopped where I was, right outside the library, and rubbed at my eyes with my knuckles, hoping nobody'd seen me.

That was when I heard the clip-clop of hard-soled shoes on the walk. Looking up, I saw Mrs. Trask coming my way. For how stoop-backed she was, she sure moved quick.

"Are you hurt?" she asked when she was just a couple feet from me. "What ever is the matter, child?"

I didn't know what to say, so I just shrugged and tried my best at a smile. From the way her eyes got soft, I knew she didn't buy it.

"Come along," she said, reaching out and hooking her fingers over my shoulder, pulling me to her side. "Let's get you inside. I seem to have left my hanky on my desk."

I let her take my arm as we walked to the library and up the steps to the door. As fast as she'd come to me, I figured she'd worn herself out.

"I believe I need to sit down," Mrs. Trask told me once we'd gotten beyond the big wood doors. "Would you be a dear and help me to my chair?"

I told her that would be fine and did as she asked.

She held my hands real tight as she lowered her backside into the chair. I couldn't tell if the creaking was her knees or the chair taking on her weight. I knew it wouldn't have been proper to ask.

"I was dusting the shelf over by the window," she said. "When I saw you crying, I came as fast as I could."

"You didn't have to do that, ma'am," I told her, letting her keep hold of my right hand.

"Oh, I know that, my dear." She smiled up at me.

"Then why did you?"

"I have long been of the opinion that when one sees someone in need, one goes to them," she said. "If one sees a friend crying, one goes as swiftly as is possible."

She'd called me a friend. I opened my mouth and tried to tell her even a little bit of what'd been troubling me. Seemed, though, I couldn't figure out where to start. If I'd told her about one thing I'd have to spill the beans about all of it. Sorrow never did come in small bits. Instead, it arrived as a mass of sadnesses all stuck together.

I closed my mouth. Mrs. Trask wasn't one to pry and she wasn't the kind to impose. She wouldn't force me to say a thing. Mrs. Trask was a lady, and a kind one at that.

"Whatever it is," she said, patting my hand. "It shall be made right, my dear."

"Yes, ma'am," I answered.

Goodness, did I ever hope she was right.

Chapter Thirty-Nine

I took longer than I should've, walking home from the library. I hoped maybe Mama'd gotten to feeling better and that she'd be up and getting supper together for us. Even then, I wasn't sure which Mama she'd be. The way her moods went up and down, I never could know from one minute to the next.

When I finally turned on the corner of the main street and Magnolia, I thought real hard about just walking round back and heading straight through the woods to Aunt Carrie's house. No matter the day of the week or the kind of weather, Aunt Carrie was the same. Kind, smiling, and warm.

For about the thousandth time I wished Aunt Carrie was my mama. And for the thousandth time I felt guilty all the way to my bones for thinking such a thing.

"Hey, Pearl," a voice I knew belonged to Bert called out to me. "Over here."

Turning, I saw him and Ray standing inside the pigeon coop, looking out at me through the chicken wire–covered window.

"Come on," Ray hollered.

Seeing as how I didn't want to go home just yet, they didn't have to ask me a second time.

"You two look like you went and got locked up," I said, crossing the street and walking directly to them. "Sassy get out and trap you boys in there?"

"Nah, she's still in here," Ray said. "Bert thought she was a little lonesome."

"Probably why she's always running away is 'cause she's in here by herself all the time," Bert said. "She just needs a little company."

"Come in," Ray said. "There's room."

The boys shifted positions in the coop so I could join them. Sure enough, that bird was still in there, perched on the ledge just above Bert's head. Her feathers were puffed out and her head pulled in tight to her chest. I wondered if she really was sleeping or just pretending with hopes that those boys might leave her be.

"You wanna know a story one of the boys told us today?" Bert asked. "Go on, Ray. Tell her."

"Nah." Ray rubbed at the back of his neck

and looked at the ground. "It'd just give her bad dreams is all."

"It's just a ghost story."

"No it ain't." Ray shook his head.

"You too scared to tell me?" I asked, crossing my arms.

There wasn't a story ever told that could get goose pimples raised up on Ray Jones's arms. But, boy, did he like scaring the willies out of me whenever he got the chance.

"I ain't too scared," he said. "It just ain't a ghost story. It's real. Bob said so."

"Since when do you believe anything Bob says?" I asked.

Bob was full of ghost stories and old town gossip that nearly never proved to be true. Why anybody'd listen to him was beyond me. Whenever he got to telling one of his tales, I'd just roll my eyes and walk away.

Besides, any story Bob told usually ended up giving me nightmares for weeks, Ray was right about that. I sure didn't need the help.

"Bob's dad told him," Bert went on. "He said it's a true spook story."

"You really wanna hear it?" Ray asked, looking me in the eye and shaking his head. " 'Cause I ain't fixin' to get you mad at me for tellin' you somethin' that'll keep you up all night."

"I guess so," I answered.

I leaned back against one of the posts that held the coop together. Bert scooted nearer to me, resting on the same post. It took all my power to resist the urge to put my elbow into his side to make him give me some room.

"From what Bob says, ten years ago there was a whole bunch of folks here in town that ran with the Klan," Ray started. "You know what the Ku Klux Klan is, right?"

"Course I do," I said. "I'm not stupid."

"My dad wasn't one of them," Bert said. "He's always been friendly with the coloreds."

"Most men didn't join up, I guess," Ray went on. "But there were enough for them to have meetings and cause a little trouble."

"You know whose dad was in the Klan?" Bert's nose wrinkled like he smelled something rotten. "Delores Fitzpatrick's."

"Everybody knows that," I said.

I sighed and looked away from Bert and blinked long and slow at Ray, hoping he'd think I was getting bored with his story and get on with it.

"That's right. Bob told me that, too," Ray said. "He wasn't one of the bosses, I guess. He never had enough money to be a boss over nobody."

"Who cares?" I asked. "What's it got to

do with anything?"

"Well, seems the Klan around here never had much chance to do nothin' excitin'," Ray said. "Weren't no Negroes livin' around except the farmhands and such. Never did cause them boys trouble on account the farmers protected them. They never did go after the Mexicans, neither. They'd pick at harvest for hardly anything. Wouldn't make sense to drive them outta town. And there weren't no Catholics for them to go after except for in Adrian, and that was too far. So, the Ku Kluxers just sat around playing poker."

A picture formed in my head of a handful of men in those white robes and pointed hats like I'd seen in the news reels. They were all around a table dealing out cards. With their faces covered up, I didn't figure they'd have to worry about holding a poker face.

"One day a man and woman came to town and moved into a house on Astrid Street. You know the one." Ray turned his head and spit on the ground. "They come lookin' for work and such."

"Nah, they came because her family lived here," Bert said.

"Didn't neither."

"Sure they did. My dad said so."

"What's it matter?" I asked. "Just go on with the story."

"All right. I will," Ray said. "All the folks in the houses nearby watched them movin' their stuff in. Wasn't long before the Klan boys got word that the man was colored and his wife was white. They didn't like that too much. So one night they went over and put a cross up on the front yard, burning so bright most the whole town saw it. Then they went in and dragged that man out. The Fitzpatrick man, he had something to prove, I guess on account he was poor."

Ray stopped and cleared his throat and shoved his hands into his pockets.

"What'd he do?" I asked.

"Well, he got him a rope outta somebody's truck and strung it around the Negro's neck. Hung him right up a tree that was in the schoolyard." He leaned forward. "Hung him till he died."

I looked Ray right in his eyes. If I hadn't known any better I might've thought he was about to break. But he blinked and turned his attention to the pigeon as if he was waiting for her to do something real special.

"Wife of his?" Bert said. "Died of heartbreak that very same night. Their spirits haunt the house. You know, the one that's all boarded up."

"Why'd you tell me that?" I asked, with my eyes still on Ray.

He didn't answer me, just kept his eyes on the bird.

"Ray, I'm talking to you," I said, my voice near a holler. "Why'd you tell me something so awful as that?"

Bert tried putting his hand on my shoulder. I hit it away.

"Don't touch me," I said.

"It probably ain't true," Ray said, turning toward me. "You know Bob's stories ain't never true."

"Well, don't tell me any of his fool stories anymore, Ray," I said, looking up at him. "Just don't."

"I'm sorry," he said, and I knew he meant it. "Why're you so mad?"

What I told him was that I didn't know. But that was a lie and he knew it. The truth was I didn't know how he could tell a story about a man hanging after what his father'd done. Seemed to me, that picture of his own pa strung up in their old dugout back in Red River would've been plenty enough to keep him from telling something stupid like that.

"I never meant to —" Ray started. Then he stopped talking.

I could've sworn he was about to start

crying.

Seeing Ray cry would've broke me for sure. I pushed past Bert and out the door of the coop, not caring that it slammed shut behind me. My eyes stung, but I willed myself not to cry for a second time that day.

Across the street and up the steps, I opened the front door of our house and stepped in. There was no smell of supper cooking. The dining room table hadn't been set. On the kitchen counter was a half cup of black coffee that'd turned cold. The door to Mama's room was open and I peeked in. Her bed was a mess and her shoes weren't lined up against the wall where she always kept them.

"She's gone," I whispered, my heart beating fast. "She left us again."

My stomach turned and I was sure I'd be sick. I rushed to the kitchen, surprised that I didn't trip over my own two feet getting there. Every thought in my head stopped and then started twirling fast as ever, making me feel like I was going to collapse from the dizziness. My chest tightened up and I couldn't seem to get any breath.

"Pearl?" Ray called from the living room. "Where're you at?"

I stepped out from the kitchen. I must've

looked like I'd seen a ghost for the way he rushed to me and shook his head.

"I didn't know the story'd bother you so much," he said.

I shook my head. "It's not that."

"What then?"

"Ray . . ." I said, feeling the burning of tears in my eyes. "I knew she would. I just knew it."

"What're you talkin' about?"

"She's gone."

"Nah," Ray said. "Bet she's just takin' a rest. Did you check her room? Or maybe she had to get to the store for somethin' she forgot."

"I looked." My eyes clenched shut and the tears rolled down my cheeks. "She's not there."

"You stay here," Ray said. "I'll take a look-see around. All right?"

I did as he said, standing right where he'd left me. All through the house, his bare feet slapped against the floors. Up the stairs, through the hallway, back down the steps, across the living room.

He checked the whole house twice over and still didn't see her. Finally, he went to the back door and pulled it open.

"Pearl," Ray called. "You best go get your daddy."

I gasped for breath, opening and closing my mouth like a fish that'd just got hooked and pulled up from the water. I used the backs of my wrists to rub at my eyes.

"What is it?" I asked, my voice coming as nothing more than a whisper.

"She's here," he said before stepping out.

All of me stopped feeling. The racing feet and speeding mind slowed. In dreams I'd sometimes glide over the floor and that was how it felt just then. Like gliding. In a dream I might've twirled or the room might have grown longer so I'd never seem to reach the back door.

But it wasn't a dream, I'd pinched myself to be sure. And I did reach that door and step through. Mama hadn't left us.

Mama was still at home.

CHAPTER FORTY

She was leaning against the edge of the back porch, Mama was, both hands on either side of her belly, her face pulled tight like she was in pain. Her feet were spread wide on the ground. Ray'd hopped off the porch and stood in front of her, his face close to hers.

"Get Mr. Spence," Mama said through her teeth. "And get the doctor."

Ray looked up at me, "Go on. Get your daddy," he said.

"What's wrong?" I asked.

"It's too early," Mama said, her voice a sob. "It isn't time yet."

"We'll be right back, ma'am," Ray said. "You'll be okay here?"

Mama nodded and pinched her face, breathing heavy out of her mouth.

Ray stepped up on the porch.

"Get your daddy," he said. "Quick."

"What's happening?"

"Go, Pearl!" he yelled.

It was like getting woke up suddenly, Ray yelling at me, and I turned and ran to the front door.

I ran without thinking of where I was going. Somehow I made it to the police station, up the steps and through the door, across the entry way and to Daddy's desk.

He wasn't there and I thought I might scream for all the fear that burned through me.

"Daddy . . ." I started, but couldn't finish.

"Darlin'?" he said, coming out of Mayor Winston's office. "What is it?"

"Mama." It was all I managed to get out.

He didn't wait to hear more. He took my hand and we rushed, fast as we could, all the way home.

Ray sat on the front porch, Bert standing beside him. Both boys had their eyes on the grass as if they were watching it grow. Daddy let go of my hand and went up the steps past Ray and into the house.

I made to follow him in, but Ray stood, blocking me.

"Let me by," I said.

He shook his head.

"Come on, Ray." I moved to one side to get around him, but he just went in front of me again. "I gotta see to Mama."

"My dad's in there," Bert said. "He'll help her."

"We should go," Ray whispered to me. "Maybe go for a walk in the woods. See Mr. and Mrs. Seegert for a bit."

I turned toward him, not really understanding what he was saying.

"Come on, Pearl," he said.

"We never had supper," I told him.

"We'll be all right." He put a hand on my arm. "I'll bet Mrs. Seegert's got something left over we can have."

"But Mama . . ." I looked back at the front door.

"Pearl," Ray said, taking my arm and giving it a tug.

"I'm not going anywhere." I tried making my voice fierce so he'd know I meant business. But it just came out as a squeak. "I don't wanna leave Mama."

"She'll be all right," Bert said. "I promise."

"You can't promise that," I told him. "Nobody can promise something like that."

"Come on, Pearl." Ray was gentle with me like he always was. "It's no use stayin' here. You can't go in. You can't."

"But she's my mama."

"I know it," he said.

Just then I heard Mama cry out. I tried pushing past Ray again, but he was stronger than I was. Always had been, and I was sure he always would be. There wasn't any use, me fighting against him. I couldn't win.

"Let's just go for a walk," he said.

I let him take my one hand, Bert my other. The three of us walked to the tree line together.

We stepped into the woods.

It seemed the only thing to do.

Chapter Forty-One

The path through the forest squelched under my shoes. I thought it might be warm enough for bare feet, so I took them off, rolled my socks down, and put my toes right in the squishy mud. Seemed about forever since I'd walked around without shoes on.

Just thinking of how long I'd kept my feet covered made me feel like a part of my wild nature was taming. Sure seemed an awful shame to me.

We walked quiet as we could, taking our sweet time getting to the hiding cabin. Seemed when I was under the reaching arms of the trees I could forget about all the happenings at the house on Magnolia Street.

I decided right then if things got bad enough I could pack myself a bag, fill it with warm clothes and a couple cans of beans. I'd need to bring along an armload of blankets and my pillow. Maybe take a box of matches from the drawer in Mama's kitchen. If I had to, I could stay out in the hiding cabin until winter came again, or longer if need be. I thought sure Ray would teach me how to build a fire. When I ran out of food I'd taken from the pantry, I'd just pray that God might see fit to do as He'd done with the Israelites in the wilderness. I'd always wondered what manna tasted like.

"Go on," I told the boys once we reached the cabin. "I wanna be alone for a bit."

They looked at each other and then asked if I was sure. I nodded and they went up the path toward the farm, leaving me to the quiet of the woods.

I sat on the porch of the cabin, letting my feet swing just over the ground.

A robin redbreast hopped along on the ground in front of me as if I wasn't bothering her at all. Uncle Gus'd told me those birds were a sure sign that spring had come to stay for a bit. I was glad to see her.

She tilted her head like she'd heard something before bending down and grabbing a beak-full of dried up grass and flitting off to someplace. I imagined she had a good start on a nest, one placed high enough in a tree that no raccoon or possum would bother climbing up to get the eggs. She'd be sure to have put it on the sturdiest branch she could find.

From up in the treetops I heard a trilling, squeaking, chirping song. I looked up so I might just see which kind of feathered critter was singing. Sun beamed its way through the still bare-naked tree branches and warmed my face.

Shutting my eyes, I pretended that bird-song was calling the mama bird with her mouthful of twigs back to the nest. Back to home.

My eyes snapped open when I heard a crackling of twigs not too far from me. Craning my neck I saw Aunt Carrie coming my way, wearing an old pair of galoshes and an oversize barn coat I thought must have belonged to Uncle Gus.

"I didn't want to scare you," she said.

"It's all right," I told her. "You didn't."

"I'm glad." She stopped in the middle of the trail that led to the apple orchard behind her house. She had a book in her hand, one of her fingers stuck between the pages to keep her place. "The boys told me you were out here."

I let my shoulders slump.

"Do you mind if I come sit beside you?" she asked. "You don't have to talk to me. I brought a book. I could read to you if you'd like."

"It's all right," I said.

"Thank you." She continued on toward me, her forehead wrinkled and her eyes soft. She sat next to me on the porch, letting her feet swing right along with mine. She, too, turned her face to the treetops, squinting at the sun.

"Sometimes when I'm troubled I come here," she said.

"You do?" I asked.

"I do. It's nice and quiet. A good place to just think for a little bit."

I understood what she meant and told her as much.

She turned her face and looked at me sideways. "You've never read anything by Shakespeare, I don't think."

"No, ma'am."

"One day you will," she said. "And I think you'll love him."

I wasn't sure who that Shakespeare was she was talking about, but if Aunt Carrie said I'd like him then I was sure I would.

"He wrote a play I'm particularly fond of," she said, holding up the book. "*As You Like It*."

"Is it funny?" I asked.

"Some parts are. Now, I don't want to tell

you too much about it," she said. "But I will tell you that there's a forest in it. The forest of Arden."

I whispered the word after she'd said it, liking how noble and strong it sounded coming off my tongue.

"One way or another, all of the characters end up in the forest," she said. "It becomes a haven for them. A place where they may forget the troubles of the real world."

"It's nice to have places like that," I said.

"Yes." She nodded. "But soon, in the play, they realize that the forest is full of troubles all its own. A hungry lion, terrible weather, a lack of jobs."

"Did they stay in the forest of Arden?" I asked.

"They did not," she answered. "At the end, they go back to reality. They go back home."

She stood and offered me her hand, pulling me up. Then we stepped onto the porch and she pushed open the door to the cabin.

"I sometimes come and stand here," she said, stepping in and going right to the middle of the floor. "I look around at the walls and the windows and the floor and think about the history of this place."

I let myself think of the slaves that ran away, who stayed in that cabin for a night or two before heading to their freedom in Canada. I wanted to let her know that I was thinking on it, too, so I took her hand again. She squeezed mine real gently.

"They ran to this forest, the runaway slaves did. I like to think of it as a sort of Arden for them, a temporary haven." She looked down at me. "They didn't stay, though. There were too many dangers here for them if they did. They had to venture out and face adversity if they ever wanted to find home."

"Did they all make it?" I asked. "To Canada?"

"I don't know," she answered. "I suppose I'll never know that. But I hope they did. If not to Canada, to another place where they could live free."

We stood there another minute, only the sound of the woods filling our ears. Birds and chattering squirrels and crackling tree branches. A breeze so gentle I wouldn't have heard it if I'd not been listening closely.

"Something's wrong with Mama," I whispered. "And the baby, I think."

"The boys told me," she said.

"Ray and me, we found her," I told her. "She said it was too early."

"Oh dear."

She let go of my hand and put her arm

around my shoulders.

"Is she going to be okay?" I asked.

"I hope so, Pearl," she answered.

"And the baby?"

"I don't know."

We left the cabin, Aunt Carrie pulling the door to behind us. She held my hand all the way down the path that led to the apple trees.

I couldn't hardly help thinking of Mama all the way as I walked down the trail. I imagined she was in her bed, covers pulled up to her chin. I hoped maybe the doctor had given her something that might help her rest.

I asked if God would see fit to let her be all right.

I prayed it more than half a dozen times, just in case He hadn't heard the first time.

CHAPTER FORTY-TWO

Aunt Carrie cut slices of leftover meatloaf and put them between pieces of bread for Bert, Ray, and me. She'd asked if we wanted it warmed up, but we'd told her it was fine cold. I didn't want to tell her, but I was so hungry, I wasn't sure I'd be able to wait long enough for her to heat it. I knew the boys would be just as starved as I was.

Once she put the plates on the kitchen table she went to the living room where she kept the telephone to call Daddy to let him know where we were.

"They're eating a little supper," I heard her say. "They can stay as long as you need them to. I can send Bert home with Gus in a little bit."

Then she was quiet, only making a few noises and saying, "I see" every once in a while. I wished I could hear what Daddy said on the other end.

"That's fine, Tom," she said. "I'll see you

in a little bit."

I'd only finished half my sandwich by the time she came back into the kitchen. By then, though, I found I couldn't take another bite. I pushed my plate in front of Ray.

"Is Mama going to be okay?" I asked.

"Your daddy will tell you more once he gets here," she said. "He shouldn't be too long."

Bert didn't want to leave when Uncle Gus had said it was time. I could tell by the way he poked around, walking slow out to the car. I waved at him out the living room window as Uncle Gus pulled away.

Aunt Carrie set me up on the davenport with a couple magazines. Ray worked a puzzle on the floor. The only sound was the clock ticking away the time before Daddy came to get us.

I flipped through the pages of one of the magazines and looked at pictures of women with their finger-waved hair and silky dresses.

I couldn't keep my mind on any of the words next to the pictures, though. Resting my head against the back of the davenport, I looked out the window, watching for Daddy to come.

My eyes eased out of focus and my mind

wandered, trying to think what could've happened to Mama and the baby. All I could think was if the baby came too early he would just be real small. We could take care of a tiny baby, I knew we could.

I heard Daddy's truck before I saw it coming up the drive to the farmhouse. Closing the magazine, I put it in the basket where Aunt Carrie kept them and stepped out onto the front porch.

Uncle Gus's dog came from around the side of the house toward Daddy's truck. He didn't bark because he knew Daddy belonged there. His tail went a mile a minute and he ran alongside the truck until it stopped.

Daddy climbed out of his seat and started toward the house. Just from how weary he looked, I knew something was wrong.

"Hey, darlin'," he said.

He made his way to the porch and put both hands on my cheeks before kissing me on the top of my head.

"Is Mama . . . ?"

"She'll be all right," he answered. "In time."

He pointed at the porch steps and I knew he meant for us to sit there. He lit himself a cigarette, smoking it slow and not saying anything right away.

I kept my eyes on the yard between us and the road. Soon Aunt Carrie would plant her flowers in the beds on either side of the porch steps and ringing the trees. The irises, she'd told me, would come up on their own out of the bulbs she'd buried years ago in the ground against the south side of the house.

She'd told me I could help her when it came time to plant. And she'd promised to let me pick out a couple seed packets to sow in the garden. I'd hoped for cucumbers and watermelon.

"Pearlie," Daddy said, catching my attention from the yard.

"Yes?" I asked.

"Your mama lost the baby."

I scrunched up my face, trying to make sense of the words. I just couldn't. They had no meaning. Mama lost the baby. How could anybody lose a baby? Then I thought of how Peter Pan had flown away from his parents right after he was born. Flown away so they never saw him again. And Aunt Carrie saying they wouldn't have been able to stop him even if they'd tried.

But that couldn't be right. Babies didn't fly away. That was nothing but a fairy tale.

"Do you know what that means, darlin'?" Daddy asked, putting out the stub of cigarette against the wood porch.

I shook my head.

Daddy reached into his pocket for another cigarette. Holding it between his lips, he lit a match and shielded the flame from the breeze. Once the end of his cigarette was lit, Daddy flicked his wrist, making the end of the match turn from flicker to smoke. He tossed it to the side on the ground.

"Sometimes . . ." he started. "See, babies can be fragile."

"Like Beanie?" I asked.

"Yup. Like Beanie." He nodded and took a pull on his cigarette. "But we got lucky with Beanie. I guess some folks might not say lucky. They'd say a miracle isn't anything less than the hand of God."

"Meemaw would say that."

"I do believe you're right about that, darlin'." Daddy rested his elbow on his knee and leaned his lips against his hand, the smoke of the cigarette curling up right in front of his face. "This baby, it wasn't strong enough, I guess. I don't know."

But it had been. I'd felt his kicks. If I tried real hard I could feel them still, bumping into my hands through Mama's skin, through her dress. He'd been so strong.

"It's hard to explain, Pearlie." Daddy tossed his half smoked cigarette to the ground. "I'm still trying to make sense of it myself."

"Where's the baby?" I asked.

"Doctor Barnett took it," Daddy said, not looking at me. "He said he'd take care of it."

"He can't take the baby." I shook my head. "He's ours."

"Pearl —"

"It's not right, Daddy. If Mama doesn't want him, I'll take care of him. I'd be good at it. It doesn't matter if he's real small."

"Darlin', hush now." Daddy said it in his softest voice. In his kindest way, not as a scolding. "What I've gotta tell you is hard to say. And it's going to be hard to hear."

If I'd had any will left I would've run off to the forest and pretended it was my Arden. And I'd never have had to know what made Mama so scared in the back yard or Aunt Carrie so quiet after Daddy'd talked to her on the telephone. And I wouldn't have had to hear what Daddy said. But the strength was all gone out of me.

"Pearl, the baby passed on," he said. "It died, darlin'."

He put his arm around me and let me cry. Not once did he shush me or tell me it was going to be all right.

Chapter Forty-Three

Aunt Carrie said Ray and I could stay at the farm as long as need be. She'd said it might be best for Mama, not having to worry about taking care of us just then.

"I'd be happy to have them here," she'd said.

Daddy drove us back home so we could pack up a few things. Just enough to last us until he came to get us again. A couple changes of clothes. That was all we'd need. And a book or two. Maybe my hairbrush and the nice clip Mama'd given me for special occasions.

It seemed impossible, thinking about what to take when I knew Mama was downstairs in her bed. Daddy'd said she was in a deep sleep, that Doctor Barnett had given her some powerful medicine so she wouldn't have to feel any of the pain.

I wondered if he had anything in that doctor's bag of his that might deal with all the hurt that was coming once she woke up and remembered why her stomach wasn't round anymore.

"You need help?" Ray asked, standing in the doorway of my bedroom, his few things crumpled in his hand.

"I'll manage," I answered.

He came in anyway and sat on my bed. I thought how Mama would've gotten after me if I'd bunched my clothes like he had. She'd have grumbled at me for making a mess of my blankets if I'd sat on my bed the way he did. But she'd never scolded Ray, not really. Not in all the time he'd been with us.

"It'll be like we're on vacation," he said.

"What?" I asked, turning toward him.

"It's like we're goin' on a trip," he said. "I ain't never been on vacation before."

"We're just going to the farm." I turned my back and took a couple dresses off their hangers. "It's not that far."

"Nah, you're lookin' at it wrong." He cleared his throat. "Just think of it. We're gettin' away from life in town and goin' out to the country for a spell."

I shrugged, not wanting to see the sunny side of anything just then.

"We'll be far away from all the cares of the world," he went on.

"There's no place somebody can go to get away from bad things," I said. "They've got a way of following a body around."

"Guess we just gotta be faster then." He gave me a weak smile. "Ready?"

"I wanna see Mama first."

He didn't try to stop me. He knew better than that.

Daddy'd said it was okay to go to Mama if I promised not to wake her. I told him I'd be quiet as I could. I'd just wanted to look at her, to see with my own eyes that she was all right. To maybe feel with my own hands that her skin was still warm and hear with my own ears that she was still breathing.

I opened the door to her bedroom as slow as I could and stepped in on my tiptoes. She was on her side, facing away from me. She didn't move but her snoring let me know she was breathing all right. Mama never had been one to snore, not that I knew of, at least. I thought whatever the doctor had given her must have been mighty powerful.

I stepped around the end of the bed, running the tips of my fingers along the quilt and feeling the patches of cotton and the stitching like scars holding it all together. I stopped, resting my pointer finger on one of the squares, tracing the red thread heart Meemaw had sewn at the bottom right-hand corner of the quilt.

I remembered so many years ago I'd gotten sent to bed without supper. For the life of me I couldn't remember what I'd done, but it must've been bad for Mama to have me go without a meal. It had always bothered her something awful to think that Beanie or I was hungry.

That day, I'd crawled up under that quilt on my bed. It was in my room in Red River and I remembered rubbing the soles of my feet against the gritty dust on the bottom sheet. My stomach grumbled but I was too angry at Mama to admit that I was hungry, not even to myself.

Later on, before she'd sent Beanie up to bed, Mama'd come in my room. I pretended to be asleep that day, pinching my eyes hard so I would remember not to open them and give myself away.

She'd sat the end of the bed. I opened one of my lids just enough to see her there, her eyes on that square and her finger tracing the shape of the heart. Mama'd stayed there a long time, so long I nearly fell asleep for real.

But then I'd heard her sniffling. I opened that one lid again, wider that time, and saw her reach up and push a tear off her cheek.

"Mama?" I'd said.

She startled, but just a little. "I thought you were asleep," she'd said.

"Why're you crying?"

"I wasn't crying," she'd answered. "Do you know I love you, Pearl?"

"Yes, Mama," I'd answered. It'd been the truth, I did know it.

"I really want you to know that I do."

"I know."

She'd reached to where my foot bumped up the covers and gave it a squeeze.

"Don't ever doubt it, sweetheart," she'd said.

That day in the house on Magnolia Street it was Mama's foot forming a ridge under the quilt and my finger tracing the stitched heart.

"Do you know I love you, Mama?" I asked, keeping my voice as quiet as I could.

She didn't answer. Still, I hoped she knew.

CHAPTER FORTY-FOUR

We'd gone to school the next morning, much as I didn't want to. Neither of us said a word about Mama. Bert didn't either. It wouldn't have felt right, talking about something so private as that.

I wondered if we'd ever talk about it again, even between us.

After school Ray changed into work clothes and went out to the fields to work alongside Noah Jackson, repairing fences and getting the farm ready for the planting season. I wondered what it was like, the work men did that built up calluses on their hands and muscles in their arms. Whatever it was, Ray liked every minute of it even if it did wear him out.

As for me, after school Aunt Carrie and I picked a couple books and climbed up in the reading tree out by the chicken coop, our skirts tucked up so we wouldn't be quite as unladylike as we might've been.

The hens clucked at us and it sure sounded like they were laughing.

We read for a spell, the air not quite warm enough to be without a sweater, but the sun just bright enough to keep us from being too cold.

After a little bit I found myself staring off toward the woods. I let myself think through the day before. It seemed like a year had passed since I'd stepped into the pigeon's coop and since Ray had told me Bob's story about Mr. Fitzpatrick hanging that man.

"Are you finished reading?" Aunt Carrie asked.

"I guess so," I answered, turning toward her.

"It's nearly time to get supper in the oven."

But she didn't make a move to climb out of the tree so I didn't either.

"What are you thinking about?" she asked.

"Just about a story I heard the other day."

"It must have been a good one for you to still be thinking about." She closed her book and rested it on her knees.

"Aunt Carrie, is it true about the house on Astrid Street?" I asked, turning my eyes back toward the forest.

"What house?"

"The haunted one, not too far from the

library," I said. "It's gray with black shutters."

She shut her eyes and nodded her head. "I think I know the one."

"Is the story true?"

"Tell me what you heard."

I told her the story Ray had told me. The man and woman and the Ku Klux Klan and how Mr. Fitzpatrick had hung the man himself. She listened, her hands folded on top of the book, her eyebrows lowered and eyes squinted.

"Is it true?" I asked, leaning back on the branch behind me.

"Yes and no." She sighed. "It's half true, I suppose. How about we go inside and get supper started," she said. "Then I'll tell you a little more about it."

"Yes, ma'am."

We climbed out of the tree, the chickens scampering over to see if we had anything for them to eat.

"It's not time yet, ladies," Aunt Carrie told them. "I'll have Pearl come out with your supper in a little bit."

I bent at the waist and petted one of them on the back. She didn't seem to mind so much.

Once we got supper simmering on the

stovetop, Aunt Carrie warmed up some coffee from breakfast for herself and poured a glass of milk for me.

"Ruthie Bliss was my very best friend when we were growing up," she started, sitting across from me at the kitchen table. "She's the one I told you about. The one who let me play with her hair."

"Bliss?" I asked. "Like the town?"

"Yes, she was sisters with Abigail. You'd know her as Mrs. Wheeler."

"Were you friends with Mrs. Wheeler?" I asked.

She shook her head. "Not really. She was a few years younger than Ruthie and me."

Aunt Carrie went on to tell me that they went to school together, back when even the high school grades were in the same building.

"Not many stayed in school that long in those days," she said. "Many of the kids gave up their education early to help at home."

"That doesn't sound too bad," I said.

She smiled at me and looked at her fingernails. "I don't think most of the children would have disagreed with you."

"Ray would be happy if he could stay here and farm with Uncle Gus."

"Ah," she said. "But Gus would want Ray

to stay in school. You too."

I nodded and took a sip of my milk.

"Now, my friend Ruthie and I were inseparable. We'd run all over the farm when she'd come to visit. We'd hide in the barn and jump out at my brother. Charlie would get so mad at us for scaring him like that." She laughed. "The Bliss family lived in that house where the Wheelers live now. And when I'd visit her house we'd eat candies in the cellar. Abby had a sweet tooth. If she knew we had candy, she'd bother us until kingdom come to give her some. So we told her there were goblins living down there. That way we could eat our sweets in peace. And talk about boys."

"Were there goblins?" I asked.

"No. We were teasing her." She smiled. "I wonder if Abby ever thinks about that when she goes to the cellar."

"Maybe she's still too scared to go down there."

"That could be."

"What ever happened to Ruthie?" I asked. "Is she the woman in Ray's story?"

"She is. But it didn't happen exactly the way he told it." She found a small cluster of crumbs and wiped them off into her hand. Getting up, she went to the sink and brushed the specks off there. "She met Nehemiah at one of the speakeasies in Toledo."

All I knew of speakeasies were the stories Ray'd told me. He'd said they were where Al Capone sold his liquor and shot anybody that looked at him sideways.

"Was he a gangster?" I asked.

"Heavens, no." Aunt Carrie turned toward me, her eyes wide. "It wasn't *that* kind of speakeasy. No, Nehemiah never would have hurt a fly. He was one of the kindest men I ever knew."

"Him and Uncle Gus?" I asked.

"Yes. Uncle Gus is a kind man, isn't he?"

I nodded.

"Nehemiah played in a jazz band. I had never heard anyone who could play piano like he did." She put her hands to her heart. "It was as if his fingers were water, they moved so fast over the keys, making waterfalls out of the notes. He was a wonder."

"You heard him play?" I asked.

"Yes. Ruthie had me go with her to hear him play more than a few times. It was no wonder she fell in love with him."

I leaned my elbow on the table and Aunt Carrie didn't get after me to mind my manners, so I rested my head on my hand and listened to the rest of her story.

"Her parents were against it, of course, the two of them getting married," she went on. "They wouldn't even let him set foot in their house."

"Why not?"

"Because he was a colored man." She sighed. "But Ruthie was a spitfire. She wasn't one to take no for an answer when there was something she wanted. They eloped. Do you know what means?"

I shook my head.

"It means they ran off and had a justice of the peace marry them. They went to Toledo so no one could stop them. Her family vowed to never speak to her again." Aunt Carrie leaned back against the counter. "Nehemiah wanted to bring Ruthie home to Bliss, but he couldn't buy a house for her."

"Why not?" I asked.

"Well, because a colored man isn't allowed to own land in Bliss."

"Why's that?"

"Because of the color of his skin." By the way Aunt Carrie's eyes narrowed I could tell she didn't think it was a good thing. "Ruthie asked her folks if they could sign for the house. They told her they wouldn't."

"Why would they be so mean to her?"

"They said that she had embarrassed them," Aunt Carrie said. "It broke Ruthie's heart. Gus ended up signing the paperwork for them. It always bothered him how the Bliss family just cut Ruth out of their lives. Not even Abigail would come visit. More than half a dozen times Ruthie'd sit right at that table, crying over all of it."

Aunt Carrie stirred her pot before lowering the flame.

"At that time the Klan was getting strong here," Aunt Carrie said. "I will never understand the men who joined up. I'd grown up thinking they were good and honorable, the men of this town. Their fathers and grandfathers had fought against slavery, and here they were . . ."

She stopped and took in a deep breath.

"You okay?" I asked.

"It's so easy for me to feel hatred for them, Pearl, for what they did," she answered, her face as flushed as I'd ever seen it. "It's such a temptation to hate them."

I nodded, thinking I understood what she meant.

"They didn't burn a cross in the front yard and they didn't lynch Nehemiah," she said. "Those parts of the story are not true."

"Then he's still alive?" I asked.

"Sadly, no."

She told me the men were mad at Nehemiah for taking a job at the sawmill north of town that might've gone to a white man.

And a woman that could've been married to a white man, too. They'd gone and knocked on the door, meaning trouble, but they didn't have a rope.

"Was Mr. Fitzpatrick there?" I asked.

She nodded, closing her eyes.

"Did he kill Nehemiah?"

"No," she said. "You've heard the story of Stephen, in the Bible?"

"Yes, ma'am."

"Then you know of Saul holding the cloaks of the men who stoned Stephen?"

I nodded my head.

"Mr. Fitzpatrick held the white robes of the men as they beat Nehemiah," she whispered, a tear breaking loose from her eye. "I don't know that they meant to kill him. But they didn't want to get their robes stained. That was what they'd said."

"Did they kill him?" I asked.

She nodded.

"What happened to Ruthie?"

"She saw the whole thing," she answered. "I've heard that her screams could be heard clear across town."

"Then what happened?" I asked, my throat feeling tight as I spoke.

"She left. She didn't even pack a bag or leave a note," she said. Then she looked at me, her eyes wide and her fingertips raised to her lips. "I shouldn't be telling you this. It's upsetting you."

"Did those men go to jail?" I asked.

"They did not. There was no justice for Nehemiah, I'm afraid." She wiped at her face. "A few years later the Klan in this town dissolved. If ever they talked about the matter they put all the blame on Mr. Fitzpatrick."

"Is he a bad man?" I asked.

Her eyebrows pressed down like she was thinking real hard.

"Well, I don't know how to answer that question, dear," she said.

"Was it a wrong thing to ask?"

"No, it wasn't. It's just that some things are so very complicated." Lowering her arm, she wrapped it around her stomach as if she was fixing to be sick. "It should be a very easy question to answer. But it just isn't."

I took my empty glass to the sink and rinsed it out. By the way she turned toward the stove and put a lid on her simmering pot, I could tell she didn't want to talk about it anymore, so I didn't ask any more about it. I went to the dining room and set the table. By the time all the bowls and plates and flatware were out, Uncle Gus and Ray had come in to wash up for supper.

After he said the blessing, Uncle Gus

looked up at Ray and me, his face looking tired, but smiling anyway.

"I sure am glad y'all're here," he said. "Feels more like a home with the two of you sittin' at this here table."

It felt good, hearing him say that.

Chapter Forty-Five

Aunt Carrie had to run some errands in town once Friday afternoon came around and she said I could go along with her if I'd like. When I'd asked if I could pay Opal a visit, she told me she thought that was fine, just so long as it was okay with Opal.

I knew it would be.

She gave me a nickel and told me I could get a bottle of Coca-Cola to share with Opal. I made sure to tell her thank you three times so she'd know how I did appreciate it.

Opal's eyes sparkled as she popped open that bottle, pouring half into a tin cup for me and taking a swig out of the bottle.

"It's been too long," she said. "I hadn't remembered how good it was."

"I like it," I told her.

"Me too." She winked at me and tipped back the bottle for another sip. "Want to see what Lenny gave me?"

I nodded and watched her stride the few steps it took to get across the room. She tugged open the top drawer of her dresser and took out a small box. Holding it like it might crumble if she wasn't careful enough, she knelt in front of me, then lifted the hinged lid. Earrings made of blue stones sat on a tiny velvet cushion.

"Aren't they pretty?" she asked.

"Yes," I answered. "How's he got money for them?"

"They were his mother's," she said. "He said she doesn't wear them anymore. She told him I could have them. Can you imagine it?"

"Are you going to marry him?" I asked.

"Who? Lenny?"

I nodded.

"I don't know about that." She shrugged and closed the small box. "They're just earrings."

"Do you love him?"

"Love's not the word for it, I don't think." She turned to the radio and flicked it on. "He's fun to be around and easy to look at, but I don't love him."

Kneeling on the floor, she eased the dial until she found a sound that she liked. My cup of soda pop in my hand still, I went and sat on the floor beside her.

"I paid your mama a visit yesterday," she told me.

"Is she all right?" I asked. "Daddy didn't think I should see her yet."

"She's healing up. It might take a while."

"Did she say anything about me?"

"Baby, she's not saying much of anything right now." Opal leaned close to me and plucked a loose eyelash from my cheek. She held it, balancing on her fingertip, in front of my lips. "Make a wish."

I wanted to tell her I didn't believe in such things anymore. Shooting stars and birthday candles and wishbones didn't hold any kind of magic that could make even the simplest of wishes come true. It was all bunk, hooey, and nonsense. Instead, I just blew the eyelash off her fingertip.

We sat and listened to the radio. A week before I'd have asked if she could teach me a new dance step and she'd have agreed. That day, though, I was worn out. If I could've, I'd have laid down right there on the floor and slept until Aunt Carrie came looking for me.

I finished up my Coca-Cola and told Opal thanks for letting me visit with her. It sure had done me good. And I told her I thought the earrings were sure pretty, whether she loved Lenny or not.

"He's just a silly old boy," she said. She put a hand on my cheek. "You'll take care, will you? If you need anything at all, you come see me."

"Would you look in on my mama every now and again?" I asked. "Make sure she's eating?"

"I'll do that, Pearl," she answered. "I'll do that for you."

I found Aunt Carrie walking out of Wheeler's general store. She didn't have anything in her arms but a stack of mail and a book from the library.

"Did you have a nice visit?" she asked.

"Yes, ma'am," I answered.

"I'm glad." She pushed her lips together. "You know what I think would be good today?"

"What?"

"A little dish of ice cream," she said. "Do you think you'd like one?"

"Yes, please."

She took my hand and we crossed the street to get to Shirley's diner. I could've crossed on my own. I did it plenty of times without holding anybody's hand. Still, I didn't tell Aunt Carrie that.

It felt good to have her take care of me.

Chapter Forty-Six

It was the kind of Saturday morning that inspired laziness in me. The sun seemed to have taken the day off, hiding behind heavy-looking clouds that Uncle Gus had said might burst at any minute. Aunt Carrie had tried warning me off from going into the woods after I told her that was what I was fixing to do.

"Soon's I feel a drop of rain, I'll come right back," I told her.

"All right, I suppose," she said. "It isn't the rain I'm worried about. Those look like storm clouds."

"I'll be quick," I told her. "I promise."

Just to prove to her how fast I'd be, I broke into a run just as soon as I got out the kitchen door. Before too long I was on the porch of the hiding cabin, breathing in the smell of coming rain and letting my mind wander wherever it wanted to go.

Not a minute after I'd sat down, I felt a

drip-drop of wet on my cheek and got up to go home. It wasn't until I got to the tree line that I realized I'd gone the wrong way. Instead of stepping out into the apple orchard, I was looking at the back of the house on Magnolia Street.

I didn't leave the woods. Instead I stood, leaning against the trunk of what I'd have guessed was a maple tree. There was no movement inside the house that I could see, nobody walking past a window or out back grabbing the laundry off the line before the rain came. It was as if the house had been left empty. The home taken right out of it.

If there'd been a haunted house in Bliss, it might just have been that one.

The here-and-there drops of rain turned into a smatter then to a splatter. I turned so as to make good on the promise I'd made to Aunt Carrie. By the time I got to the back door of the farmhouse the clouds had stopped holding back, letting loose all the rain they'd been carrying.

It rained all the rest of that day and didn't stop until well after Ray and I'd had our baths and gone to bed. We sat shoulder to shoulder on my bed, watching the lightning crackle across the sky in crooked white lines.

"You ever wonder what'd be like to get struck by lightning?" I asked him, whispering so Aunt Carrie wouldn't know we were still up.

"Guess so," he answered. "Seems it might sting a little."

He gave me his lopsided grin and I couldn't help but smile back at him.

"You think it's true that lightning never strikes the same place twice?" I rested my head on my fist.

"Nah," he said. "I'd bet lightnin' can strike just about wherever it fixes to."

"Reckon you're right."

We sat in quiet for a minute or two before a bolt sliced through the night sky, lighting up the world so bright I could see clear to the barn. It didn't take but a second for the booming roar of thunder to sound out so loud I felt the house give a shake.

I couldn't hardly help it. That one made me curl up and put my hands over my face. My heart beat fast and I waited for the roof to fall down around us.

"Why'd that one have to be so close?" I asked, my voice a whimper.

"We're all right," Ray said. "Don't be afraid."

"I just hate it when they get that close." I lowered my hands, trying to see if the barn was on fire or the chicken coop blown to bits and feathers. All I could see was the rain tip-tap-tapping against the glass of the window. "It scares me is all."

Ray put his arm around my shoulders and told me he knew what I meant.

"We'll be just fine," he said. "I promise."

Chapter Forty-Seven

May came on gentle with green grasses and buds exploding into flowers on the tips of all the tree branches. The sun saw fit to grace us for more hours of the day, warming up the air and the ground and the very moods of all the folks in Bliss.

Ray and I hadn't gone back to the house on Magnolia Street since Mama'd lost the baby. What had started as a couple days at the farm was going on two weeks. Daddy'd bring us odds and ends we needed from our rooms, saying Mama wasn't ready for us to visit just yet.

When he'd come, he'd stay over for supper. Sometimes it was as if he was there in body, but not in spirit. His eyes looked so tired, his face drawn. When I'd ask if he was all right, he would say he didn't want me worrying.

"I'm doing good, darlin'," he'd say.

I didn't believe him for a second.

May was planting time in Bliss and most of the farm boys stayed away from school to help their fathers put seeds in the ground. Ray'd begged to be allowed to stay home with Uncle Gus so he could spend the days planting corn and soybeans and sugar beets.

Uncle Gus wouldn't hear it, though.

"As long as I'm trusted with your care, I'm gonna make sure you get to school every day them door's is open," he'd said. "I know Tom'd agree with me, too."

"Yes, sir," Ray'd answered.

"Y'all can just come on after school," Uncle Gus had said. "I don't mind puttin' you to work then. Bring that Bert fella with you sometime, too. I think he could use a little dirt under his nails."

So after school each day Ray and I walked through the woods to the farm. A couple times Bert did come, sometimes bringing Sassy along in her bird cage for fear she'd be lonely without him. Uncle Gus's tan-colored dog named Boaz wasn't so sure what to make of Sassy at first. He'd worry and whine, sniffing through the bars of that cage until Sassy pecked at his nose.

Poor Bo, he'd go running off to hide in the barn and cry over his hurt feelings.

The men'd go right out to the fields, folding pant legs up and kicking off shoes along the way. As for me, I went to the garden with Aunt Carrie where she showed me how to sow the seeds by hand.

"We'll have zucchini over there," she'd say, pointing to one corner of her large garden. "And I think the potatoes will be there."

She told me we'd have tomatoes and cucumbers, squash and peppers. I held the tiny seeds of beans and lettuce and broccoli in the palm of my hand, in awe that soon enough they'd turn into food to add color to Aunt Carrie's table.

I liked being in the garden with her, the shade of a borrowed straw hat I wore keeping the back of my neck cool. And I liked the earthy smell of the dirt on my hands. It felt nice having soil under my fingernails and my bare toes wiggling in the grass.

As much as I'd hoped to have a garden of our own in the back yard of the house on Magnolia Street, I found I was content to work alongside Aunt Carrie there at the farm. We didn't usually say a whole lot while we pulled at weeds and checked tiny growth of plants. If anything, Aunt Carrie would share a line from a poem she liked or I'd ask her which bird was singing just then from the tippy-tops of the trees. Chickadee or robin, starling or sparrow. I couldn't have picked a favorite if I'd tried.

"I could watch them for hours," Aunt Carrie'd say.

I could've too. If heaven ended up being a garden in Michigan, I'd have been happy to spend eternity right there, God's glory beaming down on me, brighter than the sunshine.

Chapter Forty-Eight

It was a Saturday and Uncle Gus had given Ray and me a couple nickels each so we could go into town to see a movie.

"You both worked real hard," he said. "Go on and have some fun."

Ray was good enough to wait for me to get on a fresh dress and run a comb through my hair. I couldn't remember when it'd happened, that it mattered to me that my hair wasn't in tangles and my clothing was clean. And I wasn't sure when I'd started to notice the hair and dresses of the ladies in Aunt Carrie's magazines. I imagined Mama would've been proud to see me that way.

"Let's go through the woods," Ray said once I was ready.

"All right," I said. "But I don't wanna get my dress dirty."

He shrugged and we walked together through the apple trees and toward the forest. As soon as we got near the line of trees,

Ray took off running.

"Race ya," he called back at me, disappearing into the woods before I could even get started.

"No fair," I hollered at him, chasing behind on the trail.

I ran fast as I could. So much for keeping my hair neat and my dress tidy. It didn't hardly matter, though. I was just glad to feel air filling my lungs and my legs moving strong and quick. There wasn't a way in all the world I'd beat Ray, but that didn't matter to me. Not really.

Besides, Ray'd always cared about winning far more than I ever had.

I knew he'd clear the trees long before I would, so I slowed down, catching my breath so he wouldn't see how hard I huffed and puffed. And I did run my fingers through my hair, just to be sure it wasn't sticking up on end.

When I finally did get to the edge of the trees, I took a good breath before stepping out into the grassy yard behind our house. It crossed my mind to go in and see how Mama was. To have a little visit. Just for a minute or two before going off to the movie with Ray.

But then I didn't know if I could walk in anymore. Seemed I might have to knock first and wait for somebody to answer the door. I worried maybe I wouldn't be welcome.

Still, I walked to the house. The closer I got the more I heard Mama's voice, raised so loud it sounded like she was standing outside and hollering. Then I saw Daddy's profile through the kitchen window. He was holding his hand up to his forehead in a way that made me think he was awful tired. At least they'd had sense enough to shut the windows.

"Come on, Pearl," Ray said. "Let's go before we miss the start of the movie."

"I wish she'd just go away," I said, kicking at the porch once I got close enough. It hurt my toes but I wasn't about to let Ray know that, so I kicked it again for good measure.

"You don't mean that," he said.

"Sure I do."

"Come on. Let's just go."

I looked in the kitchen window again, hoping maybe Daddy'd put a stop to the fighting if only he'd see we were standing there waiting. But he didn't notice me, didn't turn my way.

Ray took hold of my arm, giving it a little tug. I followed his lead around the house and on our way to the theater.

Much as I wanted to turn back to see if I

could catch a glimpse of Mama, I didn't.

I just didn't.

Bert came out of his house when he saw us, all smiles and waving hands.

"Are you back?" he asked, jumping off the porch just like Ray might have.

"Nah," Ray answered. "We're just passin' through."

"Where're you going?" Bert asked after he got across the street to stand beside us. "You two runnin' away?"

"Not today," Ray said.

"Why would we run away?" I asked.

"I don't know," Bert said. Then his eyes flicked to the house where Mama was still screaming at Daddy.

"We're goin' to a movie." Ray shrugged. "You wanna come?"

"Yeah," Bert said, happy as if Ray'd asked if he wanted a hundred bucks. "Let me ask my mother."

He turned and ran back to his house, holding the door open and hollering for his mother, letting her know he was coming with us and could he have a nickel or something.

I tried not to let Ray see how sore I was that he'd asked Bert to come along.

Mrs. Barnett came to the front door and

put coins in Bert's hand. She kissed him on the cheek and he responded by rubbing at his face like she'd smacked him with a slimy fish. She looked at Ray and me, waving like she was real glad to see us.

I waved back, thinking what a nice mother she must be with her sweet smile and bright eyes.

"She gave us money for popcorn," Bert said, showing us his handful of nickels.

"That was good of her," Ray said. "Don't think I ever ate popcorn at a theater before."

"She thought it might make you feel better," Bert said.

He looked right at me when he said it.

Before I could even stiffen up or say something hard to Bert, Ray caught my eye and gave me a half smile.

"Ain't that nice of her?" Ray asked me. "Ain't it, Pearl?"

I licked my lips. "Yeah," I said. "It was real nice."

It was kindness and I knew it. But it was kindness mixed with a measure of pity and that was hard to take.

The theater in town only showed one movie at a time so we didn't get a choice like we could've had if we went up to Adrian. Of course, we'd have been happy with just about anything. It'd been since the fall since we'd had such a treat. Ray even said he'd sit through a smooch-faced movie if he had to.

When he'd said that, Bert looked at me and I could have sworn he blushed. I would've told him not to get any smart ideas but I sure didn't want him keeping my share of the popcorn from me.

The man taking the money for the movie looked at us like we were a bunch of hobos and said we had to have a nickel each to get in, eyeballing us like he worried we'd knock him over and run on past. It wasn't until Ray slid our money across the counter that I realized how full of dirt he was. It seemed he'd packed all the soil in Michigan under his fingernails.

Bert bought the popcorn and we walked together into the theater.

The lights dimmed, so we couldn't see how shabby the carpet was under our feet or how stained the cushions were on the seats. With the near-dark of the room it seemed the most glamorous place in all the world and I walked a little taller and slower, making sure to move the way I thought Greta Garbo might.

Ray wanted to sit all the way in the very front row, right smack-dab in the middle.

"My pa always said they're the best seats," he said. "Ain't nobody in front of you to keep you from seein' the whole screen."

I just shrugged. It didn't matter to me where we sat just so long as he let me sit right beside him. He did and I was happy enough about that. Bert made sure to sit on my other side and I tried not to notice how he kept sneaking peeks at me.

Seemed we were the only ones in Bliss had the idea to come to a movie that afternoon and that was fine by me. We wouldn't have to listen to anybody sniffling or whispering during the show. And there wouldn't be anybody telling us to move over so they could have our seats, especially since they were the best ones in all the theater.

The lights lowered until we were in darkness and I couldn't help but get a flip-flop feeling in my stomach due to all the excitement.

The bright sound of trumpets busted out at Ray, Bert, and me and made me sit up straighter. On the screen a man opened his mouth and let out a gravely, heaving sound, almost like he was yelling. I'd heard a voice just like that more than a couple times, with Opal, when we'd dance to the radio in the tiny space of her apartment.

"Cab Calloway," I whispered, reading the

big white letters printed across the screen. Then his smiling face winked out at us and I thought I understood why Opal was so head-over-heels for him. He was handsome enough, that was true. And he had charm for miles.

He and his band played in the narrow space of a train car, a fast and trilling song. Old Cab, he danced up and down in the middle of all the instruments, waving his arms and bobbing his head so his hair flapped up and down on his forehead. He bounced and I didn't know if that was from the jostling of the train or the beat of the music.

When the trumpet took over the song with a ba-ba-ba-da-ba, Cab got to tapping his feet and twirling with his left arm out and his right hand on his stomach in what looked like a samba. That's what Opal had called it.

The way he moved, it was no wonder she loved him.

The song over, the man who worked on the train, the porter, told Mr. Calloway, "My wife sure likes jazz. She's a lindy-hopping ole fool."

"You want to keep your wife at home, do you? Make sure she stays true?" Cab asked. "Let her dance right in the living room."

"How'm I supposed to do that, Mr. Calloway?" the train porter asked, shaking his head. "How'll she dance without no music?"

"Go on and get her a radio, brother." Cab reached into his coat pocket and pulled out a card, handing it to the man. "Your wife will never want to leave home again."

"Yes, sir," the man said.

"Get her that radio, the nicest one they've got," Cab said. "And she'll not go out looking for another man to dance with."

The scene changed, the porter stood in the living room with his pretty wife. The two of them stood on either side of a big old radio right in the corner of the room.

"Can we hear Cab Calloway on it?" the wife asked.

"Sure we can, honey," he answered. "Sure can."

Again, the scene changed, back on the train. That old train porter had the biggest smile on his face, telling his friend he doesn't worry about his wife stepping out anymore, not since he got that brand-new radio for her.

My heart slumped when the scene changed once again. There in the porter's living room the woman sat on Cab Calloway's lap, their faces close together, lips touching.

Blinking, I remembered seeing Mama kissing Abe Campbell there in our dining room in the house on Magnolia Street. The way she didn't pull away, the way she didn't shove him from her. I remembered how she'd seemed to melt when he touched her. Just the way that porter's wife did when Cab Calloway put his hand on her waist, her back, her leg.

I thought it was a good thing I hadn't had a bite of the popcorn yet. I felt I might just get sick right there in the theater.

That train porter's wife didn't deserve a husband that bought her radios and smiled so wide at her. And that rat Cab Calloway didn't deserve a girl so good as Opal Moon. Abe Campbell didn't deserve Mama, not the way he'd left her soon as he'd known she was having a baby.

And Mama, she didn't deserve Daddy. Not even a little.

Chapter Forty-Nine

Mama'd come to church. She wore a dress that hung loose from her shoulders and skimmed right over her swollen tummy. If I hadn't known better, I might have thought she was still carrying a tiny life around inside her.

But I did know better. Her stomach wasn't near as big as it had been.

"Good morning, Mama," I said once she took her seat in the pew right beside me.

"Hi, Pearl," she whispered without so much as a hint of a smile. "How're you doing?"

"I'm all right, ma'am," I said. "How about you?"

She shook her head and shut her eyes.

"I should have known better than to hope," she said, her voice so quiet I'd almost missed what she'd said. "I should never have dared."

I was about to ask her what she meant by

that, but the organ started playing and we all stood to sing the first hymn. I tried not to take too many peeks at Mama to see if she sang along. But whenever I looked up at her all I saw was her closed eyes and tears streaming down her face.

She only moved when the sadness made her tremble.

I was real glad when the preacher stood in the pulpit, nodding at us so we knew we should take our seats. He opened the big Bible and read out loud in his calm and smooth voice. He read King David's words which he spoke to his son Solomon as he lay on his deathbed. Seemed most of what he'd said to his boy was about this person or that and I just could not follow along.

Aunt Carrie had her Bible open across her lap, her finger following along under the words. There on the page I saw a name I'd heard about at least a dozen times. Pastor back in Red River sure had liked to holler out about that woman named Bathsheba.

When I'd been younger, I'd thought she was named Bathsheba on account that when King David had first seen her she'd been taking a bath. When I'd asked Mama about that, she'd just shook her head and said I came up with the oddest things to say.

"He seen her soakin' in the bathtub,"

Pastor would say, eyes looking around at the congregation and just about bulging out of their sockets. "He called her over, lay down with her, and took her as his own."

It'd always seemed to me that Pastor got the biggest kick out of the Bible stories that had fornicating in them. Far as I could tell, there were plenty of those kind of tales to keep him busy.

From what I remembered, King David'd had Bathsheba's husband killed off and took the woman for his own, her expecting his baby.

"The Lord saw fit to strike that child born of the lust of the flesh to get sick and die," Pastor had said. "Praise God for His justice!"

King David had bawled his eyes out over that baby. He'd begged God for help and didn't eat for a good long time.

Still, the baby had died.

If anybody had asked me, I'd have said I didn't understand God making that baby sick. And I'd have told them how it didn't seem right, making the baby pay for the sins of the grown folks who'd done the sinning.

"After that child up and died, King David didn't turn to drink and he didn't wallow and boo-hoo," I remembered Pastor saying. "He got hisself up and went to the house of the Lord."

What nobody ever said was how Bathsheba felt. She'd sat with that little baby and tried tending to it, tried healing it from what the Lord had struck on it. I wondered if she'd known there was no hoping that it might live.

Sitting in the pew right next to Mama, I wondered if Bathsheba'd ever felt a fool for hoping.

Aunt Carrie insisted that Daddy and Mama come out to the farm for dinner after church. Mama'd tried saying she was too worn out and not hungry. But Aunt Carrie had looked her in the face with kindness twinkling in her eyes.

"Wouldn't the fresh air be good for you, Mary?" she'd said. "You don't have to stay long. But it would be nice for the children to have you there for a little visit. Don't you think so?"

Mama'd nodded and followed behind Daddy to the truck. She didn't say one word when I jumped in the back with Ray.

"You think she's all right?" I asked Ray as we rode along.

"Don't know," he said. "She looks tired."

"At least she isn't screaming."

Ray nodded and turned his head to watch

the countryside rush past. That was how I knew he was done talking. It was just as well. I wouldn't have known what else to say anyhow.

I turned, pushing the windblown hair out of my face so I could look through the back window at Mama and Daddy inside the truck.

Daddy was looking straight ahead, both hands on the steering wheel. Mama had her face set toward him and I could see her profile. She was saying something to him. I only wished I could read her lips to know what it was she said to him.

Then she noticed me and turned, her eyes meeting mine. They looked so different, those eyes. Empty almost. As if all the feeling she'd held in them had poured out, leaving nothing behind.

I lifted my hand and touched the glass between us and her eyes dropped to look at it.

She tilted her head just a little, but looked back into my eyes. It seemed she was hoping to find something there.

I only wished I knew what it was she wanted to see.

Aunt Carrie had put together a few pot pies for dinner. The crust was buttery as it should be and the gravy nice and rich. Green beans and orange carrots, yellow corn and emerald peas seemed like springtime on my plate. I didn't mind asking for seconds. Aunt Carrie didn't seem upset to serve them up.

"I ever tell y'all about the first time I met Carrie's folks?" Uncle Gus asked after he'd finished off the last of his pie. "I seen Carrie in town, think I told y'all about that awhile back. Anyhow, I wanted to spend a little time with her."

"I told him he couldn't court me until he'd met my parents," Aunt Carrie said. "More bread, Ray?"

"Yes please, ma'am," Ray said.

"Carrie's mother invited me over for supper," Uncle Gus went on. "Guess she wanted to see if I had any manners, bein' from down south and such."

"No, Gus," Aunt Carrie scolded. "Mother was being hospitable."

"Uh-huh."

"Oh, stop." She smiled and shook her head at him. "I'd told her you were too skinny and she said she didn't wonder, you being a bachelor and living on hardly anything the way you did."

"Anyhow, I got myself all gussied up. Put on a bow tie and all."

"You looked so handsome."

"And Carrie, she looked like a dream."

"He's being kind," Aunt Carrie said, winking at me.

"I come in and sit down right here in this very chair my behind's in today," he went on. "From the very beginnin' I could tell your father didn't think much of me."

"I was his only daughter."

"Well, he give me the hairy eyeball while you and your mother was gettin' supper out. Lord, did he make me nervous."

Aunt Carrie didn't say anything, she just tilted her head and watched him tell the rest of his story.

"Now, I gotta tell you, my ma never in her life made chicken pot pie."

"Why not?" I asked.

"I don't mind tellin' you." He leaned forward. "She was a firm believer that pie should be dessert, not a meal. Ain't that right, Tom?"

"Excuse me?" Daddy asked, looking like he'd just gotten woken up from a shallow sleep. "Oh. Yup, that's right."

Daddy tried at a smile, but failed miserably.

"So when Carrie's mother brought out the pot pie, I got to wonderin' if I was over for dessert, not supper." He shrugged. "I figured, when in Rome, do what the Romans do. So, before Carrie cut into it, I piped up and said, 'You know what I like on that? I like me a big old scoop of vanilla-flavored ice cream on top.' I said, 'There's nothin' I like so much as when it melts all over top of it. Adds real good flavor.' "

"I tried to say something, I promise I did," Aunt Carrie said, a laugh hanging in the corner of her mouth. "But my father told my mother to get the ice cream out of the ice box."

"And Carrie cut me the biggest slice of that pot pie she could've."

"Remember, I was just as nervous as you."

"I'll believe that when my goat stands up and starts tap dancin'," Uncle Gus said. "Well, Carrie's father told his wife to scoop up a nice round ball of ice cream to put on top of my pot pie. She did as he said and plopped it right on my supper."

"I will never forget how big your eyes got when you realized it was meat and vegetables," Aunt Carrie said, clapping her hands in front of her face.

"What did you do?" Ray asked.

"The only thing there was to do," Uncle Gus said. "I told her the most polite thank-you I could manage and cleaned my plate."

"He told my mother it was the best thing

he had tasted in his whole life," Aunt Carrie said, shaking her head. "She believed him, the dear."

"Then, seemed whenever I came for supper, she'd made a pot pie and put a big old scoop of vanilla ice cream right on top, just for me."

"Oh, if she'd ever known she would have been horrified," Aunt Carrie said.

"And that was why I never told her," Uncle Gus said. "A man's gotta do whatever he has to if he wants to win the love of a good woman. Ain't that so, Tom?"

Daddy glanced at Mama. "That's right, Gus," he said. "Sure is."

"Excuse me," Mama said, getting up from the table and dropping her napkin on her seat.

"Are you all right, dear?" Aunt Carrie asked.

"I just need a little air," she answered, making her way around the table and into the living room.

The screen door creaked as she went out.

Daddy went after her.

I went to the front door and watched them walk away down the drive, Daddy following Mama and calling after her.

She just kept right on going.

Chapter Fifty

I waited on the porch, expecting to see them coming back up the drive, hand in hand, to get Ray and me. They'd take us home. We'd all be back to normal. Life would be easy for the first time I could remember. It would work like magic.

I waited for them even though I knew they wouldn't come. At least not in the way I'd hoped they would.

After a little bit, Aunt Carrie came out to sit beside me on the steps. She brought with her the clean scent of washed dishes and I felt guilty for not staying inside to help her do them up. If she was sore about it, she didn't tell me so.

"Do you remember me telling you that I was never able to have babies?" she asked.

I nodded. "Yes, ma'am."

"I lost a few of them like your mama did." She reached around her knees, linking her hands in the front. "Three babies."

"I didn't know," I said.

"That's because I didn't tell you." She smiled at me. "Women don't talk about it. Not really."

"Why not?" I asked.

"I suppose because it's a private matter," she answered. "I didn't even tell Gus about the last two until later."

"Was he mad you kept it a secret?"

"No." She shook her head. "I think he was more worried about me than anything."

"Were you okay?"

She shook her head no. "The grief made me feel like I would lose my mind."

"Do you think that's what's wrong with Mama?"

"It might be," she said. She let go of her knees and took my hand. "I believe she'll come back. I keep praying for it to happen. It might take a long time, dear. A very long time. But I believe God can heal her heart."

"Did you ever feel one of your babies move?" I asked.

Aunt Carrie shook her head. "I don't believe so."

"I felt Mama's baby," I said. "With my hands."

"That must have been nice."

I nodded.

We stayed there awhile longer. It felt good

being outside and still like that, not rushing off to do something or go someplace. Just sitting and breathing in the crisp spring day was good enough for me.

Daddy came back not long after Aunt Carrie sent Ray and me up to bed. The springtime evening had made it hard for me to fall asleep, so bright and active was the world outside the window.

Even so, I'd have woken up if I'd heard Daddy's voice anyway.

I was sure he'd come to bring Ray and me home.

Up out of bed I hopped, swinging my thin robe over my shoulders. I didn't think of packing up any of my things. There would be time later for that. I couldn't hardly wait another minute to get back to the house on Magnolia Street.

"Ray?" I said. "You up?"

All I heard back from his side of the room was thick breathing with just the smallest rasp of a snore. It was all right. He could come home the next day after school for all I cared.

I followed Daddy's and Uncle Gus's voices to the living room where they sat in a couple chairs in a corner of the living room. They were both sitting at the edge of their chairs, leaning forward, elbows on knees, talking close like they were sharing some kind of secret.

"Guess there's a place just outside Detroit I could take her to. Doc Barnett told me about it," Daddy said. "I hate to do it, but I don't know that I've got much choice."

"She gonna fight you?" Uncle Gus asked.

"Might just." Daddy sighed. "I can't take care of her anymore. Not the way she is right now."

Uncle Gus nodded. "You know I hate bein' nosy, Tom."

"I don't mind telling you," Daddy said. "She went in to have a bath. Something didn't feel right."

Daddy patted his chest.

"I never have been one to get a feeling about something," he said. "Not like that. But I went in to see that she was all right."

He rubbed at the back of his neck and shook his head.

"Gus, she had my shaving razor," Daddy went on. "I swear, I thought she was going to cut herself with it. Fixing to kill herself."

"You really think she would?" Uncle Gus asked.

"Can't be sure. But I wouldn't doubt it. Not the way she's been talking lately."

I thought of Mr. Jones, Ray's father. How

he'd sat in his broken down jalopy with his gun between his legs, the end of it pointed right up under his chin. He'd wanted to die so bad, but Daddy didn't let him. Not that day at least. But Mr. Jones had found a way.

One thing I'd learned was that if somebody wanted to die badly enough, they found a way.

"Abe's been sending her letters," he said. "I found a stack of them in her drawer."

"Oh, Tom," Uncle Gus said.

"I think she's just so twisted around, she doesn't know how to feel," Daddy said. "She's not herself."

"You're leavin' tomorrow?" Uncle Gus asked.

"Planning to," Daddy answered. "Might be gone a couple of days. Winston told me to take my time."

"We're happy to keep the kids long as you need us to," Uncle Gus said. "Carrie and me, we sure like havin' them around."

"Thanks, Gus. I best get going. Mrs. Barnett's looking after Mary for a while. I should relieve her."

"You get some sleep if you can."

"Feels like I haven't slept for two years, Gus."

"I know it. Maybe when she's somewhere safe you can," Uncle Gus said.

"I hope so. I'm worn down."

"You're doin' the right thing. You are."

Daddy stood, looking smaller than I'd ever seen him. His shoulders were slumped and his face was sunk in. I didn't know that he'd been eating much, he looked so thin.

I thought of the time he told me about his father. He'd been so sick he'd slimmed down to almost nothing. He'd wasted away. Seemed worry was the sickness that was wasting Daddy away. It sure made my stomach ache to think of it.

He saw me standing there at the bottom of the steps in my nightie with the robe slung around my shoulders.

"Darlin'?" Daddy said.

Uncle Gus nodded at Daddy and said he'd give us a couple minutes to ourselves.

"When can we go home?" I asked.

"Not yet, darlin'," he answered. "Not yet. But soon. All right?"

I told him it was all right. But that was a lie.

Chapter Fifty-One

Opal told me Lenny had plans to take her on a date, just the two of them. He'd even gotten a dress for her to wear. It was the green-blue of pigeon feathers when the light hit them just right. I thought Opal would look real nice in that dress, the way it cut in at the waist and flared out at the bottom just enough so I could imagine it had a nice swing to it.

"Where'd he get it?" I asked her, feeling of the soft cotton dress where it hung on the back of her apartment door.

"It belonged to his sister. He said she doesn't wear it anymore," she answered. "I'm just glad I don't have to wear a work dress."

On the floor she had her good shoes, all the scuffs rubbed out of them and the leather shinier than I ever could have managed to get mine.

"I even got a new pair of stockings," she

said. "Lenny gave me the money for them."

She held them up for me to see.

"They're nice," I told her.

"I can't remember the last time I had brand-new. I'm so afraid to tear a hole in them."

"Where's he gonna take you?"

"I don't know," she said. "I hear there's a jazz club down in Toledo where they don't mind a colored girl like me dancing with a white boy like him. Maybe he'll take me there."

She folded the stockings and put them careful as she could on the top of her dresser beside the tiny box I knew to hold the earrings Lenny'd given her.

"I keep thinking of sitting in the apartment back in Detroit," she said. "Listening to the band play whatever struck their fancy. They could play the same song every night and it would seem new every minute or so."

"How could they do that?" I asked.

She turned toward me, leaning her behind against the dresser. "They just made it up as they went along."

"How did they learn to do that?" I asked.

"I guess they first learned the easy stuff — which note was which and how to put fingers on the keys. They used that and made up whatever they thought sounded good," she answered. "Same as with dancing. You learn the easy steps — the rock step and the double back and such — and then you just make up the rest. It's not hard."

"I don't think I could ever do that," I said.

"You might surprise yourself," she said. "You never know unless you try."

She turned toward the dress, smoothing its skirt with the palms of her hands. The corners of her mouth turned up and she hummed some tune or another.

"You love him," I said. "Don't you?"

"I don't know," she said. "Lenny's trying to get me to run off with him."

"Would you do that?"

"Goodness no." She laughed. "He's not the man for me, Pearl. Not even close."

She left the dress alone and came to sit beside me. We talked about music and dresses and when the next dance at the American Legion might be.

What we didn't talk about was Mama, and for that I was glad.

It was nice to have a friend like Opal.

Chapter Fifty-Two

Daddy took Ray and me back to the house on Magnolia Street on Thursday after we ate supper at Aunt Carrie's table. It seemed like it had been a year since I'd stepped into that house, so many things had happened. When Daddy opened the door, letting me go inside first, I noticed how dark it was. The curtains had been drawn and a fine layer of dust lay on everything.

Ray hadn't come inside with us. He'd said something about going over to see Bert. Daddy'd said he'd need to come in before dark and Ray'd told him he would.

The very first thing I did after going into the house was push the curtains open in the living room, letting in the last bit of light from the day. Second, I went to Mama's room. The door was opened wide and the bed was untidy, like somebody'd gotten up quick and hadn't had time to pull the covers tight.

Mama wasn't there like I'd hoped she would be.

"Did you really take Mama away?" I asked, standing in the bedroom doorway.

"I've got something I have to tell you, Pearl," Daddy said, standing right in the middle of the living room. "Just don't know how to do it."

"Where did you take her?" I asked. "Will you tell me?"

He nodded.

"How about you come sit down," he said, pointing at the davenport.

I did as he asked, not pushing myself all the way back on the cushion, but sitting closer to the edge so my feet could touch the floor.

Daddy pulled up a chair so he could sit facing me, our knees touching.

He didn't say anything for a few seconds, but it was long enough for my imagination to run through all the things that he might have to tell me about Mama. Of all the ideas popping and snapping in my mind, the one that came strongest and hardest was a picture of Mama with his shaving razor in her hand.

Just the thought of it made the back of my throat sting, making me think I was going to be sick.

Daddy opened his mouth like he was fixing to say something, then closed it again and reached in his pocket for a cigarette.

"Seems I remember a time when smoking these eased my nerves," he said. "I'm not sure it works anymore. Or my nerves are just too broke down for fixing."

He lit the cigarette and breathed in the smoke, squinting his eyes like it either felt good or burned. Either way, he smoked the whole thing down almost to his shaking fingers before putting it out in an already full ashtray on the side table.

One thing I'd learned was that when there was something difficult to do or say, it was made easier by holding hands. He let me take his and I felt of his rough skin against my fingers.

He pushed his lips together tight and swallowed. Then he used his free hand to push a bit of my hair behind my ear.

"Pearlie," he started, his voice quiet. "You know you mean the world to me, don't you? You're my girl."

"Yes, Daddy," I said, breathing deep after speaking, bracing myself for the bad news I was sure was coming.

"And your mama," he said. "She does love you. You do know that, right? She might not know how to show it right now, but she does."

I nodded my head even though I wasn't at all sure that she did.

"Well . . ." He stopped and licked his lips. "How am I going to tell you this?"

I gave his hand a small squeeze, but not so hard that it might hurt him.

"It's all right, Daddy," I said. "I'm strong."

He broke a smile and looked down at our hands.

"I know you are, darlin'. You always have been. Strong and brave."

Him saying that made me sit up taller. If anything I could be strong and brave for him.

"It's your mama —"

"Is she sick?" I asked.

"In a way," he said.

"From the —" I left off. "From what happened?"

"Yes, darlin'," he answered. "I guess you might say it made her heartsick. That on top of losing Beanie, it just broke her heart all over again. Doctor Barnett said he's seen it before."

"Didn't he have any medicine for her?"

"He tried," Daddy said. "Gave her a couple of things for her nerves, to settle her a little bit and help her sleep."

"It didn't work?"

"No." He stuck the tip of his tongue out between his lips like it helped him think better. "She's not herself. Hasn't been since Beanie died. But you knew that already, didn't you?"

I nodded.

"It got so I couldn't take care of her anymore, Pearl." He cupped a hand over his forehead and dragged it down his face. "I couldn't do enough for her."

"I heard you talking to Uncle Gus."

"I know you did."

"Was she really going to cut herself?" I asked. "With the razor?"

He breathed in through his nose and shook his head. "I don't know, darlin'."

"Why does anybody do that to themselves?"

"I don't know how to answer that, Pearlie," he said. "I guess she's going through a time of being weak. What she needs is us to be strong when we can. We've gotta remember that, all right?"

"Yes, sir," I answered.

"That's fine, Pearl. Just fine."

"Is Mama like Mad Mabel now?" I asked. "Did she lose her mind?"

"She's not seeing things that aren't there," he answered. "She's just got a broken heart that won't mend. That's all."

"So, you took her to the hospital?"

He nodded.

"When can she come home?" I asked.

After I asked that it was like the whole world decided right then to slow down to a snail's pace. All the sounds from outside drew out longer than usual — Bert and Ray's hollering at each other, the sound of a car driving by, the high-pitched trilling of a bird. The tic-toc-tic of Meemaw's old clock took more time between each toc-tic-toc. Even my heart seemed to pump longer and lower.

I waited for Daddy to answer, half fearing he might say that she couldn't ever come home. That she'd gone into the hospital a permanent patient. And as I waited for him to say something, I worried maybe he never would, that he'd just shake his head and keep his mouth shut tight.

When can she come home was a question that had a heavy dose of hope to it. Hope I didn't have to spend.

Daddy blinked. His lids seemed heavy and I knew it was on account he didn't get much sleep on a good day, let alone when life was harder. He lifted his eyes to mine and cleared his throat like he was about to say something important.

It was then that I knew the question wasn't when Mama would come home, but if.

I bit at my lip to keep myself from crying.

"Your mama, she's all turned around right now," he said. Where he'd hardly been able to force a word out before, now he got the words out fast and tumbling like a waterfall. "See, she's changed. Losing somebody will do that. Moving a thousand miles from your home will, too. A lot's happened. A whole lot. She's not sure who she is anymore. I wonder if that's why she took off with Abe, because she couldn't seem to remember who she is."

"She's Mama," I said, wondering if that wasn't enough for her anymore.

"When I told her that Doctor Barnett said she should go to the hospital, she was mad. She fought me. I didn't know that we'd make it in one piece. I thought sure she'd jump out the truck door while I was driving," Daddy said. "I've never seen her so mad."

"Why was she mad about it?" I asked.

"I don't know exactly. But if somebody tried taking me to a place like that, I reckon I'd be upset too."

"Is she going to get better there?"

"I hope so, darlin'," he said. "I've got to

believe she can get back to herself again."

"Can Opal come back and help us?" I asked.

"I'll have to ask her," he said. "I'm sure she'd be glad to have the work."

He held my hand tight, like it was keeping him from floating off into midair.

"Will Mama be able to come home," I asked, "if she gets better?"

"If she wants to." He nodded, looking back at me. "She'll always have a home with us. That is if she wants it."

"What if she doesn't?"

"Then we'll make do," he said. "And we'll be all right after a while."

I got up and climbed onto his lap, resting my head against his shoulder. I knew I was too big for such a thing, but the way Daddy put his arms around me made me believe he was glad I'd done it anyway.

We sat like that, not talking, for a good long time, just listening to the clock tic and toc along even though it seemed our family had come to a dead stop.

"Daddy?"

"Yes, darlin'?"

"You won't go away, will you?" I asked.

"Nope," he answered. "My home is here with you."

Chapter Fifty-Three

Miss De Weese had let us out a whole thirty minutes early on Friday. It was the last day of school until fall and she'd said she didn't think she could hold our attention a minute longer anyway.

Ray and the few other boys who'd stayed in school on account they didn't have farms to work with their fathers went off into the schoolyard with bat and ball to play a game of baseball. Hazel and her group of friends went to sit along the side of the game to watch.

As for me, I wasn't inclined to sit on the grass and pretend to be interested in either a game I would never be allowed to play or whatever it was those girls might talk about while they watched.

And I sure didn't want to go home where I knew I'd be all by myself.

Instead, I went to the library.

Mrs. Trask sat at her desk, her head hanging forward so her chin rested right on her chest. It wasn't the first time I'd caught her snoozing and I'd learned it was best to let her wake up on her own. Otherwise she'd just get confused and then embarrassed. So I made my way to a shelf where I knew I could find a good book or two. That day, like most others, I wasn't disappointed with what I'd found.

The sun beamed in through the half-open window, warming me as I sat, spread out, on the seat built right next to the glass. If I listened close enough, I could hear the cracking bat and the hollering boys from the baseball game.

I read of a woman named Ida who lived in a lighthouse on a rock right along where the ocean met the land. It was her job to keep the lights burning whenever it was too dark for the folks on the ships to see the jagged beginnings of the shore.

Seemed no matter how bright the light that spun around and around in the tip-top of the lighthouse, boats would still crash into the rocks somehow. Whether during a storm or because somebody wasn't paying enough attention, they'd wreck their ships and end up bobbing along in the waters, floating on pieces of wood.

When that happened, Ida would get right

into her rowboat and paddle her way to them. No matter how strong the winds or how wild the waves, she'd get in that boat of hers.

I imagined her bringing the folks back to the home she made in the lighthouse. She'd wrap wooly blankets around their shoulders and heat up homemade bone broth for them to sip.

"You'll stay here until morning," she'd tell them. "Then it will be light and the storm will have passed. Then you'll be able to find your way home."

The folks she saved would sleep deep and easy and they'd wake to a day that was just as Ida'd told them it would be.

I wondered if when they reached home it looked a little different to them. A little more beautiful, a bit more warm.

That night I dreamed I lived in a lighthouse. One very much like Ida's, with the light spinning on top and a boat tied to the dock, bobbing up and down until I was ready to hop in it.

A storm had stirred up the waves. High winds caused the lighthouse to sway here and there, to and fro. I stood looking out the window at the ocean as it rose and fell, splashing up on the rocks and pulling at my small boat as if it wanted to steal it away from me.

The crashing waves sounded like cymbals, the moaning wind like trumpets. Rain pittered and pattered on the roof like the tinkling of piano keys and thunder roared and banged like a drum.

There outside my window folks were paired up and dancing to the rhythm, getting drenched by the storm. The waves reached up every now and then, grabbed hold of a couple and pulled them into the ocean.

"Come in," I screamed, holding the door open.

But my hollering couldn't break through the ba-ba-booming. The music of the storm out-shouted me.

Again and again, the hungry waves took another and another. The water splashed up, wetting my shoes, my stockings, the hem of my skirt. I had no choice but to slam the door shut, leaving what few pairs remained out in the storm.

Still, they kept on dancing.

"The music," I whimpered. "It doesn't make sense."

We make it up as we go along, I heard Opal's voice along a howl of wind.

Finally, the waves licked at the legs of the

one last dancer. She had curly dark hair and a dress the color of blue-green pigeon feathers. Opal's face turned to Mama's and back to Opal's. Then Beanie's face. Back to Mama's.

It was all three and not any of them at the same time, the way people can be, but only in dreams.

"Let me in," she yelled.

I tried the door, but it was locked. Stuck. I didn't have the key or the strength to pull it open.

"Pearl," she screamed. "Please! It's coming for me!"

I pulled and pulled but the door wouldn't budge. She banged with her fists, her kicks, over and over.

"Help!" she yelled.

I sat up with a start, sweat all over me like I really had been fighting a door to get it open. I had to tell myself to be calm, to breathe deep.

My heart pounded and my head ached.

I was in my bed, I reminded myself, not in a lighthouse. The weather outside was calm, no rain in sight. And I was just eleven years old, not a full-grown woman living all by herself in a lighthouse on the edge of the ocean.

I was just a girl.

I couldn't have saved anybody.
Not even if I'd tried.

Chapter Fifty-Four

I couldn't fall asleep after that dream. Whenever I thought I might drift off again, some noise would jostle me back awake. I decided I might as well get out of bed and see if Daddy was still up. I hoped he was. Nothing could calm my spirit better after a bad dream than being with Daddy.

"Did I wake you?" Daddy asked when I came into the living room.

I shook my head.

"I had a bad dream," I said.

"I'm sorry, darlin'." He closed the book he had on his lap. One of his history books that he'd brought with us from Red River. "Come on over here, Pearlie."

I did and sat beside him on the davenport and rested my head on his shoulder.

"Wanna tell me about it?" he asked.

I commenced telling Daddy about my lighthouse dream. He listened, not interrupting me even once. He did rub my arm and kiss my temple as I told it and that helped me feel not so much alone.

"I couldn't do anything," I said. "All I could do was watch her trying to get in and hear her screaming."

"Does it have you feeling upside down and inside out?" Daddy asked.

That was just how it felt. I nodded, glad to have a daddy who understood.

"Do you ever have bad dreams?" I asked him.

"Sure I do," he answered. "I think everybody —"

But he didn't finish. Somebody'd knocked on the back door. Knocked hard enough to wake the dead, let alone alarm folks that were already wide awake.

"Now, who could that be?" he said, more to himself than to me. He got up from the davenport. "Stay right there, hear?"

"Yes, sir."

He went to the door, opening it just far enough so he could see who was out there knocking. After just a couple words, he stepped to the side. Opal came inside, holding a piece of paper in her hand. That white sheet of paper shook so hard I thought sure Opal must've seen a ghost.

"Mr. Spence," she said, her voice trembling. "I'm sorry. I didn't know where to go."

"Are you all right?" Daddy asked, looking down at Opal like he didn't know what to make of her. "What happened?"

"It's just . . ." she said, looking down at the paper. "I was gone, with Lenny. When I got home, this was stuck to the door."

She handed the paper to Daddy. He read it over and shook his head and clenched his teeth in a way I knew meant he wasn't all too happy about something.

"Any idea who would have done this?" he asked, folding the paper in half. "Anybody around town been bothering you?"

"I —"

"Tell me, Opal," Daddy said, making his voice soft. "This isn't your fault. You aren't in trouble. You have done nothing wrong."

"It could have been anybody," she said, shutting her eyes and making a tear dash down her cheek.

"You stay here tonight," he said. "Pearl, help Opal find some kind of night clothes of your mama's, all right?"

"Can she stay in my room?" I asked.

"That's fine, darlin'," Daddy answered. "Opal, I'm going to see this doesn't happen again, all right?"

I let Opal be in my room by herself to get

out of her dress and into one of Mama's old nighties. Even though the door was closed, I could hear her crying. I thought of how sometimes when I had cried real hard, Mama would bring me a washrag soaked in cool water to soothe my face. I got one for Opal, hoping it might help her feel at least a little better.

"You can sleep in my bed," I told her. "I don't mind the floor."

"I don't know that I could sleep if I tried," she said.

She sat on the edge of my bed, dabbing under her eyes with the washcloth, cleaning a bit of makeup off her face in the process.

"Are you okay?" I asked, sitting next to her.

She shook her head and told me she wasn't.

"Did somebody hurt you?" I asked.

"No," she answered then sniffled. "They just wrote a nasty note."

"What did it say?"

She squinted her eyes like she was about to start crying again and looked at me.

"It called me some bad names. Names I won't repeat to you. And said that I need to stay away from Lenny," she said. "Or else."

I thought of what the Ku Klux Klan men had done to Nehemiah Carson just because he'd married a white woman. It took a couple real hard blinks to get the picture out of my mind of men smashing their fists into Opal. Just the thought of it about made the hair on the back of my neck stand up on end.

I turned and reached for the curtains, pulling them together in case whoever'd written that letter was poking around looking for Opal.

"Are you scared?" I asked.

"I am," she said. "I should have known better. I knew nothing good could come from being around Lenny."

"Does he love you?" I asked.

She shook her head. "I think he might. But I don't love him."

She turned toward me. All the crying she'd been doing had made her eyes the prettiest color of gray-green I'd ever seen.

"There aren't many in this town that treat me like I'm just as much a person as they are," she said. "Lenny always has. You and Ray and Mr. Spence, too."

She didn't say anything about Mama, and I knew that was on account Mama wasn't so good at hiding how she felt about folks with a little more color to their skin.

"Who do you think wrote the note?" I asked.

"I don't know," she said.

"I hope Daddy puts him in jail," I said. "Whoever it was."

"What am I going to do, Pearl?" Opal asked, shaking her head.

"We'll take care of you," I told her. "Daddy won't let anything bad happen to you."

"I don't know. He doesn't need me making life more difficult for him."

"You wouldn't."

"Well, maybe not me. But there are some who'd like to see me gone." She licked her lips. "Knowing how some people around here are, they'd run me right out of town first thing in the morning if they could."

I thought about what Meemaw'd say whenever somebody got to worrying. She'd tell them they shouldn't be all bothered about what was about to happen the next day. "Today's got plenty trouble all its own," she'd said. "Tomorrow'll be another batch of trouble you don't got no idea about yet. Can't worry yourself silly over somethin' you don't know about yet, can you?"

"Can I just worry about today, then?" I'd asked.

"No, sweetheart," she had said. "Today you gotta cast your cares upon Him. You know what I mean when I say 'cast'?"

I'd started to nod, then caught myself in the lie and quickly shook my head from side to side.

"Means you gotta throw those cares and worries right at Him," she'd said. "He'll catch 'em and take 'em. Every one. He takes them cares on account of His great and perfect love, darlin'. Love casts out fear, don't it?"

I tried to think of a way to say as much to Opal. But I couldn't think of the kind of words that'd make her feel better the way Meemaw always had with me. So, instead, I thought I'd do unto her what I'd like somebody to do for me.

"Do you want a glass of water?" I asked, getting to my feet. "Maybe it'll make you feel better."

"That would be nice," Opal said. "Thank you."

I let the water run out of the kitchen faucet until it was good and cold. And I cut a biscuit in half, spreading a thick layer of butter on each side just the way I knew Opal liked it, bringing it upstairs on a plate even.

Because I cared for her.

Chapter Fifty-Five

Millard had once told me about a whole town that'd gotten itself eaten down to the nails by termites. He'd sat beside me on the courthouse steps right in the smack-dab of Red River, the two of us sucking on the little pink candies he liked handing out to the kids in town, and he told me his story.

"See," he'd said. "It all started with just one little termite. It got itself into the house of the carpenter in a load of wood. It was full up of eggs, that one termite was. Fit to bust."

Millard'd said that the carpenter carried that termite around all day without knowing it was even there. He'd gone to the baker's and the butcher's and the doctor's. He'd gotten his hair cut at the barber's and had even sprung for a clean shave while he was there. All the places he went, the termite dropped a handful of eggs.

"Other folks in town," Millard had told

me, "they had some of the same plans that day as that carpenter. And no matter where they went, they all ended up with one of them termite eggs. Good Lord, how those eggs made their way all over town. Got into all the houses even."

Then one day, all the eggs hatched at once. Baby termites bit through the wood of the walls and the tables and the chairs.

"Before long, wasn't nothin' left for nobody to sit on," he'd said. "Weren't no place for nobody to live no more. All them termites ate it. And all just from one little critter."

The gossip about the letter left on Opal's door spread around Bliss quick as termite eggs in a carpenter's toolbox. Problem was, nobody seemed able to tell the same account twice. It took on all kinds of different flavors, that story, fitting the taste of whoever happened to be telling it at the time.

All anybody knew for sure was that Lenny Miller had dropped Opal off at her door where she'd found that letter. They couldn't even agree if Lenny'd walked her up the steps or if she'd read the letter before or after telling him good night.

The folks in town put together stories of their own imagining that best fit what it was they wanted to believe. Some spread the word that Opal and Lenny were having a love affair and that she'd been stepping out on him with somebody else and that was the reason for the letter. Others said she'd tricked Lenny, playing Potiphar's wife to his Joseph. She'd slipped liquor into his soda pop and tried seducing him with her wiles. When he'd told her no she'd written the note herself, playing the victim to Daddy to get pity out of somebody at least.

Not a one of those stories made a lick of sense to me. But, I guessed it was something they had to do so they didn't have to admit there was a mean-spirited person living among us.

Daddy hadn't come home for the noontime meal, so I put together a sandwich of leftover ham from the icebox and a thermos of iced tea to take to him. Opal hadn't come back to work for us after all. Much as Daddy told her otherwise, she was scared she'd make trouble for us if she was around.

Daddy said he could handle whatever trouble might come, but that he wouldn't force her. Daddy was a gentleman.

Aunt Carrie kept us fed most of the days and I'd done my best to keep the dirt from taking over the house. Other than the laundry piling up and me breaking a couple glasses in the dishwater, I thought I'd done a pretty good job.

I walked down the main street of town, sandwich and thermos in my hands. Folks didn't pay me any mind, which was fine by me. I wouldn't have wanted to have to get at them for saying something sour about Opal. It sure would've been a shame if I'd had to drop that heavy thermos on somebody's foot.

I found Daddy sitting behind his desk at the police station, Mayor Winston sitting across from him. He had his arms crossed, Daddy did, and a look on his face I knew to mean he was past annoyed. He had crossed over to plain old aggravated.

He saw me walk in, but didn't give me a smile or tell me hello. I figured he meant for me to sit and wait, so I went to the bench, letting my feet hang an inch or so off the floor. I remembered how the long bench in the courthouse in Red River had just been an old church pew somebody'd put against the wall. But there in Bliss it was fancy with slats all along the back and curving, carved sides. It seemed it belonged in the library or the Wheelers' house rather than in the police station.

"Listen, Jake," Daddy said. "I do understand. But folks around here can't think it's all right to leave a threatening note on a girl's door like that."

"But we've got no proof, Tom," Winston said. "We don't know who did it. There's more than a few people who think she wrote that note herself. Besides, there's those earrings of Mrs. Miller's that Opal had in her apartment."

"Miss Moon worked for me nearly a year," Daddy said. "I trust her with my kids. She's never lied to me. Never stole from me. She said Lenny gave her those earrings and I'm inclined to believe her. If anybody stole them, it was that Miller boy."

"I believe you. And I'll back whatever you decide." Winston shook his head. "I just don't know how you'll figure out who wrote that note."

Daddy leaned forward and rested his elbow on the top of his desk, pinching at the bridge of his nose with thumb and finger.

"What happens if somebody makes good on the threat?" he asked. "Like they did with the Carsons?"

"We just have to pray that don't happen." Winston let out a deep sigh. "I don't like it either, Tom, but it's been simmering. Ever since the dances started. It surprises me it took this long to start boiling. We can't be too careful."

Daddy let his shoulders slump. He shook his head and let out breath it seemed he'd been holding for days.

"Well, if I see so much as one person look at Opal sideways, I'm going to have him in here for questioning," Daddy said. "She's a good girl, Jake. She doesn't deserve this."

"And I'll be right here to be sure nobody tries to interfere." Winston got up from his chair. "I'm just hoping hard that this fades away. Some things like this have a way of doing that."

"Maybe for us," Daddy said. "But I don't know that Opal can walk down the street now without wondering if she's safe. We might have a way of forgetting the kind of ugly that was in that letter, but folks like Opal have got to live with it every day."

"Don't seem fair, does it?"

"No, it does not."

The mayor got to his feet and walked toward the door. When he saw me, he stopped and took my hand.

"Pearl, you are the ray of sunshine I needed today," he said.

I couldn't help but smile and maybe even blush just a little bit.

"Lord God Almighty, give me strength," Daddy said just as soon as Winston left.

"You sound like Meemaw," I told him, getting up from the bench and carrying the plate and thermos to him.

"Sure could use her right about now." He looked at me and shook his head. "What would she say about all this mess, I wonder."

I put his lunch in front of him on the desk and sat down where Mayor Winston had been. The seat was still warm from his behind and I thought that was a funny thing to notice.

"Thanks for bringing me lunch, darlin'," he said.

"You're welcome," I answered.

He took a bite of his sandwich and made a humming sound like it was the best thing he'd ever eaten.

"Daddy?" I said.

"Hmm?"

"Why don't folks like Opal?"

"I'd say most do. It's just some don't know what to make of her, I guess."

"But why?" I asked.

"It doesn't make much sense to me either, darlin'."

"I saw the earrings," I told him. "The ones Lenny gave her."

"Yeah?"

"Do you think he was trying to get her in trouble?"

"Nah." Daddy shook his head. "I don't suspect he was thinking much of anything."

"Can't he tell somebody that Opal didn't steal them?" I asked.

"He's probably scared of getting in trouble," Daddy answered.

"I wish they'd just believe Opal."

He took another bite of sandwich and chewed it real good and took a sip of iced tea.

"Me too, darlin'," Daddy said. "It's just they're more inclined to believe a white boy over a Negro girl."

"But Opal's only half," I said.

"Not the way some of these folks see it."

"Not the way Mama sees it, either," I said.

Daddy nodded. "I know, Pearl."

Sitting there across from Daddy I realized what it was Meemaw would've said. She'd have hummed her hm-hm-hm until she had my full attention. Then she'd have looked me right in the eyes, maybe even taking my hand to be sure I really listened to her.

"Man only looks at the outside," she'd have started. "At the mussed-up hair and the wrinkly old face. All's a man sees is a stained shirt or scuffed up shoes. But that ain't what God sees. No, miss. God sees right into the heart. He's got eyes that'll see either kindness or hate. He don't miss bitterness if it's there, or love neither. He sees it all. The heavenly Lord sees all that's in the heart, darlin'."

If it was true, I knew God saw nothing but sweetness and beauty in Opal.

He saw her just the way He made her to be.

Chapter Fifty-Six

It'd taken me far too long, but I finally finished reading the Peter Pan book while sitting on the steps in the library, the painting of Wendy and her brothers flying over the river just above my head. There was no happy ending to the story. All that happened was Peter kept getting little girls to take care of him, whether they liked it or not.

Even as upside-down as Mama'd been the last year, she never would've let somebody take me away like Wendy let Peter do with her little girls.

Shutting the book, I put it on the step beside me, not wanting to touch it, let alone hold it on my lap.

After a bit Mrs. Trask called to me, letting me know it was time to go for the day. I took up the book and carried it down the stairs.

"My dear," Mrs. Trask said. "You've been crying."

"Yes, ma'am," I answered.

"It is a dreadful ending, isn't it?"

I nodded.

"Wendy Darling should have learned to lock the windows," she said. "Don't you think so?"

I nodded and smiled.

"Yes, ma'am," I answered.

I decided to walk home the long way past what'd once been Nehemiah and Ruthie's house. I hadn't walked that way since I'd heard what had really happened there. It didn't scare me anymore. What it did was make me sad.

Walking down Aster Street, I saw a man kneeling in front of the porch, putting in flowers, pushing down the soil around the plants with his hands. Yellow and orange and red flowers grew out of green stems. Marigolds. I knew because Aunt Carrie and I had planted them all around her garden to keep the rabbits away from the lettuce and tomatoes.

I stopped, watching him plant a couple more marigolds in the ground. When he turned his head I saw the scar that cut down the side of his face. I stepped back, ready to run off if need be. Then I realized who it was.

Mr. Fitzpatrick straightened up his back but still kneeled on the ground. He had on an old hat with a brim so weathered and rippled I wondered if it hadn't been run over by a truck. His stained undershirt was loose on him and the work pants he had on were covered with patches. I could see that even from where I stood.

He gave me a nod, the kind men do instead of waving.

"You Delores's daddy?" I asked, even though I knew for sure he was.

He nodded again but didn't smile at hearing his daughter's name the way I'd thought he would have.

"Will you tell her I said hi?" I asked. "I'm Pearl."

His eyebrows pushed together and he blinked real fast a couple times. I didn't think he could've been any older than Daddy. Maybe even a year or two younger. Still, he wore the look of a man who'd seen a whole lot of hard times.

"Trial and tribulation got a way of agin' folks," Meemaw had told me one time. "But the burden of the Lord Jesus is easy and light, Pearl. You know why? On account of Him takin' most the load on His own back, darlin'."

Standing there not ten feet from Mr. Fitzpatrick's worry-lined face, I wondered if he'd ever had somebody like Meemaw to tell him nice things like that.

"I'll tell her," he said before turning back to his planting.

What I wanted to do was stay there, watching him do his work. Then I thought I'd ask him why he was doing it. But Mr. Fitzpatrick didn't seem the kind to talk all that much, and besides it wasn't any of my beeswax.

Anyway, I thought I knew well enough.

Seemed to me there must've been about a hundred ways to say sorry.

Chapter Fifty-Seven

It had been more than a couple weeks since somebody'd put that letter on Opal's door. Folks in town all but forgot that it'd ever happened. They'd moved on to talk about how this person or that had lost their home to the bank and how that person or this had moved away.

It seemed to me gossip flittered about like a moth. Landing here one day and lighting over there the next.

Still, Opal stayed to herself. Daddy had told me not to bother her too much, so I hadn't gone to her apartment. I sure did hate to put upon folks.

But once two weeks had passed, I decided it was time to pay her a visit.

Opal had her door propped open to let a little breeze in. She had her radio playing and the song poured out to me as I climbed up the steps to her apartment. When I got to the top I saw her kneeling on the floor with her back toward me.

What few things she owned were lined up on her bed, an open suitcase resting on the floor. One by one, she lifted pictures and dresses and her old tin cup and a book, placing them each with the very most care into the suitcase.

I reached my fist to the door and gave it a knock.

"Hi there," she said, looking at me over her shoulder. "Come on in."

She turned the radio down so it wasn't so loud, but we could still hear it.

"What are you doing?" I asked, my heart feeling like it was fixing to drop all the way down to the soles of my feet.

She pushed aside this and that so there would be room on the bed for us to sit. When she patted the thin mattress I sat down.

"You're leaving," I said. "Aren't you?"

She nodded and then took my hand in her own.

"Bliss never was ready for a girl like me," she said. "I need to go somewhere people might understand me a little."

"I understand you," I said, not knowing if what I said was the truth or not. "I try to, at least."

"I know you do, Pearl." She squeezed my hand.

"But you're still going?"

She nodded again.

"Pearl, meeting you was one of the very best things to ever happen to me," she said. "I'm telling the truth."

I couldn't remember a nicer thing anybody had ever said to me and I had to hold real tight inside my throat to keep from crying.

"If my getting stuck in Bliss only happened so I could have you in my life, then it was worth it." She sniffled. "But this town has never been home to me. I need Detroit. The busy streets and the sidewalks full of people rushing to one place or another. And I need my family. I just miss them so much."

"Remember how you told me about listening to the music from the jazz club?" I asked.

She smiled and nodded.

"Was that true?" I asked.

"Yes. On weekend nights we didn't sleep until three in the morning sometimes, the music was so loud," she said.

"And you never cared, did you?"

"No." She smiled and pulled in her bottom lip. "I never did."

"Do your folks still live in that apartment?" I asked.

"I hope so."
"What if they don't?"
"I'll find them," she said. "Even if it takes the rest of the year. Or the rest of my life."
I didn't ask her why she'd spend all the rest of her life looking for her family. Didn't have to. I already knew.
They were her home.

Daddy offered to drive Opal back to Detroit. She told him she'd already bought a bus ticket. She wouldn't hear of anybody seeing her off. No goodbye suppers or cake or pie. She didn't want a fuss.
She left Bliss the way she'd come, quietly and without many noticing.
But I noticed. And I cried the better part of the day.
Lying in bed that night, I imagined how it would be for her, getting to Detroit.
The bus wouldn't get there until the middle of the night. She'd climb down the steps to the platform and wait for the driver to pull her suitcase out from under the seats. It wouldn't take long on account there weren't too many travelers that time of evening.
She'd remember the streets, the tree on this corner and the funny looking dog that lived at the house on that corner. Nobody

would be out, not really. Most folks would be inside sleeping, resting up for the next day's work.

Somehow, she'd get herself turned around. It'd just been too long since she'd been home last. So she'd close her eyes and listen as close as she could. Listen until she heard a ba-da-bum of drum and wah-wah-wah of trumpets. She would listen for the meow of a clarinet and the trill of a flute.

She'd follow the music, letting it lead her home.

Chapter Fifty-Eight

I spent the better part of the day with Aunt Carrie in her garden. Opal'd been gone a full week and I'd finally started to feel like I would be all right without her after all. Besides, she'd written saying her folks still lived in the apartment across from the jazz club. They'd been glad to see her. Her mother had cried. Her dad, too.

"I can't say I wish I'd never left," she'd written. "But I'm so very glad I came back."

The hurt of missing her was muted by the happiness of hearing she was happy.

After Aunt Carrie and I finished pulling weeds and picking whatever we found ripe — beans, sweet peas, carrots, and the like — we sat in the soft grass, our heads tipped back to watch the clouds.

"It's a walrus," she said, pointing. "Do you see its tusks?"

"Yes, ma'am," I told her. "And he's eating a tulip."

"Oh yes. I can see it."

We sat for a little while longer, being lazier than we had any right to be. Still, we enjoyed the day.

"Aunt Carrie?" I asked.

"Yes, dear?"

"Pastor back in Red River said one time there wouldn't be any clouds in heaven," I said. "Is that true?"

"You know, I've never pondered that before." She shut her eyes and pushed her brows toward the middle. Then she opened her eyes and looked at me. "What do you think?"

"Well, I don't know. I hope there are some there," I answered. "Sure would be nice to sit up there and see stories in clouds."

"I think so too, dear." She leaned back, letting the sun warm her face.

"I'd find Beanie," I said. "Meemaw too."

"Wouldn't that be something?"

"I'd be sure you got to meet them." I smiled. "They'd like you, I just know it."

Aunt Carrie reached over and cupped my cheek with her hand. The way she smiled let me know I'd said the right thing.

Ray was in his room by the time I made it back from the farm. I knocked on the door and waited for him to answer. But he didn't.

"You in there?" I asked.

"Nope," he answered.

I pushed the door open to find him sitting cross-legged on his bed and staring out the window. He was watching Bert and Doctor Barnett, a box of tools between them and what looked like a makeshift bird cage sitting in a wagon.

"What're they doing?" I asked.

"Riggin' up a wagon so Bert can show that bird off in the parade," Ray said.

I leaned down just in time to watch Bert smash himself on the thumb with the hammer. It wasn't right to laugh at a thing like that, so I covered over my mouth with my hand.

"Looks like they need some help," I said.

"I ain't up for it."

I climbed onto his bed, crossing my legs up under me. "You sad today?"

"Don't know if that's the word for it."

I waited on him to go on. He would if he wanted to. If he didn't, I wasn't going to be the kind of friend to force him to. Ray'd never been one to say a darn thing unless he wanted to.

He reached into his back pocket and pulled out an envelope. It'd been folded in half. Handing it to me, he turned his face so he could watch out the window again.

Unfolding the envelope I saw Ray's handwritten address. It was a letter he'd sent months before, sent right back to him. Next to his mother's name, Luella Jones, was penned "RETURN TO SENDER" with an arrow drawn to show there was more on the back. I turned it over. In a neat hand was written, "This person, Luella Jones, has not resided at this address for nearly three months. She left no forwarding information. Please stop sending mail to her at this address."

"How many letters did you send her?" I asked.

"One every week," he answered. "That's the address she give me."

"Well . . ." I started, but didn't know what else to say.

"I don't even know what all that means," he said, flicking at the envelope with his middle finger. "Can't understand them bigger words."

I knew he meant he didn't know how to read them. He didn't like to say out loud that sometimes letters didn't stay in order when he tried sounding out words.

"You know what they say?" he asked.

"I think it's saying that your ma moved and didn't tell anybody where she was going to," I answered.

I couldn't bring myself to look at him. Just kept my eyes on that neat handwriting and the words that were bound to break Ray's heart all over again.

If I'd have known Mrs. Jones's address, I wasn't sure I'd have given it to him. What I'd have done with it is write her a letter all my own telling her how she needed to stop hurting Ray the way she did. And I'd have told her to leave him alone for good.

It was my firm belief that he was better off with us anyhow.

"Where would she've gone?" Ray asked.

I knew it was the kind of question he didn't expect an answer for. Still, I tried thinking of something to say to him.

"Maybe she got herself to California after all," I said, scooting myself forward so we were knee to knee. "You know she wanted to go out there. Maybe she heard about a job and got a ride with some folk headed that way. I bet right now she's picking big, fat oranges off somebody's trees."

"Bet them oranges taste like summer," he said, his eyes down still, but one side of his mouth pulling into a smile.

"Bet they do." I nodded. "Maybe she got a job cleaning some movie star's house, too."

"Maybe Shirley Temple's house," he said.

"Picking up a hundred dolls that girl plays

with all day long," I said. "Bet your ma's gotta iron all the dresses for those dolls. Can't imagine Shirley Temple'd let her dolls wear anything with so much as a tiny wrinkle in it."

"Yeah." He looked up at me.

"And there's gotta be a thousand empty rooms in that place. She'd let your ma have her pick of one, I'm sure of it." I leaned forward. "Probably got her own bathroom, even."

"She'd like that," Ray said. "With a flush toilet?"

"Sure."

We sat in quiet a minute or two. Out of the corner of my eye I saw Bert had gotten that bird out of her cage and was holding her loosely. She didn't make to fly away. She just stayed put right there in his hands.

"Seems he got that bird to feel to home," Ray said, nodding at Bert out the window.

"Yup, seems that way."

"I seen her sittin' on them wood eggs I made." He smirked. "Darnedest thing, ain't it?"

"Sure it is."

The two of us kept on watching Bert walking around the yard with that bird like he wanted to show her around. His mouth moved around words I couldn't hear but I would've bet a nickel he was talking real gentle to her.

"You ever think you might go looking for your ma?" I asked.

He shrugged, his eyes still following Bert.

"Wherever she is, I bet she's finding a way to be happy," I said.

Ray breathed in deep through his nose. "I just hope she's all right."

"I have faith she is," I whispered.

"How do you do that?" Ray asked, leaning his face against the window frame and looking at me.

"Do what?"

"Think up stories," he said. "Like the one you made up about my ma."

I shrugged and turned my face toward him. "Just do."

"It's special," he whispered, looking me right in the eye.

I shook my head and looked down at my hands, hoping he didn't notice a blush in my cheeks.

"Guess y'all got stuck with me a little longer," Ray said.

"We don't mind," I answered.

And that was the whole truth.

Chapter Fifty-Nine

Daddy brought Mama home the day before the Fourth of July. Between Ray and me and with a lot of help from Aunt Carrie, we'd cleaned the house as best we could so Mama wouldn't have to worry about it for a good while yet. We'd even made a cake. Vanilla with powdered sugar sprinkled on top. Mama's favorite.

When I heard the rumble of Daddy's truck I felt sick with worry. It would have been horrible if she came back worse than she'd left. Or if, like I'd seen in a movie, they'd electric-shocked the sense right out of her head. And I worried she'd be home for a day or two just to take off again, making us feel the loss of her all over again.

Ray had run out to meet them, in case they needed him to carry anything.

As for me, I stood in the middle of the living room, still as could be so as not to wrinkle my dress or mess my hair. I wanted to look the perfect lady for Mama. I wanted to make her proud of me. And I did all I could not to sneak a peek out the living room window at her. I wanted my first look of her to be when she stepped inside.

"Go on in, sugar," Daddy said.

I shut my eyes like I was hoping to get a surprise.

Mama had worn hard-soled shoes that day. They clipped and clapped against the wood floor. Lavender-scented powder and the feeling of a body close to me made me open my eyes.

Mama stood right in front of me, her real smile spread across her face.

"You've grown another inch," she said.

"Yes, ma'am."

"And what a beauty you're becoming."

She put her hands on my shoulders. How warm she felt and how near. I reached my arms around her waist, she wrapped her hands around my head, feeling of my hair and kissing the top of my head.

Mama was home.

She tucked me into bed that night. It'd been so long since she had, I didn't know what to do with myself. When she came in, I was still sitting up and looking out the window at the woods, trying to see the tip-top of the twisted tree through all the branches heavy with leaves.

"You want to say your prayers?" Mama asked, sitting sideways on the edge of my bed.

I shrugged.

"Don't you say prayers anymore?" she asked.

"Not the rhyming ones."

"Oh. I guess you're too old for them."

"Maybe."

She turned her eyes to her lap, smoothing the flowered fabric against her thighs.

"Pearl, I did you wrong," she said.

"Mama —"

"No. I did." She swallowed. "I put the blame on you because it was too heavy for me to bear."

I waited for her to go on, not understanding what it was she was getting at. It took her a little while, she swallowed and sighed and brushed a tear out from under her eye.

"I should have been the one to come after you," she said. "The day of the big duster. But I . . . I told Beanie to holler out for you. I told her to find you. I never expected her to get lost."

I felt the sting in my eyes and I tried to fight the crying, but I didn't think I'd win.

"I thought it was just a normal one," she

said. "I didn't know. Still, I never should have sent her."

"You couldn't have known."

"It should have been me," she said, lifting a hand to hold her head. "She would still be alive."

I wrapped my arms around my bent knees, digging my nails into the skin of my arms to remind myself not to cry.

"And I tried finding every way I could to blame you," she went on. "I told myself if you never went off, she'd be all right. If I could blame you, I'd be able to live with myself. But I couldn't do it and it made me so angry."

"Mama, don't."

"It was my fault, Pearl." She shook her head. "Mine. I thought if I left I could forget about Beanie. I could forget I'd ever had a family at all. I could start over."

I wanted to beg her to stop, not to go on. It was too much. But I found I couldn't hardly open my mouth, let alone form the words.

"But I couldn't." She gasped, holding a hand over her mouth. "All I could see was Beanie. And you. The way you looked at me after I slapped you. You were so scared. And I hate myself for that."

She shook and sucked in shallow breaths.

"I never wanted to be like my mother," she said. "I never wanted to do to you what she did to me. But I did. And I can never hope that you might forgive me."

I couldn't hold back. Not anymore. I moved so I was close to Mama and put my arms around her, let her rest her head on my shoulder, held her while she shook.

"I forgive you, Mama," I whispered, hoping it was loud enough she could hear it.

"I don't know why you ever would."

"You're my mama."

It was all I could think to say.

By the way she held me tighter, I thought it was right.

Chapter Sixty

I couldn't have been asleep long. Maybe a half hour, an hour even. But something had woken me, the creak of a floorboard and the sound of voices. For once, the words of Mama and Daddy weren't angry or sad.

It sounded like they were singing.

When I got up from my bed and out the door I saw Ray standing at the top of the steps, already listening in.

"What are they doing?" I whispered.

He shrugged.

I nodded for him to come downstairs with me.

Once we got to the bottom we saw them, Mama and Daddy. She was in one of her nighties, one that looked like something a lady would wear in the movies. Her hair was down and looked soft with the curls falling perfectly down her back.

They had their arms around each other. And they moved in time. Together.

Their faces were so close that it seemed they might kiss at any moment. But they didn't. Instead, they both sang about wishing on the moon and stars.

Daddy reached his hand up and held Mama's neck, pulling her head near to rest on his chest. He had his eyes shut and I saw how he had tears on his face. But he wore a smile.

Ray took my hand and the two of us went back to our rooms, shutting our doors.

I slept better than I had in a real long time.

Chapter Sixty-One

I stood in my bedroom, looking at my face in the mirror. Touching my cheeks and nose and jaw. I thought there hadn't been too much change in me, not yet at least. It might take time, looking twelve years old. I couldn't hardly expect to on the evening of my birthday.

In my closet was a brand-new dress Mama'd made for me to wear at my party. It was a light shade of blue that she said would look nice with my eyes.

"You'll have to wear a slip under it," she'd told me. "Soon enough I'll have to take you to get a brassiere."

I'd thought I might just faint from embarrassment. Good thing Daddy and Ray weren't anywhere near enough to have heard her say such a thing. I thought I would've just died.

I slid the slip over my head and hoped I could avoid a brassiere at least a little while longer. Even at twelve I still wasn't ready to be a full lady just yet. I stepped into the dress and buttoned up the front of it. It fit just right.

"Do you have it on yet?" Mama asked through the door. "I want to see it on."

"Yes, ma'am," I answered.

She opened the door and tilted her head from one side to the other, checking to be sure the dress laid right and the hem was even.

"Spin around for me?" she said.

I did and she nodded.

"I like it, Mama," I told her.

"It makes you look so grown." She crossed her arms. "Now, don't let me catch you climbing a tree in that dress."

"Yes, ma'am."

"And I won't have you galloping around in the woods wearing it."

I nodded.

"You look beautiful," she said.

I couldn't help but smile.

Mama'd made a cake for me, even though I'd told her she didn't have to. I knew she'd have to skimp on something to buy the sugar, but she'd said it was worth it. She'd even found the candles she'd used the year before that still had a little length on them.

They all sang to me as she carried that cake from the kitchen, twelve candles brightening up the room. Uncle Gus added his booming voice, and Aunt Carrie lent her sweet one. Daddy sang and so did Ray. But the voice that made me smile was Mama's. Clear and light and altogether lovely.

She put the cake on the table right in front of me and I waited until they finished singing before shutting my eyes to make my wish.

I'd thought on that wish a real long time. And I knew just how I'd say it in my mind, careful not to so much as mouth the words for fear it wouldn't come true.

I wasn't all the way sure that wishes did come true. Not too many that I'd made before had come to be. I'd never become an Indian princess or gotten a pony of my own. But, then again, a couple had.

Ray was still with us and Mama had come back. Millard was still alive and happy down in Red River and Daddy smiled easy again.

Once they finished singing I filled my lungs and held it as I thought the wish into the air.

Fast as I could, I let the breath push out of my body, through lips shaped like a circle. All the flames flickered and went out with just one stream of air. The smoke curled up toward the ceiling, carrying my wish along with it, I imagined.

I sat beside Daddy on the front porch of the house on Magnolia Street, his booted feet right next to my bare ones. It was just how we had sat together a hundred times before. I thought back to when I'd wriggle my toes in the grit of the porch and how Mama'd holler for me to wipe my feet off before coming in so I wouldn't track dust all over her newly swept floors.

A bubble of ache welled up in my chest. I sure did miss Oklahoma something awful. It didn't seem likely I'd ever get the chance to go back there, it being so far away and all. Besides, with all the dust Millard said still blew through, I didn't know that it'd look like home anymore. Far as I knew our house there right beside the church building could've gotten buried in the dirt or knocked over flat by the wind.

"Whatcha thinking about, Pearlie Lou?" Daddy asked, crossing his arms over his chest.

"Just about home, I guess," I answered.

"Red River?"

"Yup."

"You missing it?" he asked.

"Yeah." I rested my elbows on my thighs

and held up my head on the palms of my hands. "I miss how the sky was wide and how I could see fifty-sixty miles if the day was clear."

"Bet you miss how hot it gets," Daddy said, winking at me. "And the way a horny toad runs when it's scared."

I smiled and shook my head. "Nah, I couldn't miss those critters if I tried."

"I can't imagine you would."

"Daddy?"

"Yes, darlin'?"

"You remember the day you found me?" I asked. "Back on the day I was born?"

"I do." He looked at me the way he did when he got what Mama might've called sentimental. His eyes were crinkled in the corners and were just enough watery that I feared he might cry.

He didn't cry and for that I was real glad.

"When you took me into the house, did Mama hold me right away?" I asked.

"She did," he said. "She looked you all over real good, counting your fingers and toes and checking to be sure you were breathing okay."

"And I was?" I asked. "All right?"

"Better than all right," he said. "You were perfect. She gave you a bath and found one of Beanie's old baby outfits to put on you.

Boy, did you holler like the dickens through the whole thing."

"I did?"

"Sure. That's what newborn babes do." He scratched his fingernails under his chin. "Once she got you all dressed and wrapped up in a warm blanket, she held you close as she could and worked at soothing you."

"How'd she do that?"

"The way any mama would," he said. "She sang to you."

Daddy lit himself a cigarette and I stayed by his side. A man walked past our house and tipped his hat at Daddy. A chug-chug-chugging jalopy shimmied down the road, so loud I didn't know how the fella driving it didn't go deaf. Across the street Mrs. Barnett was taking in the day's last load of dry laundry. Inside our living room Ray had the radio playing some funny show or another.

It sure was busy that evening. But I closed my eyes to all of it, wanting to picture Mama holding me on that first day I was alive.

The blanket would've been a white one with dots of yellow flowers all over it. Mama'd shush me, hoping to calm my screeching. Holding me close to her chest, she'd rock one way and then the other, swaying in rhythm with her hushing.

She'd open her lips, letting out her sweet-sounding voice that got me to quiet down. She sang me a song of welcome, one that came from deep in her heart. She sang out of love and care and of wanting to keep me for her own.

I imagined that was when she'd known I would be hers for the rest of forever. In that moment she'd become Mama to me, and I was her Pearl. I pictured a tear, just one, tumbled from her eye all the way to her soft jaw. Her voice might've caught in her throat for the swell of feeling that grew in her chest.

But she wouldn't have stopped, not for anything.

She just kept right on, singing me a song of home.

DISCUSSION QUESTIONS

1. This story begins with Pearl reimagining the tale of "The Pied Piper of Hamelin." She thinks up a better ending, one which doesn't end so tragically. Which childhood story ending would you like to revise? How would you change it?

2. In the first chapter, Ray hears about how his parents fell in love. The happier-days story surprises Pearl, who only knew Ray's folks to be abusive and emotionally absent. Why might Ray's parents have undergone this kind of transformation? How is Pearl's perception accurate? How is Pearl's perception lacking?

3. Some folks in Bliss weren't keen on the mixing of races at the dances. What might have led them to feel that way? How were times different then? What echoes of that mentality did you witness in your own

childhood? What echoes do we still witness in our culture today?

4. When Mama calls on the telephone, Pearl asks her if she's coming home. Mama responds, "It's not that easy." What do you think she meant by that? What do you think of Pearl's reaction?

5. Daddy goes to visit Mama, only to come home with a broken heart and a busted lip. What do you think happened during the visit? What might have happened if Mama had come home with him that night? How might that have changed matters for Pearl?

6. The children at school are especially cruel to Delores Fitzpatrick. Why do they single her out for teasing? Why is it that Ray feels protective of her? Think of a situation from your childhood when you or a classmate was bullied. How was the situation handled? How can a child survive such torment?

7. Delores uses a vile word for Opal Moon. Where had she learned such a thing? How is something like racism passed down from one generation to the next? Are there

any negative family cycles you've been able to put an end to?

8. Opal tells the racial history of cakewalks. Did you know this history before? Do you know of other seemingly benign traditions that had racially charged beginnings? Perhaps look up the practice of blackface as well as racial stereotypes in film and literature. How might these have proved detrimental in the way our culture views people of color? How should we respond once we know of such history?

9. How did you feel when Pearl described Mama coming home? How about the compromising situation Mama found herself in? Did you expect a different reaction from Pearl? Or from Daddy? What might you have done under those circumstances?

10. As in life, most characters in the Pearl Spence novels have suffered hardship. Why does hardship change some people for the worse while it refines others to become stronger, better people? See 1 Peter 1:6–7. Which characters came through the process "like gold"?

11. Throughout the story we see several examples of forgiveness and redemption. Identify which one resonated most with you and explain why. What aspect of Pearl's story best reflects God's forgiveness and redemption through Jesus Christ?

12. What would you guess happens next in Pearl's future life? How about Ray, Mama and Daddy, or the other characters? How would you write the next chapter for them?

AFTERWORD

The Swing Era came on the heels of an especially tumultuous time in American history. The 1920s saw a resurgence of the Ku Klux Klan and with that a slew of violence aimed at African Americans. Most schools, even in the northern states, were segregated, and Jim Crow laws ruled in the South. It's no stretch to say that, at that time, black people were considered less human than white people.

In the mid 1930s jazz music rose in popularity, as did the various styles of swing dancing. It was not uncommon to see white and African American musicians playing together on the bandstand or lindy-hopping in pairs on the dance floor. Folks who couldn't attend church together due to racial differences could gather at the nightclubs or community dances.

It is tempting to see this history through idealistic lenses and assume that jazz healed the racial divide, that music had the power to end strife. If only that were so. While there were great moments of unity and equity, racism didn't end. In fact, many black musicians were not fully recognized for their accomplishments.

Although the Swing Era did not prove to be an end to racism, it did provide moments of hope that people of all colors could one day live in peace, community, and equality. And that is still our hope today, even through our own struggles to live in unity.

To learn more about the Swing Era, watch the BBC's documentary *The Swing Thing* on YouTube.

ABOUT THE AUTHOR

Susie Finkbeiner is a stay-at-home mom, speaker, and author from West Michigan. Her previous books include *Paint Chips* (2013) and *My Mother's Chamomile* (2014). She has served as fiction editor and regular contributor to the Burnside Writers Guild and Unbound magazine. Finkbeiner is an avid blogger (see www.susiefinkbeiner.com), is on the planning committee of the Breathe Christian Writers Conference, and has presented or led groups of other writers at several conferences.

The employees of Thorndike Press hope you have enjoyed this Large Print book. All our Thorndike, Wheeler, and Kennebec Large Print titles are designed for easy reading, and all our books are made to last. Other Thorndike Press Large Print books are available at your library, through selected bookstores, or directly from us.

For information about titles, please call:
(800) 223-1244

or visit our website at:
gale.com/thorndike

To share your comments, please write:

Publisher
Thorndike Press
10 Water St., Suite 310
Waterville, ME 04901